W9-CLV-477

IVORY JOE

OTHER BOOKS BY MARTYN BURKE

The Commissar's Report

Laughing War

IVORY JOE

MARTYN BURKE

BANTAM BOOKS
NEW YORK · TORONTO · LONDON · SYDNEY · AUCKLAND

IVORY JOE

A *Bantam Book* / March 1991

Grateful acknowledgment is made to reprint an excerpt from *Cyrano de Bergerac* by Edmond Rostand. Translated by Brian Hooker. Copyright 1923, 1937 by Henry Holt and Company, Inc. Copyright 1951 by Doris C. Hooker. Reprinted by permission of Henry Holt and Company, Inc.

Book design by Charles B. Hames.

For information address: Bantam Books.

Library of Congress Cataloging-in-Publication Data

Burke, Martyn, 1942–
Ivory Joe / Martyn Burke.
p. cm.
ISBN 0-553-07182-3
I. Title.
PS3552.U7233I96 1991
813'.54—dc20 90-19150
CIP

Published simultaneously in the United States and Canada

Bantam Books are published by Bantam Books, a division of Bantam Doubleday Dell Publishing Group, Inc. Its trademark, consisting of the words "Bantam Books" and the portrayal of a rooster, is Registered in U.S. Patent and Trademark Office and in other countries. Marca Registrada. Bantam Books, 666 Fifth Avenue, New York, New York 10103.

PRINTED IN THE UNITED STATES OF AMERICA

BVG 0 9 8 7 6 5 4 3 2 1

TO FREDA AND LES

—and their love letters that are still glowing. After all these years.

Your name is like a golden bell
Hung in my heart; and when I think of you
I tremble and the bell swings and rings—

CYRANO DE BERGERAC
by Edmond Rostand

PONIES

1

New York—1954

Leo is pounding on the door telling us to let him in. So far he's been nice about it. But now he's starting to remind us that he's our father. We all know that. We know that's trouble because most of the time Leo can hardly remember he's got two daughters. Leo should have had boys. We all know that. Some runty little Leo Junior he could take to the fights at Madison Square Garden. Someone to turn his companies over to when he gets old. But that's not our fault. Ruthie is stalling for time. She's cooler than I am. She always is. "How do we know it's really you, Daddy? How do we know you're not just some man that sounds like you?" she says staring right into the door. Ruthie is older than me. Thirteen. "If it's really you, tell us what our names are."

Why can't I think of a good question like that? Half the time when he's cruising around town being Mr. Broadway in his Cadillac with his girlfriends Leo can't even remember our names. I've seen it happen. His eyes get sort of all jittery when he has to introduce us to one of them—his *doxies* as Mother calls them. He tries to cover up not remembering our names and he makes it all a big joke. He calls us Rapunzel and Rebecca. Or Betty and Boopsy. And some of his doxies are so dumb they don't know he's blown it and is still trying to figure out what he named his own kids. "Well hello Rapunzel," they'll say looking at us all gushy and sappy. Like this is the way our new mother should act. But we know they'll just be around until Leo gets tired of them. A month makes them veterans.

"Christie, Ruthie, open the door." Now we *are* in trouble. We've got to open the door. Even though Mother has told us a zillion times never to let Leo in the apartment when she's not there. It's all part of the war between them. But Ruthie and I know what the real problem is. They just love each other too much. It's that simple. But do you think either of them can see it? Fat chance. I unlock the door and open it. Leo stands there in his silk suit grinning at us. We *know* he's the handsomest father in the whole world. The light in the hallway shines down, catching the sharp edges of his face. Most of those edges got there from the times he was beaten up. But if they were trying to make him ugly it didn't work. The more they broke up Leo's face the better he looked. The only problem is that when he doesn't smile he looks like the Aztec mask over in the museum beside Central Park.

"Where's Mother?" asks Ruthie.

"She's fine. I'm going to be looking after you tonight."

This has never happened before. Not like this. And when Stanley comes huffing out of the elevator, we know something is definitely weird. Stanley is Leo's driver. Almost his friend. Leo always sits in the front seat beside Stanley. Right now Stanley has his tongue sticking between his lips. He is carrying a big silver tray with white napkins covering some lumpy stuff underneath.

"I had Stanley go out and get us all some dinner."

We've got to be the only kids in all New York and probably the world to have food sent in from the Copacabana. But Leo can be sneaky sometimes. Not answering you directly and hoping you'll forget. "When's Mother coming back?" I ask.

"Tomorrow morning." Leo musses up my hair. I like it when he does that.

"Where is she?"

"In jail," Leo says with a big smile.

"Not again," says Ruthie.

2

Even before we finish our Copacabana dinner we can tell something big is going to happen. It's going to be another one of Leo's doozies. He's telling us that we have to go to bed at the regular time and not pay attention to the noise. What noise? we ask him. Oh, just a few friends dropping in, Leo says as Stanley is putting away Mother's vases and calling Steinberg's Deli ordering take-out for sixty people. Leo is being extra nice, which also means trouble. Whenever he knows he's going to have a fight with Mother he turns on the charm. He wants us to take his side. That's one of the ways they fight with each other.

Leo carefully explains that he was supposed to throw a party tonight for his best friend Arnie Dalitz. But because he's looking after us he can't have the party at his place. That makes sense doesn't it? Ruthie and I nod and look at each other. Mother's place where we live is a lot nicer than Leo's apartment. But that's only because Leo hasn't unpacked most of his furniture even though he's been there two years. Home-type details don't mean much to Leo. Even when he was living here all he ever did was leave little bundles of money around to look after whatever had to be done. Our apartment is really big. One side looks out on West End Avenue and all the bedrooms are down a long hallway. Mine looks down on 81st Street and if you press your face against the window you can see the boats going up the Hudson River.

Arnie Dalitz has been Leo's best friend since they were my age. They both lived in the Bronx and were poor. Now Leo owns a big company and Arnie just got out of Sing Sing penitentiary yesterday. Arnie has been locked there for three years. He's in the rackets. But Leo will never tell us what the rackets are. Just a bunch of guys having fun he says. A lot of Leo's friends are in the rackets. Mother always kept warning Leo his friends would get him thrown in jail someday. When I remind Leo of this he says but look who's in jail tonight. Your mother.

Leo has an answer for everything.

Mother's in jail because she was picketing Leo's company again. This used to happen even when they lived here together. Every time the International Ladies' Garment Workers' Union went on strike against Frolic Frocks, Inc., Mother was there with all the little Italian and Polish ladies who worked in the factory. She'd take food down to the picket lines. And sometimes Leo would come home to find half his factory eating dinner in the dining room. Once he walked in while they were voting on his offer. But Mother picketed lots of places. Once she took me with her on a freezing cold day. We went to a big warehouse building on 28th Street where steam roared from the windows high up. It was like smoke from a dragon's nose. The steam came from the pressing machines inside the factory where a lot of foreign ladies were sewing clothes. It was so cold inside you could see their breath. They were all bundled up in ragged coats and gloves with the fingers cut out so they could sew. A lot of them were coughing. The owner came roaring in. A big fat man. The kind whose arms stick out at his side like flippers. He started yelling at Mother, telling her she'd be arrested for trespassing. Mother never took that kind of guff from anyone. She started chasing the man around his own factory. Yelling at him to turn on the heat. Three weeks later Leo brought the fat man home to drink some whiskey after they'd been out gambling. When he saw Mother the fat man went white like a fish. But Mother just smiled sweetly.

Mother is like that. If she sees a milkman beating the horse that pulls his cart, she'll go over and start hitting the milkman. It's nothing personal. Even Leo knows that. But Leo has made sure *we* know what the problem is. The problem is that Mother started leading pickets around Morgen's restaurant. Morgen's is the place at the bottom of the garment building on Seventh Avenue. Leo and all the other big garment guys in the building eat lunch there. They eat their steaks and then suck things out of their teeth and tell each other how bad business is. Leo says it was a mistake for Mother to do what she did. To teach the picketers to stand outside and yell insults about the waistlines of the big garment guys. Enough is enough, Leo says. Your mother is breaking the law. But Mother says Leo and his friends played poker with some policemen one night. They let the policemen win a lot of money and drink a lot of whiskey. The next day Mother was in jail for trespassing.

It's midnight. Ruthie and I can look down the long hallway and see them playing poker and dancing with the models. The whole living room is packed and the smoke looks like a fog rolling down the hallway. Leo must be winning because we can see him laughing a lot. And Arnie Dalitz is there in his new shiny suit, drinking whiskey and putting his arm around all the girls. Like a lot of the men there he calls them all *sweetheart*. They say the word out of the side of their mouth. The whole place is filled with *sweethearts*. But I've never heard Leo say that.

The ponies finally show up. They're always the most fun. The ponies are the short dancers at the Copacabana. The tall ones they just call showgirls. It's real interesting to watch Leo around the ponies. A couple of them know his weak spots. One little blonde goes over and musses up his hair while he's playing cards. And rubs the back of his neck. Leo pretends he's too busy playing poker but when she goes to get him a drink you can see him watch her over the top of his glasses. The pony is probably thinking of what kind of wedding dress to wear. And checking the living room to see if it would hold all her bridesmaid ponies. Fat chance. That doxie. Sometimes Leo can be so dumb. For your information Ruthie and I are both ponies.

There's some kind of noise coming from the hall around the corner. It sounds like one of the radiators has burst again except the heat's not on. Ruthie and I creep around the corner in our nightgowns. It's coming from Mother's bedroom. But the door is closed. So we run to the spare bedroom right next to Mother's. There's a bathroom with doors on both sides and even as we're tiptoeing through it we can hear Arnie Dalitz. And one of the ponies! In our *mother's* bedroom! "Oh baby, it's been three years," he says. And you can hear her giggle and say he hasn't forgotten anything.

Forgotten what? Ruthie tells me to shut up as she puts her face up against the door and opens it a tiny sliver. She spins around and even in the darkness I can see her mouth is wide open and her eyes are like pinwheels. "He's got a boner," she gasps. A what? I ask. "Stupid," she hisses. "Don't you know anything? That's what Margie Lewicki says her brother calls it." Ruthie dives back to the door and I crawl under her to watch too.

I can't *believe* it!

There's Arnie Dalitz, all hairy like Mrs. Knightley's dog, rolling all over Mother's bed with nothing on. And the pony! He's tearing off her clothes. I can't tell for sure if she likes it but I think she does. It's a good thing Mother's in jail.

Then Ruthie starts making funny noises. Something's wrong. She's trying to whisper something but she just makes these noises and points to her mouth. She's stuck to the bathroom door. Her braces are caught in the string bag Leo stapled to the door to hold his magazines when he lived here. How am I supposed to know what to do? I'm starting to panic. Ruthie is making gurgling sounds and I can see Arnie Dalitz's white bum going up and down like he's doing some kind of exercise on top of that pony in Mother's bed. He's hurting her. I can tell because she's moaning and he's not even stopping. All I can think of is Mother and the milkman's horse. So I grab a towel and push open the door. Ruthie lets out a howl. Arnie Dalitz is howling too and so is the pony. I start hitting Arnie Dalitz with the towel, yelling at the pony to get away while she can. Ruthie is rolling all over the floor holding her mouth.

Lights go on all over the place and people start running through the whole apartment. Arnie Dalitz is hopping around like a stork trying to put his pants on. Leo comes racing in with a whole bunch of his friends who are holding their cards. Everybody's yelling at once.

And then everybody stops yelling. The phone is ringing. Leo tells everyone to be quiet. He looks at the phone like it's a bomb. It rings a lot and then it stops. Leo looks relieved. Then it starts ringing again. Leo shouts at Stanley to answer it. The whole apartment is very quiet. You can hear Stanley talking on the telephone but you can't hear what he's saying. Leo is shooing everyone out of the bedroom and making shushing moves with his fingers. Then Stanley yells in a real phony voice.

"Leo, are you awake? It's Tina."

Leo's eyes go a little wider and he hurries back to the living room. Suddenly Ruthie and I are left alone in the bedroom with the pony, who looks like she's been running in a rainstorm. She just sits there on the bed breathing hard through her nose with her little red lips clamping tighter together. Staring at me. Just staring. Can you believe it? Not even a thank you.

You're very welcome I say, marching out into the hallway. In the living room everyone is very still like a painting. Only Leo moves. He paces back and forth staring at the floor as he talks to Mother. All the poker players are pretending to watch him when I can see they're really trying to look at each other's cards. "Tina, I'm really glad you're okay," he says. "I was worried about you. . . . Of course I do. . . . I didn't mean what I said about you either. . . . You know, out there on the street. The part about being a communist. . . .

Look, I know. I know. You're just doing what you feel you have to. . . ."

This is *really* something. Leo hasn't talked like this to Mother since before he moved out. I *knew* they'd get back together again!

I rush into the bedroom to tell Ruthie but she's standing over the extension phone like a cat over a bug. Ruthie! I whisper as loud as I can. You can't listen to them. That's personal!

"It's our lives too, you know. Besides, nothing Leo ever does is personal," says Ruthie, staring daggers at me. She lifts up the phone real real carefully. I figure what the heck, if she's listening it's not going to make any difference if I do too. So I go and horn in just in time to hear Mother ask if the girls are okay.

"Sound asleep. Just tucked them in. You know I was looking down at them while they were sleeping and thinking Tina and I sure made a couple of great kids." Honestly, Leo.

"Leo, it makes me feel good to hear you say that. You know there's no need for you to sleep on the couch. Why don't you use my bed?"

"Aw, Tina, thanks. But you know. There's too many memories. And I . . ." I think I'm going to barf. Can you *believe* it? Like he's searching for words. While Arnie Dalitz's pony is spread all over the bed. Along with Leo's memories. "How are the Tombs?" Leo says.

"Like usual. Dirty. Stinking. A lot of prostitutes. And about twenty of us." Mother's voice is a little shaky.

"Well, at least you'll be out in the morning."

"Leo, I've been thinking about a lot of things."

"So have I."

"Leo, can you talk? I mean is Stanley around?"

"He's in the next room. I just had him drop over with some milk for the girls." Hah! Booze for the doxies you mean.

"Maybe we could talk things over. I mean, things between us."

"Oh God, Tina. I would really like that." Ruthie and I look at each other. He means it.

"Leo, I think I'm going to post bail. I can be home in an hour."

"Honey, that would be great." *Great?* Are you nuts, Leo? It would take us all night just to scrape up the stuff that's been spilled. "Listen Tina, why don't I come down there and . . ."

"What, Leo?"

"I just thought of something."

"What?"

"Nothing."

"Tell me."

"I . . . I was wondering if it's right to get out of jail when your fellow strikers would still have to stay behind till morning. No! Tina, Tina, forget I said that—"

"Leo, wait. Maybe you're right. I can't leave them, can I?"

LeoLeoLeo. You sneaky cad you lousy rat you weasel you. But what did I tell you? Leo has an answer for everything. The party keeps going like someone has pulled a switch. The racketeers and the big garment guys and the ponies are having a great time. And Leo keeps winning. But something weird is happening! The whole room is spinning around. Ruthie and I are grabbing on to the walls that keep turning in circles. We can't even put our mouths around the straw to drink the chocolate milk that Stanley gave us. It's not exactly chocolate milk. It's chocolate and something else. Stanley keeps saying would we like to go to bed and I see Leo waving night-night. Actually I see two Leos.

When the phone rings it sounds like the fire bell at school going off in my head. The whole living room freezes again and the Leos motion for the Stanleys to answer the phone. "Hello," says Stanley and then he looks real funny before he says, "She's not here. Any message?" Then he stares at the phone and hangs up.

"Who's that?" asks Leo like someone has stolen one of his aces.

Stanley still looks kind of funny. "Some guy," he says. "It sounded like a Negro." He says it knee-grow like he's chewing over the word. *Negro?* For Tina? A couple of big garment guys check their watches and look at each other, raising their eyebrows. "Three jacks," Leo says quickly. Everyone acts real weird.

Boy are they dumb. Ruthie and I know who it is. It's Ivory Joe. But the walls are doing cartwheels.

I've got to go to bed.

3

What a headache.

Ruthie and I are both feeling around for aspirins. We have a lot to do this morning. We're going to get Leo and Mother back together again. It's definite. At least that's what we tell ourselves until we go out into the living room. It looks like Camp Wig-A-Mog on laundry day. Boys' laundry day. A disaster. There's food everywhere. And those crummy-smelling cigars piled up like dog doo in the ashtrays. I hate the things. And Leo's playing cards, the ones with naked women on the back, are all over the floor. I catch Ruthie holding one of the cards and looking at herself sideways in the mirror. No contest. Ruthie loses. She gets real upset whenever I even tease her about that stuff so I shut up. We find a nylon stocking. Which starts me thinking that maybe we'd better do a check like they do at Camp Wig-A-Mog. To see if any campers got left behind. Good thing we do. I find Mr. Kampelman wedged between the wall and the back of the couch. Smelling of booze. And with lipstick all over his white shirt. He's easy. Just a shot of Grandma's smelling salts. The tough one is the pony in the bathtub. The same one who never thanked me for helping save her from Arnie Dalitz. She's a goner. Lying there snoring with a pillow under her head. Her sweater is pulled up almost to her shoulders. It's a good thing Ruthie's cleaning up the living room. Otherwise she'd really get weird when she saw the pony's chest and then looked at herself in the mirror.

When I announce it's time to leave, the pony looks at me with one eye and then goes back to sleep. I say it again. Take it from me. I'm polite. But you should see what *she* does. She opens that same eye and tells me to do the most unbelievable thing to myself.

Not even garbage mouth Louis Makin at school would say that. Even when he had a crush on me and was trying to impress me. I tell her I'm not going to take any guff from her. But she's already asleep again. So I just let her have it with the shower. Full blast. Cold only, and in our apartment cold is cold, believe me. All of a sudden she's like a seal at the zoo. Sliding all over. Feet in the air like flippers and making gagging noises like when you put your fingers down your throat. Boy does she ever get a soaker.

The pony I can handle okay. The real tough one is Leo. He's up at least. He's always up. Leo only sleeps four hours a night. He used to drive us nuts when he lived here, roaming around in the middle of the night, coming into our room and asking "Can't you sleep?" when we were sound asleep. Without anyone to talk to Leo can sometimes get real goofy.

But right now Leo is convinced he's dying. Every morning of his life especially after he got old and turned forty Leo is convinced he's dying. Which he probably is. You would too if you had half the booze the girlfriends the cigarettes the nightclubs the parties and the gambling that Leo has. And that's on top of being one of New York's smartest businessmen. Leo is sitting up in bed looking the color of the sheets. "I don't feel so hot," he says. "I think it's serious this time, Christie."

This time? I mean honestly.

"Have you seen my black bag?" Leo asks in a voice that sounds like he's ninety. Leo's black bag goes wherever he goes. It's the kind the doctors carry, but he doesn't put the same kind of stuff inside. It's crammed with pills. There are dozens of bottles of them in all different colors and sizes. Everything from aspirins to vitamins and a whole bunch of other things. I get Leo's black bag and he starts pouring out the fistful of pills muttering when he can't find the Royal Queen Bee Jelly pills. So he settles for the blue pills in the little bottle marked *up*.

Ruthie and I clean like crazy, vacuuming the carpets opening all the windows and getting the guck off the dining room table. There's no way Mother's going to walk in here and find out what was going on last night. Not when there's a chance that she and Leo can get back together. Even Leo gets into the act. He starts drying all the dishes, which is real unusual for him. A good sign we figure. And he also changes his doctor's appointment. Every morning he gets an injection of vitamin B. To fire up the engine he says. But today Stanley is sent to bring Dr. Taffler over here in case Mother arrives early. Dr. Taffler handles a lot of the gamblers who are friends of Leo's. I wouldn't let him even look at my tonsils because he's real creepy like he should be running a funeral parlor. He's kind of bulgy with hair stuck over his big bald spot. The only time he smiles is when Leo pulls some money out of his pocket and slaps it into his hand. Leo doesn't even count the money.

Then we wait for Mother. Leo is fine now. Which means he's like a Coke bottle when you shake it too much with your finger over the top of it. He walks back and forth looks at his watch makes a phone call and then does the same thing all over again. Ruthie and I are proud of the job we've done. The apartment looks perfect. Now it's up to them. About 9:30 we get a phone call from Mother's lawyer. This afternoon he says. They're late with the bail hearings. That means we have to go to school which means we need a note from a parent saying why we're late. We explain this to Leo who looks like he can't figure it out. He's on the phone asking about dress sales to Macy's and the horses at Aqueduct. With the phone to his ear he gets a note pad and some carbon paper which he puts between the first two pages. He scribbles something stops scribbles again mutters into the phone and shakes his head. Finally after we start bugging him he tears off the pieces of paper and gives us one each. I get the carbon copy. It says: *My kid is sick today—Leo K.* On the bottom is some more writing. It says: *Misty Maiden—3d—$500///Southern Dancer—6th—a thou.*

At school Mr. Alwyn just stares at the note when I hand it to him. Then he looks at me. Then at the note again. That's all. But his Adam's apple bobs up and down over his bow tie a few times. I go to the School for Ethical Studies right on Central Park West. There's a bunch of rich kids there. Their parents all want to have kids who are brains. My best friend Susie Leggat is a brain but her parents aren't loaded. She got there on a scholarship because the school needs *real* brains otherwise the rich kids won't be sent there. Susie's not even Jewish. But a bunch of kids aren't. And me I'm half.

So who can think today? About the stamen and the pistil and what Abe Lincoln said at Gettysburg and what 12 times 15 divided by 3 equals. When your mother's getting out of jail again.

I pray for lunch period. Instead of hanging around I walk up Central Park West to the museum where I sit eating my sandwich looking at the dinosaur skeletons. The museum is where I go when things get real nutty. It's nice and quiet in there. Most of the time in the museum I make up stories about whatever it is I'm looking at. This is where Leo is great too. He started coming here to the museum with me sometimes. At first he didn't want to. He thought it was too much like school which he got kicked out of. But I got him learning about this stuff. The way to do it is make a bet with him. When I bet him who could remember the most kinds of stuffed monkeys in the glass cages the game was on. He cleaned me. He has what he says is a photographic memory. He got twenty-nine out of thirty-two. I only got nine. So I had to pay him a nickel. Leo loved it because he had a daughter he could make bets with. Almost as good as a son. I keep Leo going on our nickel bets. Sometimes it goes to a dime. Already he's learned all the Indian tribes in the Southwest the birds of Asia and the names of all the major stars in the sky at night. He's great fun to learn with. He loves it. But what he loves most is when I have to cough up my nickel. Of course later he gives me a dollar for an ice cream cone that costs a dime.

And last month I decided to risk the whole dollar on the different kinds of totem poles. I caught Leo with three library books on totem poles. And I heard him on the phone bragging to Uncle Morris that *he* was teaching *me!* The joys of betting. Is Leo ever out of it sometimes.

After lunch our class gets to go over to Central Park and play a lot of girl-type games while the boys play softball. Mostly we just watch the boys in our class who are playing Mrs. Levine's class. Both Sara Kramer and I have a big crush on Tubby Wilson. He may sound fat but he's not. He used to be. He's pitching and is going to win up till the Manny Singh fight. Manny's real name is Amand or something. But in this school naturally he gets called Manny. His father's a big wheel from India at their embassy here. Manny wears a turban and can hit home runs. This time he belts one of Tubby's pitches. It should have been a homer for sure. But when he was racing around second base that dirty Louie Makin grabbed part of his turban. It started coming undone with Louie hanging onto it like a water-skier. Manny was almost at shortstop when he realized what was happening. He went berserk. He ran back trying to pound Louie Makin, yelling and holding onto his turban like crazy. But the worst part was that the ball was thrown back to Louie Makin while Manny was on the ground wrapping his turban. So Manny got called out. You should have heard all the yelling. And then while Louie Makin was laughing at him Manny kicked him right between the legs. Louie Makin bit the dust. All the boys on Manny's team were yelling hey right in the nuts and stuff like that. But Mrs. Levine came and told us to get back to our girl-type games right away. Later we found out that Manny was awarded the home run. And both he and Louie Makin have to take ten extra ethics classes after school. It serves Louie Makin right. He was just trying to impress me and Sara.

Finally school ends. I race down to the corner pay phone and call home. Mother answers. I say hi mom how was jail and she laughs and tells me how much she loves me. I keep fishing around to find out if Leo's there. Without actually asking her. It's obvious he's not. So I say bye and hang up and call Frolic Frocks. Mrs. Weissman who's been there for a million years answers with that voice of hers that sounds like when you take an old bandage off fast. That rat Leo is still at the office. But Mrs. Weissman gives me some line about him being tied up in a meeting with some buyers. I tell her I'm about to be kidnapped by the Seven Dwarfs who are right outside the phone booth. Sneezy's holding a gun and Grumpy has the ransom note. She says she'll check to see if he can come to the phone. Leo comes on with his usual hi baby. I say listen you'd better be back home when Ruthie and I get there. Otherwise big trouble because we didn't clean up all that stuff for nothing. And Mother's already waiting. Leo goes through his ohmygod I forgot about the time routine. Which I recite silently while he says it. I know it as well as the Pledge of Allegiance.

Tonight everything is perfect. Dinner around the table. Leo carving the roast. Him and Mother staring at each other over the candles. And Ruthie and I kicking each other under the table every time we see them do anything. Leo's on his best behavior. He gave her a kiss when he came in. He told her how pretty she looked. For an ex-con he added and they both laughed. Best of all he brought her a beautiful pair of earrings. You can always tell the presents that Leo buys himself from the ones he sends Stanley out to buy. Mother is real pleased. She gives him a big hug and Ruthie shoots me a wink. It's just like the old days. Actually I never saw *those* old days. Ruthie says she remembers them though. But she gets fuzzy on the details.

After dinner we're told it's early bedtime tonight. Usually we'd moan but we know they want to be alone. Besides one wall of Ruthie's bedroom is against the living room so we put drinking glasses up against it and then put our ear to the glasses and listen. We can hear a little bit. A few words. But we can hear them laughing which is good. But something bothers me. I don't know what it is. It makes me nervous.

So I go into my room and listen to *The Shadow*. *The Shadow*'s my favorite radio show where *wealthy young man-about-town Lamont Cranston has the hypnotic power to cloud men's minds.* I always wanted to be Margo Lane *his friend and companion the only person who knows to whom the voice of the invisible man belongs.* Friend and companion my eye. She's obviously his girlfriend. So why don't they say it? Tonight The Shadow actually takes the bullets right out of the guns of the criminals before they know he's even there. I yell to Ruthie to come and listen but she's doing her chess exercises. Ruthie has a chessboard taped to the ceiling and lies on her bed making moves in her head. She's a brain.

We hear Leo and Mother head for the bedroom. In a flash we're pressed up against the door to the hallway like another coat of paint. They're giggling. Ruthie's mouth is open. I make a circle with my thumb and first finger. They go into the bedroom. We even hear the bedsprings twang. You owe me one Leo I say to myself. There's a lot of mushy remarks. Then there's a silence.

Then Mother is yelling.

Leo starts yelling back. It's all muffled until Mother opens the bedroom door and roars out into the hallway. She's holding something. Leo comes running out. "Well whose are they?" she yells.

"I don't know, I don't know," Leo yells back. The truth.

"You son of a bitch. You've pulled this once too often," Mother yells. "Get out." She throws what she's holding at Leo. It falls to the floor like a dead butterfly. Like a frilly lacy dead butterfly. A pair of pink underpants.

The pony's revenge.

4

Ruthie and I listen through the closed door. How could we blow it again? When we almost had them back together and now they're yelling at each other? Ruthie throws herself on the bed. "Checkmate," she says. "Time to clear the board and start a new game."

Now they're both yelling about Ivory Joe. Leo says, "Oh yeah, well who was that guy who called at one A.M.? Huh? Sounded like a Negro." *Kneee-gro.* Mother tells him it's none of his business and boy that really does it.

Actually Mother doesn't even tell us that much about Ivory Joe. She never says who he is or what he does. Or why he phones her so much now. But I talk to him sometimes when he phones and she's out. He has this great voice that sounds like cotton candy coming out of the phone. "Is your mama there?" he says. *Mama?* No one else ever called Mother mama.

By the next morning everything's back to normal. Leo's living at his place and we're here. But something different happens. When I get home the phone rings. It's Mother. There's something important I have to do she says. In the top desk drawer is a big envelope with GHOST LOVER written on it. I have to find it, get money out of the glass jar in the kitchen and then get a taxi to deliver it to the address she tells me. It has to get there fast.

The taxi goes down Columbus Avenue and I'm staring at the big envelope. It's not her writing on it. And what's GHOST LOVER? The address turns out to be the side of Carnegie Hall. There is a glass sign beside the elevator that says REHEARSAL HALLS. I think the elevator man scowls a bit when I tell him which room I'm going to. I get out of the elevator and walk down the hall that smells kind of musty like old linoleum. Some of the doors are open and you can look into the rooms where people are playing music. In one of them four people are sitting playing big fat violins. They don't look like they're having much fun. Further down the hall I look into a room and see a lady with a harp. The whole place is filled with music. The kind that Ruthie would love. She's a classical music nut.

When I get down to the room where Ivory Joe's supposed to be the door is closed. But you can hear music coming from inside. Different music. Not like the harp lady's. Or the people with the fat violins. This stuff is faster and louder. Sort of like a pounding sound. On the door there's a piece of paper that someone taped there and wrote on.

We would appreciate you continuing
to keep this door closed. When left open
it makes it impossible for us to
practice because of the noise.
signed
The Alhambra String Quartet
(and others)

I'm real nervous now. I know Ivory Joe's on the other side of that door. I start imagining what he looks like. Maybe big and scary like the Negro boxers in that gym Leo once took me to when he had to pay back some money. Or maybe all chuckly like Rochester the butler on the *Jack Benny Show*. I hope so. I knock on the door but not too loud. No one answers. So I open the door and look in.

There's Ivory Joe. Pounding away on the piano. He's definitely not like Rochester. He's looking down at the piano keys and scowling. Negro people really know how to scowl way better than we do. I get twice as nervous just looking at him. I figure maybe I should just leave the envelope on the floor and go. He's still just playing the piano as if I wasn't there. His hair is all slicked back and shiny and his face is the color of the toffee we buy at the drugstore for a penny. He's got on this suit that's also sort of shiny and a red shirt that I try to imagine Leo wearing but can't.

It's like I'm not even there. Ivory Joe's in a world of his own and that's okay with me. Time to go. But then I realize he's been watching me out of the corner of his eye. And the scowl is gone. "Hey girl, how are you doing?" he says in that cotton candy voice.

I try to smile but I can't. I'm fine Ivory Joe I say. I walk across the big room to give him the envelope. He starts playing jerky funny notes on the piano. I realize that he's playing one note for each step I take. Jerky funny notes that match the way I'm walking. In jerky funny steps. I can't help it I'm nervous. So I stop. He just grins and plays the same note over and over again. I start walking again this time real elegant. He starts playing something real fruity. Every time I put my foot down he plays a note. If I'm walking the way he sounds I gotta look real dumb. I stop again. I'm getting real peeved at him. But he just keeps grinning. I try again. This time I walk real fast just to get it over with. His fingers fly over the piano keys. I slow down. He slows down. He's definitely starting to bug me seriously so I stamp my foot. He pounds the piano.

Stop that I say. He just laughs. I'm getting madder and madder. But why am I starting to laugh too? I don't want to laugh. I want to be mad. But I start thinking about me walking like I was and this makes me laugh. It's not fair. Ivory Joe is really laughing harder now because he sees he's got me laughing. And this makes me even madder. But what can I do? He holds out his hand. "Please to meet you, Chrissie." *Chrissie?* Nobody calls me that. I've never shaken hands with a Negro person before. But now I'm just laughing and I forget about being mad. I like Ivory Joe right away.

Inside the envelope is a bunch of pages with music and writing on them. He looks at them and starts muttering to himself, plinking notes on the piano until he really winds up and starts playing something in-*cred*ible. I've never heard anything like it before it's so loud and so fast. It makes me want to jump up and down. He starts singing the words, something about a ghost lover who was never there. Some of the words I can't make out, like when we sing *The Star-Spangled Banner* at school. Then all of a sudden he just stops and grins.

What is that I ask.

"My song," he says. "I forgot to ask your mama to bring it when I saw her last. I'm still writing it."

What's my ma—I almost said it myself—mother doing with you? Way back in my head I can hear Leo making me ask all these questions. The rat.

"We're sort of partners," he says. Leo is practically yelling the questions now but I clamp my mouth shut as Ivory Joe goes back to fooling around on the piano. When he stops I ask if he's playing jazz.

"Ain't jazz," he says. "Friends of mine are calling it rock 'n' roll." I've never heard of rock 'n' roll before. "Tell me which you like best. This," he says playing something with his left hand. "Or this," and he starts playing something else with his right hand. I can't believe he's asking *me*. In music class Mrs. Kelcher thinks I'm a dunce but Ivory Joe doesn't because for a long time he's asking questions and listening like I know what I'm talking about when I tell him what music makes me want to jump around and what puts me to sleep. I'm having a great time when the phone rings. It's Mother and I listen to Ivory Joe talk to her in that neat way he makes his words curl all over the place. I can hear her laugh.

She hasn't laughed like that with Leo in a long time.

FIGHTERS

5

In the months immediately after their marriage ended it was always Leo who made the phone calls telling Tina they *had* to meet. There were problems. Braces for Ruthie's teeth. A different school for Christie. Which summer camp to send them to.

"Leo, where have you been for the last ten years?"

"What do you mean where have I been? Is this a trick question or what?"

"Last year you didn't think any of this was a problem. Or the year before. Or the year before that."

"Well, I didn't know about it. You should have told me about all this stuff. . . . Tina?"

"Yeah, Leo. I probably forgot to mention it."

"Hey. It happens. No problem."

Tina insisted they meet up in Washington Heights where she often went for long walks beside the Hudson River. Leo would always arrive with a few awkward jokes and a smile that would fade as he looked around at the trees and the bushes. They would walk together, suffocating in politeness until some tiny remark would fall on the tinder of stored-up resentments, exploding all over again. During one of their fights, Tina suddenly fell silent for a moment, staring at the shimmering river. "I want to be free, Leo," she said, walking toward the river. "Free of it all."

"Terrific! Great! Me too!" yelled Leo. "Where the hell are you going?"

She ripped off her blouse and threw it behind her. Then her shorts.

And the shoes were kicked off. All without missing a step on her march to the water.

"Are you crazy?" Leo tore off his seersucker jacket trying to catch up and cover her with it. Water was already over his ankles. "Look, you want a bath? I'll drive you home!"

Tina swam the Hudson. Past cruise ships and yachts that circled and called out asking if she needed help, she churned toward the New Jersey shore. Leo ran back to the car, his drenched pants slapping at his legs. The Cadillac raced south, screeching into the George Washington Bridge where Leo hurled a five-dollar bill at the toll booth attendant and roared off without waiting for change. They arrived at the same time, Tina climbing exhilarated from the water as Leo skidded down the grassy hillside yelling, "You've only got your underwear on! Remember you're a mother!"

Tina collapsed on the shore laughing. Leo stumbled and fell, rolling down the hill with her clothes whipping behind him in the blur of arms and legs that pinwheeled to a halt beside her. Leo tried to be angry. But he couldn't make her stop laughing. So he got even angrier until he started laughing himself, even though he tried to stop.

She reached out and held his hand but couldn't stop laughing. "Goddamnit. Where did it all go wrong?" said Leo, lying back in the mud and staring up at the sky.

Tina did not reply.

Tina phoned a Hungarian photojournalist she met while Leo was away during the war. Everything was *of course*. Of course he remembered her. Of course he would love to see her. Of course she would come to work for him. And when they met for a coffee she found herself once again staring into the same bemused smile that both infuriated and intrigued her. Within minutes after they met she made sure she conveyed how happily married she was. "But *of course*," he said. With the same twinkling shrug. "A lucky man, this Leo of yours." And then he told her of the beautiful Scandinavian actress he was now in love with.

"Of course," said Tina and the following day she went to work for Summa, the news photo agency established by the Hungarian and a dozen other famous photojournalists. She loved the work. The days were filled with a pandemonium fueled by the intense camaraderie of conflicting personalities locked into a common purpose. It was Tina who mediated, soothed and occasionally argued with the photographers to whom she had to hand out assignments, sometimes contacting them in distant countries by terse telegrams or static-filled phone calls. She juggled schedules and egos, negotiated with magazine editors and matched wits in the company of the worldly and anarchistic photographers who were nominally her employers.

And most of all she loved the pressure filling her days with a joyous chaos that left no room for the aching thoughts of Leo that crowded the edges of sleep almost every night.

Sometimes when she worked late she would hear music coming from an office at the far end of the corridor. It was a piano being played in ways she had not heard before. The rhythms were not jazz or even Latin. But there was a movement to them unlike any music she heard on the radio. And a man's voice, what she thought must be a tenor, could be heard singing in powerful bursts that rose and faded with the music. When she locked the door to the office at night, she would stand in the corridor listening to it.

The music came from behind a door that said CENTURY SPORTING CLUB INC. During the day, older men smoking cigars entered and left, sometimes accompanied by young men with corrugated noses and muscles that showed through their shirts. At night the door remained closed.

Over several months, Tina followed the progress of three tunes from stray chords to completed songs. In the empty corridor, she would pause, urging on the rhyming process when it stalled at *ever so cruel*. She mentally flipped through the possibilities. *Duel. Fool. Cool.* But a week later she listened to

And I was ever so cruel
Back when I knew all
That heaven could hold

sung to a pounding beat that filled the hallway with music that made her want to dance. When it stopped she knocked on the door, but the cascading rumble of low piano notes erased all other sounds. She tried the door, opened it and saw a Negro sitting at a scarred old upright piano covered with boxing trophies. He was several years younger than she, with distinct features that made shadows and reflections across his face as he played under the single harsh light. He looked up for a moment, just stared and kept playing.

"Can I help you?"

"I just work down the hall."

"Am I disturbing you?"

"No. Not at all." With the same composed stare he kept playing until he came to a difficult passage and looked down. "What if I said you *were* disturbing me?"

"Then either I'd have to stop playing. Or you'd have to stop listening."

"I wouldn't want either to happen."

"Me neither."

He smiled, more out of politeness than appreciation, and when Tina left she thought she had never met anyone so quietly self-assured. Several weeks later *Collier's* magazine was racing a deadline on a story about James Dean and the movie *East of Eden*, which he was filming. Tina returned to the office after putting Ruthie and Christie to bed and promising she wouldn't leave the old babysitter there all night. She stood in the corridor outside the Century Sporting Club Inc. listening for music. There was silence. While the negatives were being developed, she heard a door slam. She opened the door to the Summa office listening for any sounds from the corridor. Notes and ragged piano chords drifted down the hallway and then stopped. For as long as Tina remained in the office, there was the same incoherent barrage of music that ebbed into silence and then began again. When it was very late she knocked on the door of the Century Sporting Club Inc. Single notes sounded softly. She opened the door.

There was a moment of shock from which she recovered when he looked up at her. His face was swollen, with one eye almost closed and a swath of raw skin tracing the outline of his cheekbone. One hand, bandaged, hung at his side.

"What happened?" she said, trying to sound as casual as he looked.

"What do you mean, what happened?"

"Your face."

He looked down and played three notes again and again. "Earning a living," he said.

"Are you a boxer?"

"Why you surprised?"

"What on earth are you doing that for?"

"Because I'd make a lousy janitor."

"But you're a singer."

"Maybe."

"But if you lost like that—"

"I *won*." His one open eye flashed in momentary defiance.

"Well, that is really stupid," Tina said, slamming the door behind her and marching across the room. Her lips came tightly together the way they did whenever she lost her temper at Leo. "You and some other idiot bashing each other's heads in. Of all the ridiculous—"

"Who do you think you are, lady? Coming in here and sticking your nose in my business."

"It's my business if I have to listen to what you're playing."

"Hey, it's real simple then, isn't it? All you have to do is leave."

The tune he was playing on the piano whenever it was her turn to talk suddenly filtered through her anger. It was a nursery song, *The Teddy Bears' Picnic*. She had sung it to Christie when she was younger. "Are you making fun of me?"

"If I am, I apologize," he said. There was a trace of a sly smile.

"If you are, you're playing it badly."

"Hey, what are you going to do when the machine doesn't work?" he said, pounding several keys that were either dead or badly tuned. "But then it's a poor workman who blames his tools."

"So get a different piano."

"Working on it. But this one's free."

"Nothing's free."

The following morning she walked down the hall to the Century Sporting Club Inc. The old man with the porkpie hat and the cigar stub jutting out over the huge double chin that settled like a wreath around his neck answered in grunts as she told him Summa wanted to do a photostory about boxers. His eyes showed nothing buried in his face. He pulled a clipboard from his desk and started calling out the locations of their upcoming fights. One at the Garden. St. Nick's. The Diamond Belt in Philly. A bunch of Police Athletic League stuff. She stopped him, asking about the boxers involved. It turns out there was Bobo. And Kid. Davey. Max. Fergie. Bugs. Johnny. She asked about the fighter who just won a few nights earlier. In the really bad fight.

"Bad? We didn't have no bad fight."

"Where they really beat each other up."

"That was a great fight. Who told you it was bad?" He leaned over and let a ball of yellow saliva plummet from his lips into the spittoon beside his desk. "You talking about the colored boy?"

"Yes. I suppose I am."

"Joe. Ivory Joe Coulter. Lemme see." He scanned the list, flipped a page and then said, "Yeah, he's fighting in two weeks. Thursday. Near the top of the card. At the Holcomb A.C."

"Why is he fighting so soon? After the way he got beaten up?"

"It's a free world, lady. He can always quit."

"Of course."

When Tina left, the old man watched her, wondering if here was just one more white dame who had the itch to go colored. A dime a dozen.

The Holcomb Athletic Club was a fetid relic. Its Romanesque facade was coated with generations of grime from the air and the streets near Cooper Square on the lower East Side. The stone columns on the squat portico that had been built in the previous century were now chipped or missing, replaced by wooden beams. What was once an attempt by lesser merchants of some stature to have a gentlemen's club like their wealthier counterparts on upper Fifth Avenue had deteriorated into a raucous hall populated by the kind of rabble the old merchants would have avoided even more than their own employees. The beveled glass in the door had given way to plywood replacements and the parquet floors of the foyer were now linoleum checkerboards. The Ukrainians of the area would come to see their contenders matched with whatever Pole or Puerto Rican brawler came downtown. But now it was the Italians from the tenement canyons around Mulberry Street to the south who showed up in the greatest numbers. In the rank murkiness of a fight night, the club was a testing ground for young fighters controlled by the various Mafia families. Profaci, Anastasia and Gambino were all represented. And Tommy Eboli still kept a few fighters that the Genoveses controlled. As each fighter walked into the ring through the crowd of several hundred or maybe a thousand people, he passed the gamblers who had determined the odds of his success. And gambling was as much a part of the event as the fight.

Tina was the only unaccompanied woman in the club. She remained near the back of the hall as far from the ring as she could get. Men with creased faces and huge hands made remarks to her and then about her. Tina ignored them and the shield of purpose around her soon convinced them she must be the wife or girlfriend of one of the fighters. The first two matches were booed because there was no knockout and hardly any damage done. They were matches between teenage boys with dreams of St. Nicholas Arena or even the Garden. The older boxers fought under made-up names and came from New Jersey or Pennsylvania, fleeing boxing commissions that had suspended them for fear of permanent brain damage. They were at the desperate end of their careers, with clogged minds barely able to remember the kind of hope driving these young opponents to sacrifice downy faces against their fists.

Ivory Joe was in the third fight. A young boxer with short blond hair and a broad Slavic face waited in the ring as he pushed through the crowd escorted by two Negro trainers. One of them was bald and heavy; the other had a full head of tightly curled gray hair and moved a toothpick around his mouth in quickening circles. The name Red Leg was sewn on the front of his shiny trainer's shirt. Reaching the main aisle, Ivory Joe saw Tina and for a moment stopped, causing Red Leg to run into him from behind. Then he disappeared back into the packed aisle as Tina strained to watch. As he climbed into the ring she wanted to call out telling him to stop. Anger overtook her, driving out the sounds of the ring announcer and the babble of men yelling about the odds and passing money back and forth. It all became silence. She was alone with her thoughts, echoing soundlessly in the tumult. She saw the first punch and then the others that battered both men but heard only *The Teddy Bears' Picnic.* Ivory Joe staggered backward.

If you go down to the woods today
You're in for a big surprise

Somewhere far away the bell sounded and they returned to their corners, Ivory Joe disappearing behind the big Negro with the shaved head who ministered with towels and ice until it all began again and the other fighter landed a punch that sent the big gamblers at ringside leaping to their feet, cheering.

If you go down to the woods today
You'd better go in disguise

It all slowed down, the world around her running on a different rhythm, stretching out every gracefully arcing punch that crashed in their faces.

Picnic time for Teddy bears

Ivory Joe was pounded back against the ropes. Tina quickly turned and forced her way out to the aisle, pushing through bursts of liquored breath until she reached the foyer and the roar from the hall suddenly burst in her ears. It rose and fell in waves. She walked angrily back to the door but didn't open it. She leaned against the mildewed plaster wall. She stood on the linoleum floor under the neon light. She walked in tight circles, watched by an arthritic old ticket taker. And then it was over, the hordes pushing past her, spilling into the street in an exuberant flow, leaving behind a silence broken only by a few angry voices inside the hall.

Most of the lights were being turned down, leaving the ring an island of whiteness in a gathering gloom that was occasionally blurred by the shuffling presence of the cleaners. The angry voices pulled Tina toward a corridor and the dressing rooms. Two white men in suits, wearing fedoras, were standing in the corridor confronting Red Leg and another Negro, who blocked a dressing room door. The door opened and Ivory Joe appeared, still dressed in boxing trunks. Except for a welt across his forehead, his face was unmarked. One of the men in suits began yelling at him.

"You doublecrossing son of a bitch. You better be able to run real fast. And real far."

"I don't go in the tank for anybody," said Ivory Joe.

"You do what you're fucking well told."

"Well, I guess I got it all wrong, then, didn't I?" said Ivory Joe, his voice calm and even.

"You're fucking right you got it all wrong, nigger. You know how much money you cost us?"

"Excuse me, I have to change."

Ivory Joe started to close the door but the taller of the two men kicked at it. All the voices sounded at once, congealing in a contagious anger. "Get out!" yelled Tina, storming down the hall. "Out! You heard me!" The two men in the fedoras were taken by surprise, turning in toward this female voice that was so out of place. And the wild, furious eyes that bore down on them, drawing an unreasoning bead that no words could deflect. "Who the hell are you, lady?" was all they could muster, amazed to find themselves backing up.

"That's none of your goddam business," snapped Tina. "Now get out of here!" The taller one reached out and shoved her, thrusting a palm onto her shoulder, pushing her back for the instant before she slapped his face with a noise echoing like a rifle shot in the corridor. He reached back to hit her but the other man grabbed his arm.

"Freddie, you don't hit a broad. Not in here," he yelled, pulling the taller man back as Tina advanced and slapped him again. "Jesus Christ, you stupid bitch, are you looking to get your head taken off?" The two men were wrestling with each other, backing up into the hall as Tina advanced, yelling at them to get out and never come back.

At the dressing room door, Red Leg and the other trainer were grinning until Tina turned around and their faces simultaneously erased all expression.

"Excuse us, please," she said, pushing past them. Ivory Joe was standing just inside the dressing room as she marched in, slammed the door and stared him in the eye. "You have no business being here," she said.

He laughed. "Me? Lady, have you got any idea who those two guys were?"

"I couldn't care less."

"Yeah? Did you ever stop to think that they might just get you killed before you walk out of here?"

"You were the one they were arguing with first."

"If I jumped over a cliff, would you follow?"

"So, who are they?"

"They're two-bit punks trying to be big-time gamblers. But next time find out who you're yelling at. Now, you do happen to be standing in my dressing room, so if you'll excuse me . . ."

"Not till we talk about business."

"I'm not aware we have any business to talk about."

"I'm making you an offer. I'll manage you as a singer. I'll finance a rehearsal hall. With a proper piano. Take care of living allowance until you get some bookings. Handle travel and all the deals."

"Why?"

"Maybe I'm bored with what I'm doing. And maybe I can't stand to see some idiot throw away what you've got."

"Look, lady, I *won* out there tonight," said Ivory Joe, angrily pointing to the doorway.

"It's good you told me that. And by the way, were you any good?"

Ivory Joe started to answer but stopped. He leaned against a bench. "I stunk," he said. "I was the favorite. I should have won easily. Which is why those two hoods wanted me to go in the tank in the fourth round. Everyone else was betting for me. So they bet against me. And offered me two hundred dollars. I just grinned at them and told myself I was going to flatten their boy because of that. But it was all I could do to stay on my feet. And he's not very good."

"So what does that make you?"

Ivory Joe was looking at the floor, his hands braced against the edge of the massage bench. He shook his head slowly, as if waiting for an answer to appear. Finally he looked up and said, "You know what you're letting yourself in for?"

FROLIC FROCKS

6

In 1934, at the age of thirteen, Leo Klein was expelled from school for the second time and was bringing home more money than his stepfather. He had staked out 170th Street and Jerome Avenue in the Bronx as being the place to make his fortune shining shoes. Within a week he was averaging ninety cents a day. Within two weeks the word had spread and there were shoeshine boys up and down the block. Leo was down to thirty cents a day. Even worse, a price war was developing on 170th Street. One afternoon, Arnie Dalitz, the oldest kid in grade eight, showed up and announced to all the shoeshine boys that they needed protection.

"Against what?" he was asked. Arnie Dalitz gave them the answers he heard his father had given bar owners before he was found shot. When Arnie Dalitz came to Leo's corner, Leo punched him in the mouth before he could start talking. The fight ended when neither of them could stand up. They lay on the sidewalk, blood streaming from their noses and Arnie Dalitz fingering a wobbly tooth. Leo looked at his brushes and polish strewn in the gutter and made a decision.

"I'm going to help you out."

"You're going to help *me*? Since when do I need help from a dick like you?" said Arnie Dalitz, trying to stand up.

"Yeah? Well, why do you think you came here in the first place? Because *I* found this place. I have this talent, see? I can spot great shoeshine places. I'll find other places and you set up your own shoeshine boys."

"What's the catch?"

"We split fifty fifty."

"You putz. I'll beat the shit out of you before I—"

"Okay, ten percent. But I keep this block for myself."

"Deal."

"You drive a hard bargain," said Leo, knowing that he had won more than he hoped for. But he also wanted to leave Arnie Dalitz thinking that he had won. *Whip 'em but let 'em think they've done it to you.* It was to become his code in life and business. To which he would later add: *unless there's no other way out.* Within another week Leo was back up to ninety cents as the sole shoeshine boy at 170th and Jerome. He soon became bored with the ninety cents and began competing against himself. He printed business cards that said SATISFACTION GUARANTEED OR YOUR MONEY BACK even though no one had ever paid him until he had finished the job. He bought a folding chair and a rack on which he hung the day's newspapers. The well-dressed men of the area were soon making detours to spend a few minutes catching up on the news while they had their shoes shined. And for those who weren't interested in the papers, Leo always had a joke. He prided himself on sizing up the personality of his clients after three sentences. He could tell those who would like the dirty jokes from those who were strictly the priest, the rabbi and the minister types. He was never wrong. Business was soon up to a dollar seventy a day. He stopped seeing his daily total merely as money. It became a means of measuring the score. A part of the game where the opponent was always yesterday. He bought another chair and shoeshine box and set up his older brother Morris in business right beside him. Morris was pleasant, serious, and had none of the charm that Leo used to draw in customers. Leo noticed that Morris shined shoes with more care than anyone he had ever seen. He applied the polish in precise little dabs that never got on the laces. But the customers still preferred coming to Leo.

Arnie Dalitz and Leo became closest friends and would laugh about the first fight. A broken tooth for a broken nose. A draw. But each secretly claimed victory. Leo scouted the Bronx and came up with four more hot shoeshine blocks which Arnie Dalitz franchised out. With the money they made, they played fierce games of gin and poker, and sometimes they would bet the day's profits playing pool at the Avalon. The Avalon Billiard Hall was owned by Herman Pinsky's father, who spent most of his time at the track. Neither Leo nor Arnie Dalitz understood Herman Pinsky the way they did each other. Herman was heavy, with short black hair that lay flat on his head, and wore big glasses, magnifying dark eyes that could look right through them. But when Herman laughed it was like a chain reaction through his whole body. Parts of him started quivering and then shaking until everything was in motion and he was holding his stomach groping for a chair. Arnie Dalitz and Leo would take turns trying to make him crack up. They would place bets on how long it would take.

Herman never bet on anything. Once he had money he kept it, and by the age of thirteen he was rumored to have enough to buy a new car. It was Herman who came up with the gambling scheme. Why not get others involved in the card games? Outsiders. The next day Leo told no jokes while shining shoes. Instead, he told tales of card games that made men fortunes. Sworn never to reveal the location of this amazing game, he would make an exception just this once. "For you, my best customer," he said, thirty-five times that day, in a low voice, looking around him.

The back room of the Avalon was soon packed every afternoon while Herman's father was at the track. Leo, Herman and Arnie Dalitz took turns forging notes from their parents to get out of school. Sometimes all three of them would be running the games. And afterward counting the piles of money. One day, when they were still setting up the tables, a large car drove up in the alley behind the Avalon. "The game's not on for another hour," said Herman to the two men wearing suits and fedoras. When the games became a success, Herman had immediately adopted a tough way of talking, the way he thought the real casino owners talked. The two men ignored him, walking around and counting the chairs. Leo and Arnie Dalitz exchanged puzzled glances. "I said the game's not on yet," snapped Herman. One of the men picked up a folding chair and smashed it into a table.

"It's not on, period," said the man, whose left cheekbone looked pushed in.

"Says who?" said Leo, trying to sound tough. And failing.

"Look, sonny, you tell whoever's running the game that Charlie Lucky has taken over from the Dutchman. And he doesn't like people horning in on his business." Then they left.

Only Arnie Dalitz understood what had happened. They had been visited by two enforcers working for Lucky Luciano, the Mafia boss who had moved into the numbers and gambling rackets across large areas of New York City. He had taken over from Dutch Schultz, whose empire was crumbling while he spent most of his time fighting tax evasion charges. *Luciano.* The mere name struck fear into all of them. But their puny games? Attracting the mighty Luciano's attention? As fearful as they were, they also felt a little more important.

"So what do we do?" said Herman, who had stopped talking tough. Just then the door opened and several of their regulars entered, sat down and started cutting the cards.

"We'll go for one more game," said Leo. "Who'll notice?"

"I dunno," said Arnie Dalitz, looking worried.

Other men entered, waved hello and sat down to play. "Come on," said Leo. "We can't kick them out now. Besides, who's gonna know? Just one lousy game."

The game went on.

That night, as Herman Pinsky's father was closing the Avalon Billiard Hall, several men entered, drawing the blinds over the front windows. Before being beaten senseless by the men, Herman's father yelled that he knew nothing about any gambling. *At the Avalon? Bullshit! And what fucking kids? Were they crazy? A front for what? And who the hell'd be crazy enough to cross Charlie Lucky?* When Herman Pinsky's father regained consciousness, his left arm had been broken, two teeth were knocked out and every one of his pool tables had been hacked to pieces. After getting out of the emergency ward and refusing to talk to the police, he used his one good arm to beat Herman across the rear end with a pool cue that left welts for a week.

And then he vowed the worst revenge on Leo he could think of. He phoned his mother.

7

Leo never heard the phone call from Herman Pinsky's father. He was barely aware of the staccato footsteps on the stairs. In the farthest reaches of his unconscious those footsteps went off like the pistol shots he was dreaming of. Lucky Luciano had come for his revenge. He awoke yelling into the fearful mask of his mother's face.

And wished it had only been Lucky Luciano.

Leo's mother was known to most people in the neighborhood as Mother Ackerman. She had, at various times, also been Mrs. Klein, Mrs. Berman and Mrs. Ackerman. With one husband dead, another fleeing with an eighteen-year-old chambermaid and the current one working in docile servitude as a baker, Mother Ackerman was more imposing than any of her husbands. Standing six feet tall, she often wore three-inch heels. And on Sundays she would convene the various branches of her extended family in the living room, where she would sit in a high-backed chair mounted on a two-inch platform. Behind her was a portrait of the emperor Franz Josef, her political idol from the moment she had been told he had passed laws prohibiting gentiles from attacking Jews.

Mother Ackerman gloried in her contradictions. Fiercely Zionist, she had not been to a synagogue since she was twelve years old in Austria. She had refused to go no matter what threats her parents tried. The impoverished Austrian worshipers stunk, she said. None of them had taken a bath in a week. A fervent socialist, she played the stock market passionately, cheering the good fortunes of U.S. Steel and General Electric. And the advice she solemnly passed down to her sons was: Buy diamonds. Because who knew when the next exodus would be. And *then* what good would your uncle Herbert's Brooklyn real estate be?

She alone was the reason why Leo even kept up the pretense of going to school. Being expelled from school struck terror not because of the gray-faced little principal who hissed out the direst of futures for Leo and Arnie Dalitz. Instead, it was the towering stare of his mother that intimidated him in ways he didn't understand. Even entering the city junior billiard championship left him fearful that her wrath would descend on him for associating with the wrong element. Always it was *the wrong element*. Arnie Dalitz was. Herman Pinsky was. His cousin Arnold the Brain was not. And the pool hall crowd definitely was. So when Leo won first prize shooting pool, the newspapers announced that an L. Smith had won the trophy. The trophy stayed hidden under Leo's bed.

It was Mother Ackerman's Sunday-afternoon rituals that Leo grew to loathe. They seemed endless, filled with talk of philosophy and politics. His cousin Arnold the Brain would show off his mind like it was a new car. Arnold was pale and skinny with spidery fingers and limp hair. He was one of the Berman part of the family. Leo loathed the Bermans. Arrogant weirdos, all of them. He couldn't figure out why his mother had anything to do with them after her second husband ran off with the eighteen-year-old. But every Sunday they would show up like a troupe of traveling undertakers and subject Leo to the agonies of Hegelian analysis of the labor movement. Or a reevaluation of socialism in Russia. Leo couldn't believe it. Sometimes he would catch himself muttering under his breath. When there was a ball game they could all be listening to. Or crap games down the block. But this shit?

During one of the most painfully prolonged examinations of historical empiricism, he caught his cousin Arnold staring out the window at the laundry on the clothesline. It was mostly filled with his mother's underwear. "Hey Arnie, I'll bet you spend a lot of time in the bathroom with the door locked," Leo whispered.

"The name is Arnold." In that fruity voice. And looking down that long nose which Leo wanted to flatten. "And for your information, I was engaged in an activity you never do."

"Hey Arnold, is that why your hand's on your crotch?"

"I was referring to thinking."

"No shit."

"If you persist, I'll tell your mother."

"And I'll bust your face, Arnold."

"Leo, you've never gotten over not coming from our side of the family, have you?"

"I've never gotten over having to *be* with your side of the family, you dink."

"There are three of us in college. That's why you dislike us, isn't it?"

"Stick your books up your ass, Arnold—if there's any room left. I'm gonna make it big. On my own, too."

By the time he turned twenty, Leo was wondering where he went wrong.

With a tenth-grade education and no prospect for advancement, he was pushing racks filled with dresses up and down Broadway. Fighting the traffic. Watching the older men with big bellies and fat rings on their baby fingers come out of Morgen's while he scrambled for a danish to go at Dubrow's. Fighting for elevator space on Seventh Avenue and being yelled at by old Italian cutters when the cloth got rained on. Shooting crap for nickels with the other rack boys who made lewd remarks about every woman who passed by. Leo hated it all. He hated the powerlessness. And the confinement. It was worse than school. At least there he never felt the stench of failure.

And seeing Arnie Dalitz made it worse. A regular bona fide success story. Arnie Dalitz was walking all over the block dressed in his sharp suits. He could stroll into any one of the dozens of manufacturers at 525 Seventh Avenue and just eat it all up. Watching all the big cigars twice, three times his age, come running over to him like he was the man himself.

Arnie Dalitz was a kind of glorified messenger boy. But he was smart enough to know it. And he was sure enough of himself to know he would not stay there for long. He had been taken to meet Meyer Lansky, who had killed more people than most of the Sicilians in the Mafia. And now Lansky was working with Luciano and Vito Genovese. A Jew in the mob, said Arnie Dalitz, with a sense of wonderment and pride. Arnie Dalitz loved his work. It was his job to stand around the lobby of 525 Seventh Avenue for a few hours a day and take in all the requests for loan-shark money. Manufacturers scrambling to cover payrolls or buy whatever fabrics they needed to bring out their spring lines would come to Arnie Dalitz with nervous eyes and big smiles that never quite worked. Five thou. Ten. Fifty.

For a week. Ten days. A month. It was all noted down in Arnie Dalitz's own code in his little notebooks. For small amounts he would simply nod and then go for the cash. For larger amounts he went to a pay phone, dialed a number and just gave the name and amount. That was all. The manufacturers got the money that no bank would ever lend them. And then they struggled to pay back the huge interest payments that compounded every week.

On the night Arnie Dalitz took him to Al Cooper's steakhouse, Leo was going to quit. "Yeah? And do what?" asked Arnie Dalitz.

"Shine shoes. I'm better at it."

"What's with you? Huh? You want to know about problems? You should be Shapiro."

"Which Shapiro?"

"The Frolic Frocks guy. Real asshole. Can't even make the juice. On thirty G's only. The prick."

Leo remembered Shapiro, frantic, yelling all the time, cursing him for delivering the wrong kind of velvet when he had merely delivered what the shipper had told him to. Shapiro, spilling out over his pants, bald except for a fringe of stringy hair low on his head. Gambling for hours on end when they shut the doors to the show-room. And losing constantly.

The next day Shapiro was found shot to death in a phone booth. Leo was pushing a rack of dresses along 40th Street when he saw the police cars parked all over the intersection, whipping flashes of red light around in the gloom. And a crumpled figure contorted in the bottom of the phone booth as blood trickled under the door and congealed in the fine powdery snow.

"Did you know this was going to happen?" Leo almost yelled at Arnie Dalitz when he found him in a bar.

"Leo, everyone knew this was going to happen."

"Did *you* know it was going to happen?"

"Are you out of your goddam head? Don't ask me questions like that."

"Arnie, we're friends."

"Look, Leo, this ain't shoeshine time. This is the big leagues. People get hurt here. So don't go asking too many questions."

"Did you kill him?"

"No." Arnie Dalitz looked Leo in the eye. "But they put me in charge of getting rid of his company. We're holdin' paper on it. I'll do you a favor. I'll sell you the joint for six grand."

"Are you crazy?"

"Probably. Shapiro ran it into the ground anyway. It's got three thousand ugly dresses that no buyer will touch. That's what started his troubles."

"Some favor."

The blizzard the next day started just before lunchtime. By two o'clock the snow was ankle deep on the streets and pedestrians were being blown over by the wind. The three dozen dresses on Leo's rack snapped like flags in a gale as he fought his way up Seventh Avenue. The wheels on the rack kept freezing and his bare hands burned when he gripped the metal rungs. He heaved against the rack, throwing his shoulder against it and then leaning backward and churning his legs on the snow. He tugged the rack around onto 40th Street just as the wind shifted, wrenching the dresses from the rack. Before Leo could grapple with the twisting mass of fabric, the dresses shot from their hangers in volleys that hurled them into the air. They soared into the blizzard or were plastered across third-story windows. Leo threw himself against the remaining dresses, trying to stop them from coming loose. The rack slipped off the sidewalk, toppling into the gutter. And taking Leo with it. He crawled across the filthy dresses back to the sidewalk, where he stopped and stared as if a vision had appeared before his eyes.

Looming in front of him was the phone booth where Shapiro was murdered. Leo stumbled to his feet, holding his hands under his arms and jumping up and down in the freezing wind. His eyes never left the phone booth. He circled it. He began talking to it.

"Hey, Shapiro," he yelled. "It wasn't me. Okay? Got that? I had nothing to do with you getting whacked. You listening, Shapiro?"

People who had hurried past, leaning into the sleet, stopped and looked back at Leo. Then they went on.

"I didn't know it was gonna happen. Understand? If it was me I wouldn't have done it. So whadya say, Shapiro?" The phone booth stood mute in the settling grayness as Leo yelled at it until the streetlights came on. Then he went and found Arnie Dalitz.

"I'm gonna buy Shapiro's company."

"Leo, I was kidding, you know."

"I'm not. You said six grand. I'll get it."

That night Leo woke up his brother Morris with stories of a fantastic dress company that was going for a song. He left with a check for all the money Morris had, twelve hundred dollars. One of the Berman part of the family, a pale nervous cousin of Arnold Berman who had always envied Leo's aggressive flair, was persuaded that his thousand-dollar savings bond was far safer with Frolic Frocks, Inc. than with the U.S. Government. That was it for the family. Two thousand two hundred. There was no way he could go to Mother Ackerman. She would have made him return what he already had. The next day Leo got dressed in his only suit and went to a building on West 37th, where the big cigars had the hottest Friday-afternoon card game. In a fourth-floor showroom he bought into the game for two hundred dollars and left after winning nine hundred. He found Arnie Dalitz and put three thousand in front of him.

"Leo, don't do this to me. You're my friend."

"I'm buying the company."

"Six G's, Leo. I don't control that. Vito does. Lansky does. But not me."

"Fine. Six G's. Here's three. And I'm borrowing the other three from you guys."

"Are you thick or what? Leo, they kill people who don't pay them back. An' you ain't got a fuckin' prayer of even making the vigorish."

"I will."

"Yeah? How?"

"I dunno yet. I'll think of something."

"That's what Shapiro said. And he got whacked for it."

"I'm not pushing racks anymore, Arnie. Now, you gonna do this deal or do I go see Franky Dio? He'll arrange it."

"You got a death wish? He's carving notches on his belt."

"Okay, so I'll go to the bank."

"Leo, you obviously ain't got a clue. You just try going to a bank to borrow the money you need just to keep the goddam company alive long enough to put out your spring line. You know what's in the bank, Leo? Sitting behind some fucking big desk with a poker up his ass? A Protestant who thinks garment guys are all greasy thieving wops and yids. You got more chance of him giving you his sixteen-year-old daughter than any of the dough in his bank. So now you're out on your ass, absolutely up the creek and who do you turn to? *Me*, Leo. You turn into one of the zillion garmentos coming to me asking for Vito's money. So I run my little errand to the Genoveses, get you the dough. And then you sweat. 'Cause God help you if you don't pay it back. And before you know it my guys have got you by the nuts."

"So what's the problem, Arnie?"

"Leo, you're a total moron. You know that?"

Shortly after eight o'clock the following Tuesday evening, Leo walked into the big garment building at 525 Seventh Avenue, took the elevator to the eleventh floor and walked down the corridor past the doors with names like Miss Liz Fashions, Mayinette Designs, Gay Paree Styles and Princess Patterns. With the key he had just been given, he opened the door of Frolic Frocks and went inside. It was his.

His elation lasted until he found the light switch. The showroom was a mess. Dumped ashtrays. Disintegrating mirrors. Filthy sales tables. And a rack of ugly dresses made from an imitation brocade.

In the back, past the cutting tables, were hundreds, thousands of the same dull gray and green dresses hanging from racks. Like mossy tombstones with Shapiro's name on them. Or his own. "Oh my God, Leo, you couldn't give those away on Eleventh Avenue," said Morris, when Leo brought him in. "I know I'm your brother, but is it too late to get my money back?"

"You're my vice president in charge of production."

"I don't know a thing about the garment business."

"You start tomorrow."

It was several days before Leo could bring himself to sit in the chair behind Shapiro's desk. The office was a still life of commercial chaos. Files and accounting statements piled in yellowing mounds of paper. Cups with dried coffee. Smudged invoices disappearing under paper plates encrusted with moldy food. Inside the drawers were pencils with the ends chewed, bottles of Alka-Seltzer, Bromo Seltzer, Milk of Magnesia and Pepto-Bismol. Several packets of condoms. *Sunbathing International* nudist magazines. And a small black address book. Inside the book were the names of women with only their phone numbers and a price for each ranging from twenty to one hundred dollars. Occasionally there were penciled comments beside a woman's name. *For Harry from Seattle. Great bj's. Lou from Philly wants her. Will put on a show—$100.*

It was one week until he had to make his first payment to Arnie Dalitz's boss. Already he needed more money just to stay open. The pale nervous cousin of Arnold Berman was squeezed around the shoulders and told he would lose every cent of his original thousand. Leo was expecting it all, first the look of condescension, then the watery eyes and the high-pitched anguish. He would just wait it out and then steamroll back in with the very same bad news. He left with another eight hundred dollars. For two days he and Morris slept only a few hours a night. They cleaned the offices, agonized over the accounts payable, fought off collection agencies and, with the one employee they could afford, an old Italian cutter named Mimmo Franco, they got ready for the fall collection that was to be shown that week.

Hundreds of buyers from the big stores all over America were arriving in New York to purchase the fashions that would be sold in the fall. "I'm gonna sell every one of those dresses by Friday," Leo announced. Friday was the day of the payment to Arnie Dalitz's boss.

"Hah. *Buona fortuna,*" said Mimmo, shaking his head and staring at the dresses. "My mother, she ninety-one. She no wear those to pick tomato."

"Yeah, well, you're gonna fix them so she'll be begging you for one. So she can go out and dance the tarantella, Mimmo."

"Whaddayou think? Me design?"

"You said you'd done everything for Shapiro. So do it for me, too. Design something. Anything. Just fix it."

While Mimmo fretted over changes in the ugliest dress he had ever taken the pinking shears to, Leo walked into the Waldorf wearing his only suit, his hair slicked back and a silk handkerchief displayed like a medal. "A suite, please," he said casually to the desk clerk, who looked at him as if he was crazy. The lobby was packed with arriving buyers. Big-time manufacturers shouted greetings, embraced, flattered and handed out engraved invitations. Leo was given a small room overlooking Lexington Avenue. He cleared the beds out. He hung a sign on the door saying WELCOME TO FROLIC FROCKS—AFFORDABLE LUXURY FOR THE STYLISH WOMAN. He smuggled bottles of whiskey and gin into the room, saving the money he would have had to pay room service. And he phoned all the girls he knew until he found one who was a perfect size eight. She became his model in exchange for the promise of a free dress. When she saw the dress she walked out until Leo ran after her, talking desperately of candlelight dinners and weekend trips. It was Monday. Nobody came.

On Tuesday, Arnie Dalitz showed up with a case of French champagne that had been destined for the Dior party on the twentieth floor. The House of Dior had made the mistake of using a cartage company secretly owned by the Genovese family. Leo stood outside the Dior reception handing out business cards and telling buyers that there was free champagne on the sixth floor. And *spectacular* dresses. There were hundreds of buyers at the Dior reception. Less than a dozen showed up at Frolic Frocks. They looked at the dress, exchanged glances or muttered polite good-byes and left. Only two even bothered to drink any champagne. Leo stalked the corridors of the hotel. Galanos was packing them in. They were applauding every Claire McCardell or Norman Norell dress that came out. Morris phoned from the office. The other showrooms were packed with buyers. Neiman Marcus, Henri Bendel, Blum's, Best & Co., they were all there today, attracted by the big showing at Louis Winston's factory display room three floors below Frolic Frocks.

Carrying the case of champagne, Leo raced out onto Park Avenue looking for a taxi. In front of the hotel was a line of eight parked Cadillacs. A small sign said YOUR LIMOUSINE TO THE LOUIS WINSTON COLLECTION. "I'm taking the champagne for Louis," Leo told the chauffeur. "Put it in the trunk, will you." He found himself in a Cadillac with four women. The youngest was at least fifteen years older than him. Before the limo had even reached Grand Central Terminal, he decided they were definitely all from places that had never even heard of Lindy's deli. But each of them clutched leather binders and order books and talked of the huge purchases they had made for their stores back in Kansas and Ohio. Leo looked from one woman to another, telling himself that any one of them could save his life. With just a flick of the pen, a simple little signature on the right order form. "I hear the big action this year is at Frolic Frocks," Leo said. The conversation stopped cold. "Eleventh floor of the building we're going to." Another silence. "Free champagne, too."

"Really?" said the oldest of the women, peering at him through horn-rimmed glasses that magnified her steel-gray eyes. Her skin was loose yet wrinkled and her double chin moved with a delayed action whenever she turned her head. Thin hair dyed an unnatural black hung sparsely across her forehead in bangs and the expensive silk dress was arranged in flowing loose folds to camouflage a belly that shifted when she moved, like a half-used sack of flour in Levine's bakery. Leo decided she was probably the ugliest rich woman he had ever seen. "And who are you with?" she asked in a voice like dried leaves being walked on.

"I'm with Dalitz and Genovese."

"Really? Strange. I've never heard of them. Have you, Doris?" Doris hadn't. Neither had Polly. Or Virginia.

"Very big in the Bronx and Brooklyn," said Leo.

"My, my. And here you are. So very young," she said, those steel-gray eyes impaling him like talons. "My name is Muriel."

"Muriel. Great name. Pleased to meet you."

Leo dressed Mimmo as a waiter and made him stand in the hallway serving champagne outside the Winston offices. A sign taped to his tray said FROLIC FROCKS JUST THREE FLOORS UP. Mimmo smiled through clenched teeth and muttered insults every time Leo stepped off the elevator to greet strangers as if they were old friends. But every time his one model clomped out from behind the curtain there was an immediate exodus from Frolic Frocks. Mimmo returned with his tray of champagne. "What the hell are you doing back here?" yelled Leo.

"Nobody there." Mimmo tore off his bow tie. "*Finito la commedia.*"

"What day is today?" Leo asked, sinking into a chair and downing a glass of champagne with one gulp.

"Thursday," said Morris.

"I think I got a few problems." Leo's voice was low, almost a mumble.

"Yeah. Too much cheap champagne left over," said Mimmo.

"They're gonna kill me. I owe them three G's by tomorrow. This place has got Shapiro's curse written all over it."

Mimmo started to reply but the expression on Morris's face stopped him. A silence settled across the three of them and seemed to go on forever.

"Well, well, dear boy," said a rasping voice from the entrance. "I thought I might find you here."

It was Muriel.

She sat on a single chair in the middle of the showroom, her silk-encased body spilling comfortably over the edges. Her perfectly manicured nails drummed out an impatient cadence on her leather binder. She leaned forward, squinting through the thick glasses, and when the model came out her features seemed to come to a point around that large, sharp nose. Instantly she assumed command. "No, no, turn *around*," she snapped at the model. "*That* way." Leo almost held his breath, looking at Morris and then Mimmo.

"I might be able to take a few," she said with a sharp smile.

Leo exhaled in a loud rush of air and for a moment he said nothing, pacing across the showroom. Her eyes never left him. "Look, Muriel, I'm gonna level with you. I've got to sell a thousand of these or it's game over for me."

"A *thou*-sand?" In a dry laughing voice that sounded to Leo like bones rattling together. "Of *that?* Dear boy, my company does have thirty-seven stores, but even the ones in Arkansas . . ." Her voice trailed off for a moment. Her eyes lost focus as if she was thinking, until she looked over at Leo, appraising him the same way she had looked at the dress. Then she crooked a finger at the model. "Child, come over here. I think we might be able to make some improvements."

For almost an hour she snapped commands that sent Mimmo and Morris racing into the cutting room making sashes or bows that could improve the imitation brocade dress. Or at least hide its worst features. "Dynamite!" Leo would exclaim with every change, but Muriel would just shake her head and order something else to be made. Finally a wide cloth belt was produced, gathering the dress at the waist. "Not bad," said Muriel, walking around the model. "Not bad at all."

"Beautiful!" said Leo.

"Yes. Yes, I could live with that."

"Me, too." Leo was grinning, clasping his hands together and walking in bouncy little steps. "Me, too."

"But I have to think it over," she said, putting on her coat.

Leo stopped in midstep. "Think it over?" he asked, his voice suddenly enfeebled. "You said you liked it."

"Oh, I do," she said, writing something on her business card before she gave it to him. "I'm probably leaving tomorrow. But we'll no doubt be in touch before I go. Thank you so much." With that same corrosive smile, she left.

"But Muriel . . ." Leo said, as the glass door closed behind her. He slowly sank into a chair watching her get on the elevator. "I've just seen my whole life flash before my eyes." Morris looked away and the model hurriedly departed. Only Mimmo broke the silence, pacing around his cutting table and muttering to himself. "I'm finished," said Leo.

"No *finito*," yelled Mimmo.

"What?"

"No *finito!* She's-a-gonna buy!" he yelled, bunching his fingers up almost under Leo's nose. "Where's-a-card? Lemme see." Leo held out the business card, which Mimmo grabbed and pointed to the handwritten note under Muriel's name. "Whatsa say here?"

"Essex House hotel."

He stared at Mimmo, who broke the momentary silence with an irritable muttering that suddenly exploded. "You no *capice*. Shapiro, he *capice!*" Mimmo started pumping his arm back and forth, making little whistling noises with each thrust. "*Fungule!*" he yelled.

"I think he means she wants to get laid," said Morris.

"So? We'll get her some old guy."

"No-no-no-no-no!" yelled Mimmo. "You! She want you!" He laughed gleefully.

"Are you crazy?" yelled Leo. "Do you know how old she must be?"

"What does she look like?" asked Arnie Dalitz, who had entered without being noticed.

"A six-day-old pizza. The ugliest woman I've ever met."

"Leo, I'm here on sort of official business. They told me to come. They expect payment tomorrow."

At seven o'clock that evening, Leo paced back and forth on the sidewalk beside Central Park. Across the street was the Essex House hotel. A car pulled up and Mimmo rolled down the window, passing the flowers and the champagne to Leo. He blew a kiss and sang *That's Amore* as Leo crossed the road.

The door opened and Muriel smiled demurely when Leo handed her the flowers. She was dressed in a silk caftan that merged with the shadows of her dimly lit room. "For me? You are *such* a dear boy," she said, reaching up and brushing his cheek with her hand.

And, preceding Leo into the bedroom, she removed the caftan, letting it drop to the floor, a vision of gelatinous punishment that sprawled nakedly across the bed. Leo stood in the doorway feeling faint and wondering if maybe religion had a point to it after all, if there really were sins he was atoning for, as she raised her knees and looked at her watch. "I have an appointment at eight-thirty, dear boy. Well?"

It was her smile that Leo focused on, hanging on, clinging to, that fierce jumble of teeth that beckoned him closer, anything to avoid staring into the chasm between her upraised knees.

From somewhere far away he could hear *That's Amore* being sung with great joy.

LOVERS

8

One of the few times Tina had much in common with Leo Klein was the night they met in New York.

It was New Year's Eve, 1941, at a club on 52nd Street, and all the elegant young men were getting fashionably drunk, toasting the war they were about to fight. Hitler was booed and Harvard was cheered. Princeton and the New York Giants were somewhere in the middle. The big band that overflowed the tiny stage played a jazz version of *Yankee Doodle Dandy* sending the undergraduates clamoring onto the tables arming themselves with champagne geysers aimed at an uproarious enemy ambushing them with confetti grenades.

Tina sat watching as if she were at a play. Then she quietly left through a back door, walking around the block several times and not wanting to go back inside. Nineteen months earlier she had left for Spain over the furious objections of her father who had tried to have the police stop her as she boarded the ship. As an untrained nursing assistant, she sailed with a dozen other members of the Lincoln Brigade, all but one of them men—boys as she called them, most just barely out of their teens and filled with talk of their fight for liberty and truth and justice in the civil war. Thirteen months later, Tina returned to New York, no longer talking of truth. Or of the savagery she had seen from both sides in the little village near the town of Huesca in the Pyrenees where she and a Spanish peasant girl had run the clinic, working endless days and falling asleep, exhausted, in the straw on the dirt floor. In the months since she returned, the still, cold faces of the young men she had helped bury kept seeping up from the darkness of her sleep. And now, as she shivered on 52nd Street, the faces of the young men inside the bar seemed somehow obscene.

"Tina!" Her cousin Lois teetered across the ice at the end of the block, her coat wrapped around her like a shawl. "What happened to you? You just disappeared! I've been looking all over!"

"I just went for a walk. I'm going home."

"No way."

"You stay. I don't want to be here."

"I put too much work into this. C'mon." Lois tugged at Tina's arm. "Please. For me." Tina hesitated and then nodded and followed Lois back inside.

Earlier that day they had come into Manhattan together on the subway, getting off at a stop on Lexington Avenue and walking through the freezing twilight winds, their borrowed silk dresses snapping like flags around their bare legs and their precious nylons clutched in the paper bags that shielded their faces from the snow. They made it over to the muted opulence of the St. Regis Hotel, reassembling themselves in the washroom just off the lobby and then waiting for their dates under the soft light of the chandelier. Lois wanted it like that. There was no way she'd ever let Philip Barrington know she lived in a Brooklyn walkup where the laundry was hung out the front windows. Not after she'd worked Columbia University all fall, taking the subway over there every football weekend, trawling the shoals of eligible young patricians and talking vaguely of a family fortune of her own.

Tina's blind date had a last name for a first name. It was Harrison or Harriman or Harrington. She never got it right. He was something somebody III. So she just called him The Third. He was tall with creamy delicate skin and blond hair framing sharp cynical eyes that inspected Tina as they shook hands. "Myyyy, how chaaaaarming," he said, drawing out his vowels as he heard the British upper classes do. The Third was heir to a minor part of the Frick fortune, and with one year left in Yale law school, he had grimly set out to establish the mandatory reputation as a playboy, gambling and whoring with precisely the skill necessary not to jeopardize one's chance of later settling into a life of respectability. And then winking slyly whenever tales of one's youth were told over brandy.

The Third instantly decided Tina would help solidify that reputation. She was definitely the type legends could be made of. Those big dark eyes. And that olive skin. Something Mediterranean, almost tarty there. Not at all like the pastel girls at Newport each summer. One of whom he would eventually choose and marry. But this Tina! With the jet black hair. Not permed or curled like the others, but brushed back, hanging straight down across her shoulders. Pointing like an arrow to what he told himself was the most perfect ass he had ever seen. The Third couldn't take his eyes off it. Like it was a creature all its own. Was she used to having it grabbed? That's what they did in those steamy little Latin republics, didn't they? He almost whimpered at the thought.

But now The Third was crawling across the table as the band swung into *Cherokee* and the confetti grenades went off all around them. "Teeenaaaw my beloved! Don't be such a slacker. Can't you see I'm wiiiiild about you!" he yelled through the noise.

"Isn't he deeviiiine?" shouted Lois.

"You're drunk," Tina said. There was that same cool, bemused smile that had intimidated him before.

"But darling, love conquers awwwl." That same damned smile. "Be a sport. I'm off to fight the fascists. I'll come back a hero, you know."

"Who are you kidding? You're not even going overseas."

"Teeenaaaw. A mere technicality, my dearest. Washington will be a jungle too, you know. Now do be kind." He reached out, groping. Pawing. That ass, that splendid ass. Easily the crown jewel on a necklace of lesser gems he had recently plundered. "Teeenaaaw!" yelled The Third, crawling across the table toward her.

But that damned smile. The best ones were often like that, though. You just had to break them in. The Third lunged as Tina stepped serenely aside. He nosedived straight into the floor, breaking his fall on young Turnbull, a sophomore who had not even been reported missing.

The Third struggled to his feet, a glazed and crooked little grin of determination on his face. And for a moment Tina saw the room shatter into fragments of tuxedos and brass. And Ivy League types with cubist faces, florid, laughing and shouting.

A young man stood in the doorway. The man was dressed in a soldier's uniform under a khaki trench coat. He had black shiny hair combed straight back and sharp dark eyes set behind cheekbones that caught the light. He brushed past the maître d'. For a moment Tina thought he was staring at her.

"Hello, Leo," said The Third in a feeble voice as the young man approached, with that fierce stare and that smile that looked like they came from different faces.

"Harriman! My old friend!" said the young man with outstretched arms that made Tina think of a hawk descending on a whimpering rabbit. He swung his arm around The Third's shoulder in a sharp little hugging motion. "You weren't going to let your old pal Leo go off to war without paying your debts, were you?"

"Look, Leo, I *was* going to find you." No vowels dropped here. The Third had suddenly become very nervous.

"Hey, no problem, pal." Leo was both soothing and menacing at the same time. "But let's have a talk, huh?" She could see his arms tighten, steering The Third through the chaos of dancers and drunks over to an alcove near the cloakroom. There was arguing, perhaps pleading, with The Third's arms flying in all directions until the man grabbed the lapels of his tuxedo and pinned him against the wall with gentle menace. Tina watched the man through the crowd of yelling students. He was the only one in the room who interested her.

She walked to the cloakroom. "I'm leaving now," she said to The Third. "I can find my own way home."

"You can't leave," said The Third in an indignantly screechy voice. "It's not even midnight."

"This your wife?" Leo's left hand was still wrapped around a lapel.

"Good God, man! She's just a girlfriend," said The Third, looking insulted.

"Oooh, you charmer you," said Leo, patting The Third's cheek as Tina walked out the door.

The snow was piled high on the cars being pushed through drifts by drunken men wearing party hats and laughing when they slipped behind the wheels that made sizzling sounds on the ice. The clubs on 52nd Street were like blast furnaces of music and voices whenever their doors were opened. Tina had almost reached Sixth Avenue when Leo caught up with her. She could hear him running, his shoes making crackling noises on the fresh snow. He shot past her, skidding on the ice and grinning. "Happy New Year."

"Happy New Year."

"So, are you going to celebrate it with me?"

"I don't even know you." And a voice inside her said shut up. Don't push it. She stopped walking.

"Well, judging from your taste in men you can't help but do better with me." His grin was like a challenge. No way. Absolutely no way. She turned and kept walking as he called out behind her, laughing and saying okay, okay it was all a joke.

"See, I've just proved you *can* do better," he grinned, skidding past her again. But this time he tripped, his legs shooting out from under him as he hurtled into a snowbank and lay there, partly buried and very still. Tina stood there. A trick, definitely a trick. She kept walking. She stopped. He still lay there. A faint moan rose from the snowbank.

She stood looking at the tiny second hand on her watch. Ten seconds. Twenty. Nothing. Thirty. She bolted. Racing toward him, pulling him out of the snowbank as a gurgling noise came from his throat. And cradling his head on her knee saying over and over how sorry she was. Oh dear God she was sorry.

His eyes suddenly snapped open. "Okay, you're forgiven."

9

For Leo, New Year's Eve was to have been spent tracking down rich dink Harriman Solesby III and getting the money he had been owed since November when Solesby started hanging around McGirr's pool hall on weekends. Trying to convince some Vassar girl that he knew all the wise guys. Leo decided on the spot that the dink was not just a fool, he had to be a rich fool. The kind of spoiled idiot who grew up surrounded by servants, who couldn't tell him to shut up. For two weekends, Leo let the others have him. On the third, Leo slaughtered him. It was all done straight. No shills. No cool-off men. And almost no hustle. He merely insulted Harriman Solesby III in front of the Vassar girl. It always worked with dinks. They were always looking to thrash the disrespectful. Two hours later when Leo sank the final ball there was eight hundred dollars in cash and IOUs for twice that much on the table. Almost enough for a Cadillac.

The dink would pay, no question about it. With juice, the IOUs had gone up over two grand. But all Leo had to do was stare hard and Harriman Solesby III went to jelly. Thinking about the broken kneecaps and mobsters that hung around the edges of that relentless stare. Leo had practiced staring into the mirror until he got it down cold. On the New Year's Eve he went looking for Harriman Solesby III, Leo used the car mirror to rehearse his stare before going into each of the clubs on 52nd Street.

And this girl? Tina. A definite bonus. How often could you walk away with a mark's money *and* his girl? She was beautiful. At first that was all there was to it. But by the time they got to the Onyx he started thinking maybe this one was different. She *knew* things. She talked of Paris like he talked of New York. And it wasn't to impress him either. She felt no need for that. You could tell. And at first this pleased him. A nice change from all the perfect size eights who were chained to their compact mirrors. But by the time they got to The Famous Door, Leo was starting to feel insecure. Maybe she was bored with him. He started trying to impress her in little ways that made him feel phony. Like making sure she saw Buck and Freddie and the others in Basie's band nod hello to him. She'd have to figure that this was not just your average garmento she was out with when she saw that. How many stiffs knew jazz hotshots like these? Negro jazz hotshots. If she was one of these liberal types, he'd be chalking up points like crazy. But it was so hard to tell. She reacted as if it was all just normal and then excused herself, walking over to the bar to order a drink. And *paying* for it. No woman he'd ever been with had paid for her own drinks. Not in clubs like these.

Leo knew he was in trouble. He was in love.

Ridiculous, he told himself. But he didn't care. He just wanted the night to keep going, and by the time they left the second club Leo was on the verge of phoning that rich dink and telling him to forget the envelope tomorrow, keep the damn money, you've paid it back. They had been talking about the army and the war and somehow she seemed worried. She'd looked across the table, those vast dark eyes locking on him when he had made a joke about being back home by next summer. After all, what chance did that putz Hitler have when he and the guys from the Bronx got over?

She had instantly reached out, putting her hand softly across his arm with an urgency that stopped all his words.

After midnight, they kept going. The Famous Door. Hickory House. Basin Street. Bartenders called out to him. Musicians winked over their trumpets and clarinets. And older men in expensive suits and sinister creased faces got up from corner booths to put their arms around him and tell him to be careful when he went off to war. Leo would make jokes and introduce Tina as his newest best friend who had just found him in a snowbank. The older men would look her up and down as if they were figuring a price on stolen goods. Then they would nod politely with a tiny smile they reserved for women who existed merely to service a friend on whatever night they were introduced. Women they would never meet again. Tina loathed them all.

When they were outside again leaning into the wind-driven snow, Leo was exuberant, unpredictable, sometimes pelting passing police cars with snowballs and making her laugh as he shot past her, arms folded, on the icy streets. And when all of 52nd Street echoed with the chorus counting down to midnight, he put his arm around her, rubbing the back of the flimsy cloth coat she was wearing. *Happy New Year!*

It seemed like a natural thing to do, to lean over and kiss her, embracing her, drawing her in against him until he suddenly felt her pull away for that one instant when he thought he had made a mistake, crossing some shifting boundary that she had redrawn between them. But then in another instant it was Tina who came to him, encircling him with her arms, kissing him fiercely.

All around them the street had filled with laughing, drunken revelers. Even the cops who had sneaked out the side door of one of the clubs were cheering the New Year with the free beer they had been given. Someone had built a snowman on their police car. The snowman had been given a little pocket comb for a mustache, exactly like Hitler's, and its arm was raised over its head in a perfect *Sieg Heil* salute. It was Leo who threw the first snowball at Hitler. Everyone joined in, laughing and yelling about what they would do to the Nazis in one mere month. A week even! The bastards would be wiped out. Just like the snowman. Hitler was demolished by the snowball artillery led by women who hoisted long dresses up with one hand and threw with the other. Men slipped on the ice laughing and clinging to party hats. Only Tina did not join in.

And later, driving back in his Packard that somehow didn't seem to impress her the way it did other women who had been in it, Leo realized that whenever he talked about going off to war she would press herself a little closer to him. And whisper something he could not quite hear.

So he talked about going off to war more than he had intended.

IVORY JOE AND THE CLASSICS

10

Leo can be so weird. Sometimes it's like having two daughters is just too much for him. I'm willing to bet that if Leo ever talks to God the first question he asks Him after who's going to win the third race at Belmont is why He didn't give him boys. Or at least one boy. Leo is definitely a son type of father. Sometimes when it's Leo's turn to be with us for an afternoon I've noticed that Mother will do her own weird stuff. If she's mad at him she'll make sure we're all dressed up in our pink dresses. Lots of lace and bows. With our white knee socks and shiny black shoes. And our hair curled up like Goldilocks. Then she sends us off to meet Leo like two frilly torpedoes. When we meet Leo he can't hide the look that comes on his face. It's the same look as we must have had the time we thought the Goldblatts' watchdog was on a chain only it wasn't. Leo will clear his throat a lot and play with the knot in his tie while he's saying things like "Well, how's it going, gang?" Then he'll buy a bunch of hot dogs from a street vendor to keep us busy eating while he figures out what to do with us. But he does try hard. He takes us to all kinds of tourist places like the Statue of Liberty or the Empire State Building and gets real nervous if we don't act excited. Ruthie and I always come home wiped out from acting real excited.

A couple of times Leo figured out Mother's frilly dress plan and got back at her by sending Stanley his driver to be with us for the afternoon. Have you any idea what *that's* like? He's worse than Leo because he doesn't know what to do either. And because he's not our father we don't bother acting excited. So it's four silent hours of ice cream parlors. Ruthie and I used to love ice cream.

After we'd gotten stuck with Stanley a couple of times Mother stopped putting us in the dresses and Leo came to call for us again. Somehow it makes everything easier when we wear blue jeans and our old T-shirts. Then we just go roaring around Central Park while Leo sits on a bench and reads the *Racing Form*. If we want he'll take us rowing in the lake in the middle of the park. The time he fell in and got a soaker he laughed as much as we did. Then he dumped water on us. It was like he had two temporary sons, but with longer hair.

In the last couple of weeks Leo is acting strange again. Ever since Mother being in jail and him finding out about Ivory Joe. Once in a while he'll sneak in a question about *this Negro fella* trying to act like he really isn't all that interested. But he is. Leo's problem is that for someone who likes having fun, he's too much of a family man. It's like he's afraid Mother's going to do something to make us not like him. Then of course he's still crazy about Mother but that's a whole other story.

Last weekend was my birthday. Last year he sent Stanley over with a stuffed panda and an envelope with fifty dollars in it. But this year he goes real big time. Last Saturday afternoon Ruthie and Leo and I get out of his car in front of the Copacabana nightclub. "This is to show you that your old man really loves you, kid. And you too, Ruthie," Leo says. As if we thought he didn't. Inside I couldn't believe it. It was like my class at school was being held in the Copa. They were all there. *Surprise!* they all yell. The orchestra starts playing Happy Birthday and ponies come roaring out onto the stage and start dancing. At first I'm just standing there with my mouth open but I realize Leo is watching me so I start acting excited. And I am but not in the way he wants me to be. There's Sara Kramer and Susie Leggat and all the others who have never even heard of the Copa sitting there drinking Cokes like the doxies who come here all the time with Leo's rich friends. Big butter and egg men he calls them. Chiselers Mother calls them. Even Mrs. Levine our teacher is there clucking around Leo who turns on the charm. Now *that* I can't believe. We always said her face would crack if she smiled but there she is acting like a real simp as Leo pulls one routine after another. Meanwhile his secretary poor old Mrs. Weissman walks around in a daze holding a clipboard and checking off the names of the kids who came. Guess who did all the work?

But I really can't believe Mrs. Levine. She'll be in Leo's lap next. What a hussy she's turned into.

As the orchestra is blaring away I figure a couple of things out. First is that the music they're playing is nowhere near as great as Ivory Joe's. The second thing is that there's no boys here. Not one. Leo's always warning us about boys. Like when Tubby Wilson asked if he could take me for a malted two Saturday afternoons ago Leo almost had a conniption. He wanted to follow me and Tubby in his Cadillac. When I got mad at this he said okay he'd stay at least a block behind us. I got madder and said what for? He said it was in case Tubby tried something. Tried what? I asked him. Something. You have to watch out for boys, he said. Typical Leo. Just like he's always telling us how important school is.

But Uncle Morris has told us what Leo was like in school.

11

My problem is that when I'm with Ivory Joe I still keep hearing Leo's questions. *This Negro fella, what's your mama—your mother doing with him?* In my head I keep telling Leo that all she's doing is organizing things for Ivory Joe. Doing all the business stuff so he can get his group together.

Last night me and Mother and Ivory Joe sat on the floor of his studio and chose the name of the group. I loved it. I loved it because they actually asked me what I thought. That doesn't happen often. Except at school. Mother wrote the names on cards that we spread out on the floor. We had Ivory Joe and the Shadows. The Dominoes. The Cools. The Ebonies. The Phantoms. The Velvets. But we finally decided on Ivory Joe and the Classics. Or at least Ivory Joe settled on it. Anything about music he decides. But when it comes to money he leaves it all up to Mother. She's going around talking to agents and the club owners. You can tell she really loves what she's doing. It's like running a business only it's fun.

. . .

Today I found out where the Negroes live. I get to go up to Harlem with Ivory Joe while he looks for someone to be the bass singer in the Classics. Mother said I should think of it as part of my education which is the way she thinks about things like this. I'm riding with Ivory Joe in his old Chevrolet and we're way up past Central Park and pretty soon when I look out there's no more white people. I'm the only one. I ask Ivory Joe what happened and he just laughs. I tell him I'd like to live up here because there's hills. I didn't know New York had hills like these. Sometimes Ivory Joe's real serious like something's going on in his mind. I can ask him questions and he doesn't hear. That's when you can see the muscles in his arms bulge out under his shirt. I ask him if there's a Mrs. Ivory Joe and he just keeps driving. But most of the time he's teasing me, saying that he's going to make me a singer in his group. He knows I sing worse than old Mrs. Foster in apartment 8D.

We stop at a store in Harlem with a lot of junk in the window and a sign saying RECORD SHACK. Next door is a place that fixes cars but it's not like a normal garage because they're fixing the cars right on the street. There's pieces all over the sidewalk. Inside the store everybody laughs and sort of shakes hands and then Ivory Joe introduces me as his assistant. They all shake my hand. I feel very important. Ivory Joe starts asking where he can find Clarence. That's the bass he's looking for. While they're talking I look around the store. There's tons of records and photographs stuck up on the walls. They're all Negroes and I've never heard of them.

But there's also photographs of boxers and everybody's heard of them. Joe Louis. Sugar Ray Robinson. Ezzard Charles. All the champions that Leo and the big butter and egg men go to see fight at Madison Square Garden. But then I see a photograph of another boxer and I can't believe it. It's Ivory Joe. And under that one is a photo of him in the ring hitting some other boxer whose face is all munched up by Ivory Joe's glove. Ivory Joe is that you? I yell. Of course I know it is.

"The old days," he just says.

"Last winter," says that fat funny man behind the counter who laughs and hits Ivory Joe in the shoulder with his fist. But not hard.

When we get back in the car he says we're going to Wadleigh High

School which of course I haven't heard of either. It's down on the flat part of Harlem and looks like a weird old castle with high walls and pointy windows way up on the roof. It's almost dark and as we get close to it I can hear people singing real fast with voices all sounding like one. "They're just kids," Ivory Joe says, but they look like they are in at least eleventh grade to me. When they stop another bunch starts. They sing real slow and go *doooo-waaaah doo-waaah* a lot.

Another group starts singing something that says *baby-baby* all the time. It's like a contest they're having and all around the courtyard other Negroes are clapping or cheering for their favorites. Ivory Joe takes my hand and leads me back out onto the street. We walk around the block and I stay real close to Ivory Joe because it all seems darker at night here, like there's not as many streetlights. But there's people all over the block just standing around. We have to go around the whole block to get to the other side of the school. Before we even get there we can hear Clarence. *Dooom-dat-da-doom-dat-da-doom-doom-doom.* He sounds like a foghorn that's taken music lessons. We go into a different courtyard now, a real small one with lots of echo, and there's Clarence all by himself. He's real black but even in that darkness I can see he's big, way taller than Ivory Joe but without the muscles. Sort of lumpy-looking. He sees us and stops. "Clarence," yells Ivory Joe in a real happy loud voice.

"Hey, Joe," says Clarence softly. His eyes look scared like Goldblatts' dog's after they smack it.

"You been hidin'," says Ivory Joe in that same voice. It echoes. It's not like him at all.

"Ain't hidin', Joe." Then he mumbles something. He has a funny way of talking where all the words go together. It's like listening to a foreigner speak.

"So? C'mon, Clarence. What's the problem then?" Ivory Joe starts singing something from *Ghost Lover.* "Sing it, Clarence," he yells. He's ordering Clarence.

"Cain't, Joe. No use."

"Sing, dammit." Ivory Joe is singing the same part over and over trying to get Clarence to join in. Clarence tries to walk away but Ivory Joe grabs him by the jacket and all of a sudden Clarence's eyes change. Like from a hound dog to a wolf. He looks real mean and starts pushing back at Ivory Joe who just starts laughing while he sings. There's more pushing. And laughing. "Can't do it, huh, Clarence?" He's making Clarence madder and madder. You can tell because those eyes of his are making me back up and I want to yell to Ivory Joe that we should be going. But then Clarence starts doing a *doom-dat-da-doom* not the same as before but one that blends in with what Ivory Joe is singing. And even though they both look like they're going to kill each other they're sounding great. They keep going until right in the middle of it Ivory Joe suddenly stops. "C'mon, Chrissie." Just like that. Suddenly we're leaving but I'm walking backward watching Clarence go back to his hound-dog eyes like if his master was leaving for good. "Hey, Joe," he yells.

"What?" says Ivory Joe opening the car door and sounding real bored.

"I'll think about it."

"Forget it."

"I'm good, Joe. You know it."

"Yeah? But what good's that gonna do you, Clarence? Someday you're gonna be an old man tellin' people how good you were. But they ain't gonna know cause no one'll have heard a note you ever sang." He started the car. Clarence leans in the window.

"I'm your man, I tellya, Joe. Man, I'm sorry. But I gets scared."

Ivory Joe just looks him right in the eyes like he's trying to find something. At first nobody says anything. "Hey. Nothin' to be scared about." Ivory Joe chuckles. Clarence looks relieved and holds out his hand. "You're a Classic now, Clarence," says Ivory Joe. Clarence sort of smiles.

We're driving along in the Chevrolet and Ivory Joe isn't saying anything. Just looking at the sidewalk like he's expecting to see something. After a while he says, "Chrissie, you understand?"

Understand? Understand what? Is he going to think I'm a dummy if I tell him the truth? That I don't even understand what it is I'm supposed to understand. Nope I say.

"Stage fright. Clarence is the best. He was probably singing bass when he was your size. Down in Alabama. Never seen anyone scared like him before. Scared cause he's angry and can't figure out what to do with it all. Can't read. Can't write. And he's nineteen now."

How's he going to sing if he's scared?

"That's our job. To make him not scared." I like it when he says *our*. We're driving along a wide street in Harlem with some hills on it and he's still looking for something.

Are you going to be the heavyweight champion, Ivory Joe? I ask.

"Middleweight," he says. "But I quit that."

Why? I ask.

"Because." As if that's an answer. Then he says, "I knew I could never be the *best*. You follow me?" I nod. But I don't. Not really. Ivory Joe suddenly sees whatever it is he's looking for and turns the car around on the hill. He parks in front of a store with curtains over the windows and a bunch of Negro men just hanging around outside. Right away I can tell he doesn't want me to go inside with him just by the way he explains that he is looking for someone who's a tenor but it's not a place for little girls. Fine! I say in my best Ruthie voice. He looks sort of glad that I agree and gets out of the car. He's walking over to the door waving to the men on the sidewalk when all of a sudden he stops and looks back at me. He comes to the car again and says even though he promised my mama that he wouldn't leave me alone he's sure I'm going to be all right. Okay with me I tell him crossing my arms in front of me. So he leaves me again and this time he gets right inside the door before he turns and comes back and wants me to know he's not going to be long. Okay with me I say. And he gets upset. "Why do you keep saying that?" he asks. What am I supposed to say? He grabs my hand and says we're both going inside. No way I tell him. I know when I'm not wanted. That's when he starts talking in a low voice with his teeth together. But smiling. So *I* start talking in a low voice with *my* teeth together. But smiling. This makes him laugh.

We go down this long hallway toward a room where there's lots of noise and smoke. The room is filled with men and a few ladies all of them Negroes and it's sort of dark but everywhere I look I see money. There's a pile of it on a table and some men are handing it to people holding pieces of paper with writing on them. In a corner some man is counting another pile and music is playing real loud on the phonograph. Other men are coming in and out holding more paper. A lot of them have long white handkerchiefs hanging from their back pockets. I ask Ivory Joe what's going on. "The digits," he says. "The rackets. They're betting." He's walking through the crowd and people are looking at him and then at me like I'm the man from Mars. We get to a table in the corner where some men are playing cards. When they see Ivory Joe they all start laughing and slapping at his hand. One of them is called Zoot. He's younger, kind of skinny with a real big mouth and funny grin that sticks out on either side of the cards he's holding up in front of his face. "Hey, nigger, howya doin'?" he says.

I can't believe it. *That* word! My mother would wash his mouth out with soap. There's gonna be trouble I know it because Ivory Joe's not going to stand for that. But I look up and he's just grinning right back. "Fine, Zoot, just fine." Then when Zoot looks over at me he says, "This is my assistant, Chrissie."

"Pleased to meet you, Chrissie," says Zoot his long arms coming out toward me all loose and snaky like a hose. I shake his hand. "But what's such a pretty child as you doing with a highsider like this?"

I don't know what to say but another man who's bald and fat and wearing a suit starts laughing. "Hey, Zoot, I do think you should reconsider seeing as your old lady got a terminal dose of the uglies." *Uuhh-gleys* he says. They all laugh including Zoot who says, "Tell me, Henry, is it true your woman is so scrawny she looks like six o'clock?"

"Hell, Zoot, when your woman stands still on the street drunks come up and lean against her asking why the light's gone out. I swear. I seen it!"

I'm not sure but I think I'm supposed to laugh. They all are. And pretty soon they're saying awful things about each other's mothers and fathers and cousins and brothers. I try to imagine Leo sitting down and telling Uncle Morris that Aunt Ida looks like a fire hydrant except even the dogs won't go near her. Or Arnie Dalitz telling Grandma that with a nose like Grandpa has she'd better not let him stand around the flowers because nothing grows in the shade. I really don't think it would be the same. They'd all be punching each other and yelling even worse things. But Zoot and Henry and all the men at the card table are just laughing themselves right off the chairs.

I see Ivory Joe watching Zoot real carefully and after the others have gone off for drinks he sits down and says, "I hear you ain't going with the Royales after all."

"That's right, Joe," Zoot says, just looking at his cards.

"I'm putting together another group. Real good one. Bringing Clyde over from Newark. Clarence is in. Need another great tenor."

Zoot puts his feet up on a chair and keeps fiddling with his cards. "You askin' me, Joe?" Ivory Joe just nods and stares right into his eyes never letting go. "Tell you the truth, Joe, I'm getting tired of working here as a runner for Bumpy. Havin' trouble holdin' onto the green. I just blow it all first game o' cards I get myself into. The cards gone cold on me. But then I could always hold a note better'n a full house. Besides, I been thinking about the fun we had making all that devil music." He starts laughing and slapping Ivory Joe on the shoulders. Then he remembers I'm there and says, "Excuse me, darlin'." No one's ever called me darling before.

Ivory Joe is getting ready to leave. But now I'd like to stay because I don't feel much like the man from Mars anymore. People are actually talking to me. Henry shows me a card trick and he introduces me to some of the other Negro men at the table. There's Red Leg who's old with white hair. A toothpick is always moving all over his mouth without his hands even touching it and he doesn't look you in the eyes. There's Cool Curtis. And Dipper. They both look real tough till they smile. They're dressed in expensive suits and Dipper has a fedora on his head. Then there's Bama who's got no hair at all but he can make the ace of spades come out of his ear. He says he'll teach me to cheat good enough to play against So Black. This makes So Black laugh. His voice is real deep. It seems to come out of his boots. He's got a pot belly and a lot of wrinkles and they all say he can look real dumb when he has to. So Black gives me a poker chip and says I should take it home to my daddy. I should tell my daddy it's free as long as he comes and plays him and Dipper in a poker game. They're all laughing but all I can think of is tell my daddy. Leo? Are they crazy?

I don't even want to think about *that*.

12

Ivory Joe is driving Leo crazy and he's not even trying to. When we come back that night after finding Zoot and Clarence, Leo is actually parked in front of our apartment waiting for me. When Ivory Joe stops his car to let me out we don't even see Leo at first. I'm saying good-bye when all of a sudden the car door flies open and there's Leo grabbing my arm and staring daggers at Ivory Joe. "Are you all right?" he practically yells in my ear like he's saving me from being murdered or something.

I really blow it. Guess where I've been I say thinking he'll be glad. Ivory Joe took me up to Harlem. Right away I can tell that's not what I should have said. But what's the big deal about Harlem? Leo starts yelling at Ivory Joe who just sits and stares as cool as he can be.

"Where the hell do you get off taking my daughter up to Harlem?"

I had fun I say.

"Now, Christie, honey, you stay out of this." He says *honey* like he's going to spit something out.

"No harm done," says Ivory Joe. "She was looked after."

"I'll decide that," yells Leo. "Now you stay away from her or there's going to be trouble. Understand?"

If there was going to be trouble like a fight or anything it would be Leo who'd be in for it. Leo doesn't exercise much anymore. Ivory Joe is a lot younger too. But all this is starting to upset me and when I start to cry Leo that jerk yells, "See! See what you've done to her," at Ivory Joe.

Ivory Joe's my friend I say to Leo. I feel stupid because people on the street are looking now. Which I hate. It's none of their business. But I'm sniveling away like when Louie Makin stole the class hamster. And that was three years ago.

"Christie, that's enough. Come on. We're going inside to straighten this out with your mother." Straighten it out? Fat chance. Leo is standing over near the doorway and I'm between him and Ivory Joe. Right now I want to go with Ivory Joe.

Ivory Joe figures out what I'm thinking. "Chrissie, he's your daddy. He knows what's best for you." I turn around and see Leo looking even angrier like since when does he need Ivory Joe to get me to do what he wants.

Upstairs. Boy Leo is really straightening it out. Ruthie and I can hear the whole thing from her bedroom where they put us while they fight. "Harlem," he's yelling. "She's up in Harlem with some *Negro* for christsakes."

"Well, who do you expect her to go to Harlem with? An Eskimo?" says Mother.

"Checkmate," says Ruthie, who's lying on the bed staring at the chessboard taped to the ceiling. She's playing eight people at once by mail. But she had to change her name because people always quit when they found out they were playing a girl. So every week mail comes for Rudy Klein. Ruthie says she's had it with men. But she's beating every one of them.

After Leo meets Ivory Joe lots of changes start happening. Leo decides he's getting his own place fixed up so we can go and stay there for a couple of days at a time. This was supposed to happen years ago but there was always some excuse. But now it's like where have we been all his life? Leo is all of a sudden real nervous that this thing with Ivory Joe is more than he thought. Ruthie thinks he's jealous. Of what? I ask her. He's scared that Mother likes Ivory Joe. What do you mean *likes* I want to know. You know *likes* she says but of course that's stupid. Why is that stupid? I ask her.

"Don't you know anything?" Ruthie says in that chessmaster voice she's got sometimes. "He's a Negro, you dope." Oh yeah I say thinking about it for a while. Then she says, "Besides, Leo'd kill *any*one who came near Mother."

I don't know for sure. Maybe.

Next weekend we show up at Leo's apartment on the East Side and he opens the door like he's going to take us on a tour. You can tell he's glad that Mother came up with us because he wants to show her around to prove that he's changed again. I can't believe it's Leo's place. It looks really nice. And neat. Like no one lives in there. There's a lady who comes in a Miss somebody or other who Leo says is his Interior Decorator. She talks to us in a cutesy voice like we're idiots. She gets real anxious when she takes us to our room. The Children's Area she says. It stinks. It's all pink from top to bottom with frills and lacy things all over. It's like living in a petticoat. And dolls everywhere. Where were they five years ago when we needed them? This Miss somebody gets real nutty when I even *touch* one of the dolls. She rushes up and puts it back in its place. Ruthie and I look at each other. Boyohboy this is great I say. Look at all the walls we can draw on with our crayons. The lady starts having kittens. But Ruthie and I lay it on. By the time we're finished her mouth is all drawn up like the top of my little change purse when I pull the string and all Leo wants to do is get her out of there.

At dinnertime Stanley shows up with food from the Copa. Leo is being the good father. The phone rings and I run to answer it. There's some woman on the line who's real surprised to hear me answer. It's one of your girlfriends I yell and Leo scrambles over to grab the phone away from me. He says, "Oh, Carol, hi baby, I was just going to call you." And all those other fibs. But he's really good at it. And pretty soon you can tell he's got this Carol believing that he hadn't really forgotten he was supposed to take her out tonight. It's just that the family is over. All of a sudden Leo's Mr. Family and she's buying it but she's still not letting him off the hook. He keeps telling her that of course they'll still go to the party. Then he hangs up and starts walking back and forth running the palm of his hand up across his forehead. That's the sign. Big troubles.

Ruthie and I eat our Copa roast beef and look at each other. Then she comes out with the line we're taught at school.

Oh what a tangled web we weave
When first we practice to deceive

she says in a flutey schoolteacher voice. Leo says, "Girls, girls, please. This is serious." Then he smiles like he's got some bright idea. He dials Stanley's number and waits and waits like the phone is stuck to his ear. When no one answers he stares at the phone and says, "Can you believe it?"

"It's his night off," says Ruthie.

"He isn't even there," says Leo like he's amazed.

"Amazing," says Ruthie. "You'da thought he'd be there waiting for you to phone him on his day off."

"Yeah," says Leo like his mind is stuck in the phone or something. Then he gets another big idea. You can just see it coming. He dials the phone and says, "Phyllis? Hiya, howya doing? Great. Listen, let's get together tonight, huh?"

We're floored. What's he going to do with *two* of them? This Phyllis shows up all decked out in lipstick you could see in the dark. She's chewing an awful lot of gum and she's another one who checks the place out to see what she'll change when she takes over. I feel like Ruthie and me are watching a movie for the second time. Then Leo comes rushing out and says, "Phyllis, honey, I've got an emergency at the office but I'll be back in a little while." Just when Phyllis is about to do a footstamper, Leo whips out a little velvet box and says, "Honey, I bought them just for you."

Here we go again. The old fake pearl earring trick. Leo's got a dozen boxes of them stashed away. Uncle Morris got them when some company went bankrupt. If Phyllis lasts till July she's going to be asking Leo why all the gold is wearing off. Ruthie and I realize that Phyllis is really here just to be our baby-sitter. Which makes us really mad because we're old enough not to need one.

Phyllis and I end up playing canasta all night. She's not bad if only she didn't chew so much gum. Phyllis asks me a lot of questions about Leo and about what kind of emergency he could have on a Saturday night. I tell her that you never know with Leo. Everywhere he goes there's an emergency. Leo gets home long after Ruthie and I fall asleep. We wake up next morning in this frilly pink Children's Area. I feel like we should be sleeping in Macy's window. Of course we start hearing the groaning pretty soon.

"This is serious," Leo groans as he lies in bed with his bathrobe and his sunglasses on. He has an ice pack on his head. It's always serious. I get Leo his black bag with all the pills and tonics in it. "I'm sure it's tuberculosis," he says sounding like he's ninety. Last week it was diphtheria. He forgets. Never ever is it a hangover. He looks through the black bag pouring pills out and muttering to himself. Dr. Taffler shows up just after Leo has taken a drink of the juniper juice. I clear out so Leo can get his vitamin injection from creepy Dr. Taffler. Do you know that he walks with his baby finger sticking out sideways?

After Leo decides he's going to live we go out for one of our Sundays. At the movies we see *Abbott and Costello Meet the Mummy* which of course Ruthie thinks is dumb but me and Leo love. Ruthie never wants to admit it but you can learn a lot from movies. Like you can always tell when the girl's going to get kissed before it even happens. She always pushes the sleeves of her sweater up. About halfway to her elbow. Just watch Elizabeth Taylor or Marilyn Monroe when their boyfriends are around. I told this to Ruthie once. She just *tssked* and said it was dumb.

But a couple of days later I saw her go to school with her sleeves pushed up.

RACKETEERS

13

We like being at Leo's. But there's a problem. It's Ruthie. She's in love even though she'd kill me just for saying it.

All Ruthie wants to do is get home to Mother's so she can stare at her chessboard taped to the ceiling over her bed. She's got some guy from Chicago almost checkmated. She figures that with one more move she'll win. Every day she's been running to the mailbox to see if he's written her with his next move. His name is Dr. B. W. Lewis. But Ruthie and I have decided his name is probably Byron and most likely he looks like Errol Flynn. Or maybe Clark Gable. I tell her that maybe she should send him her next move in the mail with a note saying *P.S. I'm a girl.* He'll probably be so impressed he'll ask her to go steady I say. But Ruthie just gets mad and says how dumb I am for even saying that.

But later she pushes the sleeves of her sweater up again. BYRON AND RUTHIE—TRUE I write on the refrigerator and this just makes her madder. Brains don't like to be teased about stuff like that. But you can tell she just wants to get back to her chessboard. Leo can figure out something's wrong. He comes into the Children's Area and says, "Hey, gang, we had a great time today, didn't we?" and we make sure to yell "Yeaah!" But he asks it a second time just to make sure. And then he tells us that his family is real important to him. Real important, he keeps saying.

Why do I feel like I'm right in the middle? Somehow I've got to get Ruthie home to the chessboard and Byron and without getting Leo all upset and thinking we like Mother better. My mind is working like crazy. And I'm better at this than Ruthie even though she's a brain. All of a sudden I figure out what to do. I remember the amazing thing that happened to Annie Conklin, Ruthie's best girlfriend's older sister, last year when she got what they called her period right in the middle of gym class. None of us even knew what a period was until then.

I tell Ruthie just to do what I tell her. Act real tired I say. And say you've got a fat headache. She doesn't get it. But she does it. Ruthie's a great actress. She walks out into Leo's living room where he's reading the *Racing Form* and her legs are all wobbly and she moans about feeling hot and then cold. Leo keeps reading for a minute until suddenly he figures out what she's said. Then his face goes all crinkly and he drops the *Racing Form*. He carries her into the Children's Area and tells her to get into bed. Then he makes a signal for me to go out into the hallway and talk to him. But the phone rings just then and he starts talking to someone about the sixth race at Aqueduct.

I peek into the Children's Area and tell Ruthie to keep acting like she's got a temperature. When I go out to talk to Leo he's already forgotten about Ruthie. He's still talking on the phone. He puts his arm around me and gives me a goobery kiss on the cheek. He knows his whiskers always itch like crazy. But I still like it though. I know what Ruthie's problem is I say to him.

But he doesn't even hear me. He's too busy talking on the phone about putting two hundred on Quiet Dancer to show.

So fine. I drop the bomb. She's started her first monthlies I say. Leo nods and keeps talking about horses. But then he stops.

"Huh?" he says. His eyes get real wide.

You know. Her monthlies.

Leo looks like Abbott and Costello did when they met the Mummy. His mouth falls open and makes a little squeaking sound. Then he yells into the phone, "Freddie, I gotta go. I got a goddam emergency!" Bang he hangs up and then grabs my hand and almost drags me into the Children's Area where Ruthie is still lying under the covers moaning. But she still doesn't get it. When I talk about her monthlies in front of her she almost sits right up and stares daggers at me. But she figures out it's too late to change. Leo is already pacing all over rubbing the palm of his hand across his forehead. What do we do? I say sort of wailing.

Leo panics. "Jesus, you're asking *me?*" He hurries out to the living room and grabs his little black book, the one with all the doxies' names in it. He dials three different numbers walking around in little circles muttering, "C'mon, c'mon." No answer. Then he finally gets Phyllis. "Phyllis, honey, I'm so glad to talk to you, my God, you can't imagine. Listen, I need you to come over here. I've got an emergency—"

I can hear the *click* even from where I'm standing. Leo stares at the phone. "Can you believe it?" he says into the phone.

After you gave her those nice earrings too I say and Leo agrees as Ruthie comes out with a loud moan from the other room. She's really getting into the part.

"Ruthie?" Leo yells, "Hang on. I'm calling an ambulance." He actually starts dialing before I can yell that she doesn't need an ambulance. The jig would really be up then. He paces around some more and then you can see the light bulb go off in his head. He dials the phone again. It turns out to be that creepy Dr. Taffler. "You know the curse. The monthlies," he says. "Christ, do I have to draw you a diagram?" Then he listens some more. "So what do I do?" His eyes get real wide again. "Buy her *what?* Me? Go into a store and ask for those? Are you crazy?" This keeps on while Ruthie moans some more. "What the hell do I know about how you use them?" he yells into the phone. I'm starting to look for a way out of all this. But it might be too late.

Leo slams the phone down and runs around the apartment trying to find his tie which he always wears when he goes out. "You're coming with me," he says. We go racing up Madison Avenue to the drugstore. Leo's almost dragging me off my feet when we go in. It's one of those places with a soda fountain where a bunch of people are having milkshakes on one side and the drugstore part's on the other side. Leo goes over to the cashier in the middle. She's an old lady. Leo starts talking to her in a low voice but she calls out "What?" in a voice that sounds like when you scratch your fingernail across the blackboard.

"Cigars," yells Leo right away. Pretty soon Leo's bought a box of cheap cigars. And then some aftershave lotion. And a hot water bottle. In between, he drags me up and down the aisles.

What do you need those cigars for I ask and he just gets more crazy telling me not to talk so loud. He's talking out of the side of his mouth. He stops in front of a whole shelf of blue and white boxes. He's staring at them when all of a sudden someone calls out his name. It's like somebody stuck a pin in him. It's Mr. Kampelman and two other men I've seen. Leo acts real funny when he's talking to them about the next Rocky Marciano fight at the Garden. They say sure Leo and go for a coffee at the soda fountain. They keep staring at him. Leo looks from the blue and white boxes over to me and back again.

"Here's five bucks. Take one of those boxes down from the shelf and go up to that lady and pay her."

And where are you going to be I ask stalling for time.

"Outside waiting for you."

Uh-uh. I shake my head.

"Okay, okay, here's ten bucks." I don't know what to say to him. I just stare at the money. "Fifty then. But that's my last offer."

I gotta get out of this fast otherwise pretty soon he's going to be sitting on Ruthie's bed reading the instructions on the blue and white box. Hey maybe we should take Ruthie back to Mother's place I say. Just when he's reaching for another fifty.

All of a sudden he starts smiling. "Yeah!" he says, looking like Quiet Dancer just won the jackpot. "Maybe we should."

14

Stanley drives us home. When we get there Mother's not in but that's okay because she wasn't expecting us. Ruthie is happy just to be back with her chessboard. And thinking about Byron. I go into the kitchen and call the taxi company that Mother uses. It's a TRafalgar 7 number like ours so it's there right away. When I tell the driver I want to go to Small's Paradise up in Harlem he looks at me real strange. When we get up past Central Park on Seventh Avenue he asks me if I know where I'm going. He says he's willing to skip the fare if I've made a mistake.

I say thank you but it's okay.

When I get out of the taxi the streets are filled with people mostly

Negroes. Some are going to Count Basie's place across the street. I'd been there with Ivory Joe. You can hear the music from the street and a big crowd is lined up at the door outside Small's Paradise. The Negro man at the door is dressed in a suit and tie looking very very rich. He says, "Hey, little girl. Who you with?"

Ivory Joe and the Classics I say. I can hear all kinds of people in the line start talking and making wisecracks. And my mother I say. The Negro man grins and takes me inside down a long corridor toward loud music. All of a sudden the hallway opens up into this big nightclub with a stage in the middle. They've even got ponies here too dancing and kicking their legs at the same time while the band at the back is playing like crazy. The whole place is what Ivory Joe calls jumping. Even more than the Copacabana on my birthday. Way more actually.

There's only a few white people in here. The man is still leading me through the crowd when someone turns a spotlight on me and the Negro ponies on the stage all start waving for me to come onstage. But I'm too embarrassed. Besides I've got spots in front of my eyes even after the light is put back on the dancers.

All of a sudden an arm reaches out and stops me. I look into two piggy little eyes behind big fat glasses on a big fat face. "Ain't you Leo's kid?" It's Herman Pinsky and I know I'm in trouble because he'll tell Leo. It figures.

Herman Pinsky's a racketeer. Mother says so.

Mother isn't quite as pleased to see me as I thought she'd be. Everything's going crazy backstage and she's got her hands full with the Classics. There's Clarence who's saying he can't go out and sing in front of a crowd. He's too scared. And Clyde the new guy with the real high fluttery voice when he sings is jumping all over waving newspapers in the air saying that the smoke from Zoot's skinny cigars is wrecking his voice. But Zoot just keeps puffing and playing cards with old Red Leg who still doesn't look right to me. Red Leg's toothpick just keeps moving around in his mouth like it was on a handle somebody was turning from the inside. It looks like they don't even notice Clyde who keeps roaring around saying the smoke is the breath of the Devil. Clyde talks about the Devil a lot. He used to sing in a church before Ivory Joe got him into the Classics. Not the kind of church we go to. It's one where the Negroes are all jumping around and singing and waving their arms. Ivory Joe took me there three Sundays ago.

Mother is over in the corner talking to some white guy in a fancy suit. I can tell she's not sure if she likes him because she keeps using his name. *Mr. Goldin.* She says it the same way she says Arnie Dalitz's name. Everything about Mr. Goldin is shiny. His hair is shiny with a big fat wave at the front. His face is shiny. His suit is shiny. His shoes are shiny. He's tall and he looks like a movie star who's getting old. He's holding up pieces of paper in front of Mother and he keeps saying he wants her to sign something. Mother starts reading the papers and you can hear her arguing with him until the music from the big room gets too loud.

Over in the corner Ivory Joe has his hand on Clarence's shoulder. He's talking to him real tough. But Clarence just gets twice as scared. He keeps saying he can't go on. "Too scared, Joe," he keeps saying. You can tell things are getting bad. Ivory Joe sees me and says, "Chrissie, you get yourself over here, please." He sits me down in front of Clarence and says, "Boy, you telling me you're too scared to sing right this minute to this little girl here?" What else can Clarence say? He's got no choice but to look angry and say, "Joe, who do you think you're calling scared?" "Then sing, dammit," says Ivory Joe. So Clarence looks right at me and starts singing his *doom dat da doom ooh wa wa* part. I know he's nervous so I act extra impressed and this kind of settles him down and by the time he gets into the *Were you ever/More than the mist/More than the love/I thought I had kissed* part of it he's starting to enjoy himself. Ivory Joe stops him and says, "So what's the problem here, Clarence?"

Clarence and Ivory Joe come to an agreement which makes me feel important. I'm supposed to sit right in the front of the audience so Clarence can look straight at me and pretend no one else is there when they're singing. Red Leg takes me out into the audience grumbling away to himself. His toothpick is still going all over his mouth like it's trying to find the way out but can't. Red Leg must know half the Negroes here. Hands keep shooting out making shadows in the spotlight. Red Leg just shakes them and mumbles something without even looking. On the stage the Negro ponies are kicking up their legs all at once and the band is so loud I almost have to hold my ears.

We get to a table in front where two chairs have been put for us. I can look through the ponies' legs and see Herman Pinsky and the racketeer he's with. They're on the other side of the runway. The racketeer's with a doxie. You can tell she's peeved the racketeer isn't paying any attention to her. Herman Pinsky and him are just staring up at the ponies and talking to each other out of the side of their mouths. Sometimes they laugh but you can't hear them. Herman Pinsky looks like a fat white mouse with glasses. I don't know how someone like Leo could have someone like him for a friend. I don't like him.

The Negro ponies leave and the man with the microphone says, "Ladies and gentlemen, Small's Paradise in the heart of Harlem is proud to present the newest act on its way to stardom . . ." and a whole lot of other stuff but I stop hearing it because I'm so excited until ". . . *Ivory Joe and the Classics!*" And everyone's cheering like crazy. Ivory Joe is the first one out. They look great. All dressed up in those neat white suits. The band is already playing. Zoot's next and right away Red Leg starts laughing and slapping himself. Clyde and Clarence are right behind and I see Clarence looking like he's getting sent to the office to get the strap. His eyes are going all over looking for me. He can't find me. It's like he's going to run away. So I go *Psssssssst* and wave. He sees me. Already they're starting into *Train to You* the real fast song. Clarence starts singing and staring at me and his eyes are a fire. But he's doing it. They all are. Singing and moving like they're all one person. All around me Negroes are yelling and clapping. Even the white people are too. Not like the Copa where Mr. Podell will throw you out if you get too carried away. Sometimes the Copa reminds me of school.

Ivory Joe's voice is the loudest. It's beautiful. High but not real high and singing about wanting to take the fastest train back to see his girlfriend. And there's Zoot and Clyde and Clarence pounding away making train sounds moving their arms back and forth at the same time. Zoot is having a great time grinning like he's just won a poker game. Sometimes for a split second he grins down at Red Leg who's stamping his feet in time to the music. Clyde seems like he's still in church with a dreamy look. But I can't look at them too much because Clarence needs me to look at him. As long as I'm staring right at him smiling and clapping like everyone else you can see he feels okay. When they finish *Train to You* they all bow at once and even Clarence is starting to smile a little.

They do two more songs. Just when you think people can't go any crazier after *So Blue* they go into *Ghost Lover* and that does it. When they make their voices start floating all over the whole place gets real quiet all of a sudden and then Ivory Joe cuts in. It's like he makes his voice swirl around the room. It's real spooky but when their voices all come together the place goes wild. Cheering waving dancing in between the tables. They're doing it all. And Clarence doesn't need me anymore. He's looking all over the room grinning as he sings looking like a big bear. In the middle of all the craziness I look over and see Herman Pinsky trying to yell to the racketeer. He's opening a briefcase and taking out some papers. They both look excited too.

The only person who isn't going crazy is Mother. I see her back in a corner where the curtains meet the stage. She's just standing there in the shadows watching. You can't tell what she's thinking of. But it makes me think of Leo. I know what he'd be thinking.

Afterward we go backstage and it looks like the lunchroom when Louie Makin let the snake loose. People are jumping up and down and hugging and shouting. A lot of the ponies are all of a sudden real friendly to Ivory Joe. Too friendly if you ask me. Where were they when he was just plain Ivory Joe? It's all very amazing that the Negro ponies are just like the white ones Leo hangs around with. Mr. Goldin is talking to Mother again holding that same piece of paper which he gives to her. They're shaking hands when Herman Pinsky and the racketeer come roaring in and walk over to Ivory Joe like they've known him for years. "Son, you were great. Incredible. With the right help you could turn into a big star. By the way, I'm Herman Pinsky, president of Avalon Records. You probably heard of us. We've got the Vee Tones, the Good Knights and Little Philly."

He's talking real fast. He reaches out and shakes Ivory Joe's hand but Ivory Joe keeps looking over at the racketeer. "Do I know you?" he says.

"Son, this is my business associate, Mr. Eboli. Tommy Eboli," says Herman Pinsky.

"Weren't you in boxing?" asks Ivory Joe.

"Been in a lot of things, Joe," says the racketeer with a big smile. He's got real bushy eyebrows.

"Now, Joe, is there a place we can talk? Cause I got a contract here that'll make you a guaranteed fortune."

Herman Pinsky's trying to get Ivory Joe away from figuring out where he's seen this Mr. Eboli the racketeer. You can just tell. He's trying to steer him away from all the other people waving the contract in the air.

"You have to talk to our manager," says Ivory Joe.

"Manager? You have a manager already?"

Ivory Joe nods.

"Well, where is he?" says Herman Pinsky.

"She," says Ivory Joe.

"She?" says Herman Pinsky. And when Ivory Joe points to Mother you'd think Herman Pinsky has just run full speed into the goalpost. He stands there gawking. Then he tries to act like he's glad to see Mother. Fat chance. "Tina baby," he says. "How nice to see you."

"Hello, Herman," Mother says in her great drop-dead voice. Herman Pinsky must be thinking of the time Mother made Leo stop the car so she could throw him out when he was drunk and making rude noises in the back seat. Or when she caught him stealing a silver spoon at home. Leo kept saying it was all an accident but Mother wouldn't let him in the house again.

"This is really a stroke of luck, Tina. See, I'm prepared to make the group here an offer that'll make everyone rich."

"I don't think so, Herman."

"Now listen, Tina, Avalon has got the best race records of any company. We know the Negro, Tina. Hell, look what we did with *Dew Drops* and *One Hour Man*."

"Herman, right now it seems that Mr. Goldin and I are close to an agreement."

Herman Pinsky and the racketeer see Mr. Goldin for the first time. He's sort of faded away. "Hi, Herman. Tommy," he says looking real strange like he's not happy to see them.

"Well, well. If it isn't George," says the racketeer. It looks like nobody's happy to see anybody else. Herman Pinsky just stares at Mr. Goldin. Then he says, "George, I can't believe it. You keep getting in the way."

"Look at it this way, Herman," says Mr. Goldin. "We're all after the same thing."

"What's that?"

"Fine young talent."

"If you say so, George," says Herman Pinsky looking like he's stepped in something soft. Then he really blows it. "Tell me, Tina, does Leo know you're doing this?" like he was saying he'd snitch if she didn't watch out. Boy is he ever talking to the wrong person's mother.

Afterward Ivory Joe, Mother and me walk down to Wells Restaurant. I'm so tired I'm starting to wake up again. The place is packed even though it's real late. A lot of white people are there and everybody knows everybody else. Ivory Joe introduces me and Mother to some people who were just singing over at the Apollo Theater. I sit there at the table by the window eating fried chicken and waffles like everyone else. Red Leg comes in and sits with us. He doesn't eat. He just makes his toothpick go round in his mouth. They start talking about the racketeer and I can see Ivory Joe doesn't want to say too much in front of me. But Mother wants to. She says it's all part of our growing up. So we'll be well rounded. Ruthie and I are going to end up so well rounded we'll be circles if Mother gets her way. Leo's the opposite. He thinks his daughters have to be protected from everything. But in the end just being with Leo makes you well rounded.

"Racketeers," says Mother talking about Herman Pinsky and the other man. It's one of her favorite words. Then she starts worrying about signing the contract with George Goldin. She's not sure he's the right record company for Ivory Joe and the Classics to be working with.

"Hell's bells," says Red Leg. "They're all crooks but anything's better than Pinsky. Ain't you figured out who he's tied in with?"

"This a quiz?" says Ivory Joe.

"Vito Genovese," says Red Leg. I want to know who this Vito Genovese is. For a little while there's just the sound of Red Leg's toothpick going around.

"Big Mafia man," he says after a while.

15

It's me who answers when Herman Pinsky phones. It's our weekend to be at Leo's place and of course he's not here. He's stepped out. *Stepping out* is one of the things Leo says when he really means something else. Leo doesn't really just step out. He goes for hours. He never plans to. He just does and then remembers he's supposed to be somewhere else. It's like *nightclubbing*. That's Leo's very own word that means he's out spending the whole night drinking even if he's never anywhere near a nightclub. Or *ladyfriend*. That's some doxie he's never met before but who's *stepping out* with him to go *nightclubbing*. You have to know these things.

I tell Herman Pinsky that Leo's stepped out and I hear this creepy little white mouse hairless voice of his asking me to write down that he's called. He's spelling it out so slow that I'm finished while he's still halfway through Herman. Does he think I'm in the second grade?

Then he tells me how nice it was to see me with Ivory Joe at that place in Harlem. He really brownnoses like crazy. Just like Mother said. Herman Pinsky and the racketeers are trying to get a hold of Ivory Joe. It was nice to see you too I say and hang up.

"Hah!" yells Ruthie who's flat on her back staring at her chessboard that's taped to the ceiling. "The black bishop advances on the white queen." She sees life as one big fat chessboard now that she beat Dr. B. W. Lewis of Chicago. Byron as we call him. He's written back asking for a rematch. Ruthie practically had kittens. She's still afraid to tell him she's just a girl. In her letter she wrote *Regards to the wife* trying to look like a man, all sloppy with lines going all over the page. We're waiting to see if he writes back with his next chess move and a p.s. saying *Myrna says hi* or something. If he does Ruthie'll be crushed. It's Byron this and Byron that. I'm sick of hearing about Byron. Her room is filled with mushy love letters she's written to Byron but she never mailed. I found them once and started reading them and she had an absolute conniption. ". . . and Byron I know it will be an adjustment but darling if our love can shine like a flower at night . . ." Boy oh boy. For a brain Ruthie's really gone off the edge of her chessboard. I teased her and told her Byron is probably some old guy all hunched up with a greeb hanging from his nose. Like fun he is she yelled pointing to a photograph of some actor she cut out of a magazine. On the bottom of the photograph she's written *Byron* but when I peeled it off a little bit to see who it really was it said *Marlon Brando*. But I'm glad for Ruthie but he'd better change his T-shirt before meeting Leo. Already you can see changes in Ruthie. She's bugging Mother about getting the braces off her teeth. For when she meets Byron. I'm being careful not to tease too much right now. Maybe later after the next letter arrives.

Ruthie's got her chessboard out and she's giving the players names. Like Mother's the White Queen. Leo is the White King. Ivory Joe is the White Knight. The Classics are something called Rooks. Me and Ruthie get to be Pawns. Herman Pinsky and the racketeers are all on the black side along with a bunch of ponies and stewardesses and ladyfriends. Ruthie starts moving them around the chessboard but I can't follow what she's doing.

The only important thing I tell her is to get the White King and the White Queen back together again.

Ruthie and I start figuring out what to do. We've decided that Mother and Leo just *have* to get together even though last time was a big fat zero. We know they both still want to. Each of them keeps asking us lots of little questions about what the other one is doing. It's not like *Which floozie is your father hanging around with now?* It's always *Honey pass me the flour and I'll bet your father doesn't have time to bake you apple tarts like these I mean him being out all the time* as if we're supposed to blab on Leo and say yeah Mom you shoulda seen the doxie he was out with last night wow! But it's okay because they both do it. Leo's getting even worse. No more stuff about *This Negro fella*. Last time it was *that colored character* and him looking right at us instead of making like he wasn't really interested. Ivory Joe is really getting to Leo and we're worried something awful might happen. Leo can get real mushy when he's been nightclubbing and he might just get mad enough with Mother to make himself fall for some doxie who'd marry him right on the spot. And then wake up the next morning to find out he really just meant to step out.

While we're trying to figure out what to do the White King himself comes in. He's been nightclubbing even though it's only Saturday afternoon. Probably over at Mr. Kampelman's playing gin. "Hey, how's my girls?" he says. Like he hasn't seen us for a year. "Now the party really starts, huh?" I look at Ruthie and roll my eyes. I know what's coming. There's nothing we can do. It's like being tied to the train tracks and Leo's the train. I just stand there as he comes over and gives me the biggest goobery kiss right on the cheek. Then Ruthie gets it. The deadly bourbon kiss. You almost bite the dust from the smell.

Leo notices that we don't have the TV on and this makes him nervous. He just bought it last week. He told us it was a present just for us so we acted real excited. Actually we were. Most of the kids in my class don't have TV. You can split the class in half. Those who know what *I Love Lucy* and *The Ed Sullivan Show* are and those who don't. Knowing who Sergeant Friday nabbed last night is very important. After Leo got us watching the TV that first day in his living room Ruthie and I suddenly figured out it was another one of his fast ones. We looked around and he'd stepped out. The TV set was like Stanley his driver. It was to keep us company when Leo went nightclubbing. We now call the TV set Stanley Number Two. Leo sees the piece of paper where I wrote down Herman Pinsky and right away he goes over and dials the phone. At first everything is fine. It's the Leo and Herman show as Ruthie says. There is all the usual *Still making millions?* and *Where you been hiding?* that Leo and his friends always go through before they start talking. But then the trouble starts. We just watch Leo's face get angry and right away we know that rat Herman Pinsky is telling him all about Mother and Ivory Joe being at Small's Paradise in Harlem.

"She what?" Leo yells into the phone. Ruthie and I beat it. Back in the bedroom we can hear Leo start yelling into the phone and I know the rat is telling him I was there with Ivory Joe and Mother. I start to get real nervous. Once in a while Leo scares me when he gets extra mad. He's not like the Leo I know. We hear him yelling even more and it's for real. But Ruthie is the cool one. She sneaks back out and comes in with her chessboard. "It's all a matter of logic," she says.

"Ruthie it's also a matter of making sure that Leo doesn't go up to Small's Paradise tomorrow night," I say. "Ivory Joe's playing there you know."

"Fine," says Ruthie like she's talking to Byron. "How do we get a checkmate situation?"

I tell her I don't know what she's talking about but she just keeps thinking up this big plan. Leo's been supposed to take us up to Camp Wig-A-Mog to register for the summer. But for three weeks he's come up with excuses even though he promised Mother. She's worried stiff about us staying in New York in the summer and using swimming pools and getting polio from them. So Ruthie moves the White King around the chessboard and says we just have to use rational thinking on Leo. We tell him he *has* to take us to Camp Wig-A-Mog tomorrow. That way he won't get back in time to cause any trouble up in Harlem. Ruthie's got the White King and the White Knight on different sides of the board.

"*Christie!* Get in here!" Leo yells while he's still on the phone. I know what he wants.

Ruthie is Miss Logic. Saying don't worry about a thing. Just use reason like I do. She's moving the chess players all over. I can't follow a thing she's doing.

"*Christie!*" This is definitely not the Leo I know.

Ruthie picks up the chessboard and puts it in my arms. "Just explain it the way I told you. There's no way he can argue against it," Ruthie says. "It's airtight."

Well I'm not. I'm going to wet my pants I say. It's true. I'm so scared I just want to hide. But Ruthie opens the door. I walk out to face the monster holding the chessboard in front of me. I don't know why I'm doing this.

"Christie has something to explain to you," Ruthie yells out. I could kill her. But I need both hands for the stupid chessboard. Leo's still on the phone. Like a dog tied to a short chain. He's walking back and forth all red and angry.

He starts shouting. "You never told me you were up in Harlem with that colored singer. At some club! And your mother too. Well?" I stare at Leo. Then I stare at the chessboard. My mouth won't work.

"Christ, Herman, hold on a second," Leo yells into the phone. Then he turns back to me. "Well? What business have you being up in Harlem?" I look down at the chessboard trying to remember all the logic. The White Bishop. And the White King. But who's the Black Knight again?

"Dammit, are you deaf?"

That does it. All of a sudden I start bawling my head off. It just happens. I drop the chessboard. "You want us to get polio!" I yell at him. I don't know why. It just comes out.

"Herman, shut up for a minute, will you. I got problems here."

"You do you do," I yell at him. "You want us to die." I'm sniveling like a jerk but I can't help it. Then Miss Logic jumps in and starts bawling too. "You want us to be crippled," she yells. When Ruthie cries she gets snotty real quick and it's awful looking at what's under her nose. She makes me cry even more. And then *I* make *her* cry even more. Leo all of a sudden looks like the guy Sergeant Friday shined the flashlight on.

"What are you talking about?" Leo says. No more Mr. Tough Guy now.

Ruthie and I can't stop. "I'm going to be in an iron lung because of you," I blubber. "*Mother* loves us. Even if you don't. I wanna go home."

"Herman, do I tell you how to handle your life? Look, I'll call you back."

The next day Leo takes us to Camp Wig-A-Mog. He's like a big pussycat the whole time and no one says anything about yesterday. We have to drive way up the Hudson River and then turn off the highway going down roads with nothing but big pine trees and some farmers' fields. Pine trees and fresh air are really tough on Leo. If he's not around traffic and card games and a deli he gets real edgy. Especially with us. He can't just go stepping out over to Arnie Dalitz's or Mr. Kampelman's. It's when he realizes he really doesn't know anything about girls. You can almost see him wishing our names were Irving and Morty. Last summer when Leo finally stopped sending Stanley up to see us and came himself he looked like he didn't even want to get out of the car when he saw one whole acre of little girls. But that was before he met Miss Crawford the head counselor. In a bathing suit Miss Crawford is really something. What a chest she has. We all wanted to ask her if she ate anything special when she was our age. Leo all of a sudden would love to know everything about how the camp was run and Miss Crawford explained it to him.

He couldn't even pass his Junior Hiker's unless there was a crap game at the finish line. But he goes walking all over the forest in his big thick business shoes and his suit like he's Tarzan nodding at everything she says. The next week Leo comes up dressed like he's hunting lions. In the back of his Cadillac is a tent. And a huge pile of corned beef and pastrami sandwiches from Lindy's. The mattress from his bed is in the trunk. And a copy of the *Racing Form* and a little roulette wheel. Wilderness supplies says Leo. That night Ruthie and I watch Miss Crawford's cabin like a hawk to see if she's there. No light ever comes on in her cabin. I can't believe it! Miss Crawford! She even leads us in the camp anthem every day!

But that was last year and this is now. There was no Ivory Joe then. Ivory Joe is like a fourth person in the car even though he's not here. He's the real reason we're going up to the camp. Leo wants to get back home in time to ditch us and then go up to Harlem and cause trouble. But Ruthie and me are stalling like crazy. We take turns having to go to the bathroom and wanting to stop for something to drink which makes us have to go to the bathroom again. Leo keeps looking at his watch. It's afternoon when we get up to Wig-A-Mog and the minute we find out Miss Crawford isn't there this year Leo wants to leave. No matter what we do we can't keep him there. We get signed in, choose the weeks we want to come there and then presto we're back in the car. We don't even get to look at the lake. Trouble. But this time it's me that comes up with the idea. We're driving through some little town and all of a sudden I remember what we did last summer.

Hey. Let's play the policeman game I say.

"Not now, Christie," Leo says. He's got both hands on the wheel which means he's really in a hurry.

Aw why not? And Ruthie figures it out right away. She joins in with a little *aw* of her own.

"Girls. Look. I'm late for something."

"You used to do it all the time last year," Ruthie says.

"The policeman game needs a lot of time. You know that," Leo says. That's why we play it. In the policeman game the rules are that Leo has to do something totally nutty while he's driving. And it has to be right in front of a cop. Then we get to see him talk his way out of it. He does it every single time. When Leo turns on the charm every cop in the whole world would be faked out. You see them stick their head in the window with sunglasses instead of eyes and that Sergeant Friday voice that means you're going to jail for the rest of your life mister. But Leo wipes them all out. Last summer when he drove across the front lawn of the police department in some little town we thought he was a goner for sure. Red lights flashing like the Fourth of July. A prowl car racing over. Sirens blaring. But Leo's ready for them. He goes into his Ohmygod officer what have I done! routine. The best part is where he says how he's just overcome with emotion. Because of us his two little daughters he hasn't seen in over a month. He pulls out baby pictures of us. And then when we were two years old. The cop always tries to stay being a tough guy. But when Leo is almost starting to bawl you can see them start to cave in too. Leo always offers to pay for the grass. And go quietly to jail. When he asks the cop if he could find someone to drive his little girls home safely that does it. The cop is almost bawling too. Especially if he's a father. Leo always lays on a lot of *my little girls.* One time he got a cop who was just getting divorced and had some little girls too. Pretty soon both of them were sniveling away and the cop was asking Leo to go for drinks after work. Every time Ruthie and I grade Leo's performance from one to ten. That time we gave him a ten. But when the cop had gone Leo still kept on acting like a simp for about half an hour. Ruthie said it was because good actors always get into their role but I'm not so sure. Anyway it was still definitely a ten.

But today when we really need to play the policeman game and stall for all the time we can get he won't do it. So Ruthie throws a real sulk. She's a great sulker. You can almost see the black cloud over her head. I can't do it like she can but I try. Right now I'll try anything. Pretty soon Leo figures out that he's got two silent sulkers on his hands. If there's one thing that drives Leo nuts it's silence. It makes him real nervous and usually Ruthie and I have to keep talking just so he won't feel like we're wishing we weren't with him. After a day with Leo you can get really pooped. But right now we just sit there. Leo turns on the radio. It's lousy reception all static except for the two stations that have church music on them. So we drive through little towns listening to church music until it makes Leo crazy and he switches it off. Silence.

"Look, we don't have time to play the policeman game," he says all of a sudden.

"Fine," says Ruthie. Does she ever have a great way of saying one thing but letting you know that she's really saying something else. If she marries Byron he's going to have his hands full.

We keep driving. Leo looks over at us a couple of times. When we go through a little town there's a police car driving up to a red light as we go through the green light. We can see Leo looking in the rearview mirror. Ruthie jabs me with her elbow but we keep looking straight ahead. Leo slows down a little still looking in the mirror. We're almost outside the town now. We're coming up to a crossroads. There's a big empty field off to the side. Leo puts his turn signal on and looks in the mirror saying something dirty under his breath. Then he drives right off the road and across the field.

When the siren goes on behind us, Ruthie and I cheer for Leo. He looks mad and happy at the same time.

THE WAR

16

A month after they met, they were married. Leo came home on a three-day pass and Tina threw herself into his arms before he had taken the final step down from the train. The wedding was on a Tuesday. On the Monday night they broke the news in hurried phone calls to Arnie Dalitz, Mother Ackerman, Morris and various aunts and uncles. Mimmo worked all night making a dress for Tina and demanded to be a part of the wedding party. He arrived at City Hall with the dress and four members of his family, all of whom cried joyously during the brief ceremony.

The celebration afterward was arranged by Arnie Dalitz, who called in favors. A restaurant on Mulberry Street was told to close for the evening. A private party would be held that night. And an orchestra and the best food were to be provided. The reception turned out to be more lavish than even Arnie Dalitz had expected. The owners of the restaurant had obviously decided to take no chances.

Not when the request had come through the Mafia family of Vito Genovese.

Arnie Dalitz had thought of everything. He had Lindy's deliver a few trays of kosher food, which enraged the Italian cook but pleased Mother Ackerman, who was adapting uneasily to her secondary role and was wondering why her strongest son hadn't married a girl who was more submissive. They all danced until the musicians were exhausted. And even as they laughed and changed partners on the dance floor, there was an unspoken urgency between Leo and Tina. Every moment was too precious. And no one mentioned the war. And Leo's departure on Thursday.

They drove to the country in Pennsylvania, arriving just after dawn. They undressed one another and until Thursday morning they spent most of their time nude in bed. Their exhausted fitful bouts of sleep were interrupted when either of them awoke and aroused the other with long slow caresses, then kisses that swept the contours of their bodies. And once, when they were making love, Tina looked up and cried out as Leo's face passed before her, a fleeting mask, a gaunt face, not his at all but one with ancient eyes and at the moment they surged against each other in the uncontrollable gasping waves, she burst into tears, pulling his head down, pressing her lips fiercely against his until her tears ran off his face, falling down across the pillow.

She had decided she would not stay in America while Leo was overseas. The waiting wife or the riveter at the aircraft factory on Long Island were not roles she could imagine for herself. She could at least get to England in this war. They would need nursing assistants. Teachers. Secretaries. Whatever it took to be closer to the action. To Leo. But the time to tell him was later. By letter.

On Thursday afternoon, they were apart for the hour it took Leo to meet with Morris in the office. In the year that Leo had been in secret training in Maryland, he had managed to stay in touch with Morris enough to keep Frolic Frocks barely operating. Morris, whose poor eyesight kept him out of the army, was running the company with his meticulous production skills. And what he did not know, Mimmo was teaching him. But with Leo gone, there was no outside man, no one with the flair to handle the buyers and the designers. With the war everything was different. The fashion capitals in France and Italy lay under enemy control. Survival, not style, counted now and what fortunes there were to be made came from the millions of military uniforms that were needed. It was a khaki world of government contracts, bidding, sealed tenders and forms in triplicate signed by some unknown colonel.

Frolic Frocks was equipped for none of it. Merely to keep the company alive, Morris had begun desperate trips to the big harbor warehouses, wheedling, bribing his way into possession of an occasional precious shipment of raw cotton that was not going to the military. The cotton was turned into flimsy blouses that were sold instantly to big department stores bidding against each other for anything that could be sold to the women working in the war factories.

But the problem was the raw material. The cotton. Wool. Anything that could be made into a garment. On most days Morris was now returning from the harbor warehouses with nothing and the machines and the cutting tables stood silent, unused, as Mimmo paced among them, muttering to himself in Italian.

When they met, Leo instantly sensed that Morris was trying to shield him from the bad news. And staring out the banks of wire mesh windows, he had no answers to give. With the train leaving from Penn Station just after dark, and Tina waiting for him, Leo could only look into the worried smile of his older brother and nod when he was told everything would be fine.

They both knew it wouldn't.

On the platform at Penn Station, Leo embraced Tina until the train was pulling out, shouting his love over the steam-driven roar of the locomotive. He arrived in Washington late at night and was met by a car that drove seventy miles northwest of the capital into Maryland where the secret training base was hidden in the Catoctin Mountains. When he arrived he was directed to a colonel's office where he was given his posting. At first he thought it was a joke.

A war going on all over Europe and he was being sent to Cairo?

17

At the secret base in the Catoctin Mountains, Leo had been trained by the OSS, the new American intelligence unit. There had been courses in almost everything he would need. Codes and ciphers. Lock picking. Making and planting explosives. Parachuting at low levels. Secret radios and listening devices. Even killing an enemy with your bare hands. He was prepared for everything.

Except for Cairo.

Even in wartime, the rituals of elegance in the Cairo society were played out like nowhere else in the world. There were the endless rounds of parties in the jeweled clubs of the Egyptian nobility, titled Englishmen and Greek millionaires. And polo matches at the Gezira Club where the long line of Rolls Royces, Cadillacs and Buicks were incessantly polished by the hordes of chauffeurs who convened almost daily, waiting for their masters in any of a dozen routinely opulent locations. There were cricket matches. And field hockey at the British barracks by the Nile. And afterward, cool gin drinks with the officers at the Turf Club. Theatrical diversions had been curtailed since the outbreak of war. Now that the Italians were the enemy, La Scala no longer sent their singers from Milan to perform at the Opera House. The Royal Shakespeareian Company had also ceased their annual visits.

Not that they were missed by Leo. The only theatrical event he cared about was the pageantry of the opening of Parliament. There was nothing like it in America. From the Abdin Palace, all along the route of the procession, the crowds of Egyptian men in red fezzes and the women in veils cheered their young King Farouk, once dashingly handsome but now descending into fat and decadence. With his queen, Farida, the king was preceded by the outriders of the Royal Lancers and the Household Cavalry, the clatter of the hooves being the signal for the roar from the crowds. The open carriage appeared through the thicket of riders whose shining breastplates and plumed helmets caught the sun in a volley of reflections. Behind it came the open carriage of the British High Commissioner, who held the true power over the affairs of Egypt in the name of King George VI of England. It was only the foreigners who cheered when the High Commissioner rode past. The Egyptian crowds fell almost silent. Cairo was a city of intrigue amid the opulence, with the Egyptians quietly and politely seething over the British domination of their country.

Even in the quietness of his large apartment in the European section called Zamalek, Leo felt as if it was all unreal, as if the pieces of what he saw never quite came together in his thoughts. He would look out over his walled garden, emblazoned with bougainvillea and jasmine, and wonder why he had trouble remembering that there was a war going on. Yet every day the British military train would arrive with a fresh load of dead and wounded brought in from the carnage where the forces of Montgomery and the Nazis under Rommel pounded each other in the desert that seemed so far away from the elegant parties.

Leo was stationed in Cairo with only two other OSS men. Both of them were Americans of Yugoslavian descent and were involved in their mission with a passion that made Leo feel like a spectator. Food and ammunition were being airlifted from Cairo to the struggling partisans fighting the Nazis in the mountains of Yugoslavia. But for reasons that no one in Washington understood, the shipments were not arriving. Whatever the cause, German sabotage, theft or British red tape, it was the job of the three OSS men to get the supplies into the mountains of Yugoslavia. As the *kamsins*, the dust storms, settled on Cairo, Leo labored in the choking grit supervising the loading of supplies. By night, when the air had cooled slightly, he wove his way into the life of Cairo, gathering information requested by Washington. And very late at night, in the high-ceilinged bedroom with stark white walls and shuttered windows, Leo lay across the huge old bed and wrote letters that he mailed to Tina every week. *Maybe I should be like the British and wear those short pants the Arabs all laugh at. But at least they're comfortable. Listen to me! Complaining when all those poor S.O.B.'s are getting killed out there in the desert. Have I told you that I love you? And God how I'd like to be back there with you. Tell Morris hi for me. What news there? And you asked me a question so I'll give you an answer—No I don't think it's a great idea for you to go to England. They're sinking ships in the Atlantic you know. Hey let's go to Pennsylvania for the weekend. Last time was just a rehearsal. Now we really get down to serious business. But about England . . .*

It was six weeks before the letter reached Tina. Like the other letters she kept in a pile beside the bed, she read it again and again, imagining Leo's voice and trying to figure out what was in the parts crossed out by the military censors. A day later she would take the letter up to Mother Ackerman's house and read them the parts that were not too personal. At first Mother Ackerman had sat in the raised chair demanding that she be shown the letter. But Tina refused. There was too much of Leo's writing that was meant for her alone. For the first few letters it was a test of domestic supremacy. Mother Ackerman sat sternly listening. To the words of *her* son. Whom *she* had raised. Who else could have controlled Leo during all those hell-raising years? And now suddenly it was *tell Mother hi and lots of love* coming from the exquisite mouth of this little interloper.

And even worse, the attention of the entire family was shifting to

Tina. No longer were the rarefied debates about social or political matters the reason for them all coming together. Now it was simply Leo's letters that drew them to the house. Even disdainful cousin Arnold Berman, now training in psychiatry, would arrive with various members of his family. During the reading of the second letter he whispered a sly remark to his cousin. Tina looked up sharply and asked if there was something the whole family should hear. She had developed an immediate and instinctive dislike for Arnold, stronger even than that felt by Leo. But Mother Ackerman noticed that Arnold now treated Tina with the fawning reverence he had once reserved only for her.

Mother Ackerman's anger remained a silent presence in the room. But the day after the fifth letter, Tina phoned her saying, "I would like to see you. Just the two of us." They met in a small restaurant near the 59th Street station of the Third Avenue elevated railway, exchanged polite, awkward greetings and mandatory pleasantries until Tina put the letter down in front of Mother Ackerman. "Read it. Please," she said.

"But you read it to us last night," said Mother Ackerman. It was all a matter of control. Of course she wanted to read the letter. And all the others. But at her own initiative. Not when it suited this new daughter-in-law. "Please," Tina said again.

She read it until the end of the second paragraph *and all I can think of is you and me rolling in bed at that little Inn. Am I going (sex) crazy? But honest to God I miss you for your mind too. And . . .* Mother Ackerman folded the letter and replaced it in the envelope. "These letters are for you alone to read," she said.

"I know," said Tina. "But I wanted you to know that I wasn't holding them back from you for any other reason."

Mother Ackerman stared at Tina for a long time. "Yes," she said finally.

"I need some advice." Or do I say it simply? she thought. That for the sake of my husband, I want no feuds with you. This is my opening to you.

"I've never been sure of that."

"Perhaps because we've never really talked before. But look what joins us now. Your son, my husband." And what joins us, separates us.

"Tina, my dear, you must understand that I am happy for both you and my son. Leo is very strong willed. And you are, too, I suspect."

Suspect? "I want to talk to you about my plans. Ever since Leo and I got married, I've been thinking about going to England. I've inquired at the embassy and the Red Cross. There are ways I could get there and I've already set some of them in motion."

"Isn't that dangerous?"

"Not once you're there. But I think I'm going to change all those plans. There's something I want to tell you. Before anyone else. So you can tell the rest of the family." My offering. Let the hierarchy prevail as you need it to.

"Is there something wrong?"

"Not at all," Tina beamed. "You're going to be a grandmother."

"Oh, my darling girl!" Mother Ackerman exclaimed with joy and threw her arms around Tina.

When Tina's letter reached Cairo, Leo spent everything in his pockets on drinks for his gambling companions in the Royal Automobile Club. In Arabic, Greek, French and English, toasts were made to the health of the mother and of the child. It would, of course, be a boy.

Leo had backed into a mission that he never fully described to Tina in his letters. There was no way he could explain it without making it sound as if he was having a great time. Which he was. Except for missing Tina, he had concluded that his own war was so shamefully enjoyable that it must be kept as secret as possible. Otherwise every other sane, pleasure-loving enlisted man in the American military would demand to get in on the fun. And there was room for only one. When the emergency airlift shipments finally reached the Yugoslavian guerrillas they contained nothing but useless junk and used summer clothing. The OSS contingent in Cairo was ordered to investigate the possibility of sabotage by Egyptians sympathetic to the Nazis.

While the other two OSS men stalked the dusty native *souks* in search of information, Leo worked the clubs. The Cairo clubs were more elegant than anything he had ever seen in New York. Only with embassy assistance, a dinner jacket and a vague story of personal wealth and power back in America was he even able to get through the doors. There were only two clubs that really interested him, both imposing structures in the center of old Cairo. In the Mohammed Ali Club he stepped into the marbled foyer with the carpeted stairs, the billiard room and the two dining rooms where teams of waiters in starched uniforms served the finest Ottoman and French cuisine. Under Orientalist paintings Egyptian pashas played bridge in hushed splendor. A scattering of British knights, local princes and rich Jews made up the rest of the membership.

From whom Leo extracted enough winnings at the billiard table to cover the costs of his lavish entertaining.

But it was the Royal Automobile Club a few blocks away on Kasr-el-Nil that Leo preferred. There were younger members. Including women. Parties were held. And the sense of excitement extended to the ferocious poker games where the local Greeks, Jews and Egyptians gambled away small fortunes to one another, and occasionally to outsiders like Leo.

Sometimes King Farouk would arrive at the Royal Automobile Club seeking the pleasures that were slowly destroying him. His presence was signaled by the royal Rolls parked outside, the only one in all Egypt that was painted maroon, the king's personal color. Sitting at the gaming tables or in a special chair just off the dance floor, he would peer at his kingdom through small eyes encrusted in fat and hidden behind dark glasses. A plate of rich cakes was kept ready awaiting his signal and each empty glass of Coca-Cola, never alcohol—despite rumors—was swiftly replaced by a full one. His aide-de-camp remained discreetly by his side, alert to the slightest wishes of the king. Such wishes were conveyed as commands, often to whatever beautiful young woman Farouk had decided should share the royal bed back at the Abdin Palace. Married or single, it made no difference to Farouk who the woman was. Or whom she was with. No Egyptian was ever foolish enough to refuse the aide-de-camp's quiet announcement. And the foreigners who did were told to leave Egypt before the following sunset.

In the midst of the intrigue and the gambling Leo thrived. His skills at the card tables drew small crowds whenever he played. He became known, even liked, in the clubs. Old pashas gossiped slyly with him, their innuendoes filling the reports that Leo sent back to his OSS superiors. Who praised him for having such superb sources. The Greeks at the clubs came to like Leo for the explosive way he expressed himself, and for his passion around the card tables. The British considered him to be a little too American. The Syrians and the French remained aloof. Until the night Leo learned of Ruthie's birth. He bought drinks for all and toasts were made in a dozen languages. Joyous arguments raged over the name of the child. At various times during the raucous evening, Ruthie was called Edith Piaf, Karyoka, Vera Lynn or Um Kulthum. Leo kept buying drinks. And wondering what the hell he would do with a *girl.* They didn't play baseball. Or poker. Or chase women. Or even take over their fathers' businesses. But those problems were for later.

Morris's letter arrived. Frolic Frocks was on the verge of bankruptcy. They could not get the cotton they needed to make the dresses. Larger companies with big military contracts had offered to buy their steam pressing machines for a good price. It would at least keep the doors open for a while. What should be done?

Sell nothing! wrote Leo. He paced around his bedroom far into the night, muttering and rewriting his angry letter to Morris until the distant chatter of the *fellahin* in the streets simmered into silence.

A week later a short pudgy man with wire-rimmed glasses and an assertive stare approached him in the Royal Automobile Club. Without a word of explanation or introduction, he handed Leo his business card. In embossed, ornate lettering, the card read A. W. HAIBUR. "You are to meet me tomorrow afternoon at two P.M.," he said.

"Why?"

"Because I have a message for you. From a Mr. Arnie Dalitz. Good day."

18

The address on the business card was an elegant department store on a tree-lined street called Kasr-el-Nil. An Albanian doorman in gleaming boots and cape ushered Leo through the polished brass doors, directing him to the offices on the fourth floor where A. W. Haibur ran the store from behind an ornate eighteenth-century French desk. He rose when Leo entered, standing behind the desk holding out his hand and smiling with the kind of dead eyes that reminded Leo of mobsters he had met.

"Let me preface our discussion. I do not wish to become involved in whatever matters you will find yourself embroiled in as a result of our meeting today," Haibur said in a clipped and correct form of English. The phone rang, Haibur picked it up and snapped something in French, the language he obviously spoke the best. Then he hunched over the desk, his hands held prayerlike in front of him. "I have become involved as a matter of expediency for our company. That, my dear fellow, is the *only* reason. Now, then, I am to give you this." He handed Leo a letter and a small parcel.

Hey you dumb schmuck what's taking you so long to get back? Schtupping the Arabs? The broads I mean began the letter in the unmistakably bad handwriting of Arnie Dalitz. The letter was being sent by unusual channels to avoid the military censors, the FBI and whoever else had the power of arrest and detention. Arnie Dalitz did not know the whole story *so I'm telling all I know. It's calling in markers time Leo. Big time stuff. The highest. They need a favor from you seeing how your the only one we know now over there. The boys here want to scare the crap—and maybe more—outta some Greek named Sperdakas there. This greasers been giving big trouble to some real close relatives of one of the Brooklyn boys. You can probably guess who. If not ask the guy who gives you this. He's been told to help.*

Leo had met Sperdakas. He was tall, nearly sixty years old, and was always tanned, wearing a lot of jewelry and shouting at anyone who displeased him. Like many others, Sperdakas had benefited immensely when the British rounded up all the Italian men in Egypt at the beginning of the war and put them in concentration camps in Fayed and Ismailia. All Italian property was confiscated and sometimes found its way into the hands of those with official connections and the money for bribes. Within a month of the mass internment Sperdakas rode onto the cotton fields of an Italian named Luigi Greco and announced he was the new owner. At five thousand acres it was one of the largest cotton-growing operations in the Nile delta. Surrounded by guards and holding papers stamped and signed by various government officials, Sperdakas had ordered Greco's pregnant wife and her children off the property within two hours.

Sperdakas's acquisition of the five thousand acres was the best business deal of his life. Yet there were two terrible flaws to his newfound fortune and he was aware of neither. The first was Greco's wife. Her brother, Tony Strollo, lived in America, in Brooklyn, where he was underboss in the Mafia family now headed by the infamous Vito Genovese. When word reached Brooklyn that Marilena Greco, the sister of Tony Strollo, was living impoverished in a small apartment in Cairo with her three small children, the Genovese organization set out to change the situation *which is why they wanted me to get you Leo cause your the only one who can get this fucking Greek greaser. Don't back out Leo. They'd do it if someone did likewise to Tina. Get what I mean? Besides, you'll be helping save this greasers own family cause Tony wants to whack them all right now.* The second flaw was Sperdakas's family, his wife and three sons whom he had sent to America shortly before the war. They had moved in with his brother. In Brooklyn. And the Genoveses had found them. Leo finished reading Arnie Dalitz's letter. He then opened the small parcel that had accompanied it. He examined the contents, mainly photographs, and knew immediately what he had to do. "So why are you involved in this?" he asked Haibur.

"I've already told you."

"No, you haven't." Leo matched Haibur's stare.

"My business affairs are none of your concern, sir."

"I got news for you, Mac. There's some heavy IOUs being called in around the world for this one. I'm not doing anything until I know who I'm talking to."

Haibur's smile thinned out into the folds of his face. "Let us just say that your Mr. Genovese has been most helpful in helping us to obtain some of our finer merchandise."

My Mr. Genovese. Suddenly Leo understood. It was obvious. All that fine Italian leather that was somehow still available on the second floor of Haibur's store. And the olive oil that no other store in Cairo could obtain. And the Italian automobile tires with what looked like military designations on the side. It was all part of an efficient operational triangle with corners in New York, Cairo and Naples, where Vito Genovese had fled ten years earlier to avoid being prosecuted in America for murder. Even though Naples was now an enemy city, Genovese's power was still felt on the streets of New York. Orders were mysteriously conveyed through Mafia channels that rendered the war merely an inconvenience. From Naples, Genovese ran one of the most powerful black market operations in the Mediterranean. Supplying Haibur's department store with stolen or smuggled goods was merely a normal part of business.

"I am instructed to tell you that you must communicate all developments through me."

"So who else would I tell?" said Leo.

A few weeks later, as another trainload of dead and wounded rolled in from the Libyan desert, the Royal Automobile Club held what local history would record as its most glamorous New Year's Eve celebration. King Farouk's maroon Rolls was parked in front for most of the evening. Rita Hayworth arrived, spending the evening shyly answering questions about Hollywood and sometimes dancing to the big-band music played by British regimental musicians. Leo had wanted to dance with Rita Hayworth. Just to have his hand in hers. Arnie Dalitz and Herman Pinsky would never believe it.

But for two crucial hours he never left the card table in the room off the ballroom. He sat smiling at Sperdakas, fencing over a few preliminary games of gin that Leo made sure he lost. Then they switched to poker and he made sure he lost there, too, putting Sperdakas in an even more arrogant mood than usual. Leo dreaded what had to be done and losing somehow made it so much easier. He threw the cards down and slapped Sperdakas on the back. "Hey, Sperdakas! A toast to your children!" he yelled over the music.

Sperdakas reacted with disdain and irritation at such familiarity. Typically American. Leo drank the toast on his own and then pulled a photograph from his pocket, thrusting it at Sperdakas before disappearing onto the dance floor, lost in the crowd of a dozen nationalities as the orchestra played Glenn Miller music. Sperdakas stared at the photograph and his knees buckled.

Leo was lost in the arms of Rita Hayworth. He had cut in on the short Englishman who was waltzing when he should have been foxtrotting. Rita Hayworth seemed almost relieved. Or so Leo thought when he saw her smile when he cut in. But conversation had been difficult, almost painful, even when he tried to tell her how much he enjoyed her movies, especially *Only Angels Have Wings.* Her silence made Leo talk even more. And wonder why it was not what he thought it would be, dancing with Rita Hayworth, his hand placed lightly across the silk dress, feeling a warmth that strangely reminded him of another New Year's Eve.

He was suddenly spun around by Sperdakas, who grabbed his arm. "Where the hell did you get this?" he yelled. Rita Hayworth receded into the crowd as Leo turned to yell to her that it was nothing serious, that she should wait. But she vanished and his words sank into the swirl of music and dancers. Sperdakas shoved him and thrust the photographs in front of his face, yelling something Leo could not understand. "So kiss your wife and kids good-bye, Sperdakas. And your brother Nick, too." Leo cuffed away Sperdakas's hand and threaded his way over to the bar, ordering double shots of whiskey that he was suddenly in desperate need of. He had thought his loathing of Sperdakas would be enough. But it was not. Threatening a man's family pulled images of Tina and Ruthie out of the darkness and the loathing turned inward. He cursed and envied Arnie Dalitz for having it easy, for having that killer instinct, those cauterized emotions that could destroy the Sperdakases of the world, and all their children and wives, without even a second thought.

Sperdakas reached through the crowd to grab him. "I shall have you arrested," he shouted into the noise.

"Unlikely," Leo said, cuffing his hand away and smiling to make it look as if it was all a joke as the partygoers pushed past them. Then he pulled a battered American passport and another photograph from his pocket and thrust them at Sperdakas.

"That is my brother! And my son!" said Sperdakas, waving the photograph and passport at Leo.

"I know who they are. Now listen very carefully. I have a message for you."

"You never tamper with a man's family!" Sperdakas was shaking with an anger he could barely control. His words exploded in little balls of spit.

"Hey, no kidding. Maybe you should have thought of that when you drove Luigi Greco's family off their land."

"That was business!"

"So is this." The smile dropped from Leo's face and he reached out, pushing Sperdakas back into the chair. "You blew it. Mrs. Greco's brother is one of the bosses in the Genovese Mafia family in New York. You've heard of them? Genovese? Lucky Luciano?"

At Luciano's name Sperdakas nodded, the sharpness fading from his eyes. "And this guy didn't like hearing that his sister and her kids were pushed off their own land. So the Genovese family is willing to make you a little trade."

"Trade? What is there to trade?" But this time without anger. The best that could be summoned up was a faltering indignation.

"Your family."

"*My* family?" Astonishment now, almost panic. "Have you no decency?"

"Hey. I'm just delivering the message. And it's real simple—you mess up their wives and kids and they're gonna do it back to you in spades. So here's the deal. You give the Greco family back their land and one hundred thousand dollars for the money you've made off it. In exchange, the Mafia in New York will agree to . . ." Leo pulled a piece of paper from his pocket and read like a lawyer dryly reciting the terms of a will. ". . . *not* kill your brother Nick, your wife Theresa and your three sons. Nor will they set the two restaurants you own in Brooklyn on fire. Or your apartment building on West 55th Street. Or the homes that you and your brother own on Nostrand Avenue." Leo looked up and smiled serenely. "See? A simple little business deal. I'm told that you have two days to make up your mind. Happy New Year."

Leo disappeared onto the dance floor with Sperdakas now yelling after him, trying to follow him into the crush of dancers who were now counting down the seconds to the new year.

Two days later the Albanian doorman nodded crisply opening the brass doors for Leo to enter. Haibur was waiting, twirling an ebony letter opener in tense little circles on his desk. Leo told him there had been no reply. Haibur nodded and looked at Leo for the first time since he had entered. "I'm sure something will happen." The following day Sperdakas's prized Bugatti automobile was blown to pieces in the courtyard of his home in Heliopolis. And hearing the news, Leo revised his assessment of Haibur. Up there with the best of them. Genovese knew how to pick his associates. The same night Sperdakas's garage filled with rare cars, including a Cord, a Rolls and a Packard, was destroyed by fire. The next day he sat in front of Leo and mumbled his agreement to the deal.

"But there's a kicker now, fella."

"A kicker? What is a kicker?"

"A little change in the deal. You have a boatload of cotton being loaded in Alexandria. Going to Brazil. Well, it's going to New York now. To a company called Frolic Frocks."

19

The cotton was diverted to New York and Frolic Frocks began the best year of its existence. Morris wrote excited letters with stories of buyers from Macy's and Best & Co. bidding frantically against each other to get the simple dresses they were turning out by the thousands. And everyone wanted to know where they got all the cotton. *Incredible!* wrote Morris over and over. *You're a genius, Leo!*

In Cairo Leo read the letters and then put them beside the pile of Tina's letters that had accumulated on a shelf in the cupboard. He no longer stored her letters on the night table because they had drawn too many questions from the women who had occupied the bed with him.

It was now more than two years since he had left New York. And even though he still became anxious when Tina's letters were delayed, he found it more difficult to respond. His letters were shorter, written in awkward segments. Even though he told her in every letter how much he loved her, his words gradually became more automatic. In one of her letters, Tina wrote back saying that when she read his letters now, she could hear the lyrics but not the music. Leo replied with all the hurt and indignation he knew he should feel but didn't.

But on mornings when he was alone, he would often remove one of the letters from the cupboard and read it. And occasionally he would be startled to find himself talking to her as if she were there.

The women sharing Leo's bed ranged in tenancy from one night to several months. There was the Belgian widow; the Italian woman whose husband was interned at Ismailia; the wife of a colonel in the Free French forces; several of the afternoon tea set at the Gezira Club; and presently, Pamela, a British nurse. On the evening they met, Pamela's cool and very proper facade had cracked when she summoned up her worst insult to describe him. *Typically American,* she said to his face, after he told her to quit playing the martyr and let go. Tall, blonde, with porcelain skin and faintly red cheeks, Pamela had been schooled from birth in the British upper-middle-class meaning of honor and duty. As a nurse treating the casualties unloaded from the grim trains that rolled in from the war's desert carnage she had been trained to smile. Smiling was one's duty around the wounded. To keep up morale. No matter how torn the limbs, or how hideous the burns, one smiled. And woe betide any of the local civilian women driving the ambulances who did not smile also. Pamela enforced the reign of cheerfulness ruthlessly. And saw some patients survive because of it.

They met at a party in the desert of La Cité des Tentes out past the Sphinx and the pyramids. The embassies and most of the fashionable foreigners owned plots of land in a community of tents where feasts were held far into the night. The Bedouins put on shows and belly dancers gyrated to their music while lambs were roasted over an open fire. Pamela smiled during the entire evening. No matter what Leo said to her the smile stayed in place as if it were welded on. The next time they met, the smile remained and when Leo took her aside it was like talking to a mannequin. They were outside in the cool desert night where the sand dunes were like monstrous waves frozen still in the moonlight and her anger was drowned out by the Bedouin music in the tents. She tried to slap him but stumbled and slipped down a dune. He followed, kicking up plumes of sand as he ran to her. Crying, she lashed out at him but he pulled her toward him and she collapsed, sobbing against his shoulder. Their lovemaking was filled with the same intensity, an explosion of stifled emotions as they writhed across the rugs in their big tent. She undressed like no other woman he had ever met, as if she was peeling away one personality and revealing another. It was all done with a sense of defiant purpose, staring him in the eyes as her nylons and then her brassiere were held momentarily aloft, libidinous banners that fluttered gently to the carpets.

No matter what they promised each other, they both knew it would end. Their time together became more intense, and Leo's letters to Tina grew even more difficult to write. He ceased his affairs with other women and called Pamela at the hospital several times a week. From waiting in the corridors, watching the diseases and the death all around him, he began to dwell on his own vulnerability. Whatever illness he encountered on any given day was the one that played across his thoughts. He was soon spending days finding Arab doctors who claimed to have cures for the pains he was sure he felt. The pains were mainly hangovers and exhaustion from drinking all night or gambling till dawn.

With no warning, the orders from OSS headquarters came in three words—*Naples. Proceed immediately.* A horn-blaring struggle through the traffic of Kasr-el-Nil until he reached the hospital. Then racing through the corridors until he found her, turning around in her blood-spattered operating gown, her eyes looking out over the surgical mask and signaling in an instant that she knew.

Leo choked out an explanation but she stopped him. For a few desperate moments, standing at the side of a chaotic and teeming corridor, they held hands until she was called back into the operating room. She kissed his cheek and shook away tears, hurrying back into the maze.

A door swung behind her and Leo kept staring at it, expecting her to reappear.

20

Toward the end of the war, Leo's letters from Cairo arrived only every second or third week. Usually they were only one page long, ending with *Sorry the letter's so short but am real busy now. Will explain all in next one.* But the next ones never did. Tina still wrote every week, her own letters filled with stories of Ruthie's first steps and the problems of getting the landlord to fix the pipes. But whatever was important she left out. Her frustrations circling into occasional fury. Her feeling of abandonment. The empty nights. And the memories of the way she used to be.

Late one night Morris called saying they needed a model for a fashion show the next day. In the suite at the Waldorf which Morris had hired on Leo's instructions, she wore a red evening dress in front of the buyers from Bergdorf's, Henri Bendel, Saks and a dozen other stores. On the way back a photographer stopped her and asked her to pose for several pictures. He was from *Life* magazine, doing a story on wartime fashions, he explained. The next day, before Tina left the Waldorf, the photographer arrived with enlarged photos of her in the red dress. She agreed to meet him later. At a small club in the Village they danced and he told her stories of his home in Hungary and his travels around the world. He had melancholy eyes and a warm smile, and dark hair combed almost straight back with features that were coarser than Leo's but animated. She enjoyed the diversion, the feeling of being out with strangers unconnected to any part of her life, to Leo, to his family. They talked of Spain and the war there. Something kindled memories that had lain dormant. He had been to Madrid, photographed the battle of Huesca, suffered shrapnel wounds in the trenches. And Normandy, landing with the Allies. And Cairo? A glorious zoo inside a brothel. Or was it the other way around? Tina drank and wanted to dance. Something slipped away. They laughed and danced and closed down two clubs before he asked her to spend the night with him. "Of course," she said.

But at the entrance to the Commodore Hotel she stopped, apologized and said she couldn't go through with it. He put his hand on her shoulder, smiled and said he understood. When she declined his offer to escort her home, he kissed her on the cheek and for a moment watched her walk toward Broadway. She walked several blocks feeling the appraising eyes of loitering men. The wind blew across 42nd Street as she turned into the neon blaze of Broadway. *Capitol Theatre, Planters Peanuts, Pepsi-Cola, Hotel Astor* flew at her in words and colors that never formed thoughts. Streetcars clattered past. Cars honked. She was grateful to him. Even excited. Even though she told herself it was ridiculous. Just because a man paid attention to her. After the years of staying home caring for Ruthie. Who was now with Mother Ackerman for the night. And the years of waiting for Leo. She thought of the letters *explain all in the next one.* But what was there to explain? About a brothel inside a zoo? She wondered if Leo would still find her attractive. After Cairo. After Ruthie.

She went over to a phone booth that stank of smoke and dead breath, dialed the operator and asked for the number of the Commodore Hotel. Twice she hung up before the phone was answered. But when she arrived at his hotel room, he was waiting for her with a bottle of champagne which remained unopened in spite of murmured predawn intentions that faded into exhaustion.

And the next day she could not get past the opening page of a letter to Leo that she tore up in tearful fits of anger whenever she came to the part about how lonely she felt.

The war ended and Leo returned. On the night before his boat docked, Tina sat up with Ruthie showing her how to wave and yell Hi Daddy. They practiced in front of an old photograph of Leo. Hours later when Ruthie was asleep she put another photograph beside Leo's. It was one of her taken by Leo in the same month he left for Europe. She stood in front of a full-length mirror and wondered if she looked the same as she did three years earlier. Maybe better? Certainly not heavier. But maybe a little too . . . Too what? This is ridiculous, she thought. But after removing her dress she went back to the mirror for another look.

Through the maelstrom of emotions at the Brooklyn harbor they saw each other and pushed into the crowds of returning servicemen and families and Ruthie yelled Hi Daddy to everyone in uniform. They flung themselves at each other, weeping and laughing, with Ruthie chattering between them and Morris and Ida and Mother Ackerman circling, shouting, kissing. That night in the silence of their bedroom they lay listening to Ruthie's soft cries from the other room and laughing with hushed plans of their life ahead. The dead weight of the past years vanished from her thoughts, pushed aside by the rasping gentleness of his hands, softly tracing the curves of her body until some inner carousel was whirling out of control and she pressed herself against him once more.

Tina spent most of the next afternoon preparing a welcoming dinner for Leo, who arrived almost two hours late. Bursting through the door with apologies and kisses that smelled faintly of bourbon drowned in mints. And to show her that he was sorry he brought a present. A beautiful present he said, opening a flat box. Inside was the red dress she had modeled. And been photographed in. He mistook her reaction for speechless gratitude, gave her a big kiss on the cheek and insisted she try it on. At first she refused but his cajoling persistence carried her into the bedroom where the dress settled around her in opulent folds and she remembered the Hungarian as Leo kissed the back of her neck.

It took almost a year for Tina to admit to herself that the myth she had created was not Leo.

Tina became pregnant again, sending Leo into a prolonged fit of paternal joy, exulting in the son he would have, and always careful to buy a perplexed Ruthie more presents than she knew how to play with. The idea of a family, a dynasty, drew Leo closer to Tina for the few intense and fleeting moments when he was not careening through a life of business deals, parties, nights at the Copa and gambling with Arnie Dalitz, Herman Pinsky or men like them who seemed to have lost all sense of innocence. Tina participated in none of it. Nor did she want to. Frolic Frocks grew under Leo's flamboyant shrewdness and their lifestyle changed with it. They moved into the large apartment on West End Avenue. Leo missed the moving day, claiming a crisis at work. The crises merged one with another and whenever there was tranquillity it was stamped out like some disease. Leo thrived. Christie was born and Leo gave away only half of the cigars he had bought for the occasion. The footballs were cleared out of the nursery to be replaced by whatever dolls could be bought with the blank check he had signed and left for Tina. There were precious interludes when Leo would suddenly burst in announcing they should all go to the Catskills or Miami or Havana. But even days on white beaches leaving memories of the girls' delighted squealing as they played horsie with Leo in the shallow water were not enough to fill the looming emptiness of the nights on her own. Waiting. For Leo. For the averted eyes. The defensive anger at the most harmless question. Followed by the apologies. The infuriating jokes that she tried not to laugh at. And finally did, silently cursing herself while leaning thankfully into his kiss as he pressed gently down upon her. And sometimes, the faint trace of another woman's perfume that she told herself was his cologne.

One afternoon Morris called, his voice strung with tension. The model hadn't shown. There were buyers from Macy's due in an hour. Tina was flattered. After Christie was born she had exercised until she could wear the clothes she had bought a year ago. A model's size eight. And being asked to help out was a kind of secret validation. At Frolic Frocks she modeled several dresses, the burgundies and the mauves accentuating her olive skin and gleaming black hair. She could feel the eyes of the buyers watching her more than what she was wearing. Leo returned, entering the showroom, and the flash of fierce glances at her and then Morris stopped her in mid-turn. In the changing room she could hear Leo and Morris arguing in low, tight voices. With Morris backing away as always. She was suddenly aware of another presence, a tall blonde breathlessly carrying a model's oversized bag. She stared at Tina indignantly and then barged into Leo's office telling him he had given her the wrong call time. It was not Mr. Klein. It was *Leo.* There was something about the blonde that Tina recognized. It was the perfume. That she had told herself was his cologne.

Leo made convoluted explanations after the blonde was hustled away by Morris. The garment business was no place for a wife. For a mother no less. You mean for anyone with eyes and a brain, said Tina, storming out in the dress she was supposed to be modeling.

On the way down the elevator stopped at a floor where men came running up and held the doors open, yelling in a language she did not understand. From somewhere down the corridor she heard screams. Women were running along the corridor, short stubby women, with flat faces showing anguish and cheap dresses drenched in sweat. From out of one of the doors came two men who held a writhing woman, trying to carry her to the elevator. The left side of her face and body had been almost seared away. Tina stepped out into the corridor and turned away, closing her eyes as they passed, the screams ringing in her ears long after the elevator's doors slammed shut. She was alone, pressed against the wall in the long bare corridor. She remained there, listening, waiting. Then she walked uncertainly toward the door from which the woman had been carried. She opened it and heat plastered against her in damp waves that took her breath away. Steam billowed from a pressing machine that had blown up. Clouds of it circled the men and the women backing away in fearful clusters while the owner yelled at them to go back to work. Those who spoke English began yelling back, saying that the other machines would explode soon too. They were immediately fired. The owner saw Tina. They had met once when Leo had taken her to The Turf for dinner. He apologized for the confusion, for the bad language of these men, for their rudeness, for— Tina wound up, holding her small heavy purse by its string, swinging it around and knocking the man cold.

Leo shouted and threatened. It did no good. Tina picketed his building demanding safety for the workers. Others joined in. Then factories on the lower East Side filled with immigrants freezing or sweltering depending on the season were picketed. Photographs appeared in the *Herald Tribune* and the *Post*. Leo raged. Didn't she know how embarrassing it was? He could hardly go into Morgen's for lunch with his associates. The next day she picketed Morgen's. Later they fought and then made love with the purest ferocity of their lives.

Leo told himself the problem was over. But when the union became embarrassed because Tina was taking over their duties they sent men around to tell her to mind her own business. Tina replied by picketing the union. The union leader phoned Leo threatening to shut down Frolic Frocks. What kind of man couldn't control his own wife?

When Tina picketed a company called Braunel Dresses, orders were quietly sent down that she should either be stopped or killed. Braunel Dresses was owned by Tommy Lucchese, who was known in the newspapers as Three Fingers Brown. At five foot two he was as vicious as Vito Genovese or any of the other four Mafia dons in New York City. One of Lucchese's men passed the word to the Genovese family.

"Rein in this broad or she gets whacked. That's what they told me," yelled Arnie Dalitz as he burst into Leo's office.

Leo canceled all appointments and sought out Genovese himself asking for help. Trying to buy time, to stall Lucchese, anything. And feeling their contempt for a man who just didn't smack the bitch around and straighten her out once and for all.

"Leo, this is fucking serious," yelled Arnie Dalitz.

"*You're* telling *me?* I'm married to her, remember?"

"Well, smack her around a few times."

"What, are you crazy? I love her!"

"All the more reason to belt her, Leo."

"Look, Arnie, you and I don't happen to see eye to eye on this, okay? And leave it at that."

"Then for Christsakes talk to her. Make her listen to fucking reason."

"You crazy? That'd be like asking Joan of Arc to be reasonable."

"Joan who?" said Arnie Dalitz.

Even though it was Frolic Frocks' best year, Leo almost went bankrupt saving Tina's life. Whenever Tina picketed, Leo secretly followed her. Laying down an invisible trail of money, bribing whoever had to be bribed. Labor board inspectors. City officials. Police. Anyone who might cause trouble for Lucchese and the other owners as a result of Tina's activities. Usually it was just money Leo supplied. But sometimes it was hookers. Nights out at the Copa. Whatever it took to call off the dogs.

And stop them from killing Tina.

The fall collection sold out immediately. The buyers packed the Frolic Frocks suites at the Essex House and the Waldorf in scheduled sieges that sent Macy's into a frenzy of competition with Saks 34th and Arnold Constable on a line of quality dresses. Leo swung between the exhilaration of the hotel suites and the desperation of the factory's offices where he was given ninety cents cash on every dollar of accounts receivable from the big department stores. Leo took the money and raced off to bribe whatever officials were looking to the last company Tina had picketed.

Before the buyers left town Morris came into the office as Leo was bent over the desk waiting for Dr. Taffler to administer the vitamin injection. Morris's sagging face was like a blotter for every worry in the company. "I got a million dollars worth of orders to fill!" he yelled, smacking the thick sheaf of production sheets.

"So what's the bad news?"

"It's all bad news. You factored it all off to pay for this Tina thing. We don't have a dime to even buy the fabric."

Mimmo stood in the doorway dressed in his latest suit. In his new job as chief designer he wanted to convey more of a Continental flair than his work clothes had allowed. Leo had told Mimmo that from the neck down he looked like the Duke of Windsor. The rest was pure peasant.

"You look like a pimp," said Leo.

Mimmo grinned and pumped his arm back and forth making the sharp little whistling noises. "Of course. That's how we getta money. How *you* getta money."

Leo raced off to the hotels looking for stray buyers who had not placed orders with Frolic Frocks. Anyone who could make a down payment that would let Morris buy the fabric. All the big stores had been covered so the net was finer this time and the catch included an Alabama woman of indeterminate age and a Kansas redhead who bought for a chain of twenty stores and wore a girdle that made Leo think of whiplash while they were necking in his car just before she placed the largest order in the history of her company.

The instant Leo opened the door to their apartment he realized the mistake he had made. It was 2:00 A.M. and Tina was waiting. Nothing he could say would ever explain away the stench of the Kansas redhead's perfume that hung around him.

They stared at each other. Then Tina said, "Leo, it's over."

21

To Leo's amazement the years after the crumbling of his marriage had evoked a growing fascination with his own daughters. Suddenly he had to cope with them on his own. When Tina dumped them on the doorstep of his hotel that first Saturday afternoon after they separated, he almost panicked. What do you talk to them about? What do you feed them? Were they housebroken? And once they went through the maraschino cherries when there was nothing left in the refrigerator, what then? By accident, he discovered that walking in the park with them was actually fun. They were these two little people already wound up and walking and talking and bumping into things and asking funny questions that stopped him cold. Christie intrigued him, so utterly without guile, saying whatever came into her mind. And Ruthie, slyer but losing it all when she got flustered. Near the big pond in the park they had their picture taken by a photographer who had one of those new cameras that developed the photograph immediately. Then they started arguing over who would keep the photograph. To Leo's surprise he found himself wanting the photograph for his office. So they all ran back to find the photographer and have two more pictures taken.

At the end of the afternoon, it was Christie who announced that he didn't look like a daddy. He looked more like a Leo. Leo thought about it for a while and then told them he didn't feel all that much like a daddy anyway. So being a Leo was fine and that was what they called him from then on.

In the legal separation agreement Leo agreed to all the financial clauses in five minutes and fought Tina for months over every clause relating to Christie and Ruthie. He demanded it be right there in black and white that, in the event of Tina's remarriage, the new husband must always be referred to as Mr. So-and-So in the children's presence. Never, ever Daddy.

Leo's own lawyer tried to explain the problems in presenting such an approach to a judge. "Be reasonable," said the lawyer.

"Would Joan of Arc be reasonable?" asked Leo. And then he fired the lawyer.

SINGERS

22

Herman Pinsky always said his greatest talent was in spotting weaknesses. On the night he saw Ivory Joe and the Classics at Small's Paradise he watched the way each of them moved. He studied their smiles and the way each responded to the audience. And in the crowd backstage after the show he listened to each of them talking to friends until he made his choice. The weakest of all was Clyde. Definitely. Twenty-one years old. Away from home for the first time. Just four weeks in Harlem after singing with some gospel group in Newark. He had none of Ivory Joe's ferocity. Or Zoot's streetwise coolness. Not even Clarence's hulking power or size. Clyde was the baby. Every group had one. He was always saying *Really?* with a natural sense of wonder. He would be the one to give them the lyrics to *Ghost Lover*.

Herman Pinsky and Arnie Dalitz phoned a Seventh Avenue florist's shop in Harlem. The phone was answered by Dipper, one of the Negro controllers the Genovese family used to run their Harlem numbers operations. When Dipper hung up, he put a CLOSED sign on the door and drove over to Strivers' Row where Cool Curtis was waiting outside the home of one of his women, a widow with a big apartment. Cool Curtis was the controller the Genoveses relied on for the most difficult jobs when they needed a Negro to take care of other Negroes. Like Dipper, he wore tailored hundred-dollar suits with a silk handkerchief and a fedora that he removed in the presence of a lady or when administering a beating. Dipper and Cool Curtis set out to find Clyde. In the back rooms of the stores where their collectors were taking in money from runners, they put out the word.

Before dinner they learned that Clyde was living in an apartment in Sugar Hill where the granite outcroppings rose up beside the Harlem River like the walls of a fortress.

"I thought you'd be living in a way better place," said Dipper when Clyde opened the door. "Man with your talent."

"Who are you?" said Clyde.

"Friends," said Cool Curtis. "Friends who gonna make you a rich man, Clyde. We got a gentleman who's gonna give you a fat record contract. Even get you on the *Ed Sullivan Show.*"

"I'm with Ivory Joe. Don't do nothing without Joe."

Cool Curtis smiled. He was prepared to use force if necessary. "Clyde, Clyde, we know that. Matter of fact he's gonna meet us."

"Yeah?"

When they drove up to the Brill Building on Broadway, Clyde was thrilled. It was the shrine he had heard about even in Newark. Filled with music publishers. Promoters. Independent record companies. With hallways crammed with hustlers, the hopeful, the buyers and the sellers of hit parade music. Even the long lobby with its high ceiling reminded Clyde of the aisle in a church leading to an altar of brass elevator doors gleaming from the daily polishing of their art deco designs. It was all brass and mirrors and marble, even the entrance to the famous Jack Dempsey's restaurant off the lobby. In the empty hallway their steps sounded like slapping noises and Clyde wondered if God would punish him for not being at church on a Sunday morning. But God would understand. He was sure of it. After all, there was a chance to get on Ed Sullivan.

"Hey, Jack Dempsey was the one who fought Joe Louis. Ain't that so?" he asked on the way up to the ninth.

"Something like that," said Cool Curtis, taking off his fedora.

Suite 904 was the ABC Music Corp., a single office with a plain oak desk and several broken chairs. Two white men were waiting inside. Clyde wondered why one of them didn't smile. He was short and massive and reminded Clyde of a fire hydrant. The other one said his name was Lou and told Dipper and Cool Curtis that they were no longer needed. "I think I'll go too," said Clyde. But the massive one stepped in front of the door and locked it after they left. Clyde wondered what he had done wrong.

"Now, Clyde, I presume that you want to make a ton of money, now don't you?" He was smiling. Or Clyde thought it was a smile. He tried to smile back. "Attaboy, Clyde. We want to help you make some money. We're your friends. All you have to do is tell me the lyrics to that song. *Ghost Lover*. We got this tape recorder here that you can sing into. All we need is a rough copy."

"Oh, I couldn't do that," said Clyde, still trying to smile.

"Oh, sure you could."

"Oh, no."

"Oh, yes."

"You want to get someone else making the record first. Now ain't that it?"

"You'll be rich, Clyde."

"Cain't do it. I gotta go."

"Door's locked. There's one way out, Clyde."

"Which way?"

"The window. And we're nine floors up," said Lou, opening the window.

In the middle of the afternoon Red Leg set out to find Ivory Joe. The toothpick worked its way around his mouth at a furious pace and sweat ran down the deep lines in his face as he hobbled up the stairs to the third-floor apartment where Ivory Joe lived, not far from Columbia University. There was no answer. Red Leg's arthritis was bad today but he hardly noticed the pain, hurrying back to the waiting taxi. He got out at Small's Paradise, tearing a five-dollar bill in two and handing half of it to the driver, promising the rest of it when he returned. The club was empty except for Moses the bandleader who was checking the microphones. "Emergency," wheezed Red Leg. "Gotta find Ivory Joe." Moses just shook his head, and as Red Leg was cursing, Tina entered.

When the door to the Carnegie Hall studio burst open, Ivory Joe looked up in mid-note. He had never seen Red Leg act this way before. His arms were waving, his shirt was drenched and the indifference that hung across his face like a mask had vanished. "It's Clyde!" he said, stopping to gasp for breath.

"What's Clyde?"

"They're looking all over Harlem for him. Dipper and Cool Curtis put the word out a couple of hours ago."

They drove up to the Sugar Hill apartment and knocked at Clyde's door. A little girl playing in the hallway said Clyde had gone away with two men. Men with smart shiny do-rags right there, she said, pointing to Ivory Joe's breast pocket. Dipper's florist shop was locked. When they got to the storefront numbers joint further down Seventh Avenue, it was almost dark and the April night had turned cool enough for them to see their breath. Ivory Joe told Red Leg to stay outside. No point in getting too involved.

"Shit, Joe. Kinda late for that, ain't it?"

Dipper saw Ivory Joe first and ducked under a table heading for the back exit next to where the numbers men were bringing in the bets they had collected. He was almost out the door when Ivory Joe saw him and vaulted through the crowd, crashing into the alley as Dipper ran toward the cross street hurling garbage cans behind him. His breath shot out like little geysers of steam, his arms pumped like pistons in the air and his new fedora flew off his head from the speed at which he was running. But Ivory Joe was on top of him before he reached the end of the block, sending him hurtling into a pyramid of garbage cans behind the fried chicken restaurant. Sputtering chicken bones and black-eyed peas, Dipper pulled himself from the stinking heap, forgetting all fear when he saw the grease stains on his newest suit. "You motherfucker," he yelled.

"Where's Clyde?"

"Clyde? Clyde?" he screeched. "What's that peckerwood got to do with my suit?" He swung at Ivory Joe with a punch that went wide. He never saw the right hook that crashed into his cheek looping him back into the garbage. He threw an empty milk bottle that shattered on the wall beside Ivory Joe's head. Scrambling to his feet he flailed wildly until a precise volley of punches shattered his nose and several teeth and blasted all the breath from his body. Retching on the ground, he was picked up by the belt and the coat. "Lemme tell you something, Dipper. You better pray to any god you may have that nothing's happened to Clyde by the time we get there. You follow me?" Dipper wheezed and tried to say yes.

Headlights swung across the alley. Dipper was a collage of blood and filth, lurching to his feet and blinking into the light. "Brill Building," he gasped as Red Leg stopped the car in front of him.

Ivory Joe quickly revised his plan. He opened the trunk and flung Dipper inside. No point in having him make a warning phone call. The muffled shouts from the trunk grew louder as he backed down the alley. He slammed on the brakes and there was a clunking sound and a yell from the back. "Any more noise, Dipper, and I'll back into a wall," he yelled. Red Leg's toothpick was making the rounds at top speed and his eyes darted nervously as Ivory Joe stopped the car in front of the numbers joint. Inside, he pushed through the crowd of numbers men over to a desk where Henry was sitting counting a pile of money, the single light forming reflections on his shiny bald head. The steady rhythm of his counting remained unbroken as he watched Ivory Joe emerge out of the tangle of figures in the smoky darkness, reach over the desk and open the top drawer, removing the pistol that Henry kept in case of extreme emergency. It had never been used. "Hey, Joe, property of the house," he said, still counting.

"You'll get it back."

"Ain't but six bitty bullets in there, Joe."

"Probably won't need one of them, Henry."

"So what you need it for?"

"Going ofay hunting, Henry. Member what Al Capone said?"

"Don't think I do, Joe."

"About how you can get further with a kind word and a gun than you can with a kind word alone."

"Ain't it the truth."

In the car Red Leg looked down at the gun lying on the seat between them as if it was something alive and crawling. "Joe, don't know if I much cotton to the idea of taking this thing along."

"Me neither, Red Leg."

"You ever used one?"

"Uh-uh. But we're onstage in two hours. Gotta keep talk to a minimum, now don't we?" Ivory Joe was grinning.

He drove down Broadway past the front entrance to the Brill Building, turned west on 49th Street and pulled up to the curb. The music from a taxi dance hall on the second floor blasted out onto the street. But there was another sound, weaving in and out of the car horns and sirens. It was a cry, fainter, but unmistakably human, rushing through the neon forest of lights and then fading into the din. Ivory Joe ran along the sidewalk, looking around. It came again for a moment and then died. It came from above.

He looked up and saw Clyde being hung by his ankles from a window near the top of the Brill Building.

In the ABC Music Corp., they were about to pull Clyde inside for the second time. He was useless if too much blood went to his head and he passed out again. They were almost finished. Lou was fed up. What the hell was this all about? All for a goddam song? When the call came from Arnie Dalitz at noon, he'd been fixing his jukeboxes. That was as close as he ever got to the music business but Arnie called in markers saying they needed someone who would never be seen in the Brill Building again. Someone who understands music. Yeah, like a barber understands brain surgery, thought Lou staring down at the lines on the page he'd written as that terrified little shine screamed them out while hanging a couple of hundred feet over a patch of asphalt. But *Amazing Ghost?* Arnie said something about *Ghost Lover* but what the hell did he know? A second story man with a tin ear.

Amazing Ghost
How sweet the sound
That saved a wretch like me
I once was lost
But now I'm found
Was blind
But now I see

From the moment the short massive man had grabbed his ankles, all Clyde could think of was church and dying and God and the Devil and all the hymns he had sung with the New Lebanon Soul Stirrers, those rousing crazy numbers where the choir started belting out the fear of dear Lord Jesus when the whole place was swaying, then clapping, then going crazy and falling on the floor and wailing like some of them did when he stepped forward and started singing *Amazing Grace*. Not the vanilla-flavor *Amazing Grace* sung in the stone and brick churches where white people sang like a bunch of statues with hinged mouths. But now, hanging upside down over Manhattan, all he could hear was someone yelling about ghosts and the words all clogged in his mind, coming out as *Amazing Ghost*.

The first time they hauled him in, letting him writhe like a fish on the deck, he thought it was over. But the man built like a barrel yanked him up by the ankles again and shook everything out of his pockets. Pennies and dimes disappeared into the darkness, making little pinging sounds in the alley below. Screeching *Amazing Ghost* in strangled gasps until he almost passed out again. Then they hauled him in, blubbering in fear, his legs unable to hold him, twitching in spasms as Lou sat calmly moving his lips while he read what he had written. When he shook his head, Clyde burst out sobbing as his feet were yanked up and the whole world turned upside down again. At the moment he was about to be lowered through the window again, the whole glass part of the office door seemed to fall away like ice sliding off the side of a wall in sheets. Even upside down he recognized Ivory Joe stepping through what used to be the door he had just kicked in. The best part was the gun in his hand. But then it all disappeared as Clyde was swung out the window again. On his own, with no one asking him, he started singing *Amazing Ghost* for all he was worth.

"Go ahead, shoot," said the powerful man holding Clyde. "And your friend here is ketchup if I drop him."

"Fine," said Ivory Joe calmly. "I can wait." He sat down on a chair and smiled, his back to the wall and the gun moving slowly from Lou to the man holding Clyde. "But you drop him and I *will* shoot you. After I shoot your friend here."

What the hell was this? His buddy hanging out the window and him sitting there like he's having a beer? And *Amazing Ghost* was driving Lou crazy. He never wanted to hear another note of it again. Dalitz and Pinsky could take it and shove it all. Who needs this? One crazy nigger with a gun and another one dangling over Manhattan singing like a maniac. "Shut the fuck up!" he screamed. The singing stopped and for a moment there was just traffic noise.

Nothing was worth this insanity. For a song. A goddam *love* song. "Pull him in," he yelled. Clyde was dumped on the floor where he just made noises and tried to stand up when Ivory Joe told him to go press the elevator button. Pushing a chair for support through the broken glass, Clyde fell into the hall and crawled on all fours.

"Now then, no point in you running after us causing a scene. Is there?" said Ivory Joe in that same lazy voice. He looked over to Lou. "You. Get up. You're going out the window."

"Are you out of your goddam min—" He was cut short by the spring-loaded fury of this Negro, who, in a single chilling movement, had the gun only inches from his head. And his eyes, suddenly cold like a cat's, scanned back and forth. "I don't want to hear another word from either of you."

Lou's legs crumpled beneath him. Heights terrified him. *Any*thing else but not this. He started to breathe in quick, strangled bursts of air that turned into gagging sobs as he was lifted up and hung out into the terrifying whirlpool of blackness and lights.

Small's Paradise had been sold out for a week. It was the first Sunday-night performance since 1952 when Duke Ellington was playing that STANDING ROOM ONLY was hung on the door. Word had spread through Harlem that Ivory Joe and the Classics were returning. Even downtown, the news had sifted through the music business and agents, managers and small-time record company owners canceled their plans for Sunday night, driving uptown to see this new group. It was the stories of the strange, powerful new music that drew them into Harlem.

The show was more than half an hour late in starting. Moses the bandleader kept looking backstage for a signal. The band was already heading into *Take the* A *Train* for the second time and the restlessness in the audience was sending a buzzing murmur through the club. Once again Tina appeared between the curtains and gave Moses a five-minutes sign. She hurried back into the tiny dressing room where Zoot and Ivory Joe were standing over Clyde, who was lying on the makeup counter, shaking so hard the mirror rattled.

"I don't want to cancel this show," Tina said.

"We ain't going to."

"Oh, great," Zoot said. "But just tell that to Clyde here. He still looks like he stuck his finger in the light socket. Ain't no one going on till he gets hisself all straightened away."

"They hung me out the window, Joe," said Clyde, his voice skipping across the words in tremolos.

"Clyde, we got to go on, man."

"Cain't, Joe."

"You can."

"Cain't. Cain't stop shakin'."

"Clyde, I swear to God the Devil's gonna get you if we cancel. And you know what the Devil does to people?"

"Uh-uh." Clyde stared up from the table, never seeing the hands that suddenly grabbed him under the arms, lifting him and then heaving him against the wall where he was skewered by Ivory Joe's fierce stare. "He hangs you out windows, Clyde!"

"No, Joe—" The shaking exploded into writhing in the moment before Clyde's face resounded to the slap of Ivory Joe's hand. Instantly Clyde was still, hanging limply from where he was pinned against the wall.

The room was silent. Clyde's eyes made a jerking tour of his surroundings.

Zoot grinned. "Clyde, you look like something on the clothesline when the wind died. I swear."

"You with us now?" said Ivory Joe.

"Hey, Joe. You know I am."

"Great, so let's go on."

Zoot looked around. "Not unless we're fixin' it to be a trio, Joe," he said. "Clarence ain't here."

They found Clarence peering through the curtains at the audience. In the near darkness the bulges in his tuxedo showed patches of dampness. The sweat dripped from his face, running in rivulets across his shirt. "I ain't goin' on till I see little Christie out there. She ain't nowhere there."

"Sheee-it," said Zoot. "Now we might be down to a duet. What next?"

"Zoot, shut up," said Tina. Zoot just grinned at her and winked.

"Ain't goin' on if Christie's not out there."

"Well, of course she's out there," said Tina soothingly, wondering how she was going to make Clarence believe her when Christie was asleep in Leo's apartment. "Look. Can't you see her?" She pointed out to the audience and Clarence peeked through the folds of the curtains. "Way at the back."

"What's she doin' way back there? Why ain't she up front? Where I can see her?"

Ivory Joe and Tina exchanged a quick glance. "Liquor law," said Ivory Joe. "Damn, Clarence, you're smart enough to know that. Child that age ain't even supposed to be in a gin mill like this. That's why we got to put her way down back. See her? Right there."

Clarence looked out and never saw Tina give the signal to Moses the bandleader. It felt good knowing that Christie was out there. But where? Then he saw something that looked like pink crinoline way back in the farthest darkness of the club. Of course. It *was* Christie, and before he could duck out of the way, the spotlight swung around and froze him with a searing white beam that drove all sight from his eyes as *Ladies and gentlemen, Small's Paradise is proud to present* . . .

Before Clarence knew what was happening, he was onstage singing with the others. The circles of light rippled in his eyes but he was glad Christie was out there.

As they went out onstage Tina saw a pink and round silhouette bobbing among the tables in the audience, weaving toward the reserved table near the front. It was Herman Pinsky, his big cigar intermittently and faintly blazing in the gloom. Behind him was a middle-aged woman with hair piled up on her head in a frozen wave forever about to crest. She carried a stenographer's notepad and peered around at the crowd of Negroes with an expression of vague terror. But, Tina noted, she was overly polite to every Negro she encountered.

Waiting for them at the table was a tall, well-dressed Negro, wearing horn-rimmed glasses and already making notes on a scrap of paper. The man had been pointed out to Tina by Ivory Joe. He was the music arranger who worked for Avalon Records. Totally anonymous, highly paid and skilled at copying any melody he heard, he had copied down the music from songs written by others and changed them just enough to let Herman Pinsky put his name down as cowriter. Tina knew she had been right. The arranger, Herman Pinsky and the stenographer were there for just one reason. To steal the words and music to *Ghost Lover* and make their own record.

Herman Pinsky sat drumming his fingers on the Formica table. He was operating totally from hand signals now. Each time Ivory Joe leaned into his microphone after the applause, the stenographer would look over, pencil poised for the shorthand race through the lyrics. But after the first few bars, Pinsky's hand would slice horizontally toward her and she would put the pencil and notepad down and go back to her drink. It was driving him crazy, this waste of time. They should be in the studio right now recording *Ghost Lover.* The Icehouse was all set up this afternoon with Freddie and the Freshmen, those smartass little creeps from Jersey. A Jew, an Italian and two Yankees all thinking they're God's gift and yapping about convertibles like they're Bing Crosby already. But they all did that. And at least Freddie had that kind of smooth voice that could make the song sound white. That was the important thing. Like this new kid Pat Boone was doing with that faygeleh Little Richard. Hell of a talent, that Boone.

It should have all been over by now, everything but listening to the money rolling in. If Arnie Dalitz hadn't gotten those two idiots. Writing down a goddam hymn. And then one of them hanging the other out the window. That was bad enough, but losing control of his bowels nine floors up. It was shitting uphill for real. And who the hell was gonna stand for that crap? Herman Pinsky got mad just thinking about it. And imagine Genovese when he heard. This Ivory Joe had better be able to run like he could sing. With the audience going apeshit. Herman Pinsky broke his swizzle stick and flung it away, which the stenographer interpreted as the signal to heave her drink down and frantically start scribbling shorthand, yelling that she couldn't hear a thing. But while he was shouting back at her, telling her to shut up, he looked around and saw them leaving the stage. Impossible! They hadn't done *Ghost Lover* yet. He jumped to his feet and started yelling "*Ghost Lover!*" and booing but what was the use? "Fraud!" he screamed into the applause and then stormed off to the pay phone to tell them to close down the studio for the night.

23

Almost twenty years earlier, when the Avalon's pool tables were carved up and his father beaten, Herman Pinsky spent six days unable to sit down because of the welts across his rear end. While recovering from his father's retribution, he arrived at the fundamental business decision of his life: Money without the protection of power is useless. Dangerous, even. What good was all the money he made in the card games in the back room of the Avalon? Without power, all it got him was welts.

When Herman Pinsky took over his first business at the age of twenty-one, he made sure that power was on his side. It was a junkyard in Brooklyn with old cars piled up like rusting towers and an owner with a second heart attack and gambling debts. Herman Pinsky borrowed the purchase money from the Mafia friends of Arnie Dalitz. A week later he went back and borrowed another three thousand dollars. Arnie Dalitz tried to talk him out of it, warning of the terrible things that would happen if he did not repay. Herman Pinsky used the money to buy a huge shipment of U.S. Army surplus parts. The parts were mainly electrical relays that had never been used. Inside each relay were contacts made of tiny wafers of pure gold that could be broken off and then melted down.

Herman Pinsky hired two Polish immigrants and a Mississippi Negro, led them into the corrugated metal warehouse and, at gunpoint, ordered them to strip naked. Without clothes there was nowhere for them to hide the gold as they disassembled the relays and put the wafers into the glass jars that Herman Pinsky could watch as he sat on an orange crate with the gun on his knees and the Doberman at his feet.

After four days he repaid the money he owed to Arnie Dalitz's Mafia friends. He was careful to point out his gratitude. And to let them know that if there was ever anything he could do . . .

A few weeks later a car was driven up to his junkyard by one of Vito Genovese's men. Another car pulled in behind it. The first car was a new Pontiac with bloodstains on the upholstery and back bumper. The driver told Herman Pinsky to put the car into the compactor and crush it. It was obvious what was in the trunk. When the Pontiac had been crushed into a block of metal no taller than the Doberman that sniffed around it in a frenzy, the two men left without saying a word.

Herman Pinsky smiled as he watched them drive away. A favor had been repaid. And the powerful friends of Arnie Dalitz would know he was someone to be looked after.

He bought the small paint company across the street. One of its most profitable products was the shellac that was sold to Decca Records and RCA Victor and then mixed with carbon to make the 78 rpm records. But when war began, the raw materials for shellac could no longer be obtained from the Far East. The big record companies desperately hunted for alternatives. Even when old records were collected and melted down, the supply was never enough. But working quietly on his own, the elderly chemist in Herman Pinsky's paint factory one day discovered a substitute for shellac. It was a gum taken from the kauri tree. It could be boiled down, turned into biscuitlike chunks and sold to the clamoring record companies.

On the day that the men from Capitol Records phoned pleading for their shipment to be delivered before Decca's, Herman Pinsky sat in his office staring out the window at the compacted chunk of metal that had once been the Pontiac and was now a statue mounted on a concrete base.

Power.

Then he looked at the hard dark chunks of kauri tree gum on his desk.

Money.

What else was there in life?

"This," said Arnie Dalitz a day later, dumping a pile of paper on his desk.

"What the hell is all this shit?"

"Sheet music. It's yours."

"Now what do I want with that, huh? I ain't in the music business."

"You are now."

"What are you talking about?"

"Genovese's already got jukeboxes tied up. But he wants a music business, too. So he decided you and him should be partners. With this gum shit you're peddling you're a natural."

"Arnie, what are you, crazy? I don't know a tune from a fart."

"*This* is all you have to know." Arnie Dalitz pointed to the pages of sheet music and the word *copyright* on each of them. "Copyrights. Publishing. You tie up the music publishing and the copyrights to a song and you make a goddam fortune for doing nothing. Every time a song is on the radio or the TV the money rolls in. It's always pennies. But the pennies add up to a fortune. Especially if you have a hit record."

"So let's get ourselves a hit," said Herman Pinsky.

Eleven years later, Avalon Records still had not made the fortune that Herman Pinsky dreamed of. There had been only minor hits like *Dew Drop*, which sold six hundred thousand copies, but even that was strictly race record stuff, filling up the Negro radio stations way over at the far ends of the dial where nobody white ever listened. What Herman Pinsky wanted was a *crossover*, a hit record that started out Negro and crashed through into the big white money markets. You could tell you had a crossover when you started shipping more of the little 45 rpm records than the old 78 rpm's. Only the whites had the new record players that could handle the 45's.

In the years since the war, Herman Pinsky had lost most of his hair, grown into a smooth and pink plumpness, wore thicker glasses, and made enough money to make sure his father knew which one of them was the more successful. But still he wanted a hit. And each new record he released chipped away at his diminishing reserves of patience. A lot of goniffs had hits. Why not him? After all, everything was in place. He had built a recording studio right next to the scrapyard in a building that had once been an ice-making factory. It became known in the trade as the Icehouse, and the reverberations of the music recorded in the big tin-walled studio gave Avalon Records a distinctive, echoing sound. A distribution network had been set up by Arnie Dalitz, who looked after the interests of the Genovese Mafia family. And there was always lots of product around. The Icehouse was filled with Avalon's groups trying out new songs for Herman Pinsky, who would interrupt his scrapyard work to come in, listen to the song, make a few changes in the lyrics and then add his name as cowriter. And the singers, these chicken-bone coloreds and white-trash hillbillies, didn't have a clue. They were falling all over each other just to get through the door. And if they had anything that even scraped onto the bottom of the charts, you just buy them a Buick and charge it against royalties. Get them into debt. Let the interest charges build and keep them touring till they drop or bomb. Then hand them a bill and bury them with bookkeeping.

It was fine. It was all there. Except the hit. And the first time he heard Ivory Joe sing *Ghost Lover* he told himself he had found it.

But after the night at Small's Paradise he didn't even have the lyrics down on paper. And what you didn't know, you couldn't even steal. Late at night he raged through the Icehouse. The empty studio echoed with his loathing of George Goldin. A small-timer for christ-sakes. Scrounging for recording time in other people's studios. A dinky new label every month. Always scraping up money just to pay gambling debts. And the fucking contracts he offered were a disgrace. Giving the goddam coloreds outrageous terms. Spoiling it for the serious people in the industry. No wonder the coloreds signed with him.

And then reneging on the dumb bastards.

The next day Herman Pinsky phoned George Goldin. They met at Lindy's. Each secretly told the waiter to give the other the bill. And when they both used the washroom at the same time, each waited for the other to open the door first because of germs on the door handle. Over corned beef sandwiches, Herman Pinsky told George Goldin the offer he was prepared to make to buy out Ivory Joe's contract: ten thousand dollars and five points on next year's net.

"Herman," smiled George Goldin, "fuck you."

Even before George Goldin had turned him down, Herman Pinsky decided he truly hated him. More than hated him. He wanted to jam those silk shirts, those bullshit smiles, and those cheap gold rings on the long elegant fingers, into a compactor somewhere. Herman Pinsky looked down at his own fingers. They were like overstuffed sausages.

"Hey. Just thought I'd ask, George. To save you a lot of trouble."

"So who's got trouble, Herman?"

. . .

At 2:00 in the morning, George Goldin returned home from the Copacabana where he had spent more money than he had gotten rid of since he lost the Buick in the card game a week ago. It felt good to spend money, a lot of it. Not spending made him feel like he was losing it. The blonde on his arm had turned heads and that was important.

When he stepped out of the borrowed DeSoto at 3:00 A.M. he saw only the first man coming out of the shadows. The crack of the baseball bat across his ribs blew all the wind out of him and sent the burst of jagged pain shooting into his throat. The beating was done quickly, methodically. It was not severe. At least not in comparison with the real cripplers that turned kneecaps into shards of bone. The next day Herman Pinsky phoned the hospital to offer his sympathies. Through a wired jaw Goldin cursed him and yelled that hell would freeze over before Ivory— The nurse who rushed in grabbed the phone from his hand as Goldin exploded in a fit of coughing that sent his body cast clanging against the bed railings.

"More than one way to skin the goddam cat," said Herman Pinsky as he hung up.

24

George Goldin limped into the rehearsal hall, his body cast slapping against the walls of the crowded corridors. "We'll make a record tomorrow," he said through the wires in his jaw. Tina couldn't tell if he was smiling or if it was just the way the wires stretched his mouth.

"Not tomorrow," she said.

"Momentum!" said George Goldin. "We have it now. We have to act."

"Wait a couple of days."

"Why? What the hell for?" That same smile. But now it was a rictus of anger.

"I want to do some research," said Tina, turning and walking back into the noisy crowd. The next day Tina went out and bought every record put out by George Goldin's GeeGo label. She discovered his name was listed as a songwriter on all of them. It always appeared as G. *Goldin*, listed beside the name of the real songwriter. Tina tracked down one of them, the lead singer in the Sparklettes. She was seventeen, wore her hair in curlers most of the day and lived on 140th Street in Harlem. Her voice was on all the radio stations singing *Oooh Wah Baby* and she knew she was a star.

After all, Mr. Goldin came up with *forty dollars!* any old time it was asked for. Tina listened for a long time. A star. Hollywood maybe. A baby for sure. Maybe marry Leroy. My mama. We touring. Buffalo and places.

What places?

Places.

Tina asked if it had bothered her when she saw Mr. Goldin's name beside hers on the song. Well, shit yes, the girl said. But who cares about all those itty-bitty names on the record anyhow?

So what about your publishing rights? Or copyrights?

What? Who cares when this Mr. Goldin is gonna be buyin' a bran' new Cadillac for us.

When?

Soon. Said so, didn't he?

After seeing a lawyer, Tina calculated that based on the Sparklettes' record sales, the girl was owed eighteen and a half Cadillacs.

She phoned Ivory Joe from Pennsylvania Station and had to run to catch the train. She reached Washington after dark and stayed in a hotel three blocks from the White House. The next morning she was waiting at the Library of Congress when the doors opened. At a desk surrounded by the sharp silence of a marbled hall she began by writing *Ghost Lover* on what was called an EU form and when she was finished she had registered fourteen songs for Ivory Joe, three for Zoot and one for Clarence. When she boarded the plane at National Airport it was time for Ivory Joe to start rehearsing in George Goldin's recording studio in New York.

By the time Tina landed at LaGuardia, Ivory Joe and the Classics still had not been able to lay down even one usable track and George Goldin's throttled impatience was making him twitch. And every time he twitched, his body cast smashed into the wall of the tiny control room he had built in his office. His encased arm was suspended in front of him like a heating pipe that went nowhere. The more the *bap . . . bap . . . bapbap* showed up on the sound track of the little four-channel mixer, the more delays they had. And the angrier he became.

And the more Ivory Joe stared at the telephone waiting for it to ring.

At LaGuardia Airport, Tina phoned several times. There was no answer. The recording engineer had switched the phone off and not told anyone. As George Goldin had ordered him to. Tina ran for a taxi. In the recording studio Ivory Joe exchanged glances with Zoot, gave the count and with the tape rolling they started recording *Train to You* even though George Goldin was telling them to get on with it, to get to *Ghost Lover*. But *Train to You* was different. Not bad even. George Goldin listened to them sing harmony different from anything he had ever heard before. Instead of only the lead singer deviating from the harmony sung by the other members of the group, Ivory Joe had created a part for Clyde's haunting falsetto voice. Clyde came in on the repeated *Train to You* while Zoot and Clarence were singing the *whoooo-hooo-hooo* background. It all sounded like a steam locomotive gathering speed behind Ivory Joe's lyrics.

Is it rain
Is it tears
On that old driving train
driving train
driving train
Sending me home
To you
To you

Bap . . . bap . . . bap . . . bapbap. They stopped singing and stared in unison at George Goldin on the other side of the control room window.

"Sorry," said George Goldin through the intercom, trying to smile with his wired jaw. The rhythm had set him off thinking about the money he could be making if they were singing *Ghost Lover*. Millions. A fucking money machine. And why weren't these coloreds singing what they were told to sing?

Tina burst into the room.

Goldin saw her nod at Ivory Joe and then miraculously they went through a perfect take. Suddenly it was over. The musicians were packing up as George Goldin approached her with the same frozen smile. Dealing with women was either very easy or very difficult. You couldn't swear the same way. And acting tough was a whole different proposition.

"George, I know it's not necessary to mention this," she said with a smile, "but only Ivory Joe's name will appear on the record as writer, won't it?"

Goldin's features rearranged themselves and his eyes sought out something neutral. "Well, now, honey, it doesn't quite work that way. But don't you worry. I'll take care of it all."

"George. Answer my question."

A regular bitch, this one. "Look, Tina, there's a way things are done in this business, and—"

"I don't care how things are done in the business. I just want to make sure that no one steals any royalties."

"*Steals?*" said Goldin, inwardly pleased that there was such a word to swing the threads of his indignation around. "Listen, I'm giving these boys a break. And I've put a lot of work into them. So if I decide that I should get a little something out of it too, I don't want any crap from you."

"You're not going to put your name down as a writer."

"I damn well am."

"I don't think so, George." She handed him a carbon copy of the Library of Congress form, inserting it into the fingers that stuck out from the end of the plaster cast. He stared at it as it dangled in front of him, his lips parting and coming together before tightening like a slit. His face reddened. His eyes flickered in an anger that shot around him, slamming his cast to the door. Again and again he smashed the door in a fury as Tina stood and watched, not quite sure whether to laugh or flee.

"Are you out of your goddam mind?" he shouted, his cast disintegrating around his arms as it smashed into the wall like a creature with a life all its own. "No one pulls this kind of shit. Herman Pinsky'd break your head open."

"So then it *is* good we signed with you, George," she said through the same serene smile.

"That's it! Finished! I'm not dealing with you, lady," yelled George Goldin, stumbling over to the window trailing plaster and bandages. "Where's Ivory Joe?" He grimaced in pain, throwing open the window, his cast flapping in mid-air like a broken wing. "I can ruin you," he yelled down into the street where Ivory Joe and Zoot were loading the car. "You want this broad to wreck your career? Fine! But you think I'm ever going to record any more of your songs? No fucking way. And the contract says you can't go with anyone else for three years." He slammed the window down and clutched at his flapping arm.

"So?" said Ivory Joe, sitting at the piano in his rehearsal hall.

"So they're all thieves," said Tina.

Three weeks later, on the *Arthur Godfrey Talent Scouts,* Ivory Joe and the Classics went up against an accordion trio from Cleveland and won. The gamble was immense. To lose would have been oblivion. But at the end of the show the applause meter went all the way over to the right-hand side when Ivory Joe and the Classics took their bow. And Arthur Godfrey came over to shake their hands on national television. And in the audience George Goldin sat three rows in front of Herman Pinsky and all the usual small-timers trying to sign up any act they could get their hands on.

In the week after the Godfrey show Tina arranged a booking at the Apollo. Second on the bill after Ray Charles. George Goldin had released *Train to You* in spite of his threats and all of a sudden everyone knew Ivory Joe and the Classics.

After the show a white man climbed up to the small second-story dressing room. He was gray haired, dressed in a neatly tailored blue suit and spoke in a soft, southern voice. He was known to most of the Negro acts. He approached Tina and introduced himself as Mr. Weiman. He booked tours. The Weiman circuit it was called. It ran from Buffalo to Mississippi.

They had all the best performers. Little Richard. The Cadillacs. Chuck Berry. The Dominoes.

Would they be interested?

YO-YOS

25

Ruthie and I are like a couple of yo-yos. Up down up down. We're going back and forth between Mother and Leo like we're on a string. Right now Leo's got us. And so we get to answer all the phone calls from Herman Pinsky who keeps saying how nice it is to talk to me in that creepy white mouse voice. Nice to talk to you I say as Ruthie puts her finger down her throat like she's going to barf.

Herman Pinsky even sends us presents. A whole Lionel train set that makes real smoke when you put the little white pellets down the smokestack. But what are we going to do with a Lionel train set? He might as well have given us a catcher's mitt. But then he shows up with a record player. Herman Pinsky is brownnosing like crazy. "Tell your mom we're really nice people," he says to me when he phones to find out how I like the record player.

Mother says you're a racketeer I tell him which is the truth. He makes another little white mouse noise that's supposed to be a laugh but you can tell it's not. We know he's trying to get Mother to give him Ivory Joe. But she won't. Ever. It's all starting to give me a headache. Every time the phone rings I get nervous and try to get Ruthie to answer it. But she's turned into a simp. She just got *the* letter from Byron. Dr. B. W. Lewis. He wrote back saying he's coming to New York in a few months and wants to get together. And he didn't even say anything about a *Mrs.* Lewis. All Ruthie can do is lie on her back looking up at the letter and yelling "Get a load of this!" whenever she comes to a good part. She's driving me nuts. Even when I try to watch *Kukla, Fran and Ollie* all she wants to do is change the channel over to some soap opera.

Everything gets crazier when Herman Pinsky phones twice in a row and then comes over to see Leo. He really wants Ivory Joe as one of his singers. Ruthie and I can hear them talking through the walls. Actually all Leo says for a while is *What?* and *Are you sure?* "The jig is up," Ruthie says.

She's right. Herman Pinsky is blabbing Mother's whole plan. Mother wants to go to other cities with Ivory Joe and the Classics. And she wants to take us, too.

You can tell what's going to happen before it even happens. Leo and Mother will yell at each other. They'll fight like the cats down around the garbage and then if Leo doesn't win he'll pull something.

That's what happens. All weekend they argue on the phone and then Leo announces he's dying so at least his two daughters had better be around. Leo gets into bed with the thermometer and the *Racing Form* and the pastrami sandwiches from Lindy's and tells Mother there's no way she's going to take us away. Not now. Not when he's only got a little while left. He's even got some letter from a doctor to show that he's a goner. But we find out the doctor is Dr. Taffler so you can guess what that means. Ruthie thinks he signed a blank piece of paper and let Leo write what he wanted. If Leo ever does die it will be from all his nightclubbing.

Leo's dying backfires on him. All the doxies and ladyfriends find out and Ruthie and I end up practically running a place for nurses. They show up some of them with chicken soup and calling us dearie. Some of the others that we haven't seen for a while show up with big grins like they're just checking to make sure that Leo really is going to croak. They're the ones he dumped. But he fixes them. By the time they leave they're weepy just like the others. They should know better.

Most of them phone first and so Ruthie and I have started keeping a list of who's coming when. It's tricky. If you schedule them too close together there's problems. And sometimes one of them gets carried away like she's practicing for throwing herself across the coffin or something. Ruthie and I have to go in and say something like *He needs his rest* and pry the weepers out of there before the next shift starts. Leo that rat loves it. And in between he phones Uncle Morris to see how business is and he reads the *Racing Form*.

But dying's like everything else for Leo. Pretty soon it bores him.

He's in too deep to get out of it though so he does what he always does. He turns it into a bet. Mr. Kampelman comes over and he and Leo make a list of every ladyfriend he's ever gone out with. They bet that if more than half of them show up Leo wins. If not Mr. Kampelman wins. He comes over every few hours to check the list and bring Leo his pastrami sandwiches.

Right now Leo is losing. We've seen the list. Little red lines are drawn through the names of the ones who showed up. All kinds of them haven't though. And Leo's taking it very personally. We hear him start to sneak phone calls to the others. *Hello Doris? Doris how are you my God it's nice to hear your voice . . . oh not too good Doris.* So Ruthie and I put Doris down in the appointment book. According to the rules it's illegal though. Mr. Kampelman and Leo agreed no phone calls. But when Leo bets it's like his life is at stake. We tell Leo we want to quit the game. He says he knows that but can't we see that Mr. Kampelman's going to win if the game ends now. It's all going to be over on Friday which is the day the bet is over. Friday night is absolutely crazy and Ruthie and I are like traffic cops. That rat Leo has really snookered us again. White Pawn to White Knight yells Ruthie as she marches into his bedroom after the last one leaves. But to tell you the truth we sort of got caught up in the game. We know we shouldn't have but we did. Leo's checking his list muttering to himself. He's going to lose by one. He grabs his black book and starts going through the pages. "It's life or death," he says, grabbing the phone.

"Hello Elizabeth?" he says and then stares at the phone. She hung up. We knew she would. But he mumbles something awful and phones right back this time yelling at her not to hang up. Elizabeth is the one he really liked. But he blew it the time they had a fight at the Copa and he took her home on the subway when she was all dressed up in her mink. She didn't speak to him after that. But now is she ever speaking to him. We can hear it across the room. But he's laying it on as thick as he can about dying. He's really good at it. Too good. *She's* buying it too. Ruthie and I can't believe it. We thought she was smarter than that. When they talk to Leo they get air between their ears. Leo makes sure she understands the part about him probably not lasting till midnight. Which is when the bet ends.

At eleven-thirty Mr. Kampelman comes over looking like he's

already won. He's short and runty like his stinky cigar that always went out a long time ago. Ruthie and I are both real tired but we can't go to sleep before we see who wins. Leo is lying there on his deathbed talking about how he always knew Elizabeth was the woman for him while Mr. Kampelman just sits and watches the clock. Ruthie and I both get so nervous we have to go to the bathroom twice. It gets closer to midnight. Leo keeps on saying good old Elizabeth to us. All of a sudden there's a knock on the door and Leo throws himself back on the bed moaning loud enough that she's got to hear him even through the door. I'm the one who gets to open the door and there's Elizabeth. In her mink coat. She says hi girls and with a big smile hands me an envelope. "It's for your dad," she says. I ask if she's coming in. This is real important because according to the rules only those doxies who actually come inside the apartment get their names crossed off the list. But she just gives me a big grin and says she has to go. Then she leaves.

Ruthie and I don't know whether to laugh or get upset. But Mr. Kampelman knows. He jumps up and down like he's on a pogo stick and he cheers and shouts until Leo comes roaring out of the bedroom yelling where the hell is good old Elizabeth? Doesn't she know I'm dying? Mr. Kampelman is almost falling on the floor he's laughing so hard. He grabs the letter in one hand and scoops up the prize money with the other hand.

Leo opens the letter. It's a get well card signed Love Elizabeth and with two aspirins and a subway token taped inside.

It gets worse. You can tell Leo wants to quit the dying routine but Mother comes over the next day so he gives it one last try. But he gets careless. You can smell the pastrami sandwiches under the bed. Mother drops her bombshell while we're all around Leo's bed. She's going away. With Ivory Joe. And Zoot and Clarence and Clyde. And they're all going down South.

"With *knee-groes?*" says Leo. "Down South?" He really does look like he's a goner now. But Ruthie and I look at each other and I know what she's thinking. She's thinking of Clark Gable in *Gone With the Wind*. Leo could be like Clark Gable if he wanted. "They'll lynch you all," says Leo.

"And I want the girls to come, too," says Mother. She smiles that little smile of hers. It's not really a nice smile.

Leo's not faking now. He goes the color of the sheet. "My own flesh and blood?" That's us. Leo makes a little bubbling noise.

Mother picks up a copy of the *Racing Form*. She looks at the page where Leo has marked all the horses he thinks will win. "You're obviously going to last till the third race at Belmont on Tuesday."

"A mental exercise," says Leo. "The mind is the first thing to go."

"That's obvious," says Mother.

"The track takes my mind off what's happening," says Leo.

"It always has," says Mother, with that same smile.

"Tina, I swear to God, you're not taking my girls away from me. Not now," says Leo.

"But darling," says Mother, "there's really nothing to worry about. After all, by the time we leave for the tour, you'll be long gone." Then she gives him a big kiss on his head. "Come along, girls. We're going up to Harlem."

MIAMI

26

You'd think we were going to the moon. Leo still doesn't want us to go down South and all week he's been phoning Mother and she's been phoning him. She's already down there with Ivory Joe and the others. They haven't exactly been yelling but they're close. There's been a whole lot of the *over my dead body* stuff that Leo always pulls when they get crazy. It was bad enough just *her* going. You can tell Leo never thought she'd really go. But when she did he had a bird and spent all Saturday morning walking around the park with us talking about *your mother and this colored guy.*

It gets worse. Now Ruthie decides *she* doesn't want to go. It's all Byron this and Byron that. She's scared to miss even one letter from him. But I tell her she's got to go. It's part of the plan. "What plan?" she says. We've only talked about the plan a million times. Getting Mother and Leo back together again I tell her. Ruthie sits and stares at the photograph of Byron taped up on the ceiling next to her chessboard. This week Byron is Clark Gable. "Okay," she says.

Even though she's a brain Ruthie is there when you need her. Nothing is more important than getting Leo and Mother back together again. Not even Byron. That's why we have the plan. If we go down South Leo will show up too. We're sure of it. Then after they fight for a while they'll be nice to each other and at least they won't be in New York where Leo can step out for a loaf of bread and come back when we're all in bed even Mother.

But the big plan doesn't start off so well all because of Leo. Naturally. He pulls one of his fast ones. All of a sudden he *has* to take us to Miami before we go down South with Mother and Ivory Joe.

To *show us a good time* he says which makes Mother have a bird. Because that's what Leo always tells his customers when he's going *nightclubbing* with them. But this time Ruthie and I are the customers.

So Mother and Leo have one of their *honestly this is the limit* fights which is what Mother always says when you know she's going to lose. I know that even before I put the glass to the wall and hear him tell Mother what's good for the goose is good for the gander. It works every time. Mother doesn't like being the goose.

"Hah!" says Ruthie when I tell her. "It's our goose that's cooked." She's lying on the bed looking up at her chessboard taped to the ceiling. "Maybe the plan won't work." But I don't even bother to answer because she's obviously gone simpy over Byron again.

So the next day Leo shows up like we're on our way to camp again. Except this time the camp's in Miami. He's even packed lunches for us in case we don't like the food on the plane. We look inside the bags. There's pastrami sandwiches and some Fleer's Double Bubble gum for dessert. There's also toothpicks and some Alka-Seltzer.

Leo wants us to know what a great time we're going to have in Miami. He goes there a lot now. He gets the stewardess to tell us what a great time we're going to have. This is before we even get on the plane at Idlewild. Ruthie and I figure out that we've seen the stewardess somewhere before. Then we remember. She was one of the ones who came to see him two weeks ago when he was dying. Actually most of the stewardesses are people we think we've seen before. We probably have. They all call Leo by his first name. When the plane is taking off I can hear two of them arguing over who gets to be our stewardess. We get great service.

Ruthie and I are too tired to know what's going on. All we want to do is sleep but the plane starts bumping up and down. This makes Leo crazy. Scared crazy. He starts looking out the window to see if the wing is still there. Leo hates flying. He takes out his black bag the one with all the pills in it and starts taking the pretty blue ones. When I ask him what they're for he says they make the plane fly better. They don't. It gets bumpier. Leo orders three rum and Cokes and gives one each to me and Ruthie. I hate the taste. "Drink it," says Leo. "It'll make the plane fly better."

We're all drinking the stuff but the plane still doesn't fly any better.

Leo is almost strangling the arms of his seat and yelling for more rum and Cokes. He lights a cigarette and then he decides that we need one too. To calm our nerves he says. My nerves are so calm that everything's going round in circles. Smoky circles. Two bombed little girls says the man in the next seat and Leo tells him to mind his own business. The plane keeps bumping and Leo keeps telling us what a great time we're having.

That's all I remember. I wake up in what looks like Macy's window. It's real bright. I'm sleeping on shiny sheets and everything else looks shiny too. The carpet the lampshade the furniture. Everything. It's like a new car showroom. Ruthie is moaning in the next bed. She has a wet towel over her eyes. Where are we I ask her. She just says she has an awful headache and points to something. It says ROOM SERVICE—FONTAINEBLEAU HOTEL. I run through the door into what looks like a living room. It's all shiny too. We must be on the top floor because we can see for miles. It's all beach and ocean. I think this must be a dream.

Leo's not in the other bedroom. I pick up the phone and dial the operator. I'm looking for my father I say.

Right away the lady who sounds a little like Mrs. Weissman says, "Okay, Christie, honey, hang on and I'll connect you." I don't even have to say who I am. The phone rings again and a man answers. "Poodle Bar," he says. Poodle Bar? It's the same thing all over again. He knows my name right away. It sounds like a party going on and it's only morning.

Miami Beach is Leo's way of competing with Mother. From the moment he comes roaring in the door in his shirt with the pink flamingos on it he wants us to know that we're having a good time. Even with Ruthie lying in the shiny bed holding her head and moaning he wants to make sure that we're having fun. How can we? We haven't done anything but wake up. Leo acts like a camp counselor for about an hour. He shows us everything. The coffee shop. The pool. The beach. Everybody knows our names and Leo says we just have to sign our names for whatever we want. He leaves us at the pool and disappears into the Poodle Bar saying what a great time we're having. By noon we're bored stiff. There's no kids there our own age and lots of fat ladies way older than Mother who have blue hair and a ton of makeup. When they go in the pool they always just squat down in the shallow end with their nose in the air like they smell something bad. When Ruthie does a cannonball into the pool they all clear out fast. But we'd really rather be with Mother and Ivory Joe.

We get sunburned doing nothing. Then we go into the Poodle Bar and figure out a lot of things because Leo's in there with Arnie Dalitz and Herman Pinsky. They're all down here having a party. We should have known. You can tell Leo's forgotten all about us just by the guilty look he gets. And when we tell him we're bored he gets that look. The one that makes him come up with all kinds of crazy ideas to show us what a good time we're having but we just don't know it yet. He starts tearing ten-dollar bills out of a pile he has in his pocket. "Go shopping," he says.

Nope I say. We don't want to.

"You don't want to *shop?*" he says like we're crazy. "All the other ladies shop."

"We're not ladies yet," Ruthie says.

"So what do you want to do?"

Spend time with you I say. I know this will really fix Leo but that's not why I say it.

"Doing what?" he says getting all jittery. He walks us over to the door of the Poodle Bar talking out of the side of his mouth. He starts handing us twenty-dollar bills instead of just tens. Sometimes I *really* admire Ruthie. I'm looking at the twenties and starting to wonder if maybe there's something we could buy. But she just says "Fine!" in that great sulky voice and marches off with her nose in the air. "Come on, Christie, we've got to wait for Mother's phone call." That's her big gun. But sometimes it doesn't pay to take on Leo. He just watches her stomp toward the elevator.

"Oh, Ruthie, there was a letter for you," he calls out. "From a Doctor Lewis." It's like Ruthie's on a rubber band. In a flash she's back eating out of Leo's hand. Total jelly. It's Byron this and Byron that. But Leo's real cool. He says he can't remember what he did with the letter. Ruthie becomes even more of a simp. Leo's searching around in his pockets. Taking his time while Ruthie goes crazy. When he finds the letter she grabs it and rips it open and her eyes go wide. She starts jumping up and down. "He's coming to New

York next month!" she says over and over. Then she looks scared and says, "Do I look like a woman?"

Leo and I look at Ruthie. But Leo doesn't get it yet. He just sees the same scrawny old Ruthie not the Ruthie who's been reading all the romance and movie magazines and imagining Byron sweeping her off her feet like James Dean. Leo sort of laughs. Big mistake. Ruthie is turning to mush. She just wants to be told that she's not like the Before women in the ads in the movie magazines. *Are you sensuous? Develop a Bust. Be alluring.* I've seen her sneak looks at those ads in the magazine she keeps under her bed at home. She wants to be an After. But she's not. She's not all that different from me and I'm not even a Before yet.

Sometimes Leo might as well put his mind in a glass case. You can just see what he's thinking. He figures this is a great chance to keep us busy while he's in the Poodle Bar. "Ruthie, all you need is a little fixing up and you'll be a real woman," he says.

"What's fixing up?" Ruthie asks.

"You know. Shopping."

"Yeah. Shopping!" she says.

Hey wait a minute Ruthie I say. We're not even ladies yet. Remember? But it's no use. She's already an After riding into the sunset *on a dark and stormy night as Ruth swept across the hillside her passion for Byron beating a hole in her bosom as he pressed her close to his throbbing crewcut.* All because of shopping.

"Have your hair done, too," Leo says counting out the twenties. He thinks he's solved all his problems but he doesn't know what he's in for.

I knew it. It's a disaster. I feel awful but there's nothing I can do. Not now. Not since Ruthie came out of the hairdresser's on the ground floor of the hotel. This was after she bought all those shiny clothes like the ones the fat ladies in the pool are wearing. The whole time she was in the hairdresser's I sat there saying Ruthie are you sure this is what you want to do? She pulls her oh honestly Christie routine as if I'd never understand because I'm not a *woman*. The old biddy doing her hair agrees with Ruthie. She's all shiny too like the front of Leo's car and she chews gum and must be forty.

When Ruthie steps out of the hairdresser's I want to burst out laughing. She looks like a freak. She's had a perm. Her hair is up like some kind of beehive with curly little ends. And it's all pinky white! Like the fat ladies in the pool. Her nails are pink and her mouth looks like she fell into a pot of red paint. She comes weaving toward me in the new shoes she bought. The ones with the high heels that she had to stuff paper in. That's not all she stuffed paper in. She's got a chest! A lumpy one but it's still a chest. It's underneath that turquoise blouse with the sleeves that keep falling over her hands and down almost to her knees so you can hardly see the pedal pushers she's wearing.

At first I just stand there. Ruthie is that you? I say.

"*Byron* will like it," she says, teetering past. Her nose is in the air. Just like the ladies in the pool. So what do I do? An hour ago I had a sister. Now I've got Marilyn Monroe. I run along beside her.

Ruthie? Are you okay?

"Superb," she says. She's never said superb in her whole life.

She's walking down the hotel corridor. People are staring like crazy. Someone starts to giggle but I stare daggers at them. Ruthie just plows ahead. We pass the entrance to the Poodle Bar and some drunk comes out and starts laughing at her. She just puts her nose higher in the air and plows ahead. Leo sees her and comes roaring out with his mouth open. *Shopping* I say to him putting *my* nose in the air and marching away like Ruthie. We get to the elevator just before the doors close. It's full. It's the longest elevator ride of my whole life. By the second floor people are laughing. Someone says something about Halloween being early. I turn around and tell them to shush up. No one's making fun of *my* sister like that. But soon everyone's laughing. Ruthie just stares at the doors like she's the Queen of Sheba. When we get to the top floor she marches off the elevator handing me the room keys like I'm some kind of servant who's supposed to run ahead and open the door. I figure I'd better not ask questions so I do it. She sweeps in and the second I close the door she goes absolutely loony.

She starts screaming and jumping up and down trying to rub all the makeup off. She sees herself in the mirror and she looks like a peroxide scarecrow. She wails like the time Mr. Cooper's cat spent the night in the alley and no matter what I do I can't calm her down.

She throws herself on the shiny white couch and rolls around bawling and leaving a trail of makeup. Ruthie you look great I tell her. I have to say something.

"Are you crazy?" she wails at me. "Byron is going to laugh."

It'll go away.

"Yeah sure. In ten years. Then I'll be an old hag."

No you won't. Look at Mother I tell her. But it's no good. She races into the bathroom and slams the door. *Click*. I hear the door lock turn. Ruthie? Why are you locking the door?

"I'm never coming out. Never ever."

Superb I say.

I figure she'll be out in an hour. Because she's a brain she gets bored real fast. There's not that much to do in the bathroom. So I do what Dick Tracy did in his last comic book. I pull out one of my hairs and then I tape it across where the door opens down low near the floor. When Ruthie opens the door the hair will come unstuck. Okay seeya I say making a lot of noise as I leave. I spend a long time by the pool and then I walk along the beach trying to remember where Ivory Joe and Mother are now. When I get back the bathroom door is still locked. And the hair is still taped to the door. Ruthie? No answer. I start to get real worried. Ruthie? I yell.

"What?" she says sounding real quiet and real bored.

When are you coming out?

"I told you already. Never."

How are you going to eat?

"I don't care."

How are you going to meet Byron?

"Byron would think I'm a freak if he saw me. Leave me alone."

I can tell this is going to be serious. I go downstairs to the Poodle Bar where Leo almost jumps when I tap him on the shoulder. He and Arnie Dalitz are talking about something that must be real secret because Arnie Dalitz is very twitchy and smiles like he doesn't mean it. I tell Leo that his daughter has serious problems which he thinks means she's run out of money in one of the stores.

Leo comes upstairs but you can tell he doesn't really want to. At first he thinks it's all just a joke. He does his okay honey enough is enough number in that voice that's supposed to be chuckly but isn't. No answer. He knocks on the bathroom door again. "Ruthie?" Still no answer. This goes on for a while. He's thinking like crazy. I tell you he's never going to get Ruthie to say one single word.

"Okay, Ruthie, if that's the way you want it," he says. "I'm going to hold my breath until I die." He takes a big breath and then he pretends to hold it. After about a minute, he falls on the floor right outside the bathroom. He winks at me.

"Leo? You okay?" yells Ruthie from inside the bathroom. I tell you Leo's a genius. Now *he* doesn't answer *her*. She gets worried. "Leo?"

"Now are you gonna open the door?" Leo says.

"You tricked me into talking," Ruthie yells.

"I didn't trick you. I just want you to open the door."

"I'm a freak. You'll laugh at me."

"I won't."

"You don't really love me."

"How can you say an awful thing like that?"

"All you do is give us money. You don't want to spend any time with us."

"I'm sorry. Look, Ruthie, your father's had some business problems to straighten out. Now open up."

"Hah. Boozing with Arnie Dalitz and Herman Pinsky. We could be with Mother and Ivory Joe. Then I wouldn't look like a freak."

This makes Leo all jittery. Even the words Ivory Joe are a no-no around here. Ruthie and I talked about this. We're sure that Leo thinks Ivory Joe is the perfect Negro. Ivory Joe is driving Leo crazy without even doing anything. And mentioning him and Mother together can turn Leo into jelly. Angry jelly.

All of a sudden there's a big knock on the door and Arnie Dalitz comes roaring in. He doesn't say hi how are you or anything. He looks real jittery too. "Leo, c'mon," he says. "Quit futzing around. We gotta talk."

"Arnie, I got a kid locked in the crapper," says Leo. He's pacing back and forth.

"So come back in an hour. She ain't going anywhere. We got business to talk about."

"Look, Arnie, I ain't leaving my kid."

"Yeah, Arnie!" yells Ruthie from the bathroom.

Arnie Dalitz looks angry. "How'd she get in there?"

"She locked herself in. She won't open the door."

Arnie Dalitz shakes his head and goes over to the phone. "It's simple," he says. He phones someone named Lou. Lou comes up to the room. He's big and not friendly. He's dressed in a suit but he doesn't look like a suit kind of person.

"You got the little one?" says Arnie Dalitz to Lou who just grunts. Then Arnie Dalitz yells at the door. "Okay now Ruthie, get up on the can, okay? Stand up there on the can while Lou shoots the lock off."

"What are you, nuts?" yells Leo as Lou stands there with a little gun. "No one's firing at that door while my kid's in there."

"Yeah? Well how you going to get her out of there?"

"I'll do it my own way. Find a saw," he says to Lou.

"A saw?" Lou says in a dopey voice.

"A saw," yells Leo. "Don't you know what a saw is?"

So Lou comes back with a saw and Leo tells him to make a hole in the bottom of the door right next to the floor. Arnie Dalitz is walking around talking to himself. They make a little square hole in the door. Then Leo takes the tray of fruit from the table and slides it through the hole. "Here you go, Ruthie. Lunch." There's no answer. Just the sound of munching.

That's the way it is for the next couple of days. Leo orders Ruthie's food and then passes it through the hole at the bottom of the bathroom door. I pass her the chessboard, the letter from Byron, the romance novel she was reading and some new movie magazines. I have to use the bathroom in Leo's room but that's okay except when I can't stand the aftershave smell. Leo sort of likes what Ruthie's done. I'm sure he secretly prefers us to be a little bit crazy. That's when he understands us the most. He's more relaxed when we're crazy. Like we're *his* kids. At night he sits on the floor outside the bathroom with me and we talk to Ruthie like there was no door between us. It's all the usual what kind of day did you have? stuff. Ruthie tells us about her chess game with herself and what lunch was like. Leo even reads stories to her when she's going to sleep in the bathtub. He already pushed the pillows and blankets through the hole. It's kind of normal. In a way. But my problem is I'm sort of lonely.

I have another problem. Mother phones. She's all excited because the tour is going so well. Big crowds and the record is doing well too. Then Ivory Joe comes on the line and says hi and in the background there's Zoot and Clarence and Clyde laughing. Mother comes on again and wants to talk to Ruthie. I blow it. I get tongue-tied when I try to fib my way out of it. Mother's immediately suspicious. When I tell her Ruthie's in the bathroom she says she'll wait.

You can't I tell her.

"Why not?"

Cause she's been there for a while.

"Christie, what are you talking about? How long has Ruthie been in the bathroom?"

Three days I say. That does it. Mother wants to know what's going on. I really panic. That's when I say Mother it's okay Ruthie wasn't hurt at all when Arnie Dalitz wanted to shoot holes in the bathroom door to get her out because Leo stopped him and cut a hole in the bottom of the door to feed her when she turned her hair pink and white.

There's a real big pause on the phone. "Christie, darling, have your father call me right away. Do you understand?" I say yes. Mother's got on that real quiet voice now. The one that scares all of us.

Even Leo probably.

27

Even before Leo left for Miami with Ruthie and Christie he sensed a change in Arnie Dalitz. There was a nervousness, a forced laughter that tried to smooth over a command dropped casually in the guise of a friendly suggestion. Miami. A week at the Fontainebleau. Shoot some craps. Take a little sun. Party till you drop. And the whole thing comped. Wise guys picking up the tab.

And that strained smile stretching like a slit across Arnie Dalitz's face when Leo announced he was taking his two daughters with him.

"Hey, Arnie, it's me Leo you're talking to. Remember?" he said on the first afternoon when they met in the Poodle Bar. "We've only known each other for a jillion years. So what's with all this mystery shit?"

Arnie Dalitz finessed it. Leo pushed. Arnie Dalitz's fingers drummed on the table. His eyes flicked around the room. "Leo, lay off."

"Arnie, you want something. Or something is fucking up. Which is it?"

"Both."

They went for a walk along the beach where Arnie Dalitz felt safe to talk. There was a war brewing. Genovese was being pushed by Anastasia and people were turning up dead. Nothing big so far but all the signs were there. "The gorillas are thrashing and when that happens the whole goddam forest gets trampled," said Arnie Dalitz staring out into the ocean but not seeing it.

Leo stopped hearing large chunks of conversation after Albert Anastasia's name was mentioned. More than the other four New York Mafia dons, Anastasia trailed blood. He killed the way other men shook hands. Leo had seen Anastasia once on a street and instantly knew the purest fear of his life as those dark dead eyes in the fleshy face scanned those around him. Victims had been chosen almost by impulse and allies were as vulnerable as enemies.

"Why am I here, Arnie?" said Leo, remembering that fear.

"Cause you're involved."

"What the hell are you talking about? I have nothing to do with all that."

"Leo, Leo. You do." In a soft voice.

The problem was Havana and the Cuban gambling casinos that were making fortunes for the tightly controlled Mafia cartel run by Vito Genovese and Meyer Lansky. But Anastasia was not part of the cartel and had decided he should be. By whatever means necessary.

His plan was so simple that Genovese wondered why he hadn't thought of it himself. Anastasia intended to take over the music business. Booking agents, publishers, singers, he wanted them all. Controlling the music was like controlling the casinos. One crap table was the same as another but a great floor show with a famous singer was enough to have the customers scrambling into any casino, dropping money in their wake. And owning the publishing rights to just one hit record was worth a year of protection rackets. Just from the royalties paid every time the song was played.

Vito Genovese decided that he would beat Anastasia at his own scheme. And had sent word to Arnie Dalitz that this friend of his, this Leo, should be used. The one who had done such a good job in Cairo.

"Look, Arnie, I don't know what's going on but I do know that I ain't in that business."

"That's why they want you, Leo. Don't sweat it. It's just fringe stuff."

"I'm here for a holiday with my kids."

"Hey, Leo. C'mon, huh?"

"No way."

"Leo, Leo." That same soft voice saying don't be an idiot, no one says no. Not when you're in as deep as you are. With a word or two Frolic Frocks could be destroyed. Just by refusing to allow the garbage to be collected by *their* men. Or refusing to ship the dresses out on *their* trucks. Or canning the six-for-five financing for the spring line. Or worse. They could just torch the whole place.

Or worse.

"What's the deal?"

"They just want you to play a friendly game of cards." Always *they*. Never *we*.

"With who?"

"Some guy named George Goldin. They want to skin him alive in a game of poker."

Back in the Poodle Bar Leo drank and said nothing. "You could get a hundred guys to do this," he said when the third bourbon was taking effect.

"But you'll do it better."

"Bullshit."

"You will."

"Yeah?"

"Yeah. First he doesn't know you're a friend of ours. Second you're a killer with cards. And third you have a reason to nail him."

"Like what?"

"Like he's the one who holds the paper on those musical niggers your wife has taken up with."

"Fuck you, Arnie."

"Leo, for christsakes, whadya want me to tell you? It's the fucking truth. Tina wouldn't sign with Pinsky. She went with Goldin. *He* took her and this Ivory Joe on tour. You wanna nail him? Here's your chance."

After the fourth bourbon was gone, Leo answered. "Keep talking."

The next day Herman Pinsky arrived wearing a turquoise shirt that was emblazoned with pink palm trees that matched his complexion. "Losing's the easy part," said Arnie Dalitz. "Let him fleece you here in Miami. We know he's booked himself into a hotel in Havana on Thursday. You go with him. And tear him to pieces."

"What makes you so sure I'm gonna win?"

"In Havana? You will. Trust me." Arnie Dalitz laughed.

"So I win."

"So you bet your company against his."

"Are you nuts? You want me to risk Frolic Frocks?"

"Hey. You listenin' or what? I told you—no risk."

"You're sure?"

"Aw for christsakes, Leo."

"Okay. But what makes you think he'll put his own company into the pot?"

"He'd put his own mother into the pot."

"Okay, so I win. I get a record company—"

"*We* get the record company."

"So what's the big deal?"

"A song," said Herman Pinsky, leaning very close and talking very quietly. "Your Mr. Ivory Joe has a song called *Ghost Lover* that he still hasn't recorded. Genovese knows about it. He wants us to get it." Herman Pinsky's little smile creased his round shiny face. Leo was understanding it all now. "You wouldn't have to worry about your wife taking your kids off on some tour. I mean, we'd hold the paper on this Ivory Joe then. No way we'd allow that shit."

"*We?*"

"That's what I said, Leo," said Herman Pinsky a split second before Leo's daughter Christie yelled breathlessly right behind his head, almost making him lose his drink. Something about the other daughter locking herself in the bathroom. Herman Pinsky had always felt uneasy around children. They were a pain in the ass most of them. Too difficult to control. Not like adults.

. . .

At first Leo had merely disliked George Goldin. It took a couple of days for him to really hate the man. There was all the manufactured sleekness. The same corny spontaneous jokes rehearsed a hundred times. Walking around with his arm in a sling like he was a war hero. The sly winks to the women that were really meant to be seen by the men. And the flashing of big bills to the headwaiters followed by the nickel-and-dime tips whenever he could get away with it.

It was precisely the reaction Arnie Dalitz and Herman Pinsky had counted on.

Even before Goldin had unpacked his bags, Charlotte his favorite prostitute knocked on the door to his room as he knew she would. Room service, she said with that big movie star grin. It was the same grin that only an hour earlier had made Leo say to himself it's many a bumpy road those lips have traveled. *Charlotte the Harlot*, teased Arnie Dalitz the way he always did as he slowly peeled off fifty-dollar bills and handed them to her. And when it was information, no one could pry secrets loose better than Charlotte. She could take on a truckers' convention and still look innocent at the end of the night. Arnie Dalitz had brought her in from Cleveland two years ago and made sure she never forgot who she worked for. Or why.

Arnie Dalitz had also brought in Dorothy who was to be introduced as Leo's girl. She was short with jet black hair falling around an oval, vaguely oriental face. And with breasts bursting against the halter top. She told Leo she was Charlotte's best friend, but watching the shorthand glances that passed between them and the way they touched each other, Leo decided they were probably lovers. He spent the afternoon by the pool watching Dorothy play solitaire and wondering what she and Charlotte did when they went to bed.

When Christie arrived at the pool bringing Leo the latest news on Ruthie's confinement in the bathroom, Leo watched her give Dorothy that same appraising eye that unnerved so many of them. Dorothy just nodded and went back to the cards. It amused Leo that Christie approved of Dorothy's boredom. She always preferred the women who seemed the least interested in him.

An hour passed. "What's taking so long?" Leo said, staring up at the hotel.

"George is a weeper," said Dorothy in the same bored voice as she slapped down two more cards.

"A weeper?"

"Yeah. You know. He thinks you've been waiting for him. That he broke your heart when he left last time. So now he's got to make it up to you. You have to sit through them telling how much they really care about you. But it's okay. As long as they pay."

Goldin came to the pool, subtly maneuvered by Charlotte as she had been told to do. There were looks of surprise and waves, Dorothy reacting with skilled enthusiasm. Introductions. A few drinks. The usual small talk. The weather in New York. Business. The Yankees and the Dodgers. And then the deck of cards in front of Dorothy. Goldin picked them up and asked Leo if he was any good.

Leo had been waiting for the question, or a variation of it. There were two possible answers. "I'm a killer with a deck of cards," he said.

Goldin smiled. It was a patient smile. The kind a learned scholar gives to an endearing idiot. Leo knew instantly that he had him. "Oh yeah?" said Goldin.

In the late afternoon he drove up Collins Avenue to the Beau Rivage where Arnie Dalitz and Herman Pinsky were now staying. It was far enough away from the Fontainebleau so there was no chance of an accidental meeting with Goldin. Leo collected two thousand dollars and that night sat with a dry-cleaning millionaire from Baltimore, a dentist from Brooklyn, a machine-tool company owner from Akron and George Goldin. The game was simple five-card stud, jokers wild. Leo had planned the strategy carefully. First get the deadwood out of the game and start chopping away at Goldin. Give him a scare and watch how he plays. One of Leo's measures of a man was his ability to bluff, to go right to the edge of oblivion with nothing more than a grin. Goldin failed. For all the show of flamboyance, he parted with his chips like a banker watching loans go bad. When Goldin tried to bluff he held his cards closer to him as if he was afraid of losing them. He smiled too much and awkwardly. And his forefinger kept picking at the cuticle of his thumb.

When Leo had dropped eighteen hundred dollars, Charlotte hurried into the room. Part of the deal with Arnie Dalitz was that she would babysit Christie and Ruthie. World's most expensive babysitter, Arnie Dalitz had said. But Leo insisted.

"Your wife just showed up," said Charlotte, looking very shaken. Leo pictured the scene and knew why. "She just threw me out!"

"What?" yelled Leo, staring at the huge pile of chips in front of George Goldin. They hadn't planned it this way, at least not with Tina as the reason for breaking up the game. It was to have been Dorothy phoning with an emergency. Then there was to be all the faked panic, rushing away from the table lamenting his bad luck and demanding a rematch in Havana. But now nothing was faked, especially his panic. "Christalmighty how did she get down here? I gotta go. Shit, this is a goddam disaster is what this is."

"Leo, listen to me," said George Goldin with the same smile, the one that said hey sucker. "There's a lesson here."

"What lesson?" Leo was stumbling away from the table.

"You never run out on a friend just because you're cleaning him. So I'll tell you what. Come to Havana in two weeks. I'll give you another shot."

"Hey, thanks pal," said Leo, rushing out the door.

28

It gets worse. Our big plan to get Mother and Leo back together gets creamed.

Last night when Mother all of a sudden roared into our room at the Fontainebleau and threw her arms around me like she was an octopus I knew it was big trouble. You can always tell by how hard they squeeze you. If it's just a little hug like they've got all kinds of stuff on their minds you know you're okay. It's no big deal. But if it's like falling into the gorilla cage with big goobery kisses and loud talk you know you'd rather be out playing. Which is what this is.

Especially when Mother sees Charlotte who's sitting on the floor outside the bathroom door doing her nails and talking to Ruthie who's still locked inside. Charlotte's neat. She doesn't try to impress us like the other ones do. Charlotte and Ruthie are talking about men. Ruthie's telling her all about Byron. They've just about decided that men are no good when Mother roars in and wants to know a whole lot of things. Like who Charlotte is. And where Leo is. Charlotte won't tell her. Mother blows up and Charlotte decides to beat it. That's when the octopus routine starts.

About ten minutes later Leo shows up looking like Mr. Wasserman's dog when they were taking it for its shot. Mother's talking to Ruthie through the bathroom door and stares daggers at Leo. Right away you can tell he's going to get into a fight with her. You can read Leo like a book. His lips get kind of skinny and he smiles when he doesn't want to. They start yelling at each other about Ruthie. Mother tells him that no decent father would leave his daughter locked in a bathroom for four days. Leo naturally blows up and says that's what she wanted. "Are you crazy?" says Mother. "Well, then, ask her," Leo yells. So Mother does. "Ruthie?" she yells at the door. "Is that what you wanted?" But Ruthie's no dummy. There's not one peep from the door.

That's when Mother says, "Ruthie, you open it this minute." That's always the big warning signal. *This minute.* Mother's the only one who says it to us like that. Leo would never think of saying it. With him it could be this hour. This day. Or even next week. Compared to Mother he's a pussycat that way. You just don't fool around when Mother says *this minute.* So Ruthie opens the door.

Mistake.

Mother almost screams. But instead she just sits down real quick like all the air goes out of her. Ruthie looks like a complete freak. Her pinky white hair sticks out like icicles. That turquoise blouse looks like something a doxie would wear. And those pedal pushers. They're like britches for ponies. Ruthie stares at Mother. Mother stares at Ruthie. Ruthie starts to snivel. I look at Leo. You can tell he knows it's game over.

"Get your things packed, children," Mother says. Children? She hasn't called us children in years. But she's speaking in that real quiet voice that you don't fool around with. Ruthie and I both vamoose leaving Leo there with Mother. He blows it. He starts to get mad but you can tell he's just faking it. He feels guilty or something because when we hear him going through his over my dead body routine you can tell it's not the old Leo.

But then he figures out that Mother wants to take us away and keep us. Then it's the old Leo.

You can hear the fight all the way down the corridor.

29

On the night that Tina took Christie and Ruthie out of the Fontainebleau Hotel, Leo sat alone in his room listening to the phone ring. Then there was the pounding on the door. Leo kept drinking bourbon and staring out the big windows at the lights of distant boats on the Atlantic. The phone kept ringing. The hotel suite was suddenly very empty. The chattering voices he heard fell silent the instant he turned away from the ocean's blackness and looked around the room. There was a submerged edge of his own fear that softened under the chaos of Christie and Ruthie. The silence brought the fear back and for once he did not try to run from it.

The pounding at the door yielded to the clinking noise of a master key. It slammed open as Arnie Dalitz handed the bellhop a dollar bill and hurried into the room. "Why didn't you answer?"

"I didn't feel like it."

Arnie Dalitz stared at Leo wide-eyed. "Leo, what the fuck is this? We got Goldin on the line. He leaves for Havana next Thursday. And now you all of a sudden turn into a hermit?"

"I can't go to Havana, Arnie. Not yet."

"Leo, what the hell you talkin' about? This is no time for jackin' around."

"I'm gonna get my daughters back."

"Since when the hell are you the big father?"

"Since maybe now."

"Yeah, well, Leo, you're forgetting something. We got a whole goddam machine rolling. There's you, me, Herman, Eboli. Even Genovese. This ain't no bunch of boosters, Leo. You can't back out. I'm telling you as a friend."

It was always as a friend. They always told you that. And they became good guys protecting you from some greaser who wanted to smash your skull or take your money or whack you. But in the end there were no friends. Not even Arnie. Not now. Thirty years. Maybe forty. A lifetime. No one was closer. No one shared like Arnie had shared. The laughs. The money that was made. The crazy times. The gambling. The women. But Arnie had other loyalties now. "Arnie, I don't want to spend my life being alone anymore. I'm tired of it."

"Leo, I'll get you a broad." Arnie Dalitz grabbed the phone and started dialing.

"Forget it."

"Leo, we're not talking trash here, you know. Angie is a friend of mine. Not like Charlotte. She's class, man."

"Not interested."

"*You?*"

"Me."

Arnie Dalitz paced in circles behind Leo. Then he sat down tapping his fingers together and staring into the rug. "Leo, this is serious. You know that, don't you?"

"I know."

"Goldin's gonna be in Havana for three days. It's all set up. They even brought in Charlie the Blade. You ain't got no choice, Leo."

They sat in silence for a moment. "Yeah? So what do I do about my kids? I ain't gonna lose 'em, Arnie."

Arnie Dalitz thought. He stared out at the lights, twirling the edge of the peninsula of short dark hair that jutted out into his forehead. Then he picked up the phone and called Tommy Eboli to get the phone number of Tony Strollo whom he called by his nickname Tony Bender. When Arnie Dalitz went downstairs to the lobby telephone and called the pay phone on a street corner in Brooklyn, Tony Strollo picked it up and waited until the fistful of quarters was deposited at the other end and the operator said thank you. The guy who helped out your sister in Egypt was how Arnie Dalitz explained it. Strollo remembered immediately. "So what can I do?" he said.

"Okay, here's the deal," said Arnie Dalitz, rushing back into Leo's suite. "We've got you a judge."

"What do you mean 'you got me a judge'? I don't want a judge, I want my kids."

"Hey, what's with you, Leo? That's the whole point. Tony Bender owns this circuit court guy in New York who we use for other stuff. He's gonna get you your kids back. It's all taken care of. So now let's talk about Havana."

"Hey, wait-wait. What are you tellin' me? He's gonna get my kids back? How?"

"Easy. He'll rule that your kids are being mistreated by your wife. Then you get 'em full time."

"Are you out of your mind? Tina's a great mother."

"What the hell's that got to do with anything? You want the kids or don't you?"

"Of course I do."

"So? You gotta come up with some reason. The judge'll buy anything we tell him."

"Well, I ain't telling him *that*. Tina doesn't deserve it."

"Fine, Leo. Fine! So tell me what the fuck you *do* wanna do."

"I just want Christie and Ruthie for half the time. Simple."

"Shit."

Downstairs at the lobby telephone, Arnie Dalitz put more quarters into the slot. Problems, he said to Tony Strollo.

When he returned to Leo's suite, Arnie Dalitz talked through the thin smile that he used when he was impatient. "Okay, here's the deal. The judge is gonna say you get them half the time. But he needs something."

"Money."

"Nah. That's taken care of. He needs a shrink."

"A shrink? Hey, if the guy's got problems why don't you send him one of those special women you guys keep for weird sex?"

"Leo, the shrink is for coming up with some piece of paper saying your kids need to have you around. That it ain't working with them just being with Tina. It'll make 'em nuts or something. Mental anguish. Stress. All that shit."

"I don't know, Arnie."

"What's there to know, for christsakes?"

"I just don't want any goddam shrink fooling around with my kids, that's all. My cousin Arnold is a shrink. Swear to God he spends half his time locked in the bathroom with a piece of liver in one hand and *Sunbather's Monthly* in the other. Then *he* goes out and tells other people they're fucked up."

"Leo, Leo, Leo." The words trailed off in exasperation. "This ain't like you."

"Maybe it is like me, Arnie."

"Yeah? Well, you always been the Joe fucking DiMaggio of all the geniuses around here. You could always figure stuff out. But now you're looking the problem right in the goddam face and you don't see it."

"What's my problem, Arnie?"

"One goddam nigger, that's what. This Ivory whatsisname. He's causing all this shit."

"Yeah?"

"Yeah. And when you know the problem, the solution is simple."

"Like what?"

"You either find a shrink or you whack the nigger."

IVORY JOE

30

At the age of six Joseph Coulter became Ivory Joe. He sat down at the piano in the Church of the Holy Word and within two hallelujah hymns had the whole congregation on its feet singing and clapping until the preacher realized the kid was upstaging him and snatched him off the piano bench. Ivory Joe told himself that if God Almighty gave him a good enough voice when he grew up he would be a singer. Otherwise he'd be a boxer. But God would have to keep his end of the bargain. Because one way or another he was going to be different than the grownups he saw around him in Portsmouth. And all he knew was that people came into their house, gathering around the radio, to listen to the famous Negro singers or hear the boxing matches. No one came to hear the radio tell about plumbers like Mr. Dickson next door or shipyard workers over in Norfolk or the men working the canals in the Great Dismal Swamp that cut right through Virginia into North Carolina. Even his father, the man he most admired in the whole world, was not someone who would be on the radio. But Joe Louis was. When Joe Louis knocked out Jim Braddock on that steamy June night and became heavyweight champion of the world, Ivory Joe sat in the middle of the little frame house looking around at the cheering Negroes packed in so tight that some fell off others' shoulders when the knockout punch was announced. The celebration went on all night with corn liquor replacing the Hires root beer and those who lived out in the country being told not to get caught celebrating by angry whites on lonely roads.

Before the summer was over his father left twenty dollars on the kitchen table, walked out of the house and never came back. Ivory

Joe's world collapsed. When the rent man came there was no money to pay. That night Ivory Joe helped his mother pack what they could into the big metal tub they used for taking baths and waited till it was quiet enough to sneak through the back fence to an empty house down on Nelson Street. To pay the rent on the new house they had to sell the radio, and suddenly Duke Ellington and Louis Armstrong and Joe Louis vanished. His mother worked for the wife of a naval officer in Norfolk. Being a kitchen bitch, she called it. Bustin' suds.

After her first day at work she returned home to find Ivory Joe waiting for her on the porch. "Nothin' to worry about," he told her.

"And why is that, Joseph?"

"Cause I'm the man of the house. I'm gonna take care of everything."

"Wipe your nose."

Ivory Joe played the piano at the church every day when no one was around and he could pretend he was Duke Ellington. After two months his mother got sick. Her lady organs, she said, when Ivory Joe and his sister asked what was wrong. Their aunt came down from Newark, filling the tiny frame house with calls to God Almighty and chants and prayers even as she helped her sister outside to the backhouse. Ivory Joe practiced boxing against a mirror and picked fights with boys bigger than himself until the day his mother died.

While his sister was sent to live with a family in North Carolina, Ivory Joe was taken back to Newark with his aunt. They lived over a store on Broome Street and from Ivory Joe's bedroom he could hear the bursts of music and the shouting that flared all the way to Spruce Street. The area was known as the Bucket of Blood, and on the weekends when the drinking was heavy and husbands and wives were cutting each other, Ivory Joe could still hear the cursing over the prayers of his aunt. Suddenly almost everything in his life had become a sin. His aunt and the Reverend Herter who lived down the hall made sure he understood that. It became a ritual around the table after dinner, with his uncle sitting in a corner reading the paper while Ivory Joe had to recount the events of his day to his aunt and the Reverend Herter, who would thunder the Lord's opinion of his wicked ways. Thinking about girls was a fearful sin. Playing cards with his friend Zoot was having one foot in hell. Listening to music—Devil music!—on the radio was to be an agent of the damned. Hellfire, he could yell. Ivory Joe started having nightmares about hellfire. He dreamed he was burning up and the Reverend Herter was standing there just watching.

The Reverend Herter's wife had died two years earlier. Probably glad to go, thought Ivory Joe, wishing it had been the preacher instead. Ivory Joe hated his life in Newark. In his other dream he was a boxer knocking out the same opponent. Only once did he ever see the man's face. It was his father. Ivory Joe cursed his father, blaming him for everything that had happened. More than ever he wanted to be Joe Louis or Duke Ellington. Because of his singing voice he was conscripted into the choir at the Reverend Herter's church. It had none of the joy of cutting loose back in Portsmouth and when he played the piano he was told to do exactly as he was told. A wooden yardstick descended on his knuckles whenever the Devil took hold of them.

Ivory Joe decided the Devil had to be more fun. He discovered a back door to the church. It led to the basement which was filled with the late Mrs. Herter's dresses and huge plumed hats. It was his friend Zoot who lived over near 13th Avenue who decided that the basement of the Church of God and Christ would be the perfect place to use as a clubhouse. Zoot was skinny even though he ate all the time. He wore a battered fedora with the front brim pinned back and smoked cigars even in their clubhouse, while they were playing ferocious games of poker, wondering if the white boys did the same thing. Sometimes they would hear voices upstairs late at night and stop talking until the voices faded away.

But the best place was the whorehouse up the road. It had a piano and the whores liked it when he cut loose and sang the songs he could never sing in church. They would saunter into the big room after finishing with their latest customer and ask him to play new songs. *Different* ones, they'd say. All he could think of was the hymns he played at church, speeding them up, increasing the tempo so no one would recognize them. They were a huge success with the whores. He started adding more bass rhythm, giving his songs a pounding beat. The whores would dance to his music. And then he'd run home and have nightmares of the Reverend Herter watching him burn in hellfire. Zoot insisted on singing in the whorehouse, too. He had a natural voice and sense of rhythm but his main interest was the whores who were arguing among themselves over who should adopt him. It was Daphne, a tall, slender whore, who became Zoot's favorite. And Ophelia, the voluptuous one, adopted Ivory Joe.

"It's like having an older sister, ain't it?" Ivory Joe said one day.

"You crazy, I.J.? You couldn't stick your thing in any sister, now would you?"

Ivory Joe's mouth slowly fell open. "Zoot! You been *doin'* it with Daphne?"

"Nah," said Zoot with a grin. But Ivory Joe didn't believe him. That afternoon he went to Ophelia's room and put his hand on the part of her print dressing gown covering her left breast. She looked from his hand to his face, saying nothing. The silence rang in his ears. Maybe Zoot didn't do it this way with Daphne.

"I.J., how old're you?"

"Ten."

She smacked him across the arm and threw him out. Zoot definitely had to be lying about him and Daphne.

The worst part of the whorehouse was the fighting. When it happened it was more savage than any fight at school. Usually it was over a man. When a new whore came after Daphne with a knife, slicing her arm open, she grabbed a barrel slat and swung like Babe Ruth. It caught the new whore in the face with an explosion of blood and teeth that sent Ivory Joe and Zoot diving behind the piano until the screaming subsided. Sometimes the customers would come in and just listen to the music that Ivory Joe and Zoot made. One of them was a former boxer named Ruben who taught Ivory Joe how to punch without going off balance. Out behind the whorehouse Ivory Joe would punch into Ruben's upraised palms and try to remember what his father looked like.

He loved going over to Zoot's house, which was filled with a sense of life. Not like his own home. Zoot Sr. worked for the Passaic Valley Sewage Commission and even during the Depression he had not been unemployed. Their house was in an area that was mostly Italian with a few Irish and Negroes. The Italian neighbors were close friends and Zoot often played with their two boys, Dominic and Arthur, and sometimes was invited to the house for pasta that he was told would fatten him up.

Ivory Joe and Zoot let the Italians see their clubhouse in the basement of the Church of God and Christ. During one of their poker games a sulfurous odor drifted across the table obliterating the smell of cigar smoke. "Okay," said Ivory Joe, slapping his cards down, disgusted. "Who cut the cheese?" There was indignation on every face but Dominic's.

"Way to go, Dominic," said Zoot. "You farted." Everyone else jumped up from the table, waving their arms around.

"It's good for you," said Dominic, trying to look like he meant it. "That's what our father says. It shows you're eating good."

"Our old man must eat real good then," said Arthur. "The bathroom sounds like a drum and bugle band."

Dominic was still trying to turn defeat into victory as Ivory Joe and Zoot were waving their arms and making faces. "Don't tell me you guys don't do it, too."

"Never," said Zoot.

"Scientific fact," said Ivory Joe. "Negro people never do that kind of thing."

"Go on."

"True."

"Then it's cause you don't eat right. Like us. With garlic. And pimentos."

"And olive oil," said Arthur. "All you eat is that fried chicken. No wonder you can't compete with us." He and Dominic looked pleased with themselves.

"Now just a minute here," said Ivory Joe, thinking as fast as he could. "If we *wanted* to, we could."

"Hah!"

"Scientific fact. Negro people have special gizzards. We can do it any time we feel like it."

"Oh yeah? We'll have you a contest then. One guy's the farter and the other's the coach."

"That's stupid. How do you tell who uncorked the biggest one?"

"Easy," said Arthur, climbing onto the big table. "You pull your pants down, then you kneel on the table like this. Then you lean forward and put your head on the table like this. Then you take a cigarette lighter and reach back between your legs holding it right next to your ass. Then you light it. Then you uncork one and pow!"

"Pow what?"

"It shoots out flame. Like turning on the gas on your stove. Whoever gets the biggest flame wins. We each bet a dollar."

Ivory Joe and Zoot withdrew to their corner to discuss recent meals and stomach conditions. Chicken and biscuits lost out to Mel-O-Rol, several jujubes and a peanut butter, mayonnaise and bologna sandwich. Zoot was the first one up on the table, loosening his belt and pulling his pants down around his knees. The other three stood off to the side as Zoot lit the lighter and then several seconds later produced a jet of blue flame several inches long.

"Wow," said Arthur admiringly. It was Dominic's turn. He lumbered onto the table, his round fleshy face bunching up in concentration. He peeled his pants away and leaned forward until his mouth zigzagged up from the puddle of his cheek that spilled out on the table. He strained. Nothing happened. The lighter burned, a solitary beacon illuminating the cleft white globe of flesh jiggling in the darkness. Dominic's face went from pink to crimson. Sweat fell from his face onto the table as he grunted and strained. Zoot smiled at Ivory Joe, who turned to Arthur and with a victorious flourish plucked the four dollars out of his hand. At that exact instant, there was a roar from Dominic that sent a huge jet of flame shooting out behind him. It knocked Zoot off his feet and terrified the other two. And it set fire to one of the big plumes on the late Mrs. Herter's hats.

"A human flamethrower," said Zoot from the floor.

"Zoot, get up. We got problems."

"Damn right. I'd need to stick a blowtorch up my ass to compete."

"No, not that. We're on fire!" said Arthur. "Dominic, get up!" Dominic was lying, exhausted but triumphant, on the table, a crooked smile on his face. He sniffed at the air, rolled over and then bolted from the table with a yell. The late Mrs. Herter's hat was a fireball. The flames jumped to an elaborate taffeta dress that stood formidably on a dressmaker's mannequin.

"What the hell do we do?" asked Arthur.

"Is there anything to put it out?" yelled Ivory Joe, scrambling around the basement looking for a faucet, a bucket, anything. He found a heavy tarpaulin that he tugged loose. "Come on! Help me!" Zoot and Arthur raced over and grabbed ends of the tarpaulin and heaved it over the fire. It settled in billowing clouds of smoke that seemed to diminish.

"It's going out," said Dominic, doing up his pants. "Am I the champ or what?"

Before anyone could answer, a can of paint thinner exploded under the tarpaulin, which instantly became a sheet of flame shooting to the ceiling. They all bolted for the door, racing into the cool night as other cans exploded behind them. Windows blew out. Flames shot up the side of the Church of God and Christ. They could see a hole burn up from the basement through the first floor as if the building was made of paper. From the second floor, a window flew open and the Reverend Herter looked out, his face a mask of fear and fury. He was stark naked. A few feet closer to the back of the building another window flew open and Ophelia leaned out, her eyes wide with fear and her pendulous breasts swaying freely in the swirling light of the flames. The Reverend Herter heard her cry out and yelled at her to get away from the window. Didn't she know there were people? *Watching? Whore!* He dragged her away and slammed the window.

"Ophelia! I'm coming!" screamed Ivory Joe. He ran to the back corner of the building and started to shinny up the drainpipe, which already was becoming hot. Arthur saw him and raced through the gathering crowd, hurling himself upward. He grabbed Ivory Joe's foot, pulling him off the drainpipe. They landed in a cursing heap, Arthur wrapping himself around Ivory Joe until Zoot arrived to help drag him away from the spreading flames.

"Ophelia! Run! Run! Run!" he screamed, tears streaming down his face. Still dragged by Zoot, whose arms were pinned across his chest, he swung around and yelled at the turbulent crowd surging around the building. "Get away! Leave! So they can get out! Please leave!" But no one understood.

The Reverend Herter clawed his way to the window trying to button his shirt. "Damn you!" he yelled down at Ivory Joe. "Damn you!" The floor under him exploded in flames and he vanished.

For months afterward, wailing prayer sessions would burst forth around the dinner table. Nothing could console his aunt who still set a place at the table for the Reverend Herter. "The work of the Devil!" she would cry. Ivory Joe wondered if it was. He wished he had a photograph of Ophelia. He never went back to the whorehouse, not even to collect the music on the new song he was writing. God was probably telling him something. He found Ruben, the former boxer, working on a railroad siding unloading boxcars.

"I'm ready."

"What're you ready for, boy?"

"To be a big fighter."

"Forget it."

"Whadya mean 'Forget it'?"

"You don't understand the language, boy? I mean forget it. I don't train no one who ain't got the guts to be a champion."

"You're lookin' at one."

Ruben smiled sweetly. And then caught Ivory Joe with an open-handed slap that exploded like a thunderclap behind his eyes, pin-wheeling flashes of light and pain as he slammed back into a boxcar clinging to the only thought that he could keep in his head: *No tears*. He struggled to stay on his feet and keep his breathing under control. Slowly he straightened himself. "Thank you." His voice was a whisper. "Thank you for teaching me something," he said with his eyes downcast until the instant he turned and lunged with a right-handed punch that Ruben deflected with the palm of his hand as he laughed.

"Okay, okay. I had to make sure you were tough enough."

THE SOUTH

31

Leo's a wipeout.

It's two weeks since Mother put us on the plane in Miami. Leo got back to New York right after us and all he could talk about is how it's going to be Mother's turn to get us on Saturday. It's driving him nuts. The problem is Mother's down South with Ivory Joe and the others. You'd think we were going to Mars.

So now we're standing on the train platform in New York and he's making us promise for the tenth time to phone him collect every day and not talk to boys we don't know. And to make sure we remember that we only stay one week with Mother. Next week we're back with him. That's his deal with Mother. So why don't you come down and visit we ask him.

Leo doesn't answer. By the time the train is pulling out Leo is getting pretty sappy like he's going to cry or something. Which is definitely not like Leo. It's a good thing that Stanley his driver comes racing up with the lunches Leo ordered for us. We look inside the bags. This time it's steaks about as big as my head. And more Alka-Seltzer and toothpicks.

When we pull out of the station in New York we go past lots of factories for a long time. Then we come to a lot of little towns that are either a *burg* or a *ville*. After that there's farms and when it gets dark we really get into forests and spooky mountains. Ruthie starts feeling sick from wearing those dumb cardboard glasses for the 3-D comic book she brought. One side of the glasses is green and the other side is red and when you wear them the Space Invaders jump right out of the page. She goes to sleep. I go to sleep too and then when it's real dark someone wakes us up. Mother and Ivory Joe and all the others are there. It's like they haven't seen us in years. There's lots of cheering and hugging but me and Ruthie are like noodles. We can hardly stand up. Zoot carries Ruthie and Clarence picks me up like I'm a feather. They put us in a station wagon and that's all we remember.

The next morning we look out the window of this hotel we're in. We're in the middle of one of the *burgs* or *villes* but this one doesn't look so good. Sort of like somebody beat it up. There's hills all over. And crummy places. Mother says we're in Wheeling, West Virginia. Lots of coal mining she says. It doesn't look like *Gone With the Wind*. Too bad. Cause Ruthie's decided Byron probably looks like Clark Gable. And guess who's Scarlett O'Hara?

So now all we do is drive. Right now I think it's Virginia and yesterday it was somewhere else. It keeps changing. Yesterday we passed cotton fields. Then we stopped for a while near some small lakes with white spooky trees growing right up out of the middle of the black water. Clarence says they look like dead people's fingers reaching up to get you. They do. Clarence goes and gets in their DeSoto and locks the door after he says it.

I have dreams about those dead people's fingers. Clarence must have too. When we leave the next morning he looks worse than Leo does after he's been nightclubbing. All day he sleeps in the DeSoto and when Ruthie and I ask if we can ride with them for a while Mother acts grouchy like it's the kind of question she doesn't want to answer but she knows she has to because we'll bug her until she does.

"This is the South," is all she says. She won't say any more like she doesn't want us to know something bad just yet.

So Mother and Charlie and us stay in the Buick. Charlie's our driver. He's not a Negro either.

32

The sound of Christie's giggling and Ruthie's scolding came in muffled volleys through the closed door that joined their room to hers.

Tina remained very still, staring out the window.

From the fourth floor of the hotel she could see the sun descend behind the hills. For a few moments the light caught whatever would reflect it. Church spires. Distant windshields. Windows. Bonfires of burnished light that were all snuffed out together leaving only the grayness of night that settled across her thoughts. She felt more alone than she had since they left New York.

They had been on the road for almost two weeks, playing Buffalo, Detroit, Philadelphia, all the northern cities, before easing into the South. Already the days were fading together, seamless jumbled memories of performing in theaters and clubs, mere names on the Weiman circuit itinerary papers until only hours before showtime when they would arrive after driving two or three hundred miles from the previous city.

Ivory Joe and the others rode in the DeSoto wagon, the luggage tied to the roof and their freshly washed shirts flapping from the side windows, drying as they drove. Tina was in the Buick, at first driving herself or riding with Zoot or Ivory Joe, who would change cars. But in Buffalo they added Charlie, blond haired, blue eyed and eager to leave his bellhop job at the Statler Hotel where they all stayed. Charlie became Tina's driver, cheerful, endlessly unaware of life outside Buffalo and cautiously observant of her desire for moments of silence while they drove.

Charlie was an acknowledgment of danger. A safety precaution for the trip into the southern states. Unknown territory. When they entered West Virginia, something changed subtly in the way Tina and Ivory Joe acted around each other. All Tina knew was that the need for such precautions vaguely awoke in her their unspoken reason. A white person and four Negroes. A white woman. The need for a barrier. Protection. Against what? Against contact. And why? Because she was a woman. A silent undercurrent rose closer to the surface.

The light was dying. Out toward the hills she could see the smoke from a locomotive rising like a plume through the horizon where the bleached remnant of daylight merged with pure darkness. The noise of the train was lost in the distance. It labored through the edges of West Virginia. On this side of the train were the church spires, the streetlights, the brick stores.

On the other side was darktown.

. . .

"You mean niggertown," the old man at the gas station said, his hands tucked inside his overalls. His jowls moved in billowing slabs as he pointed with his head. "That way. Down past Billy Fulton's grocery store, right at Mr. Stanton's bank and left where the train tracks are at. That where the shacks start."

Ivory Joe, Zoot, Clarence and Clyde drove on in silence. Staring out the windows at the low brick buildings. And being stared at in return. Four Negroes riding in a car that most of the white men they passed only dreamed of owning. When they crossed the train tracks, the paved roads withered. Wood replaced brick. The small houses were clustered together, some freshly painted with picket fences, others decaying and strewn with litter across the yard.

"Where's the hotel?" said Clarence nervously. He had expressed amazement at almost everything that differed from life in Harlem.

"You're looking at it," said Ivory Joe. Back somewhere around Buffalo he had stopped trying to prepare Clarence for what lay ahead in the South. It was not worth the brooding hours as Clarence struggled with his imagination, finally lapsing into a nervous silence that not even Zoot's jokes could penetrate.

"Don't look like no hotel, Joe."

"Everything ain't the Statler, Clarence. But it's going to be fine."

"You mean we're sleeping here?"

"Yeah, but wait till you see the maid service," said Zoot.

"Where's Tina? She sleeping here, too?" Clarence shifted in the front seat, his thick fingers drumming on the side of the car.

"Hey, Clarence. This here's darktown. You heard the man. Niggertown. Now what would Tina be doing here?"

"So what's she doing then?"

"She's at the hotel. Over there. Her 'n' the girls 'n' Charlie each got rooms."

"She's there an' we're here."

"Hey, now you're getting it, Clarence."

"Wasn't like this in Pittsburgh."

"This ain't Pittsburgh. This is the South. Get used to it. Read me the names on that list Weiman sent us."

"Bunch of names," said Clyde from the back seat. "First one's

Annie Topham. Says she charges a dollar a night. Breakfast included."

"Where is she?"

"Don't say. Just says house with the blue roof next to the church. No drinking."

"Definitely shittin' in high cotton," grinned Zoot.

Clarence and Clyde stayed close together walking the dirt roads and telling each other that the fresh air was good for them. Everyone came out of the shacks and stared at them. Clyde decided that he and Clarence might as well be white—wearing their shiny shirts and shoes and walking around the puddles in the road instead of through them. Old men in overalls and rubber boots nodded. Children ran along beside them. When they got lost and wandered beside the two-lane highway, a police car pulled in front of them. A white policeman with a face that Clyde thought had been stepped on started snapping questions at them. Clarence's mumbled answers played rhythm to Clyde's screechy lead. When the police car drove away Clyde started shaking. They found the little white house where they were staying and while Clyde was running for the outhouse an old man called out to Clarence. The old man beckoned him toward the shack next door with spastic excitement. Neighbors heard and the doors opened. Clarence nervously entered the shack, followed by others.

"This you. Ain't it?" said the old man, holding up a new record so Clarence could read the label. *Read?* Clarence wanted to run away but too many people were crowding in behind him. He couldn't make out a word on the label. "Gonna play it on my piccolo," said the old man, pointing to the ancient gramophone. The needle dropped with a howl and suddenly the whole room was six bars into *Train to You*. Everyone started singing and clapping and dancing. Clarence had never heard their own singing on a record before. It thrilled him. Suddenly all these strangers were friends. He even smiled. And started singing. But then someone shoved a piece of paper and a pencil in front of him. They wanted him to *write* something. His name. Were they taunting him? Like the cop? Clarence turned and pushed his way out of the shack, the music still clinging to him like he was on fire.

. . .

Ivory Joe sat on the edge of the metal cot in Mrs. Annie Topham's guest bedroom. The cot almost filled the room. The linoleum on the floor had cracked like a dry riverbed. The wallpaper had peeled away around the framed paintings of Jesus and a sign over the door said REJOICE IN HIM. Mrs. Topham was a widow, living in the same tiny house for thirty-seven years. Her husband had worked the railroads and the family silverware was Union Pacific knives and forks, Erie-Lackawanna dessert spoons, Lehigh teaspoons with the occasional Southern Pacific remnant thrown in. Church music blared from the radio in the kitchen until Ivory Joe turned the dial when Mrs. Topham went shopping. Walter Cronkite was broadcasting the news from New York, which was suddenly on another planet.

Two blocks away, in the tar-paper and wood house, Zoot decided the girl was definitely chippy material. Fourteen going on twenty-eight. Tall and toffee colored. A sweater straining under the weight of those two melons. And eyes about as big, blaring innocence whenever she brushed against him. He watched her through the guest room window, returning from the well with a pail of water.

"I ain't so impressed with you," she said, pouring the water into a big tub in the kitchen.

"No?"

"My mamma has had lots of you people staying here."

"Yeah?"

"Ray Charles. Blind guy. And Little Richard. But he was faggoty."

"That ain't no good."

"But Clyde was fine."

"Clyde?"

"Clyde McPhatter. He slept right there where you're at now."

Zoot knew Clyde McPhatter. The lead singer in the Drifters. That beautiful tenor voice. Trailing paternity suits behind his concerts. "Clyde McPhatter ain't no faggoty type, I'll bet."

"Sure not."

"Where's your mamma, girl?"

"Bustin' suds for the white lady she work for. So why you askin'?"

"Why you think I'm asking? What's the water for?"

"A bath. You singin' at the warehouse tonight, ain't you?"

"I lost track of where we sing. They just call for me. Where they take me is where I sing."

"Gonna be some white girls there, I bet. Comin' over from Ohio in their daddys' cars. Lookin' for Negroes to stick their things in them."

"That like Negro *singers* you mean by any chance?"

"This ain't like where you're from. They set dogs on Negroes here. Just for lookin' at white women. Nigger-huntin'. Lynch 'em. An' cut their things right off."

"No!"

"I swear."

"Never much liked women of the white persuasion anyhow."

"No?"

"Naw. Most of 'em got the uglies. Not like you."

"You're just sayin' that."

"Ain't."

"You think I'm loose, I can tell."

"Never crossed my mind. Get over here."

"What you wanting? Why you takin' down my dress?"

"Helping you have your bath."

33

We get to this little town that looks like a lot of other little towns we've been through. It's got brick stores about as high as a house up and down the two main roads that meet in the middle. There's a couple of banks with big pillars and some big houses that have pillars too. The people are either nice and talk to you without knowing you or else they're real squinty. The squinty ones give me the creeps. Most of them live over in the tar-paper shacks. But not all.

Right now Ivory Joe and Zoot are walking up and down the main street which is called Main Street. They have to do this in every town. Ivory Joe always has to stop in at the Negro barbershop and the general store just to let people know that it's really him and he's in town. That's how they sell the tickets. Even though you see signs up all over saying SEE IVORY JOE AND THE CLASSICS SING TRAIN

TO YOU! no one buys tickets until he shows up. Zoot says it's because sometimes they've been sold tickets for groups that never showed up.

Ruthie is here with me in this big old warehouse where they're moving all the bales of tobacco over to one side and making a stage for Ivory Joe to stand on. Other people are putting down chairs and benches that they borrowed from the Negro church. There's a bunch of musicians from around here who are going to be playing for Ivory Joe tonight. They're all standing around listening to a record of *Train to You* on an old gramophone. It's getting pretty scratchy as they keep playing it and learning the music. The leader is an old Negro who's got lumpy skin and his face looks like blueberry jam but can he ever play the big horn he's got. The music fills the whole warehouse.

So far Ruthie's had to wear a scarf over her Miami pink hair. But now Clyde is making her a redhead. Just like Rita Hayworth. At least that's what *she* says. In the little room just off the warehouse Clyde, Clarence and Ruthie are all fixing each other's hair. Clyde and Clarence are doing weird things like putting grease all over their heads and then taking some lye and putting it on their hair. The lye burns their hair. Kills it, Clyde says. So it will be straight and wavy instead of having all those little fuzz curls. Processing is what he calls it. All the groups are doing it, Clyde says. The Cadillacs. The Drifters. Jackie Wilson. Sam Cooke. It looks like a lot of trouble to me. Clarence yells when Clyde spills some lye on his head and wants Ruthie to take over. While they're all having a good time with each other's hair Ivory Joe and Zoot come back. They look real happy. Zoot has a radio that he plugs in and tells us to listen to. It's playing *Train to You* and some man is talking about it. A white man, says Zoot. A white man in the South. The radio station is somewhere over in Virginia. Zoot wants me and Ruthie to know how important that is.

It must be important because people start showing up outside the warehouse trying to look in when the doors open or peeking through the cracks in the boards on the walls. Most of them are girls and they're making noises like a barnyard full of little pigs. They're squealing and grunting and when Ivory Joe steps up on the stage to rehearse they go crazy. I tell them to shush but they don't. When Clarence and Clyde get up on the stage wearing their handkerchiefs over their heads the squealing gets even louder. And some of them must be fifteen.

I go in to see Ruthie who's still sitting in the little room with her new red hair. You'd never know it's the same Ruthie. The brain. She's staring at herself in the mirror like she *is* a movie star. A movie star wearing braces. She's got another *Movie Fan* magazine and she shows me what Byron looks like now. This is about the fiftieth Byron. It's gone from being Clark Gable and Marlon Brando to this new one. Some guy named Paul Newman.

I look at Ruthie and all of a sudden I figure out why Leo's always saying *swear to God*. He and God must be partners on Ruthie. She's his secret weapon. Mother *has* to send us back to New York next week. All Ruthie wants to do is be there when Byron shows up. Me I'd rather stay with Mother and Ivory Joe and the others for just a few more days. But Leo knows if he gets one he gets the other. I can't leave Ruthie now that she's turned into one big mushball. She's got a calendar with the days marked off.

While I'm looking at the latest Byron I realize it's got real quiet. The music sort of wound down and there's not even any squealing. We go back out into the main part of the warehouse and there's a policeman standing there in front of the stage. He's older and has white hair but he looks pretty strong. He has a gun and a big hunting knife hanging from his belt. Everyone's just staring at him as he walks through the big warehouse. The sun is shining through the cracks in the wall now making stripes on the floor between the bales of tobacco. The policeman walks through the stripes with his feet making clunking noises on the wooden floor. All the eyes are still peeking through the cracks in the walls but now they're quiet too. Ivory Joe watches. He watches harder than the others. Then he turns to Zoot and the others and gives the signal to start singing. The band starts up too but they only play for a few seconds before the policeman waves his hand and the old saxophone player stops right away. The others stop too. Then the Classics stop singing one by one. The policeman just keeps walking around.

"I want a space right down the middle," he says to the men setting up the chairs. "I want whites on this side. And nigras on this side." *Knee-gras*. He keeps walking around. Just interrupting everything. "I don't want no jungle stuff goin' on here tonight. No suggestive wriggling. No jumpin' around. Understand? Just keep it toned down. *Civilized*. If you know what I mean." He walks around some more and sees all the eyes peeking through the wall. "And then I think it'd be a fine thing to see you jus' git. Take off right out of here."

"We already have our rooms here. We're staying this evening." It's Mother talking. Her voice echoes all over. Everyone turns to look.

"Who're you, ma'am?"

"I'm the manager of the group."

The policeman isn't sure what to say to her. He keeps walking around. "I talk to you a minute, ma'am?" he calls out. He says it like a question but really it's not. Mother looks at Ivory Joe for a second. A real strange look. She walks over to the policeman, who's not far from me. "You own 'em?" he says.

"I manage them."

"Travel with them?"

"Yes."

"Married?"

Mother just looks at him. "Yes, I am," she says after a long time. "Are you?"

It's like he didn't hear her. "Husband know you're here?"

"That's my business."

The policeman's eyebrows raise up and he smiles but not really. "Thing is, ma'am, we had some Georgia nigger come through here a while back. Called himself Little Richard. Jumping around like a fairy. Tearing off his clothes an' banging away on a piano an' screeching into the microphone. Sent those little bitches clear into heat. Pret' near had to hose 'em down."

"What has this got to do with us?"

"We don't want no problem niggers around here."

I can't hold it any longer. You have no manners mister I say. It just comes out. My voice sounds sort of screechy. The policeman looks over at me like he just ate something bad.

"Who's she belong to?" he says.

"She's my daughter." Mother smiles but not really.

"Figures," says the policeman who walks away.

34

When the sun set, shortly after rehearsal, Ivory Joe drove the Buick up to the back of the warehouse. In the glare of the headlights they dressed for the show, behind the sheets that were hung up to separate them from the giggling girls who were kept away by Charlie the driver.

It was Clarence the others were all watching. Ever since the policeman arrived he had grown more nervous. The rehearsal had been halted repeatedly when he had forgotten his lyrics, finally erupting in mumbled anger and storming from the stage until Tina hurried outside to find Christie and brought her back to sit directly in front of Clarence on one of the church benches facing the stage.

And now, in the glare of the headlights, each of them moved in his own thoughts. It was unlike the moments before any other performance. Clyde paced behind the pickup truck asking unanswered questions about the policeman. Zoot stretched out on a bale of straw flicking cards through his long fingers in elegant little flourishes that no one else noticed. Ivory Joe stared out past the headlights watching the audience arriving. Most of them were walking, the rippling motion of a thousand heads illuminated from behind by the oncoming lights of the cars and pickup trucks. Tina's eyes caught his for an instant before he looked away, yielding nothing. Christie ran over to Clarence, who sat in the shadows, with only the faint sheen of his tuxedo signaling his presence. Immediately she started talking, paying no attention to either situation or surroundings, and Clarence responded, defenseless before her exuberant impatience at his brooding. By the time the warm-up music from the band surged through the shed, Clarence was grunting replies and nodding as Christie kept talking.

"I've told Charlie to park the cars right outside the back door," Tina said in a voice quiet enough that only Ivory Joe would hear.

"Why?"

"So we can leave right away. I don't want to stay here tonight."

Ivory Joe looked away from the road. "No!"

"We could make it to Chattanooga by morning."

"I don't feel like running out of here just because some redneck cop struts around and talks about problem niggers. All we're doing is singing."

"Look, this is not a good place to stay." The old editor of the *Sentinel-Beacon* had put it more bluntly when Tina saw him in his office that afternoon. Leave now. Don't even perform tonight. After the Little Richard thing, it was too dangerous. The local Negroes had wisely kept off the back roads at night. The last lynching was eight years ago but now it was beatings or shootings, in the anonymity of lonely roads.

The old newspaper editor disregarded the rest of Tina's questions. Instead, he told her of a farm up in the hills behind the town where they slaughtered hogs as if it was an art form. The editor had looked over his glasses making sure Tina understood the skill involved. The killings had to be done at exactly the right phase of the moon, a shrinking moon in December or January. The water and lime had to be heated to a precise temperature and the hair was scraped off the bodies with zinc canning lids just before the pig was hung and gutted. The farm was owned by the big policeman, the same one who showed up for the rehearsal, and the local legends of darktown had all the Negroes who ever disappeared ending up with the hogs. That's ridiculous, Tina said, and the editor had responded with a tired smile he reserved for outsiders. Well, of course it is, he said. But so what? What matters is that an awful lot of people *think* it's true.

She returned to the big warehouse that was now sending gales of music into the stillness of the town. She drove with the windows open, the music carried on the warm, damp air that eddied around her, clung to her, and seethed with textures and smells and sounds she had never known in New York. The paved road ended and the car sucked up the dust beneath it and spewed it behind in a whirling funnel that clung like something being dragged. In the parking lot she slid to a stop between a pickup truck and a Ford, and hurried past one of the police cars that was parked with its lights on and doors open. A policeman, his young face peering out from behind its sun-wizened mask, stared at her with eyes that said nothing.

She hurried past the pickup trucks and the Chevrolets and Fords, and then past larger cars, the Mercurys and Oldsmobiles with Ohio license plates, fathers' cars driven in from the other side of the river by teenagers who had a room of their own.

Inside it was as if the place was lopsided. On one side of the center aisle was the white section. Several hundred chairs were arranged in neat rows and only half of them were filled. On the other side of the aisle was the colored section with what looked like a thousand Negroes pressed in together, standing on benches or sitting on laps, rafters or tobacco bales.

And in the center aisle, directly in front of the stage with his arms folded across the upper crescent of his stomach, was the policeman who had walked into their rehearsal.

The local musicians finished their warm-up numbers and moved back into the shadows as the cheering and whistles ricocheted off the tin walls, becoming deafening at the instant when Ivory Joe and the Classics walked out onto the stage and swept into the synchronized moves that raised the pitch of the uproar even more. Tina knew instantly what would happen, as if she was watching a huge and distant wave rolling in. A kind of frenzied, taunting energy shot out from Ivory Joe and spun through the hall. He moved to the edge of the stage and what had been rehearsed now became spontaneous. He waved for the bass player to keep the pounding, hypnotic rhythm sounding. His voice rose and fell, swooping across the audience in cadences that demanded a response. And they cried out in return.

As the policeman moved a few steps closer to the stage.

The music seized them all in a lockstep rush as Clyde spun into a religious fervor while Clarence fixed on Christie's big smile in the fifth row and for the first time *felt* his bass notes reaching all the way out there, amazed and thrilled by the power of his own voice.

Zoot was losing himself in all the craziness, that screaming rush that came from looking out and thinking my, my, all those little pretties flinging themselves all over the auditorium like they were in heat. And when Ivory Joe grabbed the microphone and swiveled around with that banshee howl, Zoot saw a thousand little pitter-patter hearts suddenly go off like firecrackers. And that silky voice of his! Going right up under their skirts and making things definitely moist around here. The cops knew it. They weren't no fools, standing there with faces like preachers facing an empty church as all their worst fears were cut loose, not just those little pickaninny colored bitches getting damp where it counted but *whites*, sweet respectable little white things screaming at this bunch of syncopated niggers up here onstage. Zoot loved it.

He let go, throwing off their tightly choreographed moves as they hurtled into the chorus of *Train to You*.

On that old driving train
driving train
driving train

It was all there, the energy, the pounding beat and the lockstep screams from the seething darkness beyond the edge of the stage when Ivory Joe flashed them a grin. Then something flew out of the darkness, arcing up out of the waving arms, a fluttering white creature that settled gently on Zoot's shoulder. It was a pair of panties.

"Hey! My kind of snowstorm!" said Zoot under his breath as others flew into the air, filling the darkness with white projectiles. "Throw 'em against the wall to see which ones stick," he said to Clarence, who showed only embarrassment as they took a bow. And Clyde—Clyde staring bug-eyed at what almost hit him in the face and muttering things about the Devil dragging them straight to hell.

But the cop down there staring in slack-jawed fury, now *there* was your average open book. You could tell what he wanted. He merely wanted to kill. So Zoot smiled at the cop, bent over, and elegantly retrieved the shiniest of the panties, folding them with a flourish and then inserting them in the breast pocket of his suit the way any true southern gentleman would replace his handkerchief.

And instantly the policeman started blowing his whistle but it went unheard in the frenzy of music as the cheering crowd merged, Negroes and whites all singing and clapping together, drawn into the chanting rhythm that Ivory Joe circled around them with *Honeychild*. The policeman yelled at the Negroes—*you send me honeychild*—pushing them back into their own side, only to be engulfed in the wave—*but you mend me/bend me*—that paid no attention to the florid bursts of his police whistle—*to your point of view/honeychild/honeychild*—

Tina ran through the crowd, cutting through an empty row of chairs, to where Ruthie and Christie were bouncing up and down, clapping—*give it/give it/give it*—and waving at a beaming Clarence. She seized them by the hand, almost dragging them toward the shadows—*live it/live it/live it*—stunned by the mesmerizing furies that she could feel unleashed by just the sweep of Ivory Joe's arm.

It frightened Tina. There was no control but his. No will but his. And suddenly it had become a weapon, engulfing the infuriated policeman, who bobbed helplessly across the surface of the chaos, blowing his whistle in strangled bursts of futility . . .

. . . until the big barnboard door behind the stage split into a barrage of splinters as the first of three police cars catapulted into the warehouse with sirens screaming almost in pitch with the saxophones, skidding onto the stage, scattering the musicians and singers and almost running over Clyde, who tripped on the drums that were blasted into the audience.

The music suddenly faltered into a discordant silence and the writhing masses grew still. The police cars whipped their red lights through the settling dust across the suddenly silent faces and the policemen took out their guns and walked slowly around, making mental note of those they could recognize.

The lights of the town flickered, caught momentarily behind the trees that bent into the gathering winds. Tina sat staring out the window, letting the darkness wash over her. She turned no lights on in the room and only the faint neon glow of the hotel sign intruded until the phone rang, a metallic rattle in the silence that almost made her flinch. It would be Leo phoning again, telling her for the second time today that the girls definitely had to be back by the weekend.

Instead it was the clerk at the front desk. "There's a nigra down here, ma'am," said the reedy voice. "Says he sposeta meet you but we stopped him, ma'am. Ain't no nigras allowed upstairs. 'Cept for the help."

Downstairs Tina marched past Ivory Joe straight for the desk clerk, a small man with blotched skin stretched too tightly across a sharp nose and moist stringy hair combed up over the bald part of his head. "Just who the hell do you think you are?" said Tina in a voice sharp enough to cut through the low murmur of the lobby. "This gentleman and I happen to be business associates and where we discuss that business is no concern of yours."

"This is a respectable hotel, madam."

"Good. Try to keep it that way, will you," Tina snapped. A volley of exchanged stares shot across the suddenly silent lobby. Tina walked over to Ivory Joe, her shoes sending out sharp little clicking sounds that reverberated off the marble. She smiled for the benefit of the onlookers, expecting someone to stop them as they walked toward the elevators.

"Don't you *ever* do that again," said Ivory Joe in a voice so quiet she could barely hear it. It came in calm, seething bursts, through lips that barely moved. She started to reply, the smile disintegrating and the words stillborn. "Wait upstairs," he said. And then he walked back through the lobby ignoring those who stared.

She waited upstairs, careening between anger and confusion, not knowing what she was waiting for. An hour passed. The lights in the distant windows began vanishing into darkness. She changed into her nightgown and then stood looking into the silence of the town square. A police car cruised in slow relentless circles around the perimeter. It seemed distant, almost innocent until there was a soft knock at her door and then everything she saw overflowed with fears. She hurried to the door and opened it. Ivory Joe entered as if it was a starting gate, his eyes still filled with anger and his voice so soft that words seemed an intrusion. "We're going to get ourselves some ground rules," he said.

"How did you get up here?"

"Not important."

"I'm afraid it is. You're obviously going to have to leave the same way."

"Fire escape."

"That was crazy. You could have—"

"Don't talk to me of crazy." His words flickered out at her. "Not after you pulled that little scene downstairs."

"No desk clerk is telling me to—"

"Well, go paste the Bill of Rights on your forehead and walk into the closest Klan meeting then. This ain't the Plaza Hotel, you know.

Where the ladies of New York can think pure thoughts over lunch and go home feeling good about themselves."

"What I did was right!" Every word came out as a perfectly formed unit of anger.

"This isn't some debating society, lady. This is where people get killed. Strung up. Negro-type people. Can you understand that?" His face was very close to hers, drawn in by anger, with his eyes boring holes in any defenses her emotions could grasp. "I ain't seen any New York ladies strung up yet. Have you?"

It was a question and a taunt. She said nothing.

"Have you?" His voice rose.

"No," she said in a whisper.

"So then. Any trouble we make down here *I* decide to make it. I don't need you to do it for me. You understand?"

"No. Not really." The whisper took on furies as it went. "I don't understand one damn bit of it. Not when I've got two daughters asleep in the next room. And when you put them in jeopardy tonight. You knew what was going to happen when we got out on that stage. Didn't you?"

"We *all* knew."

"Like hell we did."

"Look, this is the South. Or can't you get it through your head? Just *being* down here is trouble. All of us together. And *me* standing here—right here in this room, a white woman's hotel room, is enough to ring the whole damn curtain down."

"So why are you here? In a white woman's hotel room?"

They stared at each other.

"Right now I'm not sure how to answer that."

"Do you want to end the tour now?"

"No. Do you?"

"No," she said.

His hand reached out and touched her shoulder.

"I think you should go."

"I know."

The lights from the slowly circling police car wedged faintly across the room. "They're out there." His hand rested on her shoulder. And she wanted it to remain there.

"You knew that when you came in here."

"We both did." His hand slid down, brushing her arm, sending tremors through her body.

"Don't." She stared at him, struggling to get her breath.

Ivory Joe stared out the window. "I'm sorry," he said softly, "we're a long way from home."

"Is that the reason?" The words barely made it past her lips.

"No. I have to go."

Watching him steal across the rooftops, running low, a silhouette against the darkness, a memory intruded and flickered before her eyes. And for one dreadful instant she knew that she would never be free of Leo. And never want to be.

35

After the police cars had burst through the doors into the warehouse, they had hurled their equipment and clothes into the DeSoto which Zoot gunned even before Clyde had time to close the door.

In the noise and dust and confusion, they had waited at the edge of the parking lot until Ivory Joe saw Charlie signal from beside the Buick, letting them know Tina and Ruthie and Christie were safe and inside the car. They waited for the Buick to drive away, following it until they came to the side road that led to darktown, where Zoot flashed the high beams and Charlie honked the horn in response and drove ahead toward the hotel.

And then they spent hours around a lantern light and corn whiskey, trying to come down, trying to make sense out of what had happened even after Ivory Joe quietly left without saying where he was going.

And none of them could have imagined that Charlie was the one in the most immediate danger.

When Charlie parked the Buick in front of the hotel, he said good night to Tina and the girls and went into the lobby for a few minutes before deciding to go for a walk. In Buffalo he had always walked after work at the Statler Hotel and on the tour he had found it even more necessary as a way to relax. Leaving the hotel he headed across the town square, then up the main street until he saw a street with big houses and no sidewalks.

At first he paid no attention to the pickup truck following him. And he heard only part of *niggerlover* before the ax handle knocked him to the ground.

He was barely able to crawl out of the ditch on the edge of darktown where he had been thrown. One eye was almost closed by the beating, his wrist was broken where he had tried to shield himself from the ax handle and blood from the gash across his head caked his blond hair. He lay sprawled across the edge of the road, crawling a few feet at a time until Ivory Joe found him sometime after the flickering lights in the shacks had gone out.

Ivory Joe had heard only the rasping noises that sounded as if an animal was dying. He stopped, unsure in the darkness. The noises ceased, then returned. In the half light of the moon he saw Charlie trying to roll over on his back. Ivory Joe raced over to him, cradling his head until a low choking sound made him gently lay Charlie's head back in the dirt. He tried to make sense of the word *pickup* that bubbled up through the bloody mouth. Then Ivory Joe stood up, put two fingers between his lips as he had not done since he and Zoot had last lived in Newark and gave out a long whistle that carried like a rasping shriek into the night above the shacks.

Zoot was asleep when a nightmare seized him, sending him into his old fears that the preacher was coming back from hell and that Ivory Joe was trying to warn him with that shrieking whistle when —he sat bolt upright in bed.

They got Charlie back to Mrs. Annie Topham's house, trying to be quiet but not succeeding. Lights in nearby shacks flickered on and voices called out, settling quietly in the darkness. Clyde and Clarence loaded the DeSoto while Zoot bandaged Charlie's head and Ivory Joe explained to Mrs. Annie Topham why it was necessary to use her telephone, the only one in all darktown. She listened, saying nothing, a little old woman staring off into some distance that only she saw. "Will they burn down my house if they find out?" she said finally.

Ivory Joe started to answer but stopped. "We'll find another way," he said.

"No," she said. "I don't want you to."

They sent word through the darkness to a shack on the far side of darktown where a young woman named Rose was roused from her bed and guided back to Mrs. Annie Topham's where it was explained to her that her skill was needed.

"What skill?" she said, rubbing sleep from her eyes.

"Talkin' white," said Mrs. Annie Topham, handing her the telephone.

At the hotel, the night clerk was woken up by the switchboard telephone that would not stop ringing even though it was after four in the morning. "Yes, good morning," said a muffled woman's voice, "this is the long-distance operator. I have a person-to-person call for Mrs. Klein from Mr. Klein in New York."

"Husband?" said Tina, after answering the phone. She had not slept since Ivory Joe left hours earlier. The phone was suddenly almost too heavy to hold.

At Mrs. Annie Topham's, the small living room was filled with neighbors, some wearing nightshirts or patched overalls, watching silently as Rose nodded and quickly handed the telephone to Ivory Joe. Behind him a radio was turned on emitting only the static that they hoped would sound like a long-distance phone line. Over the mouthpiece they had taped a sock.

"Hello, darling," said Ivory Joe in a voice so different that the neighbors out in the kitchen looked at each other, momentarily puzzled. "Sorry to call you so late but your cousin Charlie has gotten very sick and I thought you'd want to know."

An hour later, Tina carried a sleeping Christie through the darkened hotel lobby as Ruthie put their suitcases in the trunk of the Buick. She could tell that the night clerk had listened on the switchboard phone. He hoped things would work out. It's awful when people get sick. And would they be heading back to New York?

In the Buick she let the engine warm up and told Ruthie for the second time that everything was fine as she noticed the police car idling in the darkness on the other side of the town square. *Now remember darling, to get to Manhattan turn east at the horse.* The horse? The words of their conversation were still unspooling through her thoughts. . . . *and take the little road through the skyscrapers.* And nothing made sense.

Until she realized she was staring blankly at the statue of a Confederate army general on a horse. It was at the far end of the town. Ignoring Ruthie's questions, she put the Buick in gear and cruised slowly toward the statue—turn east. On the other side of the horse was a narrow alley—small road. Last night the sun had set in the opposite direction, catching the windows of the three- and four-story buildings—the skyscrapers—so that they seemed to be reflecting fire. She drove around the lower half of the town square, stopping long enough at the entrance to the alley to catch a glimpse of the police car as it edged quietly around the far side of the square. Without its headlights on it looked to her like a distant animal with its eyes closed, waiting smugly to close in for the kill.

She turned into the alley. The buildings on either side were frame or sometimes brick stores whose loading doors showed faded signs proclaiming the local shopkeeping dynasties. Again, it made no sense—*just keep going straight but make sure not to drive through any puddles*—and she couldn't understand why she should look out for puddles when there obviously had been no rain in days, maybe weeks. The Buick jostled across the bumpy surface until the headlights picked up what looked like a long, thin puddle of water running a couple of car lengths along the left-hand side of the alley. She edged the car over to the other side, coming so close to the wall that Ruthie peered out the window and yelled that the paint would be scratched.

Behind them the police car closed off the alley, a lumbering shadow that stopped momentarily and then lurched ahead in slow pursuit. The sightlines of the alley converged on the points of red light at the back of the Buick, a scent that trailed back to the police car as it gathered speed.

Something crashed onto the alley from above. It was a brick. Then another one, grazing the front bumper of the police car. And then a small torrent of bricks scattering across the alley. The police car stopped with the wheels on the driver's side resting in the shallow puddle. One of the policemen stepped out of the car into the puddle and shone a flashlight up into the darkness. Nothing. The brick wall of the store was intact. He shone the light around the alley.

There was steam coming from the puddle. It drifted up around his shoes, curling into the beam of light in evaporating little wisps.

Far ahead the taillights of the Buick vanished and the policeman ran back to the car. In a single motion the police car slithered through the puddle and the headlights snapped on. It roared through the alley, braking violently at the junction that led to the Dry Ridge road going south to the highway. The Buick was now just flickers of red light through the grove of trees near the highway.

The tires of the police car gave out a sizzling scream as they spun across the asphalt. The car made the turn, slithering across the road, and then fishtailed off toward the dots of red light on the highway. Grinding through the gears, it closed in on the Buick.

But suddenly there were lights, other lights, on the road behind the police car, gaining on it with some kind of commotion. The policeman in the passenger seat swung around the moment before the strongest high beams he had ever stared into sent spots shooting across his vision. He shielded his face as the lights swung out to the side. Music, loud raucous music, swallowed up even the roar of their own car. Goddam jukebox on wheels, he yelled as the policeman behind the wheel looked over just in time to see the DeSoto glide past them. Cruising right up there and overflowing with the same arrogant niggers, but this time singing that jungle shit like they owned the goddam road. *Two* roads! The DeSoto shot off the highway onto the Blue Licks side road—without even signaling! Not even *white* men from up north were fool enough to pull stunts like that with the law glued to their ass.

"Get them fuckers!" yelled the policeman with the spots in his eyes and the police car screeched to a stop on the highway, laying undulating tracks of rubber that were duplicated in reverse. Smoke shot from the tires.

"What about the woman in the Buick?"

"Fuck the woman. Get the niggers."

The police car shot to the side into the onrushing whirlpool of dust spewed up from the gravel road by the DeSoto. Suddenly there was no horizon, just the endless billowing dust and the taunting music sounding above even the roar of the engine. The siren was turned on. The flashing roof light was turned on, whipping redness that was flung back at them. The policeman in the passenger seat was almost jumping up and down yelling get them, get them, get them!

Until the terrifying slapping sound coming from somewhere below them as the car began to lurch and the policeman in the passenger seat screamed above the din to slow down! *slow down!* but the other screamed back that he couldn't goddamnit! his foot was welded to the gas pedal.

In the hours before dawn while they had waited in the DeSoto for what seemed like forever, Ivory Joe sat behind the steering wheel answering Clyde's and Clarence's fearful questions as Zoot adjusted the mouthpiece of the trumpet so that it would sound the loudest when the time finally came.

The acid they had been given by Mrs. Annie Topham would eat the tires off any car ever made.

"You sure?"

"Yeah, I'm sure."

"How so?"

"Cause the late Mr. Topham used it on the railroad. Eat the bolts off a bridge if they wanted it to. She's been storing it for all these years not knowing what to do with it. Waiting for the good Lord to tell her what to do with the stuff. You heard her."

"So what happens if the police car don't stop right in the acid?"

"Think positively."

When the police car swung onto the highway in pursuit of the Buick, even Clarence forgot his fear. All he could think about was Ruthie and Christie being chased so he rolled down the back window and joined in the most ferocious version of *Train to You* he had ever sung.

Anything to save Ruthie and Christie.

Even when Ivory Joe floored it and roared up alongside the police car, he closed his eyes and sang as loudly as he could, clenching his fists and pounding them into his knees in fear and anger, grabbing the door and coughing on the dust as the DeSoto suddenly careened down the side road.

Long after sunset, the police car was found where it had come to rest, partly submerged in the swamp. Long strips of rubber from the tires guided the way. And when the car was pulled from the mud, the onlookers finally believed the policeman's story about how his shoe was glued to the gas pedal. Something had melted the sole.

36

Charlie's a mess. After his accident we drove all through the mountains and then kept going until it was almost dark. Mother says Charlie tripped and fell. Like off a cliff? I ask her but she just stares daggers at me like I said something dirty. Well? I ask he looks like he fell off a cliff doesn't he? I'm telling you everybody's real strange right now.

Charlie just lies across the back seat and makes noises. Mother doesn't want to say anything. And Ruthie and me are supposed to stay quiet. Have you ever tried being quiet when there's nothing but trees passing by all day long? But Ruthie's fine. Naturally. She's got her chessboard and that's quiet. Sometimes brains have it easy. They can sit there yapping away inside their own head. Today was one of the only times I really wanted to be a brain. Staring at trees really makes me want to talk to somebody.

When we stop for something to eat at some little shack up in the hills. Charlie's asleep in the back. Ruthie and Mother and me have to go inside and bring out food for Ivory Joe and Clyde and Clarence and Zoot. They can't go inside because a lot of squinty people are standing around just staring. Very creepy. They all look sort of pushed in. Hillbillies Zoot calls them. Ruthie says their eyes are either too close together or too far apart.

Inside the store Ruthie and I remember that we haven't phoned Leo today. If we miss by even a few hours he's already started thinking of which judge to call. He wants some court to say terrible things are happening to us. So he can get us back to New York. But Ruthie and I are always real careful to say Leo for your information everything is great and why don't you come down here? A couple of times we almost had him. All he and Mother need is a couple of days alone in some romantic place.

We know we're close.

So when we go inside the store we look for the phone. An old fat lady with one tooth is behind the counter. She sort of points to the phone on the wall. The whole store stinks and it's dark. We have to crank the phone like they do on *I Remember Mama*. When old Mrs.

Weissman answers the phone at Frolic Frocks she can't understand a word the hillbilly operator says. She must be getting deaf because she always screams into the phone. She finally figures out it's us and then she panics like Leo's going to fire her if we hang up. We can hear all kinds of screeching when Leo comes on saying yes yes he'll accept the charges. He yells into the phone. "You're three hours late. What's the matter? Are you safe?" Like we're in Africa or something. No matter what we tell him he doesn't believe us. Ruthie and I are standing on tiptoes grabbing the earpiece from each other and yelling into the other part of the old phone. "Put your mother on the line," says Leo. "I'll see you Friday."

Friday? What's Friday? Mother takes the phone. At first everything is real sappy the way they get just before they start yelling at each other. It's hi Leo how are you and I'm fine thank you. You can tell she still likes him. But then it starts. You just have to watch her face change while she's listening. She doesn't yell at him but she sure starts arguing. I look over and see a whole bunch of hillbillies standing around the store in the shadows looking like the Seven Dwarfs only taller. The old fat lady is waving them all in like Mother is some kind of show. This is private lady I say. But she just laughs without any sound coming out. Mother is really going now and we can hear Leo's voice through the phone. Mother stares daggers at us or maybe it's our imagination because we always feel like we're ratting on her when we phone Leo. But we've got to do it. Ruthie and I go outside. There's a whole bunch of hillbillies all standing around staring at Ivory Joe and the others in the DeSoto. It reminds me of Mrs. Fineman's cats looking in the bird cage. The hillbillies are wearing old overalls and staring at Ivory Joe who's dressed real nice. One of the hillbillies has a gun a big one hanging down like a third arm. Another one says something to me that I can't understand. He says it again. And again.

I finally understand. They yer niggers? he's asking. I tell him that if Mrs. Levine was here she'd wash his mouth out with soap and then I go right over to the DeSoto and climb in. Just to show *them*. Zoot and Ivory Joe look at me and then at each other. Clyde says good old Mrs. Levine in a real soft voice. Zoot says, "Christie, sugar, we love having you in the car but these nice white hillbilly folks don't like little white girls riding with us four gentlemen of somewhat darker persuasion. Specially the moron with the big gun," he says. The hillbillies are all moving around the car making their noises and looking weird. Ivory Joe starts talking in a real soft voice without moving his lips. He looks real cool. "Don't give 'em eye contact," he says. Clarence's hand starts shaking as the moron points the gun right at the windshield. That is really the limit. Just like when Louie Makin pointed his cap gun at us in the hallway at school. This was just after he stuck the sparkler in Manny Singh's turban and lit it. I went right up to Louie Makin and when he said he'd shoot I just said bullroar Louie. The moron looks like Louie Makin too. A little bit.

So I open the car door. I hear Ivory Joe say something to me. But I'm already outside. I walk straight over to the moron. He's still pointing the gun. Bullroar I yell. He doesn't move. But he does look down at me with that eye of his. It looks runny like our noses in the winter. "What?" he says. Bullroar I tell him. He looks at the other hillbillies like they're all trying to figure it out. Right then Mother comes out and you can tell she's real mad because of Leo. She says excuse me to the hillbillies the way Jackie Gleason says it to Ed Norton on *The Honeymooners*. Like she really means business. She just plows right through them. But the moron is still there and when she sees the gun Mother just says, "Oh don't be ridiculous." The moron isn't stupid. He knows he'd better not fool around with Mother. She says to us that we have to get going or we'll be late. Mom can I ride with Ivory Joe? I yell. She says of course dear and I jump in and we drive away right past the hillbillies who just stare like Mrs. Fineman's cats when the canary flew out her window.

37

Sometime in the middle of the night we're still driving and we have to stop. Charlie needs to stretch out so they put him in the back of Ivory Joe's station wagon.

Off in a field there's something on fire. It's like crosses on a church. Everyone stops to watch it. Mother says it's the clan. Whose clan? I ask her but she doesn't answer. Instead she just says there's been some trouble and tells us to go back inside the car. We drive all night. Ruthie and I are wipeouts. But I remember Mother telling us it's all part of our learning process. With Mother anything crummy is a learning process. Like taking cod liver oil. Or having to kiss Aunt Ida.

We wake up and it's still the middle of the night. We're driving down this road with trees all around. There's a big fat moon hanging right over the road. Sometimes it gets blocked out by the cotton candy stuff hanging from the trees but mostly it just hangs there in the sky making the road look shiny like the chrome on the cars. Ivory Joe is driving the DeSoto in front of us. We're the only two cars on the road and their red lights sort of float on the shiny road in front of us. It's real pretty even though we're wiped out. You can hear singing. It's Ivory Joe, Zoot, Clarence and Clyde singing *Ghost Lover* while they're driving. We roll down the windows so we can hear it better. I ask Mother when they're going to make it into a record. Soon Mother says. When some things get straightened out. That's her way of saying she doesn't want to talk about it.

For a long time we keep driving like we're going to crash into that big fat moon that gets so low it looks like it's right at the end of the road. I wish Leo was here. He'd like it even though he'd pretend he didn't.

THE SHRINK

38

"Leo, you're stalling."

"I'm telling you, Arnie, lay off, willya, please."

"For christsakes, it ain't up to me! Don't you get it? It's gone way beyond me, and Herman, and Bender, and anyone else you know. And when people don't do what Genovese wants, they have a habit of getting themselves real fucked up."

"I'm trying to explain something to you—I don't want to go to Havana. Got it?"

"Too late, Leo. Monday! *You* got it? Monday! It's all set up for you to carve Goldin a whole new asshole."

"Yeah? So why me? You can get a dozen guys to play poker."

"*You* tell that to Genovese then! Cause I ain't. Not when he remembers Cairo and the way you shook down that Greek."

"That was different."

"You wanna know the difference, Leo? You *really* wanna know the difference? Genovese and them couldn't have gotten you killed as easy. Over there you renege on 'em and it takes maybe ten days, maybe more to get it set up. Here you renege and they can whack you in ten minutes."

"All I want to do is find my kids. I don't even know where they are."

"Whadya talkin' about? They phoned you yesterday from Kentucky, didn't they?"

"That was yesterday. Today they're at some lousy music hall in Memphis. And right now they're three hours late phoning me."

"Oh, Jesus, Leo. Gimme a fuckin' break, willya."

The next morning when Leo entered the lobby at Frolic Frocks, he could see Arnie Dalitz and Herman Pinsky waiting for him in his office. The door to Morris's office was closed for the first time since they had taken over the company. From one of the cutting tables at the other end of the manufacturing area Morris looked up with a startled expression that Leo could not decipher.

"We got it all taken care of," said Herman Pinsky, stepping just outside the office and placing himself between Leo and the closed door to Morris's office.

"You got what taken care of?"

"The thing with your kids."

Leo stared into some infinity within the pile of junk and papers on his desk and with slow deliberate motions he circled it, sitting down on the edge of his chair still staring into the same infinity that Arnie Dalitz and Herman Pinsky looked for but could not see. "Herman," he said at last, "since when do you guys take care of *any*thing with my kids?"

"Leo, Leo, I told you back in Miami," said Arnie Dalitz in a soothing voice. "We got ourselves a judge on standby. And all the judge needed was some shrink to say your kids are going bananas without you being around them. Or some shit like that. And bingo! We get a court order and your problems are over."

"You telling me you got a shrink stashed in Morris's office? Is that it?"

"Not just *a* shrink. *Our* shrink. But we gotta use him before the twenty-third."

"What happens on the twenty-third?"

"Some psychiatrist shit. Some professional association our guy belongs to. Don't ask. They all fight like a buncha jealous women. This association wanna kick him out at this big meeting they're having on the twenty-third. He's too fuckin' good, that's his trouble, I'm tellinya. But as far as our judge is concerned, until then we're kosher."

Leo said nothing. He looked from Arnie Dalitz to Herman Pinsky, rapping a pencil in an aimless drumming rhythm that scratched at their thoughts until Arnie Dalitz could stand it no longer and reached out and plucked the pencil from Leo's hand.

"I ain't interested."

"Leo, it's all set up."

"It ain't fair to Tina."

"Jesus Christ, Leo!" yelled Herman Pinsky, his cheeks quivering. "Whose side you on? Yours or hers?"

"She's a good mother to my kids. I don't want to sic some shrink on her. She don't deserve that shit."

"I thought you wanted your kids back."

"I can fight my own battles, Arnie."

"Too late," said Arnie Dalitz angrily, slapping two air tickets down on the desk. "A present. From Vito Genovese and friends."

"He wants to make sure you ain't got anything distracting on your mind before the big match in Havana," said Herman Pinsky trying to act cheerful.

"C'mon. Let's go talk to our shrink. You and him are on the flight to Memphis this afternoon." Arnie Dalitz leaned around the corner and pushed open the door to Morris's office.

Sitting on the threadbare couch, with knees together, toes pointing inward and an expression that veered wildly between indignation and fear, was cousin Arnold Berman.

39

Even before the plane taxied into position for takeoff at LaGuardia, Leo had decided to declare war on this bony dink. Who now, thanks to the noted child-raising expert Arnie Dalitz, and some hack judge, was supposed to advise, actually *advise*, on how to raise kids. And not just *any* kids either. Christie and Ruthie. Leo downed the second martini. "Look, lemme tell you something, Arnie—"

"Arnold."

"Arnold. Sorry. Now I don't want to make a federal case outta this, and there's no point in you taking this personally, but I gotta level with you. I'd rather be sitting in a pile of shit than be stuck here on this goddam plane next to you."

"Typical, Leo. Typical."

"This ain't my idea to sic you on Tina."

"For your information, Leo, I am merely trying to help."

"Actually, Arnold, the person I'm really disgusted with is myself. Just because my company owes Arnie Dalitz's greaser friends a ton of money I let them dump you and all your jerkoff theories on my family. Now what kind of guy would do a thing like that, huh?"

"It may interest even you, Leo, that there are some problems your daughters are having. I've seen it for years. There's an Electra complex that—"

"Bullshit. The only Electra I know about is this plane we're flying on."

"Leo, if you refuse to even consider the nature of your own daughters' personality adjustment problems then there's—"

"My daughters are more normal than you and I put together."

"I hardly think that normality is something you would want to comment on. I am merely making the point that I've seen indications of fixated drives on the part of your daughters. I might want to see them for further treatment back in New York."

"In a pig's ass you will."

"Fine, Leo. Just terrific. That does it. I'm leaving."

"I'd like that, Arnold. Especially since you're on a plane."

"Still the Neanderthal, aren't you, Leo? It's been the same since puberty."

"Pretty touchy, ain't we?"

"I am *not* touchy. I agreed to accompany you to Memphis as a favor. To help members of the family."

"Oh, sure you did. They bought you off, pal. Now they got their hands around your Freudian nuts and I'm the one who has to listen to you yodel. What's happening on the twenty-third?"

"Professional jealousy. Some members of my own profession are envious of my accomplishments."

"So?"

"So they're meeting on the twenty-third."

"To do what?"

"I really don't feel it's necessary to discuss it, Leo."

"Hey, Arnold, tell me what your price is. What'd Arnie Dalitz buy you for?"

"Mr. Dalitz is assisting me in my defense against jealous colleagues."

"What'd you do, Arnold? Take the piece of raw liver out when someone was watching?"

"You really are crude, Leo. You've never respected intellect. All you understand is loudmouth parties."

"What's wrong with parties?"

"Nothing, if you enjoy being a slave to your libido."

"Why is this goddam plane jerking up and down so much? Stewardess?"

In Memphis before Leo met Tina at the hotel, he had made up his mind to tell her all about cousin Arnold and the real reason he was there. But the moment she opened the door, staring straight into his eyes, her black hair swirling around her shoulders, longer than he remembered it ever being, all he could say was "God, Tina, you look great." And the instant he heard his own words he knew he had blown it.

They talked for almost an hour, spilling awkward pieces of conversation out into the silence of the hotel room, each of them smiling more than they usually did and taking care to say nothing that would offend. But when Tina left to go to the rehearsal, the whole conversation broke into fragments that replayed in her mind as a puzzle where nothing fit together. Cousin Arnold? In Memphis. The dink. Who just wanted to meet the girls. For a few minutes.

"What for?" asked Zoot when they took a break while the guitar player replaced a string.

Tina's reply went on until the piano player stopped and listened too.

"Hey, Teen," said Zoot when she finished. "You come out with a lotta hot air. But you still ain't answered the question."

"I don't know," she said when she finally replied. "And let's get back to work."

They rehearsed until the saxophone player got the tempo right on *Sweet Thing*. Then Tina departed quickly, saying she had arrangements to make back at the hotel, and the moment the door closed behind her, Clarence blurted out, "I'm smellin' a trick, I swear."

"Well, you genius you," grinned Zoot.

"This Leo character's tryin' to horn in on Ruthie and Christie." Clyde's voice screeched up an octave before he finished.

"*This Leo character* just happens to be their father."

"But Joe, I don't care. Ain't no one takin' little Christie away by some trickery. Ain't fair. Just ain't and you know it."

"Well, first of all, suppose we just do ourselves some research on this mind doctor. Hey, Daddy D. We're going to be needing a favor."

The big bass player who was packing his instrument into its case grunted. "I'm listening, Joe."

"We need to crank up the Beale Street telephone."

The Beale Street telephone was cranked up when Daddy D preceded Ivory Joe into a Negro pool hall just east of the Mississippi River and cracked a cue on the side of a table until the whole room fell silent, the players staring through curls of smoke. "Joe and the boys need some assisting. Some New York mind doctor is messin' where he don't belong."

Before the sun had set, Arnold Berman was known to all of Beale Street. Every bar and club all the way up to Nootie's whorehouse became an observation post, flashing signs that Arnold Berman never saw while walking, almost stumbling, a pale swiveling figure bobbing among the zoot-suiters with their pointy shoes, and the dudes with their watch chains the size of lariats sporting these women, these *unbelievable* tawny-colored women in dresses that could have been painted on, shimmering in the headlights from the slow parade of shiny cars going nowhere as their radios filled the air with this raucous, awful music.

It was timed precisely. On the third floor of the hotel, Zoot looked out a corridor window to a phone booth on the street corner where Clyde waited for the word from Daddy D's man at the bar across from Hernando's. When Arnold Berman passed Hernando's, the word was given, Clyde flashed the signal, Zoot said, "Do it!" and the bellhop used his master key to open the door.

Inside the room, Arnold Berman's possessions were swiftly assessed in the obsessive order they were arrayed. The socks in one drawer, the underwear in another. All laid out in symmetrical perfection. The pants hung in the closet with grays and browns separated. The pens and pencils lined up in descending order of size along one side of the small desk.

The bellhop was desperately trying to remember where everything went after Zoot sped through Arnold's possessions.

"What are we looking for?"

"Clues."

"To what?"

"When we find it I'll tell you."

The breath mints, the stomach pills, the laxatives and the Life-Savers were noted and left in their place next to the Gideon Bible. The sock suspenders were passed over as the folded shirts were lifted carefully and replaced in their exact position in the drawer, whites to the left, plaids to the right. "Nothing," said the bellhop.

"There's gotta be." Zoot sat on the bed.

"Damn! You're wrinkling up the bed." The bellhop swept his hands across the bedspread and suddenly stopped. Zoot looked around and saw his hands framed around a rectangular outline bulging up through the thick bed covers.

"And what to my wonderin' eyes appear." Zoot grinned and tore the bedcovers off the bed. The bellhop yelled for him to stop until he saw the book that Zoot pulled out from the tangle of sheets. It was written sparsely in French and adorned with photographs of naked women and men.

"Well, well, well, well, well."

"Oh my."

"Damn!"

"Man oh man."

"Not bad for white folks, huh?"

"You can't read what it says."

"*Read* it? You lookin' at some of the finest examples of fucking you ever saw and you're thinkin' of *words?*"

"What's this here?" The bellhop pulled a long brown envelope from the tangled bedcovers.

"*Dr. Arnold Berman,*" read Zoot, and then opened it, removing a letter. ". . . *Psychiatrists Board . . . Notice of disciplinary hearing on charges of professional misconduct . . . July twenty-third . . .* My, my, my, my, my!"

"Is that good?"

"Here's five dollars for your trouble, my man. And where's the phone?"

40

You can always smell a rat with Leo. Whenever he's going to pull something you can just tell. He gets different. Nicer, like he wants you to know that it's not really him that's doing what he's doing. It's the other Leo, the sneaky Leo. Not the smiley one with the goobery kisses that are supposed to make you be on his side in case he and Mother fight.

We get to Memphis and he's there. We find this out when we just get into the hotel room and he phones. Like two minutes after we get in the room. Which right away should make you know it's the sneaky Leo. Mother answers it and when she finds out it's him she gets real nervous. Mother never gets nervous talking to him but now she sure is. She has to clear her throat a lot. She tells him she has a cold. She doesn't. And she actually says it's fine with her if we stay over at the hotel Leo's staying at.

After Miami we thought she'd nail the door shut if Leo ever showed up.

When Leo comes to get us you can tell he's stalling. First he says he's going to Havana on Sunday. Then he says he's come here with Uncle Arnold. Like creepy Uncle Arnold was some big friend. Mother always used to tell Leo not to keep calling him a dink. But now it's good old Uncle Arnold and we're supposed to meet him. "Why?" says Ruthie in the same voice she uses when she says *fine*. Ruthie's practicing to be Mother when she does this.

She's got a lot of practicing to do. Leo just grins. Then he drops the big one. He does it with the old by the way Ruthie there's a letter waiting for you back in New York from some Dr. Lewis. Byron isn't it? As if Leo didn't know.

Now Ruthie's my sister and you'd think I know her but I don't. I mean I *do* know that she'll turn into an instant sap when Leo the sneak just says Byron's name. But what I don't know is *how* sappy she'll get. She's almost like a cat when you're trying to pour cream into its bowl. She might as well be rolling all over Leo's feet. But what really makes me smell a big rat is when he says gee we could always call Stanley and ask him to open the letter and have him read it to us.

Ruthie the brain can't even figure out that Leo probably had Stanley steam the letter open three days ago. He probably knows every word. But I know when to keep my big mouth shut.

Sure enough Stanley just happens to be at Leo's place back in New York when they phone. Leo holds the phone up to Ruthie's ear. She starts looking like Howdy Doody. Her eyes go real wide and her mouth moves but no sound comes out. Then she starts squealing. Byron wants to know if she'd be free for a drink in the second week of August. That's only a couple of weeks away. All of a sudden Ruthie just wants to be back home in New York. Forget the tour. Forget Ivory Joe. Forget everything except Byron. The White Pawn gets wiped right off the board by the sneaky King.

All Leo wants to do is take us back to New York after he's finished whatever he has to do in Havana. Nightclubbing probably. It's driving him crazy that we're here with Ivory Joe. And Mother of course. He keeps asking how things are going and no matter what we tell him about what's been happening he always wants to know more. It's always about Mother. And us too. He always wants to know if we have as much fun when we're with him. He asks like it's a big joke and he doesn't care about the answer. But he does. You can tell.

But do you think Ruthie has ever stopped to figure all this out? The brain? Or that Byron might not even be Byron? He might be Bruce. Or Bob. Or Barry. Or that Leo would cream Byron if he ever even went out with her? After all the lectures that Leo is always giving us on men? And a *drink?* No way. Besides milk even makes Ruthie dizzy. But before I can even say anything she's got this Paul Newman's photograph up there on the hotel wall. With the name Byron written under it.

Leo just smiles.

41

It gets worse.

Creepy Uncle Arnold actually shows up. Berman the Vermin Leo used to call him. But now they're hanging out together. Sort of. Ruthie and I can't believe it. There's another rat somewhere here.

Uncle Arnold stands there in the doorway of the room skinny and all hunched up looking at us with those leaky eyes of his. He's like Goldblatts' dog when Mr. Goldblatt is around. That's when it always gets this look like it's going to be beaten. Whenever Leo's around Berman the Vermin gets that look twice as much. You can tell Leo doesn't like him even though he tries to act like he does. They both smile but not really. And when Leo slaps him on the back like he does with Arnie Dalitz Uncle Arnold stops smiling real fast.

The phone rings. You can tell it's Arnie Dalitz just by the way Leo talks. It's all that hey pal stuff. But Leo is real fidgety like he doesn't want to talk with us around. So he hangs up then says that me and him should go out for a walk. Uncle Arnold has to talk to Ruthie. By himself.

Right away I jump and say no I think Ruthie and I want to stay together. But when I look over at her she's back mooning like a simp. Off in the clouds. The Byron clouds. She'd probably agree to jump out the window right now.

Before I can say anything more Leo grabs my hand and out we go. I say Leo how can you leave Ruthie with Berman the Vermin? This makes him even more fidgety and he goes roaring back to Uncle Arnold and starts talking with his lips together like they're a zipper. Uncle Arnold gets the flutters like Goldblatts' dog did when it made the mess in the lobby. Then Leo comes back and we're off down the hallway. His hand's sweaty. And his mouth is still like a zipper.

He takes me down to the Mississippi and we walk along by the boats. Leo rents a boat with an outboard engine and a man to steer it. We go out in the river and act like we're having a good time. Which is tough when he keeps looking at his watch. The good life he says. I just keep my mouth shut.

All of a sudden he starts yelling at the man to take us in. Like the boat is sinking. Leo looks at his watch five times before we get to shore. What happened to the good life I say but it's not such a smart idea to ask that right now. Leo's in a big hurry. He just about drags me back to the hotel. When the elevator doors open he roars over to Uncle Arnold's room. But all of a sudden he stops and starts tiptoeing back to his own room which is next door. He goes *shhh* and then opens the door like he's sneaking in.

When I get into his room he's standing there with a glass pressed to the wall and his ear on the glass. I didn't know grownups knew that trick. He's listening to Uncle Arnold and Ruthie and his mouth gets scrunched up. He keeps looking at his watch until he roars out and pounds on the door yelling time's up. I hear Leo making zipper talk to Uncle Arnold who starts sounding screechy. He keeps talking about phoning some judge.

I go over to Ruthie. What happened I ask her. But all she'll say is that she talked about Byron for almost two hours. Ruthie's a goner.

Leo grabs Ruthie. Now it's my turn with creepy Arnold. Leo keeps yelling that things will be fine. Not to worry honey he says about ten times as the Vermin closes the door. Then he smiles at me. I smile back. He says how nice it is to see me again. How he's always thought I was so nice. I'm waiting to find out what the catch is. He says why don't we get to know each other better. Oh sure I say. All I can think of is Leo with the glass pressed to the other side of the wall.

Creepy Arnold wants me to talk about myself. Usually I don't mind but not now. It's hard work. I don't know what to say. He wants me to sit still instead of walking around. Easy for him to say when he's sitting in a chair with a big notepad on his lap. His legs are crossed something like an insect's. He's been writing down everything I say. He keeps asking about my dreams. I can never remember any of them past when I brush my teeth. He gets upset when I tell him this. So he asks again. And again. I'm fed up. All I can remember is the last Abbott and Costello movie I saw so I pretend that was my dream and I start telling him about how there were bad men with knives chasing me through the mummy's tomb. *Knives?* He gets real interested and writes fast with the tip of his tongue sticking through his teeth.

He keeps asking me all these dumb questions until I just want to tell him to see the movie himself. But I'm up to my neck so I can't. Instead I just clam up. He says it's real important I keep going. I have some major unresolved complexes he says. What unresolved complexes? I ask him. There's a conflict between my id and my ego he says. My what? He starts drawing me a diagram of my id. I didn't know I had an id. I want to know if it's pretty but all he says is that it's having a tough time. I ask if it's serious and he says it can be. Like the measles? I ask.

Worse he says.

42

When Daddy D's runner brought the two tweed suits, Ivory Joe hung his on a hook in the room behind the pool hall but Zoot had to try on his suit immediately. "Already makin' me feel like an educated man," he said, fingering the coat with the leather patches on the elbow. "Doctor Zoot." He grinned. "Has a nice ring now, don't it?"

"You sure we ain't gonna lose Christie and Ruthie to this New York mind doctor?" Clarence looked up from the door which he was holding steady while one of Daddy D's sign painters traced lettering on the opaque glass. The letters spelled SEXUAL RESPONSE OFFICE.

"Clarence, quit talking all them low notes. Gotta think positively," Zoot said, trying on the tweed pants. "Damn! I swear! All them scholarly types must just itch themselves into a lather wearing this shit. No wonder they're all so twitchy."

The phone rang. Ivory Joe looked through the doorway to the pool hall, put two fingers into his mouth and whistled the place to a standstill. The last of the caroming balls rolled into silence and the players stood staring into the back room while the ringing of the phone suddenly seemed as loud as church bells. Ivory Joe picked up the receiver and hesitated before saying "Response Office . . . Clyde? I can't hear you."

In the hotel, Clyde whispered into the lobby telephone and nodded in the direction of Arnold Berman who had just walked out of the elevator, heading toward the front entrance. The bellhop took his signal from Clyde and then hurried through the crowded lobby. At the revolving door he asked, "You wouldn't happen to be *the* Dr. Arnold Berman, would you, sir?" It was the *the* that did it, that stopped Arnold Berman just before going into the revolving door and drew him back into the lobby, toward the telephone receiver that lay beckoning like a reward for *the* Dr. Berman. There was a phone call, the bellhop said. From Dr. Joseph. Surely he had heard of Dr. Joseph. *The* Dr. Joseph.

Ivory Joe scanned the silent room behind the pool hall, the faintest of smiles occasionally flickering nervously from Clarence, Zoot and the dozen or so pool players who stood, cues in hand, not daring to move. "Is this *the* Dr. Arnold Berman? From New York City?" Ivory Joe said into the receiver in a voice that Clarence had never heard before. It was a rich, firm voice that sounded to Clarence like it just had to know what it was talking about—this *was* the Dr. Berman who was engaged in psychotherapy, was it not? Fortuitous. Could a meeting among like-minded professionals perhaps be arranged? To discuss research. On a major study we are intending to use as a comparison with white people.

. . . *with white people!* Exchanged glances wafted the words through the pool hall as a jumble of tinny halting sounds spilled from the telephone. Ivory Joe looked up and smiled the same smile that Clarence remembered from whenever he was beating the rest of them in a poker game. "I think what you mean to say, Doctor Berman, is . . . 'Are we Negroes?' Yes. Yes, of course we are."

From the receiver came the scrambling assurance that that was fine, no problem, absolutely, fine, and by the way . . . what exactly is the nature of this study? . . . If you don't mind my asking?

"Oh I'm sorry. I thought you'd be aware of our work here at the Institute," said Ivory Joe with just the faintest hint of professional irritation. As he winked at Zoot. "It's entitled Sexual Response in the Mature Negro Female."

Half an hour before the eight o'clock appointment Arnold Berman left the hotel and the Beale Street telephone cranked up. He never noticed the succession of eyes watching his every hurried step of the way toward the pool hall. His progress was relayed with hand signals, phone calls and once a trumpet solo of *Take the* A *Train* that came from a Dixieland bar just after Arnold Berman passed by outside, taking off his tie for the second time, smiling quickly at every Negro who looked at him and trying to blend in with the crowds all around him.

In the room behind the pool hall Ivory Joe and Zoot waited. The phone call had come from Clyde at the hotel letting them know that Arnold Berman was on the way. While Ivory Joe organized the psychology books on the shelf beside the desk Zoot went looking for tobacco to put in the pipe he had just bought. The pipe swooped down into a large curved bowl that Zoot practiced holding with studied elegance, the way he decided a real professor would. In the pool hall he peered suspiciously into a paper bag that Lukie the runner held out. "What is this shit, Lukie? Looks like you been out mowin' somebody's lawn and trying to pass it as tobacco."

"I just wish I had me a lawn of this stuff. Be a rich man."

"Smells a little wiffy. Well I'll be damned. Shocking. A man of your high repute, Lukie. Now give us a pipeful. For the sake of academic research."

The phone rang a final time telling them that Arnold Berman was a block away, but Ivory Joe had already spotted him, a gangling silhouette holding a piece of paper and squinting at the street numbers hidden by the shadows.

"What's he doin'?" Zoot's face disappeared behind a small cloud of smoke from the pipe. "Let's get this road on the damn show."

"He's looking at his watch. For the third time. Now he's walking back up the block."

"Shee-it. Dude's on white time, you just watch. Don't want to be early. And don't want to be late. Right on the itty bitty minute."

At 7:59 the footsteps sounded on the stairs, an angular shadow fell across the opaque glass and they heard the involuntary murmur as Arnold Berman read the lettering on the door. Ivory Joe did not wait for the knock. With a dignified flourish he opened the door and peered through the bifocals. "How good of you to come. I'm Dr. Joseph. And this is my colleague Dr. Zootman."

All Arnold Berman could think about was how unorthodox it was—sitting in some Memphis office next to a honky-tonk pool hall with these two tweedy Negroes. But in a way it all made sense. This Dr. Zootman expelling the most astonishing smoke rings after sucking back on that strange-smelling pipe. But then it was different here. Not at all like being with those professional hypocrites back in New York. And what a rich untapped area of research! Who would have thought? And even more incredible was what they had done with their limited resources and the meager backing from this College of the South. Or whatever it was called. *Field research!* That's what they called it. And wasn't that *exactly* what those professional hypocrites on the board were trying to pillory *him* for on the twenty-third?

"What exactly brings you down here, Dr. Berman? Research?"

"Oh no, no. Just helping someone in my family."

"Really? A personal trip then."

"Well, not really. My cousin has two daughters that his wife has run off with. So I'm getting them back for him."

"You are?" Dr. Zootman's eyebrows arched. "How wonderful."

"Just how does one do that?" Dr. Joseph stared through the haze of pipe smoke, suddenly looking very serious.

"I'm making a professional evaluation of their possible personality disorders. Something the court back in New York can use. So the girls won't have to endure some rather silly journey the mother seems to be on."

"I see."

For a moment they said nothing, Dr. Zootman stroking his chin while Dr. Joseph just stared off into space. Somehow there was a silence even though the music from the bar across the street was loud, almost deafening. Arnold Berman did not like silences unless they were from patients. "I'm doing some research that might interest you. On the problem of cathected libido and the diminished quota of sexuality."

They seemed to be thinking it over.

Dr. Zootman smiled that enormous smile of his. "Well, basically, I always figured it all comes down to the size of the thing. If you know what I mean."

"The size of the thing?"

Dr. Joseph stood up. "Why don't we show you *our* research?"

Then the three of them, colleagues really, had walked down that Negro street, the same one with the crowds and the lights, heading to this incredible place they called Nootie's. And now, sitting right at the libidinal center of *their* research with all those dark-skinned women, prowling through thoughts he barely dared think of, Arnold Berman drank whiskey and slapped his thighs as he had never done before. And this Dr. Zootman liked him now, he could tell. The man was smoking this bizarre-smelling tobacco and laughing as he smoked it. Weed, he called it. And offering the pipe to him as he laughed at everything that was said. He had never seen anyone offer his pipe to someone else, not even in the faculty rooms where they blazed away with a dozen different tobaccos.

But these Negroes were different. And might take offense. So he took the pipe and puffed away and soon he started laughing without knowing why. He reached out and draped his arm around a passing dark-skinned woman, amazed and thrilled that she stopped and rubbed up against him. He couldn't believe what he had just done —in public! Or why he was giggling with this Dr. Zootman, who was sitting there pointing and laughing and stamping his feet up and down, yelling "Research!"

"Research!" yelled Arnold in return, laughing, almost shrieking, and not being able to stop. Not even when this Negro woman was pointing at the back of his shirt as more of them clustered around, staring at something and laughing. The woman, the succulent one, was suddenly tearing at his shirt, hurling him into fits of giggling as she tore it off him while straddling his lap. And then holding the shirt up so he could see the imprint on the back reading SEXUAL RESPONSE OFFICE inscribed backward in the still-drying paint from the door he had leaned against. Someone held a mirror in front of his shirt and then everyone seemed to be laughing at it.

Even he was laughing at it, at the horrifying thought of having walked around for all these hours with *that* on his back, but what else was there to do? When this woman was rubbing her hands across him in a way that caused tremors across his lap that had nothing to do with the giggling. And then, this Zootman reached around behind the woman, tugging at a bow on the back of her dress. It loosened and the dress burst away, spilling out a cascade of breasts, like ripe dark fruit tumbling into Arnold's face.

And in the single flickering moment of conscious thought that came and then vanished, he knew that finally he was beating Leo at his own game.

43

You can tell Leo wants to get going. But we don't want him to. He's probably stepping out. With a ladyfriend. Even if he is in Memphis. But Ruthie and I don't want to get stuck in this crummy hotel by ourselves while they're all out having all the fun. So we keep him reading the bedtime story.

It's *Cyrano de Bergerac*. The comic not the book. Leo showed up with a bunch of Classic Comics. *Huckleberry Finn. The Hunchback of Notre Dame. Ivanhoe.* Culture he says. He figures Mother should read them to us. But he does it better. He gets more emotional as the heroes get themselves into trouble. He adds stuff to the story and he even starts taking bets on what's going to happen. In Miami he gave Ruthie three to one that the Artful Dodger would get caught before Oliver Twist. And Huckleberry Finn was even money to be pulled off the river by the local cops and sent home. And I won four dollars on a twelve-to-one long shot that those people would make it around the world in eighty days.

But tonight you can tell Leo is trying to speed things up. He keeps skipping pages right where this fair Roxanne was driving poor Cyrano crazy. But we keep making him go back. Because Cyrano has got this big nose and Roxanne won't even look at him. He's got the hots for her Leo says. And he says that she's bananas over this clutzy Christian who goes to poor Cyrano to help him write all his love letters to Roxanne. Leo really gets into the story. He starts yelling that Cyrano has a nose bigger than Uncle Irving who owned the bakery. And we start cheering for poor Cyrano. And booing the bad guy, this Count somebody or other who wanted Roxanne for himself.

The crunch comes when this Christian gets poor Cyrano to write the words to make Roxanne go nuts over him. Leo really gets into it. He starts walking back and forth between the two beds flipping pages and reading.

Your name is like a golden bell
Hung in my heart
And when I think of you
I tremble and the bell
Swings and rings
Roxanne Roxanne
Along my veins Roxanne

I'm jelly. And Ruthie heaves herself back against the pillows and moans "Oh Byron!" Honestly. But Leo's the biggest simp of all. He looks like he should be Cyrano. Without the nose.

That's the problem I say to him. You never say anything like that to Mother.

"I did, too," he says.

"Oh yeah?" says Ruthie. "What?" Sometimes she sounds like Mother.

I'll bet you never told her she was pretty I say. Leo starts thinking.

"Of course I told her," he says. "Your mother was the prettiest of them all."

"*Is,*" Ruthie says.

"*Is,*" Leo says.

"Oh yeah? Why?" Ruthie says. She's going back to being the brain.

"What do you mean why? She just is that's all." Leo looks at Ruthie.

Then he looks at me. We don't say anything. That always makes Leo nervous. "Her hair," he says. "That long black hair. And those big warm eyes that take in everything when she stares at you and you know you can't fool her."

Not like the doxies I say. Leo sort of grins.

"Did you ever tell Mother her name was like a golden bell hung in your heart?" says Ruthie. She asks the kind of questions I want to.

"Sure," says Leo. But he knows he's not fooling us.

44

Leo walked out of the hotel and tried to remember what he had said to Tina back in the days when they were together. He had no idea where he was headed. He walked through the pools of neon into the human blurs that whisked past him on Beale Street. He was trying to recall what he had said on the day he returned from the war. There was a ton of *I love you's*. There had to be.

Had to be? He told himself he couldn't remember.

When Tina opened the door she showed just a flicker of surprise. Leo stood in the corridor. "Tina, there's something I always meant to tell you:

Your name is like a golden bell
Hung in my heart
and when I think of you

I tremble
And the bell swings and rings"

She stared at him. "Leo? You been drinking?"

But he just stood there grinning that same outrageous, infuriating grin that came from somewhere years and years ago, back when she would have run and thrown her arms around him. "Hey, I won't stay if I'm not wanted," he said.

"Since when did that ever stop you?" Their expressions remained frozen across their faces. And then she smiled. Barely. And slowly opened the door. Leo entered.

"The tour's going okay, I hear."

"Yes. Very well."

"Are you enjoying it?"

"Most of it. There's been some ups and downs."

"You'd be bored if there weren't."

"Are the girls asleep?"

Leo nodded. "I made Ruthie double-lock the door from the inside."

"You sure you won't have to cut a hole in the door and pass her food through it?"

"Very funny. I'll let you know in the morning." Leo grinned. "I was reading some stuff to them earlier. That's where I got those lines from. The ones about the golden bell."

"You're kidding me. Gee, I thought you came up with them yourself."

"Yeah, sure. Would you have believed me if I said I had?"

"Probably. Look what else I believed."

"Yeah." Leo stared at the floor. "Yeah."

"Leo, tell me again what Arnold's doing here."

"I told you, he's just doing some weird shrink-type study."

"So he comes all this way? Just to talk to Ruthie and Christie?"

"Maybe it's a study of the effects of pastrami sandwiches on sisters growing up on the upper West Side. Who knows?"

"You're the one who said you'd break his Freudian neck if he even came near them."

"Hey, come on. He's family. Bottom line."

"Leo, who do you think you're talking to?"

"Tina, now just be reasonable and—"

"Is there some reason why you don't want to look me in the eye while you're talking to me?"

"Yeah . . . I'm scared my nose is going to grow." Leo shook his head and almost laughed. "It's a scam, Tina."

"Why am I not surprised?"

"Okay. Okay. I got myself into a mess. I rolled a pebble down a hill and before it's halfway down it turns into a goddam boulder. After Miami I got nervous about the girls, that's all. So somehow Arnie got involved—"

"Leo, you're an idiot."

"—and he paid that dink to come down."

"To do what? To make sure they weren't turned into emotional cabbages?"

"Something like that."

"Since when do you need Arnie to pay for anything?"

"Since maybe when I'm into his guys for so much money that Morris is having a heart attack twice a day."

"The man is pure sleaze."

"Hey, c'mon. It's the way things work in the garment business. You know that. You think I like owing money to the mob?"

"Probably. That's your business, Leo. But Ruthie and Christie are *my* business. And since when does Arnie Dalitz, out of the goodness of his heart, airlift your weirdo cousin in here to tell *my* kids how life should be led? Give me a break."

"I told you it was a scam."

"But you didn't tell me why."

Leo hesitated. "He thinks he's doing me a favor. Putting my mind at rest. And you know something? He just might be. I gotta meet them in Havana."

"Why?"

"Business."

"What business?"

"Look, Tina, it's nothing illegal, okay? I don't want to go. So just leave it at that."

"Oh, Leo." Spoken softly. It was the signal that Leo always hoped for. The gales of emotion suddenly subsiding. Replaced by concern. And maybe more.

"I've been thinking a lot about the old days," said Leo.

"Me, too. I still care about you. Maybe more than I want to. But the problems aren't going to change."

"Like what problems?"

"Like you."

"Aw, Tina. I've changed. I'm not like I used to be."

"Oh yeah? When was the last time you stayed out till four in the morning? *Nightclubbing?*"

"Wha— Tina, that's got noth— Why are you even bringing up . . ." His voice trailed off. "Wednesday." They stared at each other in silence.

"Hey. No problem." Leo shrugged. He walked toward the door. "One thing I want you to know. And I mean it, Tina. I'm serious about this, okay? I did *not* come here just trying to seduce you, okay? Just so you understand. Okay?"

She stared and said nothing. Leo opened the door. Then he closed it.

"Come to think of it, maybe I did." He reached out to touch her shoulder, felt her shiver as something cut loose in the instant before they were embracing, kissing fiercely and sinking across the bed.

Until the pounding noise and the deep urgent voice at the door. "Tina!"

"Clarence? Clarence, I can't come to the door right now."

"You have to, Tina. Ivory Joe wants you to come right now. Says you don't have to worry about the mind doctor no more. He's up a tree stark crazy naked."

45

The debate over which of her girls Nootie should choose for Arnold Berman had gone on all afternoon. The decision was delayed while the other arrangements were being made—the phone calls from Daddy D, and the visits from the zoot-suiters, the sweetbacks and the pool hall gamblers, all hearing over the Beale Street telephone that something was up and wanting in on it. And most of them agreed with Lightning who said Lavinia was the only one for the job. She could wear out any ten ofays ever born and make 'em cry to come back colored in their next life.

At first Lavinia had played Arnold like an instrument, easing him up and down the scales, rubbing her breasts in his face one moment and backing away the next, giggling as he chased her around the room with spiraling fervor while the others cheered. She allowed herself to be caught, and slowly she danced up the stairs to the big room in the back, feeling his hands grasping at her breasts in clumsy lunges, kneading them like pieces of dough until he fell backward across the bed and tore the bottom part of her dress away with bursts of hysterical giggling punctuated by *Shh! Shhhhh!* Lavinia began laughing, too, undressing him as he flailed and grasped at the triangulation pushing against his zipper. She tugged off his clothes until his bony white body lay like birch twigs scattered randomly across the bed. His giggling shot through into laughter and rebounded back again as he clutched at her with one hand and at his florid erection with the other.

And when she spilled across on top of him, lowering herself with swaying motions and cooing smiles, a look of terror suddenly came into his eyes, and with a gagging howl he bolted out the door.

Leo followed Tina into the yard around Nootie's. Shug and Jubal, the two Negro policemen, were yelling at Arnold to put some clothes on and come down from the roof. But Arnold clung to the chimney, veering between laughter and panic, waving something at the woman who had covered herself in a sheet and was yelling up at him. "Skinny white bag o' bones got the whore's best dress up there," said Shug.

"Influence of the weed," said Jubal to the crowd that had gathered.

"And the woman. Peckerwood can't handle neither," said a soft voice from the crowd and they all laughed.

Tina wove through the onlookers. "Zoot, how come you're all dressed in tweeds?"

"Just felt scholarly, I guess." Zoot tried to look earnest.

"You have anything to do with this, Joe?"

"Just out taking the night air. Heard the commotion." Ivory Joe looked straight into her eyes.

"Absolutely," said Zoot, but the big grin took possession of the lower half of his face until he slapped it. "Damn. Face got a life of its own."

"Your New York shrink has got himself some problems with women." Ivory Joe handed Tina a sheaf of papers with NOTICE OF DISCIPLINARY HEARINGS typed across the front page.

Ten minutes later Leo was yelling into Nootie's phone, trying to make himself heard over the uproar as Shug and Jubal dragged Arnold toward the ladder while the crowd cheered. "You knew it, Arnie! You knew he was a fucking rapist!"

"He's not a rapist, Leo. Calm down, willya? He just had sex with a few patients, that's all."

"That's all! And you sic him on my kids?"

"Leo, Leo, he only goes for old broads. Every one of the dames he diddled was old enough to be his mother. One of them had four grandkids, for christsakes. What's all that noise?"

"That noise is *your* shrink, stark naked, being pulled off the roof of a whorehouse."

"Oh Jesus."

"You wanna talk to him, Arnie? Huh?" Leo stretched the phone receiver cord as far as it would go, holding it out the door. "Do you, Arnie?" He leaned out the door, then peered up at the bony white legs that were being pulled across the edge of the roof by Shug and Jubal. And suddenly Leo started laughing. "Hey. You know what? I've been waiting for this sight all my life! And why isn't the rest of the family here to see it too? *Now* they'd believe me!" He was laughing in a way Tina hadn't heard him laugh since before he went to Cairo. "Hey Tina. Thanks."

"I had nothing to do with this." Tina looked around for Ivory Joe but found Zoot instead, trying not to look at her, puffing on some huge pipe and humming *The Battle Hymn of the Republic.* With a grin that kept growing wider in spite of his efforts to control it.

Leo hung onto the phone cord, stretching it out onto the porch, using it for balance as he looked backward and laughed while Arnie Dalitz's voice sounded like tinny little rifle shots from somewhere far away. "Leo! Leo! For christsakes! What's so funny? Leo!"

"Hey, Berman! I got Arnie Dalitz on the phone. Tell him what a great job you're doing."

Arnold's voice was screechy now. The giggling came only in throttled little fits as he was pulled toward the ladder. "Mr. Dalitz! It's going great! I got everything the judge needs to get the girls back. Ha ha ha."

Tina stepped out of the crowd and Leo suddenly wondered if the heat he felt in his face came from her eyes. "*What* judge?"

"Oh shit," said Leo under his breath.

"Leo, you there?"

"*What* judge?" And the crowd echoed *What judge?* in shades of laughter.

"Tina, it wasn't my idea."

"Leo, for christsakes, just keep your fucking mouth shut. You're gonna make it worse. Leo? You listening?"

"You were using him to get a court order? Is that it, Leo? To take the girls away?"

"Tina, it's not like that. I would never have gone through with it! Tina, where are you going? Tina . . ."

LEO, JULES AND GEORGE IN HAVANA

46

Leo caught the Pan Am shuttle to Havana. One of the stewardesses was Vikki, who used to be Vicky when she was based in New York and wasn't wearing so much eye makeup. Before the plane took off she had told Leo she was no longer living with that man and she'd be happy to do his chart any time. Leo had no idea what she was talking about and decided not to bother asking. A few minutes out of Miami she was back saying that another passenger had been asking if that was indeed the same Leo, the guy from Frolic Frocks in New York who threw all the parties at the Waldorf. Leo looked back in the direction she was motioning and saw a man pretending to be engrossed in a magazine. It was Jules. Jules something-or-other. Leo's definition of a loser. A sad lumpy face with circles under the eyes that only enhanced the aura of untold humiliation shining from them like watery beacons. His hair was parted an inch or so above his left ear and combed up over the top of his head, lashed across his baldness in oily strands. Leo vaguely remembered Jules as being a buyer for somewhere important enough that his presence had to be endured at the parties. Leo turned away but not in time. Jules looked up with an expression of carefully planned surprise and gave Leo the big beaming wave reserved for only best friends. Before Leo could bolt for the washroom, Jules was hovering over the empty seat beside him saying things like Gosh, it's Leo, isn't it? When the schmoo knows exactly who the hell it is. And then actually *sitting* in the empty seat in the same instant he asks if it's okay to sit down. Suddenly all the anguished looks came back to Leo, the ones from the salesmen who were assigned to entertain Jules. The hardship post of the garment world. In less than a couple of elapsed air miles, it's right down to business. Divorce. Ethel has left. But hey guy life goes on. And then that big hearty laugh blowing out the same stale mirthless air. But hey guy Havana's where the broads are, now don't tell me *you* don't know that. Big cazungas on them I'll bet, huh? What a lucky fluke that we met like this, huh?

Jules had never been to Havana before. Or almost anywhere else. He asked Leo which hotel he was staying in. Leo pushed the recline button, slumped against the seat, and only answered the question when he found out that Jules was booked into the Capri. Jules had heard that George Raft the movie star was working as the official greeter at the Capri's casino. Ethel had always liked George Raft. Ever since they'd both seen *Rumba* with him and Carole Lombard years ago before they were married. *Rumba* was set in Havana, too, how about that, what a fluke, eh guy? With all those gorgeous women and suave guys. Jules was going to have his photograph taken with George Raft and send it to Ethel. Let her eat her heart out. She'd come around. All she needed was time.

Leo looked out the window into the clear blue sky and thought that Charlie the Blade was a genius, hiring a washed-up movie star to stand around and get his picture taken with dumpy middle-aged losers who'd flown a few thousand miles just to show all the Ethels of the world what they'd really lost. The Capri was knee deep in marks like Jules and no wonder. Definitely genius.

In an hour the plane was over the rocky northern coast of Cuba, turning west to Havana and the pincers of land that jutted out around its harbor. Jules was excitedly leaning over Leo, staring down at the patchwork of red tiled roofs and green plazas surrounding the wedding-cake dome of the Capitolio in the heart of the city. At the airport, Leo managed to lose Jules in the chaos of a band playing *Guantanamera* for the tourists. Ramiro, the driver Lansky loaned to Arnie Dalitz, was waiting with the Cadillac. Ramiro was thin, almost skeletal, with sunken cheeks in a long face and sinews where muscles should have been, but he lifted Leo's heavy suitcase as if it was a newspaper. On the Malecon, the wide boulevard curving along the shoreline, Ramiro honked the horn and yelled at the other drivers cutting in front of him. And then cut in front of them. It was the introductory part of the Havana pageant that Leo had come to accept as routine. Across the harbor was Morro Castle with the surf pounding against the rocks beneath the battlements. The castle sat in his memory, an immovable blot of silent horror since the day he had stood with Arnie Dalitz staring at the sharks swimming in slow circles below them. Arnie Dalitz had pointed out the chute emerging from the massive walls of the castle. In the days of the terrible yellow fever, the chute had been the fastest way to get the corpses down to the waiting sharks.

But it ain't only the old days, Arnie Dalitz had said, telling of how Lansky's people had disposed of some small-time hood from Buffalo. They'd taped his mouth shut, tied his hands and then hung him by a winch off the side of a fishing boat for hours one night throwing bloody horse meat into the waters just off Morro Castle. With flashlights they made sure he saw the sharks and then slowly lowered him into the water up to his belt line. Arnie Dalitz had laughed as he told the story. On every drive along the Malecon, Leo always looked over at the castle and was sure he saw sharks. He'd never been able to separate the two images. Ramiro swung the Cadillac onto a narrow street near the Capitolio, pounding on the horn as the street clogged up with horse-drawn carts and motorcyclists. They parked near the Prado and Ramiro led Leo under the big trees where the cobblers and street vendors called out in English and Spanish and men hunched intently over games of dominoes. At a small café, Arnie Dalitz sat alone drinking coffee. His greeting was more spontaneous, more Latin, than Leo had ever remembered. He grabbed Leo's arm, almost embracing him, with a big grin as they traded the mandatory quips. "Hey, Arnie, you running for office down here?" he said and they both laughed. But Leo wondered what was really happening. The big greetings, the grand gestures always made him nervous. In all the years he had known Arnie Dalitz, they never needed to hang billboards over their friendship. Everything was understood. Sometimes unspoken. The slaps on the back were for the stiffs, the marks.

"Georgie boy is ripe," Arnie Dalitz said immediately. "We let him win last night at the roulette wheel. He thinks he's on a roll."

"Hey. You don't even want to know how my kids are? I fly all the way from Memphis and all you can talk about is this idiot Goldin?" said Leo for effect. For needling. He watched Arnie Dalitz instantly weighing the options of his response.

"Since when are you a big family man, Leo? You can hardly remember your own kids' names, for christsakes."

"Have I showed you their pictures?"

Arnie Dalitz's eyes scanned him like a searchlight. Looking for the put-on. "The three of us. Taken in Central Park."

"That's nice, Leo. Real nice," Arnie Dalitz said without enthusiasm.

"I tell you, they're smarter than any kids I've ever seen. And funny as hell. That cousin of mine, the shrink, got stiffed by Christie so bad—"

"Leo, goddamnit, we ain't got much time," Arnie Dalitz said, looking at his watch. "We got the game set up at the Nacional in a couple of hours. We gotta talk."

Leo looked into Arnie Dalitz's smile stretched thin across all the years they had known each other. Those years counted for nothing. Not now. "Hey, come on. We been hustling a million games, you and me. Since we were two. So what's the big deal?"

"The big deal is that you're gonna skin George Goldin alive."

"So what's this got to do with me talking about my kids?"

"Who said it had anything to do with you talking about your kids? Leo, what is this with you, huh? I mean, what the fuck is going on? Miami was like a goddam nursery. And now with everyone from Herman to Genovese staring over your shoulder you act like all you want to think about is baby pictures."

"Arnie, they're not babies. They're nine and thirteen."

"Order some dessert."

Leo ordered the cream cheese and guava that he always had in Havana. Arnie Dalitz slumped back with his head down, staring ahead and twirling the end of his short cropped hair. Everything was in motion. His fingers drummed on the table. His leg jackhammered up and down on the ball of his foot. At the next table several army officers were drinking wine and pounding the table when they laughed. They wore high riding boots and britches and hung their trooper hats over the backs of the chairs. One of them was a major with slick black hair combed straight back and a precise little mustache that looked like two inverted teardrops, one flaring down from under each nostril. Leo had seen the major once before, striding across Calle Zulueta on his way to the Plaza Hotel. The major had been pointed out as the most fearsome hunter of Fidel Castro's rebel guerrillas back in the mountains and had his picture in the Havana papers several times, once shaking hands with President Batista. At another table were older, heavier Cuban men filling the air with the smoke of their cigars that rose into the slow overhead fan. Leo could always tell the Cubans from the Americans, especially in the summer when a lot of the men wore the guayaberas, the shirt-coats that the Yanquis could never wear well. Especially the mobsters who always looked like they were in a costume when they went tropical.

"Leo, promise me one thing. Just one single thing." Arnie Dalitz was still staring out onto the street and twirling the ends of his hair. "When you get into that card game tonight, you're gonna be the same old Leo. You're not gonna pull out the ba— kid pictures."

"C'mon Arnie."

"I worry, Leo. Believe me, I worry."

"You always worry."

"Not true. This is a big banana race, Leo. I want it to go right."

"All this for one lousy little song."

"Look, something you gotta understand. These days a song's better than a bank job. This ain't 'Row row row your boat' anymore, you know."

When Leo met George Goldin by the registration desk of the Nacional Hotel, there was the same lobby-filling hello, the grand slap on the back, the arm-clasping handshake and the piano-key smile framed by the carefully maintained tan. And weeks after the beating not even the surgical wires, still barely visible behind the teeth, detracted from the polished surfaces of a face that Leo wanted to laugh at. And to drive that smile a few inches back. But he returned the greeting, matching Goldin in loudness and backslapping. The lobby resounded to declarations of friendship. Everything had been arranged. Goldin had just spent the day at the racetrack where he won and returned saying that the horses had been good to him for the first time in a month. The track was secretly owned by Meyer Lansky, who sent word to put the fix in. On the night before, Goldin had bet on the baseball game. The Havana Sugar Kings were playing the Montreal Royals. Arnie Dalitz had scrambled to find ways to bribe the Montreal pitcher, but the game had already started. Havana won anyway and

Goldin collected. Charlotte was flown in from Miami. The good luck charm, Goldin had called her. She was told to say she came over because she missed him. And to phone every few hours. Arnie Dalitz took her calls on the patio of the big villa in Mirimar, the suburb where they had rented several houses not far from the Almendares River. For the first three days Arnie Dalitz had stayed away from the Nacional, deciding it was better if he was seen there only after Leo checked in. Herman Pinsky had wanted to come but was convinced he should stay in Miami. And several decks of cards were expertly shaved and then replaced inside the cellophane wrappers.

Leo sat on the balcony of the huge room he had been given, staring across the private gardens of the Nacional. His eyes followed the *criollo* lines of the hotel, its silhouette stretching out like an elegant and ornate barrier that blocked the chaos of Havana traffic beyond its walls and left only the serenity of the ocean beyond the gardens. Leo did not look down. He was practicing. His hands sped casually along the edges of the playing card. A Queen. He snapped the card down still without looking. The next one. An Ace. Then a ten, an eight and a Jack. Each card went into a different pile. His fingers skimmed the cards like a blind man reading braille. Only when the last card was in its pile did he look down and check his work. Except for a stray Jack in with the Queens, all the cards were in their right pile. It was the exercise he always did with a shaved deck. Like an athlete warming up. And no one could finesse the cards better. He stared at them until the last rim of orange daylight over the hotel faded from the sky.

"I'm not going to use a shaved deck," he said when they met in the lobby.

"I beg your pardon?" said Arnie Dalitz, a blankness coming over his face.

"I'm playing head on. Clean."

"Leo, tell me something. Did you leave part of your brain in Memphis?" said Arnie Dalitz, steering Leo into a corner of the lobby. "This ain't no lark. You've got to win."

"I'm going to."

"Oh yeah? What if your luck goes sour?"

"I can still beat him."

"You're out of your goddam mind. What's the point?"

"The point is he's a donkey. A four-dollar haircut on a ten-cent brain. I don't need any help to whip him. I want to do it on my own."

Arnie Dalitz was searching for the put-on again. After a while he said, "Have you ever stopped to think what they'll do to you if you blow it?"

They. Leo looked into Arnie Dalitz's eyes that had gone dead over the years, leaving only a grim darkness, the edges of tunnels that went all the way back to some private chamber of violence. A few, the true savages, were born with those dead eyes. But for the most, like Arnie, it was acquired. Leo grinned, knowing exactly what would happen if he blew it. "Nah. Not worth worrying about," he said.

It was George Goldin who initiated the game. Just as they knew he would. Like all such gestures, it was done in the lobby, in a voice ladling an oily graciousness which Leo returned in kind. He would *consent* to another game. A *favor*, Leo. For a *friend*. One of the rooms off the main casino had been set aside. It was all to look very casual. The idea was to drift in with a few of Lansky's best shills looking as if they'd just wandered by. And if Goldin had any strays he wanted to drag in, so much the better. The shills would blow them off after a few hands and then clear out themselves, leaving only Leo and Goldin.

Everything was ready. Leo and Goldin were warming up with quips around the roulette wheel. But a voice cut through the din. "Leo! Thank God I found you. I was sure you said the Nacional." It was Jules, stepping through the crowds and patting the top of his head to make sure the strands of hair were still lashed in place. "You know what? George Raft isn't there!" He waited for Leo's response. Leo just stared. Goldin looked over at Jules, fixing on the bright blue shirt emblazoned with flamingos. "A friend of yours, Leo?" Goldin said with that same sleek smile and slightly arched eyebrows.

"Yeah. As a matter of fact, a real good buddy. Jules, meet George."

Jules shook hands as if he was being admitted into a club. "Leo, can you believe it? George Raft was advertised. They said he was there every night. And he's gone till September."

"That's a problem, Jules."

"Problem? A disaster is what it is."

"What are you going to do about the photo you were sending to Ethel?"

"*That* I got covered," he said, searching through the pockets of his baggy slacks. "I went on a tour. Right as soon as I heard George wasn't here. Someone told me to go to Zanja. You been there?" Leo had been there. Everyone had been there at least once. Zanja was the section of Havana bordering on Chinatown. "Look at this. I had it taken at the Shanghai Theater," he said, thrusting a photograph in front of Leo. It was a picture of Jules embracing two of the fat whores who did stripteases at the Shanghai. The whores were naked and laughing. One of them had her hand inside Jules's pants as he lit a big cigar with a dollar bill. "Wait'll Ethel gets *that!*"

"I'd like to be there."

"Almost as good as George Raft. Ethel gets real jealous," said Jules. "And the house is in *my* name. Hey, Leo, listen, I heard of another place. Better 'n Zanja. Called Colón, where they got everything from women doing it with other women to you name it. Right on a stage. Wanna go?"

"Can't. I'm busy here. But have a good time."

"You're too busy to watch a woman doing it with a woman? Leo, you can't see that in Peoria, you know."

"My loss, Jules. Look, I'll see you around. We'll get in touch."

"What's going on here, Leo? Little floor show maybe? Don't forget, buddy, you owe me some good times from New York."

"Look, it's nothing. A few friends of mine are playing cards, that's all."

"Hey, I love cards."

"Jules, these guys are pretty good. Believe me. I don't want to see you lose your shirt."

"You know who you're talking to? I won a bundle playing Deke Kaiser last Fourth of July."

"Uh-uh. This is different. Look, I'm sorry but that's—"

"Oh, let him play," said George Goldin with a big smile as he adjusted his cufflinks. "Jules, I'm sure you'll give us a run for our money. That's what you're really worried about, isn't it?" he said, casting a knowing look at Leo.

An hour into the game almost nothing was going as it was supposed to. Jules was winning and out of six players three remained. When there should have been only two: Leo and George Goldin. Arnie Dalitz had casually wandered in just before the game started, been publicly persuaded to play by one of the two shills and spent his time purposely losing to George Goldin. One of the shills was a slow-eyed fat man from Cleveland who Lansky had brought in because of a mind that could calculate square roots, percentages and odds the way other men told the time of day.

It had been his job to drive Jules out of the game while the Cuban shill ran interference. But Jules left them all stunned. A full house. A low straight. Four sixes. And he bluffed impeccably.

Leo watched Arnie Dalitz and wanted to laugh. All the high rollers scrambling to keep up with poor sappy Jules. And Arnie Dalitz twirling the promontory of his hairline while the fat man from Cleveland nervously licked his lips and shoveled handfuls of *turron* into his mouth. Leo flicked at his cards and like a faint charge of electricity, something leapt through his fingers. The deck was shaved. He casually turned to Arnie Dalitz, who looked away. Leo understood. The shaved deck had been slid in for the fat man. He needed all the help he could get to drive Jules out of the game. It had become a shambles with the fat man and the Cuban shill struggling to win and Arnie Dalitz doing his best to lose. He was losing in order to let George Goldin make up his losses to Jules. If Goldin became discouraged or angry and dropped out of the game, it would be a disaster.

Jules sat in front of his pile of chips, his sagging face creased in smiles as he talked about card games he had played when he and Ethel had gone over to the Lippmans' on Friday nights. Arnie Dalitz just stared. Then he excused himself for a few minutes and returned, playing with tightlipped concentration as another round of free drinks was served. Leo knew that Jules's drink would be loaded with a shot of whatever would be needed to induce progressively worsening stomach cramps leading to diarrhea and fever.

But after another hour Jules still sat there beaming as he arranged his chips in neat piles, drank from the glass set in front of him and told Arnie Dalitz how his wife would be eating her heart out if only she could see him now.

. . .

It was days later that Leo found out exactly what happened. That Jules had been punched almost unconscious in the washroom when he took a quick break sometime after midnight. And that he watched the hammer pulled back on the pistol that had been shoved in his mouth. But there were no physical marks left. The punches had been buried into the flab of his stomach and the Cuban behind the pistol had been careful not to knock out any teeth. Jules had left the game exactly as he had been told to, whining that he was tired and wanted to go to bed. Even when George Goldin accused him of running out he just muttered his own insults in return, cashed in his chips and walked out of the empty casino in his flatfooted waddle that grew more pronounced when he tried to move quickly. Strangely there were no taxis waiting outside the Nacional. He hurried a few blocks through the fetid night and never saw the baseball bat that crashed across his head. The money was removed from his pockets and quietly returned to Arnie Dalitz while he sat watching George Goldin lose.

They played all night and in the hours just before dawn Goldin changed. The big smile had dissipated and the condescending words of encouragement had been drawn aside, leaving only the bullying panic beneath the mask as Leo carved away the pieces. It was only the two of them playing now and Leo forced his will upon the game, wanting it one-on-one with no shills, no marked deck, nothing that could ever drain off the sweetness of memories he had already decreed before their source was even conceived. He played carefully, relentlessly, allowing Goldin to win the crumbs then blindsiding him on the big pots. Goldin had yelled for Charlotte, his good luck charm, to be sent down. She was brought downstairs, irritably rubbing the sleep from her eyes and holding her arms in front of her to keep the flannel dressing gown closed. Her hair was in curlers and without makeup she looked like all the women Goldin had ever left when their features grew to remind him of his own age. Leo wanted to laugh as he watched Goldin staring at Charlotte.

By first light Goldin was nearly destroyed. His IOUs littered the table. Charlotte had been sent upstairs. And Leo sat back, casually flicking three Kings in front of Goldin's suddenly haggard face. "I understand you know my wife," he said.

"Your wife? I don't understand."

"Her name is Tina." Leo let him figure it out, staring him in the eyes, not letting go until Goldin slammed the palm of his hand on the table. "*She's* your wife? The one with the niggers?" he yelled. "You knew who I was all along. You're doing this for her."

"My wife and I are separated," Leo said with a polite smile.

"This is a goddam setup."

"Don't flatter yourself. The day I have to rig a game to beat some degenerate lowlife I'll switch to crossword puzzles."

"I'm not going to put up with this crap," said Goldin, standing up and unrolling his sleeves.

"Sit down," Leo yelled, leaning into the table, his eyes turning cold. "You're going to put up with all this crap until I tell you you're finished. I've had to listen to all your big time playboy bullshit until I wanted to throw up. And right now, friend, I'm holding enough IOUs from you to enforce my own way of doing things." Goldin looked around the table. Arnie Dalitz. Leo. The fat man from Cleveland. The Cuban. Silent stares. He sat down. "How you gonna pay these?" said Leo, holding the IOUs in the air.

"I have money coming in."

"You don't have enough coming in to pay Charlotte's fee for a night," he said, watching the resentment flicker through Goldin's eyes. "Or are you going to tell me that she's in love with you? Like all the others?"

"Stay out of my personal life."

"Kinda hard to do, George. When you're broadcasting it all over any lobby you can find." Leo grinned, knowing it was going to work. Just find the pilot light of indignation and keep throwing matches at it. Goldin's mouth was like a seam as he stared across the table.

"What do you want?"

"The money," said Leo, letting the IOUs fall to the table.

"Look, I've told you, I don't have it. You knew that when you took the IOUs. So give it a rest."

Leo shuffled the IOU papers, drawing out the moment. "Tell you what, George. I'm going to give you a break. I'll give you a chance to win it *all* back. But I don't think you're going to go for it."

"And why is that?"

"Because I don't give you credit for having any guts."

"Well, supposing we find out," said Goldin, glaring into the faint light that shone horizontally through the big windows.

"I'll play you for your record company."

"Are you crazy? One hit record is worth ten times what I owe you."

"But you ain't got a *real* hit, George. Not yet. I'll tell you what, though. Let's make it all worthwhile. I'll bet my company against yours. Winner takes all."

Goldin laughed and then saw Leo was serious. He suddenly became defensive. "That's ridiculous."

"Why?"

"It just is."

"Well, isn't this interesting. The big riverboat gambler here. Tell you what, George. I'll even make it safe for you. If you lose, I'll give you thirty days to raise the money to buy the company back."

There was a silence again. Goldin shifted in his chair. "Thirty days."

"That's what I said."

"In writing."

"Any way you want it."

"Deal the cards."

GHOST LOVER

47

"I couldn't get that wonderful song out of my mind. I kept hearing its sensual lyrics in my head. That driving rhythm. Almost erotic yet tender at the same time. And I said to myself, that song just *has* to be heard by the public. Nothing should stand in the way of making this transcendent classic into a record. Immediately," said George Goldin. His rich voice coasted along on the currents of its own power, yet somehow not matching his expression, which had constricted into estuaries of exhaustion after the urgently arranged journey, flying from Havana to New Orleans and then driving part of the night to the small Mississippi town where Ivory Joe and the Classics were performing.

"Now whaddya suppose that ofay was talking about?" said Clyde after George Goldin left and drove back to the white section of town.

"Fucked if I know," said Zoot.

"Money," said Ivory Joe. "Something's happened and he needs money."

They sat on the collapsing porch of the small frame house where Zoot had rented a room. The Mississippi afternoon heat pressed down. The red clay dust seemed to congeal in the moist air and settle like a glazing across the azaleas and dogwoods. Shadows crept across the edges of the porch where the flies broke the stillness and fought crazed aerial dogfights. From inside the house came the soft moan of its owner, Esther, who was in labor with her sixth child. She lay on her side across the bed covered only by a white sheet, her eyes closed and her arms wrapped around beneath her chin. Beside her, sitting on a chair, her elbows resting on her knees, was the old midwife. A stethoscope hung across her apron and behind her on a table covered with newspapers were the chipped enamel bowls awaiting the boiling water that Clarence was heating on the fire outside. Clarence had never seen anyone so calm as the old midwife. She sat staring at Esther through thick glasses, as still and as silent as if she was watching for a petal to fall from a flower. The whole process fascinated Clarence, and when Esther had said she would name the child after him if it was a boy, he had remained in the tiny room. He sat on a bench fanning away the flies and leaning back against the crumbling lathwork wall, waiting for instructions from the midwife. The thought of another Clarence in the world pleased him and when he saw George Goldin step immaculately from the taxi he decided to send this new Clarence some money when they all became really big stars.

Before the performance in the cotton warehouse, Tina and Ivory Joe drove around the town in the least conspicuous way. Tina drove while Ivory Joe sat regally in the back seat. They had seen harried white wives driving among the shacks every morning picking up their colored kitchen help. Because a Negro could never sit side by side with a white person there was no choice but to put them in the back of the big cars as if they were being chauffeured around. When Ivory Joe had come out of the shack where he was staying on that first Mississippi morning, he had burst out laughing. "Damn, I got to get me one of those," he said.

"I could definitely get used to this," he said from the back seat of the Buick.

"Forget it," Tina said, looking in the rearview mirror. Ivory Joe gave a little wave out the side window to no one in particular. "What do you think about Goldin wanting us to record *Ghost Lover?*"

"I'll bet there's a lot of beautiful tunes floating around Heaven that never got heard. Because no one ever got around to making them into records. Let's do it. While we *feel* it."

That night after the show they headed north and then east. They drove into backwater swamp roads reeking of primordial rot where the tupelos rose from the muck like a barricade. Christie was awoken by the smell seeping through the windows and did not go back to sleep until they reached the flat alluvial plain of the cotton and soy fields. The roads resonated with an emptiness that they all filled in their own way. Christie saw goblins riding out of the night. Clarence asked about robbers and Zoot wondered aloud what would happen if they met up with the Ku Klux Klan. Man, give me Harlem any day, he muttered. Least there they don't have these shriveled little white dudes dressed up in their old ladies' bedsheets runnin' around yellin' boo and stringin' up niggers. Yeah, said Clyde, but the only trouble with Harlem is it's your old lady that'll string you up. Using the bedsheets. Fine by me, said Zoot. When they approached the towns it was the DeSoto with Tina driving that went first, like a scout checking the terrain signaling with the brake lights that it was safe for four Negro men in a new Buick to proceed. The main streets of the towns were deserted. An occasional neon sign buzzed in the darkness. Confederate memorials rose up heroically, bronzed arms pointing to past rages and glories. Courthouses, silent and solemn, stood with columns that looked to Zoot like the bars of a prison. They crossed through Alabama, going into Tuscaloosa but avoiding Birmingham. Clyde and Clarence slept in the back seat of the Buick while Ivory Joe and Zoot took turns driving, and to keep awake they talked about George Goldin and his strange transformation. The man had shown up out of nowhere with a faceful of smiles and fine words. All of a sudden he was agreeing to everything they had ever wanted. He would not even think of putting his name down as cowriter on any of their songs. He had great plans for them. There would be television shows. Dick Clark and *American Bandstand* would be a cinch. And CBS was there for the asking. Look at the *Ed Sullivan Show*. They were snapping up anyone with a hit. Sam Cooke. Ray Charles. Fats Domino. And it could all be done in less than a month. It *had* to be. All they had to do was record *Ghost Lover*. Immediately. All the record distributors around the country were lined up. And the DJs had all been greased. Calling in IOUs, Goldin said. Over and over he mentioned IOUs. "Do you trust him?" Zoot asked.

"Course not," said Ivory Joe. "But at least this time we got it down on paper."

By dawn the cars had crossed into Georgia, spewing plumes of red dust behind them until they reached the paved highway to Atlanta. Just past the bridge over the Chattahoochee River they separated, each car heading for a hotel in a different part of the city. Goldin had taken care of the reservations and meticulously drawn the maps on his personal stationery with the two embossed and ornate Gs at the top. At the Biltmore Hotel, Tina led a somnambulant Ruthie by the arm while Charlie carried Christie up to their room on the sixth floor. It was somewhere in the middle of the morning when the bar of almost white light that had been crossing the room through the crack in the thick curtains reached Christie's eyes. At first she dreamt they were still in the car and someone was shining a light on them. She awoke with spots in her eyes. She stumbled over to a chair and sat staring at the telephone until she picked up the receiver and made a collect call to old Mrs. Weissman at Frolic Frocks, who yelled at Christie not to hang up while she phoned Leo on another line.

In the two days since George Goldin lost to Leo he had worked at nothing else but raising the money needed to save his company. Even before leaving Havana the answer was obvious. A hit record. *Ghost Lover.* If it could be recorded quickly enough and a copy hand-delivered to Alan Freed at WINS in New York, a chain reaction might be started. If Freed liked the record he would demand both an under-the-table payment for playing it on the air and at least one week's booking at the concerts he produced at the Brooklyn Paramount Theater. For which Ivory Joe and the Classics would be paid a maximum of two hundred dollars for the week. But it would be worth it. Freed was capable of forcing a song onto the charts through sheer repetition of air play, and what caught hold in New York would shoot through the rest of the country in a matter of days. An hour after losing to Leo, Goldin had phoned Freed from his room at the Nacional. They had done business before, and listening to the clipped voice drifting through the static of the long-distance lines Goldin was thankful he had always delivered exactly what he'd promised Freed. This time he held nothing back. His volley of superlatives came back in questions of dates and bookings and a demand to hear the record. A day later, after talking to Tina and Ivory Joe in Mississippi, Goldin began phoning the seventeen regional record distributors who wholesaled his records around the country. To each of them he promised a huge hit song on its way, complete with Freed's blessings and national television. He would give them the record for half price. In return they would pay cash on the day Freed first played the record on the air in New York. The money could be wired or delivered in person. But no one would be allowed even one day's grace.

Before he left Mississippi, he had verbal agreements from nine distributors with three others wavering. Easily enough to pay Leo and save his company.

All that remained was the actual recording session. From his address book he took out a tattered carbon copy of a list made by another record producer who had worked in the South. On it were the names of the radio stations that had been used as emergency recording studios by independent producers who could not get back to New York or Chicago. It was a crude way of making a record but more than one hit had come out of such a session. With the list placed next to a road map, he narrowed the choices to a station in New Orleans and WGST, the radio station at the Georgia Institute of Technology in Atlanta. Next to WGST he noticed the handwritten notation *Students—very cheap* and George Goldin decided that Atlanta would be a fine place to cut a record.

48

Leo had planned to pick up the girls and head straight back to New York with them. There was no time to waste in Atlanta. Morris was complaining about the work that was backing up and had left unanswered messages of distress in Miami and Havana. But at the hotel neither Ruthie nor Christie was ready to leave. There was a problem Christie explained carefully. "Ivory Joe is finally making his big record. Can we stay and watch? Please?"

"Only as long as we're back in New York for Friday, though," blurted Ruthie. Friday was the day Byron had arranged to meet R. Klein under the clock at the Biltmore Hotel.

"Since when do people make records in Atlanta?"

"Since Mr. Goldin showed up."

"You don't mean *George* Goldin?"

"Yeah. The record guy who's always dressed real sharp. The handsome one," said Ruthie.

"Handsome? *Him?*" said Leo.

"Not as handsome as you, though," said Christie instantly. "But he keeps looking at Mother like he likes her."

"Are you nuts? They hate each other," said Ruthie, disregarding Christie's fierce look.

"I thought they were sort of partners," said Leo.

"She says he always keeps trying to rob Ivory Joe."

"Are you sure?"

"Ask her," said Ruthie, grabbing the phone and dialing as she looked triumphantly at Christie. "We'll tell her you're here and you want to watch, too."

George Goldin had hired the Georgia Tech radio station for the entire evening, the only scheduling problem being the newscasts that had to go on live every hour. But he decided they could work around the problem. They were working around everything else with a staff who had never done anything more complicated than spin records and talk into microphones. There was no studio, only the tiny announcers' booths and the outer office filled with oak desks and chairs that Goldin stacked to one side of the room. When the musicians arrived there was no place to put the drummer so Goldin made a space for him in the hallway. The saxophonist had to be put behind the opened door of a closet to balance with the guitars and bass. When Ivory Joe and the Classics showed up, they rehearsed until the positioning of the two microphones had been adjusted at least enough to let the voices be heard over the instruments. It was while he was explaining the crude mixing procedure to the student technician that Goldin realized he had passed over something. He had looked around the crowded room and failed to register a face in the chaos. At the back, behind the glass window of an adjoining room that looked out over the rehearsal, was Leo.

Goldin's response turned to stone and he no longer heard the questions that kept coming at him, even as indignation sent him walking toward the window.

It was the first time Leo had ever been impressed by George Goldin. The man definitely knew his work. He moved with crisp control, listening to the instruments, adjusting their levels, correcting them. Unlike other areas of his life, he made no grand gestures, no booming pronouncements meant to fill lobbies. The musicians deferred to him naturally and the dialogue between them was the subdued jargon of professionals.

Leo had shown up out of curiosity more than from the urgings of his daughters, even though they had been unusually insistent. It was only three days since Havana and the Morning of the Third King as Leo now called it, when he had slowly turned over the King of Diamonds and watched Goldin begin to shake so hard he could no longer hold his own cards. And now, as Goldin realized that it was Leo staring at him through the glass, a look descended across his face like a conductor hearing a vile note. He walked the length of the room through the bursts of rehearsed sounds. "What the hell are you doing here?" he demanded through the glass. "Checking up on me?"

"Checking up on what?"

"I still have twenty-seven days to pay you the money, Leo. I don't need any reminders."

"Hey, George. I'm here calling for my daughters. To take them back to New York," said Leo, staring into that suddenly pained face and the voice that had reverted, spiraling into a whine. "So what's the big deal?"

"No big deal, Leo. I'm just telling you if you're trying to shake me up it won't work. When we lay this song down the money's as good as there."

"From one lousy song? You'll make all that money?"

"More."

"*More?* What the hell am I doing in the rag trade?" Leo kept trying to give Goldin an out but it was only the arrival of the four Negro singers that interrupted his self-righteous stare. The room filled with sly laughter and languid greetings between the singers and the musicians.

Leo felt suddenly like a spectator watching his own family in a life he knew nothing about. Christie and Ruthie were jumping excitedly around the man wearing the suit and the tie with the matching handkerchief, the one they called Ivory Joe. The clothes flowed easily, almost elegantly, around the man and Leo found himself looking at his own rumpled suit reflected in the control room glass. Tina entered, handed out papers that had to be signed, joking with an easy confidence. And what was all this? Why hadn't she been that way before? Instead of all the hard-edged stuff?

Leo stared at his own reflection in the glass. It had become a screen. His daughters were performers, projected across it and given funny things to say and charming things to do. And Tina was the leading lady, as dark haired and beautifully mysterious as anyone he had ever seen in the movies. In the commotion of easy laughter, the reflection in the glass looked back at Leo and was silent except for a cry that never sounded.

None of it was right. Not *any*thing. Not this performance where he was part of the audience.

And not anything since the whole Havana thing had started. Since when did Arnie or the Genoveses have to go to the trouble of fleecing a mark like Goldin in a card game? And then giving him thirty days to buy it *back?* They had other, quicker and more brutal ways of grabbing the company.

As Leo dialed the phone the first rehearsal of this *Ghost Lover*, this beautiful haunting tune that the Negroes were singing, floated down the hallway. He tried several numbers in New York, finally reaching Arnie Dalitz at the Icehouse. Herman Pinsky came on the extension phone and chuckled when Leo told them where he was. "And you accepted collect call charges for *this?*" he said to Arnie Dalitz.

"Why not? It's your phone." More laughter. Leo had never heard them so relaxed, so playful. Not since they were all hustling as kids.

"Is that *Ghost Lover* I hear?"

Leo stared into the phone, his thoughts tumbling. "Herman, how'd you know that song?"

"Hell, I know the lyrics as well as they do. Gonna be huge, Leo. Huge."

None of it was right! "He's gonna pay off the Havana debt with it. You know that, don't you?"

"Yeah, well . . . " Herman's voice trailed off. Saying, for christsakes, Leo, were you born yesterday?

"Don't sweat it, Leo." Arnie Dalitz's voice was suddenly cold and even. Saying meddlers get hurt, Leo. You know that. "You did your part. Leave the rest to us. Just get back here, schmucko. We'll take in the new show at the Copa. Sinatra, I think."

Leave *what* rest to you? Even before he hung up the phone, struggling to bluff his way through to the end of the conversation,

Leo knew. And wished he could tear it all from whatever memory he would ever possess. The whole thing had been so beautifully set up. Havana. Goldin. And his scramble to get this song, this *Ghost Lover*, recorded. They had it all figured out right off the goddam mark. They knew Tina and this Ivory Joe character would never agree to make a record for Herman. Tina hated him. So let Goldin do the donkey work. And then . . .

He was staring through the glass window again before he even realized he had walked back into the control room. Watching blankly as this weird music was being rehearsed until the student technicians had to yell for everyone to be quiet so they could read the six o'clock news.

And Goldin, strutting around the studio, not hearing the seconds of his own life ticking away. Not even figuring out that he would step off the plane in New York triumphantly carrying the *Ghost Lover* master tape and be murdered within a week.

49

Leo stared.

The quiet campus in summer. Goldin leaving, the tape under his arm. Smiling. Muttering great work. Brilliant. Love it. Talk to you next week.

"George! Wait!"

"Something wrong, Leo?" Said like the king of the goddam hill.

"Yeah. I don't think you should go to New York right now."

"Oh, really?" The full force of that smile. The perfect teeth and the tan mobilized to overwhelm with contempt. "Why?"

"People there are gonna cause you trouble, George."

"Sure, Leo, sure. Face it. You lost." Holding the *Ghost Lover* master tape up like a banner.

"George, they're out to get—"

"Leo." That same pompous smile. "Fuck you."

The Cadillac drove away.

Leo sat in the Atlanta hotel room feeling himself fill up with fear and listening to his daughters play in the next room. For the first time in his life he did not want to go back to New York. He stared out the window into the heat that shimmered off the asphalt roof on the other side of the street and saw Shapiro, *a crumpled figure contorted in the bottom of the phone booth as blood trickled under the doors and congealed in the fine powdery snow.* And wondered why the hell Goldin couldn't see the same thing.

"I'm packed!" yelled Ruthie.

"Me too, me too!" Christie backed into his room dragging her small suitcase with the pink plastic flowers sewn on the side. Her tongue was wedged firmly between her teeth.

"C'mere."

She circled him, her head tilted in wary amusement. His hand darted out, pretending to grab her tongue, sending her into squeals of giggling as he planted a kiss on her cheek. "Not the goober! Ruthie, help! Leo's doing a goober!" She wriggled free as Ruthie ran into the room.

"When are we leaving for New York?"

"Soon."

"Soon?"

"Maybe we should drive back. You know, see the scenery."

"*What?*"

"She doesn't want to see the scenery. She wants to see Byron."

"That's a week and a half from now. Just think of the fun we can have."

"It's a rat, Ruthie."

"Girls, girls. Please. This is your poor dear old father you're talking to."

"Hah! If you can't go nightclubbing, you go nuts. Watch out, Ruthie."

Leo stood beside the car, waiting for Tina to emerge from the hotel and say good-bye to the girls. He had wanted somewhere less public, where he could talk to her. Instead he found himself in the middle of the sidewalk, with the engine running and the girls clamoring from the back seat. "Tina, there's something I have to explain." And seeing that look come over her, the old 3:00 A.M. X-ray glare as he tried to wipe the perfume away and get her to understand that he would have been back hours ago if the damn car hadn't broken down and . . . "The thing with Goldin isn't going to work out."

"What are you talking about?"

"Arnie's people are going to move in."

"Like they did with your cousin Arnold?"

"Tina, this is different. This is dangerous."

"Oh Leo, please."

50

Last year when we were in school almost our whole class became blood brothers. But instead of blood we used red ink. Even two kids who were wearing casts on their arms became blood brothers when Louie Makin made them stand on different sides of the A-bomb shelter fence and put their casts together. Then he put red stuff on their casts and told them to wait. It was red glue but they didn't know it. Then he rang the A-bomb bell that Mr. Alwyn had just put in in case the Communists dropped a bomb on us. Everyone yelled and ran around like this was really it. But those two morons were glued together and banged their casts back and forth yelling like they were being murdered. They banged so hard on the fence that they tore it down. One of them wet himself. But even when it was all over they were still blood brothers which meant they had to keep their promises.

Which is why I make Ruthie into a blood brother. I make her promise that no matter what happens she won't conk out on me just when I know we're real close to getting Mother and Leo back together. I can smell it. But I can also smell Byron and it makes me nervous. Even though she's a brain she'd give it all up just to be back in New York when Byron gets there. Brains don't think like the rest of us. They can do dumber things than ordinary people. And there's no arguing with them. If Ruthie thought Byron thought the sky was green she'd tell you it was. And she'd prove it to you too.

So that's why I made her a blood brother. Now she can't get out of it.

When Leo found out that Ivory Joe was making his record here he wanted to watch too. Which is weird because Leo never wanted to see them sing before. But you could tell this is different. *Real* different. Because Leo's never been in the same room as Mother and Ivory Joe and all the others. Everyone is very weird. Like pretending the other person isn't there.

Leo stays weird even when we're driving to the place where Ivory Joe and the others are singing tonight. It's still daylight and we drive up Peachtree Road until it turns into a highway and we keep following this map that Mother had made for everyone. Leo is looking around and saying boy what a great country this is here huh? I say wait a minute there's nothing here but trees and fields and shacks. And creepy moss hanging down in some places. It makes Camp Wig-A-Mog look like Times Square. But Leo just keeps on saying how great it would be to spend some time here.

All of a sudden we pass a police car sitting on a side road. Leo says hey let's play the policeman game and that's when we know we're in big trouble. *We* always have to talk him into playing the policeman game. Now he's the one who wants to do it. It's like he *wants* to be caught.

"Leo I don't think this is such a good idea," says Ruthie with her head turning all around like she was Mrs. Fineman's budgie. "The policemen here aren't like the ones back home."

"Yeah," I say. "They're all squinty-looking. They could keep you here for weeks."

But Leo just looks pleased when I say this. I don't get it.

We start yelling at him that we don't want to play that game. Both Ruthie and I are jumping up and down in the seat telling him to keep going. Leo doesn't know what we know now. Which is that you don't play the policeman game in places like Georgia. The policemen here have their own game and you really don't want to play with them. We tell him that but he doesn't hear us. He just looks in the rearview mirror and starts to make little laughing noises. He keeps driving and not paying any attention to us. We come up over a hill and see this dinky little town off in the distance. Just down the road is some big warehouse with a bunch of cars around it. That's got to be where they're singing. But Leo's still looking behind him too much to see what's in front. Ruthie and I get stiff necks looking one way and then the other. We think we're home free. But then Leo really does it. He steers right off the highway and plows over this field.

Ruthie and I are both yelling at him to get back on the road but he's laughing like someone told him a joke that we never heard. Sure enough we hear a *veeeeerrrrruuuuugh* noise behind us and I just put my hands over my eyes. I can't take it anymore. We're bouncing all over the field. I know what we're in for. Some big fat old policeman who looks like he just ate something bad is going to get out of the police car. Or else it'll be one of those skinny policemen who look squinty and angry like a chicken that lost its feathers.

But when I open my eyes it's not either. It's this real young policeman who gets out the car with eyes like new quarters. Everything about him looks real new. He comes over toward us looking almost as scared as we are. He's sort of good-looking and Ruthie is staring at him real closely. I know what she's thinking. Byron. She's hoping Byron looks like this.

"Guess you didn't mean to do this, huh?" says the young policeman in his real thick Georgia accent. When he talks it sounds like someone playing guitar strings one at a time.

"Matter of fact, I think I did," says Leo with a big smile. Ruthie and I look at each other. This is definitely not the way the policeman game is supposed to be played. By now he should be babbling about how he's so emotional just to be with his two little girls.

"You did?" says the young policeman looking sort of confused. "Why?"

Leo scratches his head and thinks about this for a while. "I don't know," he says. It's Leo that's not playing the game. You're supposed to help the policeman out. Give him something to make him want to let you go. But Leo just makes it worse. "To tell you the truth, I sort of felt like it," he says.

"Um, look mister, I think it'd be better if you pulled over off this here field."

"Sure thing," says Leo who drives over the rest of the field and parks on the edge of the road.

You'd better start playing the policeman game for real I say but Leo just pats my head. I hate it when he pats my head. I feel like a cat. The policeman follows and then gets out of his car and asks Leo for his driver's license. He looks at it. "Hey, New York, huh?" he says. "I lived in New York for two years. Long Island. That's where the wife's family is from."

"Where on Long Island?"

"Just outside of Glen Cove."

"It's pretty up there."

"Sure is, I tellya," says the young cop. "Didn't want to come back."

"So why did you?" Leo is really getting into it. He is such a rat sometimes. Here he didn't even try and he's going to win the policeman game. You can see it coming.

"My Uncle Frank phoned. Offered me this job here. Three months ago."

Another police car comes driving up. It's coming from the warehouse and it does a big circle on the road and stops in front of where we are. "Have the feeling this is Uncle Frank," says Leo. Right away I know we're in trouble. This real squinty policeman gets out. The chicken type. He's old and skinny with a collar that's way too big for him. It looks like he's sticking his head up out of a sewer. He comes walking over with all the stuff on his belt clanking away.

"What's the trouble, boy?" he says.

"No trouble, Uncle Frank," says the young policeman who's all of a sudden sort of nervous again. But this Uncle Frank takes Leo's driver's license and looks at it. "What are you doing here?" he says.

"Going for a drive," says Leo. You can tell Leo doesn't like him.

"Now I'm gonna ask you again. And you're gonna tell me straight without any sassin'. What are you doing here?"

Leo just stares for a second. "We're going for a drive to see some people we know sing."

"You mean like nigger-type people?" says this squinty. "Who're coming in here like they own the whole pot of lard. When they're just liable to end up cookin' in it." He looks down at Leo's driver's license. "But that figures with a name like this. Niggers an' Jews I mean."

Ruthie starts yelling like crazy. "You just watch your big fat mouth," she says. My sister's definitely not your usual brain.

For some reason I've got to join in too. Yeah you little runt I shout out the window. My father'll beat you to a pulp if you don't watch out. Leo just looks from the squinty to me and sort of smiles. Then he pats me on the head again and sort of smiles some more while the squinty starts yelling something. But you can't hear too much because another car drives by real slow with the radio turned up loud.

It's the Buick. Zoot sticks his head out the window with that big grin of his where his face looks like it's hiding behind his teeth.

"Well, well," says the squinty. "My lucky day."

51

They were late leaving Atlanta because Clyde had turned the Georgia Tech washroom into a laundry, insisting their shirts needed to be spotless for the show that night. When Ivory Joe walked slowly through the washroom, saying nothing, but making a clicking sound with his heels on the marble floor, Clyde yelled out the window to Clarence telling him to get off his fat ass and start bustin' suds too.

Ivory Joe and Zoot sat and waited with all the doors of the DeSoto open. "What do you think of our man Goldin?" Zoot asked.

"Kind of man who goes in a revolving door behind you and comes out in front of you." Ivory Joe was reading a letter. "He says here we're gonna get the Tivoli in Chicago. The Earle in Philly. The Apollo. The Howard. All the big theaters. Top of the bill. Up there with Fats Domino, Ray Charles, Little Richard."

"You believe him?"

"Yeah. If *Ghost Lover* is a hit. But any fool could get bookings then."

"You see him talking to Ruthie and Christie's daddy? I'm wonderin' if they got some deal cookin' that we don't know about. I tellya, something smells."

"Gonna be us if we don't get out of here. *Clyde!*"

It was late afternoon when they left. The drive north to the hill country town near the borders of Georgia and the Carolinas would take right up to showtime. Clyde kept computing their arrival against the time needed for their shirts to dry. In daylight at sixty miles per hour with average humidity it took an hour for the shirts tied to the outside of the car to dry. But now with the light fading, Clyde was opening the side window every few miles and muttering about going onstage with damp shirts until Zoot told him to forget it. Settling back into the rear seat, he contented himself with sneaking looks at the laundry every few minutes and asking questions about Nat King Cole until Ivory Joe and Zoot exchanged glances, turned up the radio and started singing aimlessly. Ivory Joe kept checking the rearview mirror, watching Clarence, whose eyes soaked in every fear, every uncertainty. The news that Nat King Cole had been pulled off a stage in Alabama in the middle of a performance had flashed through the circuit of singers. Depending on who told the story, Nat King Cole was either beaten badly or merely shoved off his piano bench. Was too injured to continue the performance or just shaken up by the white attackers. Was booed by the Ku Klux Klan in the theater or cheered by the mixed audience. The story ebbed and embellished itself with every telling and Ivory Joe had carefully shielded Clarence with diversions when the subject came up. Clarence was going into one of his cycles. All he wanted to do was go home. Back to Harlem. Back to crowded streets filled with people he didn't know. Where no one made you stand up in front of strangers who terrified you.

For a while Clarence had enjoyed the tour, but somewhere just before Mississippi, Ivory Joe had begun seeing that flicker of uncertainty return to his eyes. After every performance Ivory Joe had been careful to make it all seem easy, fun even. Something to be looked forward to the next night. Zoot had instantly joined in with his sly jokes that made Clarence laugh in spite of himself. Only Clyde could not understand what was happening. No matter how carefully it was all explained to him, he still chattered away about the Klan or the burning crosses or Nat King Cole and couldn't figure out why no one talked to him.

"So what happened to Nat King Cole?" said Clarence, even though he'd heard the story three times before.

"Nothing," said Ivory Joe. "Matter of fact, he might be showing up to hear us this evening."

"You shittin' me, Joe. I can tell."

"Swear to God."

"Yeah, but he's going to be disguised as a white man wearing a sheet over his head," said Clyde with his high whinnying laugh.

"Hey Joe, let's go back to Harlem, huh? I mean like now." Clarence leaned over the back of the seat, grabbing Ivory Joe's shoulder.

"Hey Clyde, why don't you just hang outside with the laundry for a while?" said Zoot, turning up the radio as Clyde laughed. They drove in and out of the sunlight that was settling behind the hills until they came up over a hill and saw two police cars on the side of the road. "Hey, I.J., slow down. Don't that look like Christie's old man getting pushed outta shape by the cops?"

"Stop," said Clarence immediately.

"Stop? You crazy, Clarence?" said Clyde. "Them cops gonna eat you for breakfast."

"Christie's in trouble! Ruthie too!" shouted Clarence, swiveling and kneeling on the back seat, straining to see what was happening.

"Easy, man. Nice and easy," said Ivory Joe, rolling down the window and smiling. "We got ourselves an itty bitty old cop and a Boy Scout here," he said under his breath. In the other car he saw Christie waving them away. The older policeman was walking toward them when Leo stepped out of the car.

"You're nothing but an anti-Semite," Leo said.

The older policeman whirled around. "I don't need no Jew cussin' at me, mister. You just made one big mistake. Billy, you watch him."

He turned back. Zoot's smile had faded. "You with them?"

"I guess we are," Zoot said, giving a little wave to Christie and Ruthie, who just stared.

"Well now, what's all this here?" he said, fingering the shirts hanging from the side of the car. "White flags?" He laughed and walked around the car. Clyde peered wide-eyed over the edge of the window at the shirts he had washed.

"This *was* clean laundry," said Zoot.

"Well, I think we should see *all* your laundry, boy."

Ivory Joe's hand was resting on the steering wheel. It went up quickly in a silencing motion as Zoot was about to reply. None of them spoke. Ivory Joe stared.

"You boys deaf?"

"We are performing tonight. Right over there. They're waiting for us."

"Lotta people waiting for you. North Georgia White Citizens Council waiting for you. Heard tell the Klan's waiting for you. Had it with all this nigger music. Had one of your type come through here not two weeks ago. This homo-type. Little Richard something or other."

"Sheee-it, not again," muttered Zoot.

"Whose car is this?"

"Ours," said Ivory Joe.

"Lemme see the papers." Ivory Joe nodded to Zoot, who opened the glove compartment and pulled out the registration papers, handing them to the policeman.

"Well, well. Ain't your car after all, now is it? Looks like what we got here is a case of automobile thievery. This belongs to one Tina Klein."

"We switched cars. She's driving our DeSoto," said Ivory Joe.

"Now who is this *she*?"

"My wife," said Leo, trying to sound as bored as possible.

"My, my. You go letting your wife consort with these coloreds? I wouldn't let my wife consort with the coloreds."

"Have you talked to her about it lately?" said Leo with a tight little smile.

"Awright," yelled the policeman. "Let's just take a look at all this laundry. You too, *Klein*." Which he pronounced Klaa-ine.

"Know what I'd do if this was New York?"

"Well that's the beauty of it all, now ain't it? This *ain't* New York."

"Billy, tell Uncle Frank here how much he'd love New York. Harlem especially."

"Billy!"

"Sir!"

The field soon became a collage of white on green. Laundry was spread out across the grass. Every suitcase was opened. Every item inside was removed and spread out. Toothpaste next to socks. Shirts next to music sheets. Underwear. Maps. Tuxedoes. Ties. Vests. Bottles of lye. Hairbrushes. Billy, the young policeman, walked gingerly through the maze, stepping around whatever he encountered. The older policeman walked right across it all, holding the shotgun he took out of his police car. Mud stains were left across the shirts and tuxedo jackets. In the distance, at the warehouse, a crowd gathered, watching. Around the field another crowd gathered, laughing and making loud remarks of encouragement whenever the policeman walked over any piece of clothing. Christie and Ruthie stood holding their father's hands and staring across the debris at Ivory Joe, who slowly shook his head when he caught them looking at him, watching for a sign.

"What a jerk," said Christie, in a voice loud enough to be heard.

The policeman ignored everything but Clarence's trembling, which had become too obvious.

"Got something to hide, boy?" yelled the policeman, holding his gun in front of him. Clarence pulled his chin in, folding his top lip across the lower part of his jaw and shaking his head, his eyes turning instantly watery. "Don't you hear, boy?"

"He's deaf and dumb," said Zoot.

"In a singing group?"

"He does rhythm."

The policeman thought about it for a moment and then nodded. In the distance the band hired for the evening was standing outside the warehouse practicing *Train to You*. "Key of G," yelled Ivory Joe and from the distance someone yelled back and waved.

The policeman circled back angrily. "I could charge you with litterin'," he said, pointing at the field. He stopped in front of Clarence. "You know that?" Clarence nodded as Zoot reached up behind him and put his hand on the back of his shoulder. "And I'm still inclined to do that. If I see any damn jungle music goin' on in there. We're gonna put a stop to you people comin' down here. For once an' fer all. Hear? But I'm gonna hold this Mr. Klein. You're charged with trespassin'. Till we investigate these here tire marks on the field. Now this investigation should take us at least till we see what kind of music your boys are gonna make over there."

Leo and Ivory Joe stared at each other across the field strewn with clothing. "They are not my boys," Leo said, pronouncing every word carefully.

"Well, now, they must be," smiled the policeman. "Here they are ridin' round in *Mrs. Klein's* automobile. Now what in hell is goin' on if they ain't yours?"

"Damned if I know," said Leo, returning the smile and motioning for Christie not to say anything.

"Well, then, you'd just better hope they know their place."

They left everything but the music sheets. The police car, with Leo in the back, had driven across the clothing in a wide circle as it turned around. There were cheers from some of the onlookers while others stood silent, impassive and watching them. Ivory Joe knew that the biggest problem was that it all looked like a joke. With this goofy old cop. About as frightening as a scarecrow. Until he picked up the gun and stood near the cheering section. It was all like stepping into a ring against a paunchy old opponent but knowing that somewhere beneath that shambling, disconnected exterior there was still the wiring to connect with a right hook that could put out the lights.

And the kid cop, Billy, wandering around looking both stern and apologetic at the same time. Stepping carefully over fragments of clothing while Leo was reassuring his daughters, telling them everything was going to be fine, that their mother would be along soon to take care of them. Ivory Joe had walked around the full circumference of tattered cloth as Leo got into the police car. "Probably see you again," said Leo.

"Probably," said Ivory Joe.

"What are you planning to do?"

"Don't know," said Ivory Joe, looking at the field of clothing.

"Yes you do," said Leo, staring at him and not letting go.

"You're right. I do."

In the back of the warehouse, with the audience already whistling for the show to start, Clarence was shaking too hard to hold a steady note when he sang. Christie and Ruthie alternately broke into tears, asking what was going to happen to Leo, while Clyde paced in circles saying he couldn't go onstage dressed in his ordinary clothes. Ivory Joe separated them, putting Clyde with Zoot and taking Clarence aside gently and then suddenly turning on him in a quiet fierce voice. When Tina arrived minutes later, Clarence was earnestly explaining to Christie that everything would be fine, that he would protect her. It was explained to Tina what had happened and decided that she would go to the jail in the Buick. Ivory Joe insisted that Charlie keep the two girls near the backstage door where the DeSoto was to be parked. Then looking through the curtains as the band stretched, he said, "We're going to convert the cops."

"How we gonna do that?" said Clyde, brushing at an unseen spot of dirt on his pants.

"We're gonna have ourselves a regular old barn burner."

52

From the jail cell Leo could hear Tina's voice. The words were muffled by the heavy doors and the snoring of the drunk in the opposite cell, but her voice sounded in notes and phrasings of theatrical anger that made him suddenly realize how much time had passed. He couldn't remember exactly. After the war? Or even earlier. When she was picketing his building. When he was so attuned to this voice of hers with its union of conviction and anger. Among the friends he grew up with, anger was merely another weapon, a device used when necessary for self-preservation. With Tina, her fury was an extension of belief, and time had dulled Leo's strange pride in her independence. It was like having something untamed that was his alone. A long time ago. Before it all sank into the banalities of domestic feuding.

The snoring abated as the drunk in the opposite cell turned over on his side. He was the only other prisoner and wore an expensive but baggy seersucker suit, a wide maroon tie with handpainted ducks on it, and a battered fedora that now almost covered a shiny face, its brim resting on a small hooked nose. Now he could hear Tina threatening the policeman with the wrath of every elected official who could descend upon him. *Governor Talmadge! Get him on the phone or I will.*

It was everything that ordinarily hardened the resolve of any southern lawman, providing the joy of watching sputtering northerners demand their rights in this, a sovereign nation still at war. But this cop, this Uncle Frank, was retreating. Leo could hear his voice turn raspy with exasperation, not at all like the curling, taunting drawl when he had driven Leo to jail, cruising slowly past all the red brick storefronts, the staring men in overalls and shapeless peaked caps. Uncle Frank was no match for Tina, yelling that all he was doing was keeping the peace. And opening the heavy door letting Tina march in. They looked at each other through the bars. The policeman remained in the doorway until Tina turned and stared at him. "I've been thinking of something," Leo said to her when the policeman left. "You know, we should be married."

"It would be a disaster. Trust me," said Tina, smiling but unable to sustain the smile. She reached through the bars and pressed her hands around his arms. "Oh, God, Leo." On tiptoes she forced herself against the bars and tried to kiss him, her lips barely able to brush against his face. They remained touching one another until the drunk rolled over and called out. "*Edith!*" yelled the drunk. "Edith, I'm sick of your father."

"I can call Arnie Dalitz for you."

"You hate him."

"No, Leo. *Despise* him. But he'd get you out of here."

"These places don't work the same as New York."

"You underestimate his sleaziness."

"Oh no I don't."

"And there's another reason why it would be a disaster. Your friends are thugs. I never could stand them."

"Haven't we been down this road before?"

"Yes. But somehow it's more enjoyable when you're behind bars and can't just get up and leave. Did you really drive over the field?"

"Of course."

"Oh, Leo."

"Hey. I was overcome by the torrent of emotion. By the sheer thrill of seeing you again. Your name is like a golden bell that—"

"Leo, it's your wife you're talking to."

"Yeah," said Leo with a smile that was somehow serious. "I know."

"*Edith!*"

"Hey, come on," said Leo. "We did better than him and Edith. Hell, look at the great kids we raised . . . Okay, *you* raised."

"Leo, our great kids are over with Charlie the driver right now. I want to get them out of this creepy little place."

"Why did you even book yourselves into this dump?"

"What did I know about where we play? We phone in to the Weiman office. They tell us where to go. And we go. It's that simple."

"Doesn't look too simple."

"It's not. It's a lot of work. And worry."

"So is it worth it?"

"If *Ghost Lover* turns into a hit—yes. We own the song. Not Goldin."

And I will have sold you down the river, he thought. Turned over Goldin's Havana IOUs to men who will hold a gun to your heads and tell you *they* now own his company. And pull the trigger if you don't like the terms. "You must feel good about it."

"I do. It's really important to me."

For an instant Herman Pinsky waved from behind his cigar and Arnie Dalitz grinned that dead-eyed grin of his and said the word he always used when he was slaughtering the lambs: *Fab-u-lous.*

"Fabulous," Leo said before he could stop the word from leaving his lips. "Look, why don't you go get Christie and Ruthie out of here. Tell this Charlie to just take off with them. And meet the singers later."

"I'm going to get you out of here first."

"It'll take too long."

"It won't."

"Tina, goddamnit, it will. A jail is a jail. I'll be out of here one way or another. But just get the girls out of town."

"Edith? Edith, is that you?"

From the other side of the door voices sounded and other doors slammed. Phones rang in quick succession and the voices became louder. Car engines started and shut off. Sirens sounded. The old policeman burst through the doorway. "I knew it!" he screeched. "I just knew it. Mix a bunch of niggers in with *your* people and look what happens!"

"What happened?"

"The niggers left nigger heaven is what!"

The warehouse had been converted into a combination storage area and concert hall in 1946 after having lain empty for most of the war years. The owner was a cousin of the Wright family, who later became prominent in the political life of the state. His proposal was unheard of. He intended to allow Negroes into the warehouse at the same time as whites. Not that there would be any mixing. The Negroes would be seated in a special balcony that was built. Nigger heaven it was called. The whites of the town were to have the main floor to themselves. But there were those who argued that the arrangement was all wrong. Negroes higher than whites? The whites should be in the balcony. The debate had never moved past the porches of the shacks and the stores. For the past few years one part of the warehouse had always remained empty. When Hank Snow or Red Foley came through with a group of Nashville country singers the balcony was unoccupied and the ground floor was packed. And those who were standing or perched on cotton bales would never have thought of moving to the empty seats upstairs. When the Negro gospel groups like Soul Stirrers came to town the balcony was packed but the ground floor was empty. It created bizarre eyelines for the Negro performers, singing with their heads tilted back in front of an open space where the portable wooden chairs had not even been unfolded. It was an arrangement that lasted until the new kind of music intruded, this rock 'n' roll that brought Fats Domino up from New Orleans singing *Blueberry Hill*, the Drifters singing *Up on the Roof* and *Under the Boardwalk*, Sam Cooke with *You Send Me* or the Platters with *Smoke Gets in Your Eyes*. Suddenly both the balcony and the ground floor filled up. The young white teenagers came in driving farm trucks or chopped and channeled pinstriped Mercs and Fords that resembled what they saw in *Custom Car* magazine. And the Negroes came walking, or occasionally in cars that were parked discreetly at the far end of a dirt parking lot. As the fervor of the performances increased, the word spread from neighboring counties and states that the problem was not an isolated one. The North Alabama White Citizens Council went on radio and television denouncing nigger music and emissaries were sent into Georgia creating the North Georgia W.C.C. that included several members of the Ku Klux Klan, who roamed the back roads after the concerts looking for Negroes to beat senseless or even run over in their cars.

When Ivory Joe stepped onstage the cheering could be heard by the distant groups of men waiting on the small roads leading away from the warehouse. Except for rehearsals, it was the first time Ivory Joe and the Classics had ever performed in their street clothes. The choreographed movements somehow felt awkward without the support of their tuxedo jackets. But by the second song, when Ivory Joe began winding up on the piano, only Clyde was still conscious of their clothing. While he sang, Ivory Joe searched out the policemen who had been stationed around the warehouse. There were three of them, over half the town's police force. The two he had never seen before were standing at the edge of the stage but it was Billy, the nephew, he was looking for. The audience was already on its feet and the forest of outraised arms had almost obscured the stairway to the balcony where Billy was standing guard. Once located, Billy became a target. Ivory Joe played to no one else. The music, the energy, the movements were aimed at him, relentlessly building through the tempo of *So Blue, Stolen Tears* and then *Honeychild* that had the audience dancing in the aisles. Ivory Joe lurched out into the crowd whipping the extra microphone cable behind him while the two policemen nearest the stage yelled for the audience to sit down. But they were all dancing, flailing wooden chairs across the floor, swaying and clapping their hands to the beat that increased steadily, hypnotically, from the second piano and the bass, finally crashing through to *Train to You* and the gyrations from the Classics that had the balcony going wild.

But Billy stood stoically on the bottom stair. Until his foot started tapping. And his head bobbed back and forth. With his two cousins he had once driven all the way to Memphis and paid two dollars at Sun Records to cut a demo record that ended their dreams of being singers. But that was before Long Island. And before coming back to be a policeman. He saw the other two cops at the front, yelling and struggling with the teenagers around them. They were older, with creased necks and tight mouths. Above him came the pounding of the Negroes. The whole balcony shook and swayed. He had been told to keep them up there. By orders of the chief of police, Uncle Frank, no one left nigger heaven once the first note was played. But Billy was now deciding there were certain problems with all that. First, the balcony was going to collapse. And second, the music was great. He'd rather be up on the stage. Or at least down there dancing. Clapping. Cheering.

They were far from anything they could recognize in themselves. Clyde was singing like he hadn't sung since the spirits overtook him in the gospel hall. Clarence was bobbing up and down, locked in some changing, clapping world of his own, plunging deeper whenever Ivory Joe increased the tempo. And for the first time Zoot was afraid onstage. He felt himself losing control and plunging into the whirlpool in the darkness out beyond the footlights—out where Ivory Joe was. The roar from out there was engulfing them all. Their own voices could no longer be heard and in a flicker of thought Zoot wondered why he was afraid.

From out of the footlights Ivory Joe moved toward them. "*Get out!*" he shouted over the screams of the audience. "*Now!*" Only Zoot understood what was happening. He jabbed Clarence, jarring him loose from some inner rhythm, and shouted at Clyde, pushing him in a way that looked like it was all part of the act. Clarence tried to ask why but the question was swallowed in the uproar and suddenly he and Clyde and Zoot were outside, trying to catch their breath around the DeSoto. "What about Joe?" gasped Clyde.

"Get in!" said Zoot revving the engine. "He wants it this way."

Billy suddenly realized that Ivory Joe was all alone up there on the stage. Just him and the music. He kept dancing further into the crowd. Totally *alone* up there. It thrilled Billy because it was as if he was singing right to him and what else was there to do but snap your fingers? One on one! Me and *him!* Further and further into the crowd! Turning to the musicians buried deep in the shadows and signaling for *Ghost Lover* as one of the support beams over Billy's head splintered and crashed to the floor.

It was *Ghost Lover* that did it. The high eerie chorus coming out of one voice, Ivory Joe's voice, peeling off into spirals of imagery, leading the roar of the crowd. One of the girls in front of Billy spun around on her white bucks, the kind Pat Boone wore on television, and sent her skirt spinning like a cheerleader's. She reached out and grabbed his hand—even though he yelled that he was an officer of the law, which made her laugh as she danced and teased in front of him while he tried to look stern and official before telling himself screw it as this Ivory Joe sang . . .

. . . *alone*! He had seen her before in the eleventh grade when he had been starting grade nine but she was different now with that V-necked sweater wrapped over an orlon pointiness that she shook in front of him even though he held out his hands, motioning her to cease all this. And showing her his wedding ring. Which just made her shake all the more, jumping up and down to the music, grabbing his hand just as this Ivory Joe suddenly surged through the crowd and sang *under* the balcony where the Negro kids couldn't see him until one of them hung down from the balcony railing. Then there were others, like bats hanging in a row from the roof of some cave. The stairway suddenly filled up with all the Negro kids pushing down, demanding to see, to join in all this lunacy until they were all *together!* Negro and white kids pinwheeling around in music and laughter—which, in the name of the law, by orders of the chief of police, Uncle Frank, Billy wondered if he should stop it all, yelling things like *You're all under arrest!* . . .

. . . until the moment when he gave in and started dancing too.

Leo heard the details told by a pack of voices in versions that changed with every telling. The drunk had staggered to his feet, introduced himself as Alonzo Bethan Jr., explained that he usually inhabited better quarters and yelled for silence as the sirens sounded. "Huey Long populists," he muttered. "They make the worst cops. No sense of poetry." His clothes showed the stains of various liquors and perhaps meals. When one of the policemen rushed through the jail Alonzo yelled, "The quality of mercy is not strained. It falleth as the gentle rain from Heaven," and then slumped against the steel cot mumbling to himself. "Edith didn't show up, did she?" he asked.

The police chief hustled Ivory Joe through the door and into the cell next to Leo as the door was held open by other policemen with silent angry stares that did not even acknowledge Alonzo Bethan Jr.'s salutations. "Evening, Luther. Regards to the missus, Tom. Howdy, Curt." The door slammed with a metallic finality and for a moment there was the silence of the three of them staring at one another until the sound of voices outside drew Alonzo to the high barred window of his cell. "Louts," he said. "Knaves. Rogues." He slumped down. "Assholes."

"A pretty stupid thing to do," said Leo with a big grin.

Ivory Joe said nothing, as if he had not heard. "I beg your pardon," he finally replied. "Or am I not talking to the idiot who drove his car over a field?"

"That's different."

"Oh, really?"

"I was impressing my daughters."

"I got news for you. You blew it."

"What do you know about my daughters?"

"I know they're too smart for that kind of shit, man."

Leo thought for a moment. "Yeah. Probably," he said.

"No probably about it."

"No fighting!" yelled Alonzo. "Now is the time for solidarity. Onomatopoeia! Synecdoche!"

"Where are my daughters?"

"They got out with Tina and Charlie. Heading up the back roads for Carolinas."

"What about your friends?"

"Zoot and the rest? They got out the back door. I got trapped in with the crowd."

"Why didn't you just sing your songs and get out?"

"What's the point in that?"

"An artist!" yelled Alonzo. "No mere trifling technician, this man."

"What did they arrest you for?"

"Mongrelization. Same thing you're in here for." Ivory Joe grinned. "At least that's what the dinky little cop says."

"Running with the purebreds here," said Alonzo. "Always a problem."

They fell silent, listening to the commotion outside. "I'm worried about Tina and the girls," said Leo.

"They'll get out okay. No one here's a match for Tina. Or Christie. You got great daughters, man."

"I know."

"Should spend more time with them."

"Who the hell are you to tell me about my daughters? If it wasn't for you and your goddam banshee music they'd be up in New York all summer."

"Bored stiff."

"Yeah, of course, if you consider museums and theaters and all the other cultural things I'm introducing into their lives. But what the hell would you care about that?"

"About as much as you'd care about bringing music and travel into their lives."

"*Music*? You call that stuff music?"

"Yeah. I do. Like Mozart, man. They used to say he made banshee music. But that's the problem people with no imagination have. Mozart was a composer, by the way."

"No kidding. I thought he was a bookie. You know something? If there wasn't two sets of jail bars between us . . ."

"What?" Ivory Joe glared in defiance.

"Gentlemen!" Alonzo sputtered. "Spare me any medieval arguments about how many composers can dance on the head of a pin." From outside came the noise of revving engines. "Speaking of medieval, the local sapsuckers have arrived. I presume neither of you gentlemen would have the short-term misfortune of being either Jewish or Negro, would you?"

"I'm Chinese," said Ivory Joe.

"I suspected as much," said Alonzo. "But try and convince the local intelligentsia here. Neither of you would happen to have a little bourbon, would you?"

They sat and listened to the noises outside. There were voices and more engines. And then a gathering silence that seemed louder still. None of them spoke. After a while low voices sounded beyond the door. They were dry and almost whispered like a rustling of dead leaves until the door opened and the policeman entered.

"Frank, there seems to have been some mistake. I was set upon by louts, manhandled severely until I passed out and—"

"Forget it, Alonzo. The only thing that was manhandled was the bottle you was drinking out of."

"I shall call my in-laws and report such impudence."

"Already talked to your father-in-law. He's 'bout ready to turn you into a field hand. Says to keep you in here overnight."

"Well, it's a good thing for the republic that we have civil code against the internecine contravention of family decency, now isn't it?"

"Forget it, Alonzo." He turned to Ivory Joe and Leo. "Lotta folks out there pretty upset about all this. Good thing you got us to protect you."

"We're very grateful," said Leo in a neutral voice as Alonzo signaled him to remain silent.

"I'm sure. Now, to show what kind of people we are, we're going to release you, which is surely goin' a ways."

"We can leave now?" said Ivory Joe.

"Uh-uh. Jes' hold on. Gotta let things calm down a little outside there. I'll be back in a while," he said with a smile that somehow didn't look to Leo like a smile.

When he had departed, Alonzo said, "Never trust an aged constable who is in need of elevator shoes and a large gun. It is all a trick, I swear. I know this town. Mean as a cornered rat when it wants to be."

For more than an hour they lapsed into fitful silence, broken only by Alonzo's apologetic history of the area. He was careful to point out that the lynchings were all done south of there. Mostly. Nothing like that had happened around the town for years. And the Leo Frank case, the Brooklyn Jew they lynched years ago, had to be at least a two-hour drive down from Atlanta. That was where most of the Negroes had gotten it. Where it was flatter. And the heat made people meaner.

"Still waiting for some good news, Alonzo," said Ivory Joe.

"The good news is they don't do that anymore. Lynching, out of fashion now. Mostly."

"I don't like all these 'mostlys.' "

"You're sure you don't have any bourbon?"

"Last time I went into a synagogue I was twelve years old."

"And I told you, I'm Swedish."

The sound of brakes was heard outside. A car door slammed. Someone ran into the jail and exclamations were heard beyond the door that opened swiftly. Billy entered, his police uniform patched with sweat. He was out of breath as he looked around at each of them as if checking on their presence. "Billy! My dear boy! Do join us for a drink," smiled Alonzo.

"You people are in deep shit," said Billy as he turned and hurried back through the door.

"No *mostly* there," said Alonzo.

Leo paced around the cell, glaring at Ivory Joe. "I'm just now beginning to realize what an absolute mess my life has been from the day I first heard about you."

"Well, now see, *that's* the problem, ain't it? You should have realized what a mess it was *before* you heard of me. And if you hadn't driven across some damn field neither of us would be in here."

"You sure of that?"

"No."

The door opened as the sound of a car engine starting was heard. Billy hurried into the cell area, at first too nervous to speak and breathing in gasps. "Okay, here's what's gonna happen to you," he said, pacing back and forth. "In an hour my uncle's coming back here. When it's real good an' late an' most people are turned in. An' the roads is real quiet like. So he sets you free an' there ain't but two roads you can take outta town. An' right now on both of those roads there's men waitin' for you. With guns. And roadblocks. They're gonna stop you. An' then they're gonna give you a fearful hidin'. Beat the living tar right outta you. They're all in hoods so you ain't never gonna see any faces anyhow. But my uncle made a deal with 'em all."

"What kind of deal?" asked Leo in a soft voice.

"They ain't supposed to kill ya. Uncle Frank don't want no murders here. Then the Feds find some excuse to come in an' start opening up the whole can o' worms. But there ain't no guarantees. Some of those boys been drinkin' a shitload. I seen 'em."

For once Alonzo appeared totally sober. He stared from Ivory Joe to Leo. "Now Billy, listen to me," he said in a firm, quiet voice. "I think you have to separate yourself from what others would tell you is your duty here. You have to help these men."

Billy's breathing continued sounding like a pump. He said nothing. He still paced back and forth looking through the bars and Leo could read nothing from his eyes. "I know that, Mr. Bethan. I know, dammit," he said, taking one very deep breath and slowly exhaling. "I already started somethin' off."

"What did you start off, Billy?"

"Can't say, Alonzo. Just trust me." He held onto the bars for a moment and then, with a large key, he opened both cell doors. "I'm quittin' here. Headin' back up north. But I'm gettin' you outta here first."

"No Nuremberg trials for Billy," said Alonzo.

"Now, see, I sent the other officer south. Told him Uncle Frank wanted the southern roads checked for roadblocks. He'll be an hour at least. So I'm gettin' you out in my police car."

"Me too, Billy."

"Alonzo, you ain't exactly in the same sinkin' boat as these people here. But if Uncle Frank's gonna hang me for two he might as well hang me for three."

"Your powers of logic are indefatigable, Billy. Now open this infernal cage." Billy opened the cell door and Alonzo shambled into the corridor adjusting his crumpled fedora.

"I'm gonna back the car up to the rear door. When you hear it round the back, you get out fast, okay?" said Billy, hurrying through the front door. When the police car had been moved to the rear of the building, they pushed against the door but it would not open. They pounded on it and heard Billy's terse words and then silence until he appeared in the cell area, running, with a key. "Shit. Forgot it don't open without this." He heaved against the door, which opened, spilling them all onto the dirt parking lot behind the police station. A single bare light bulb cast harsh light from above the door and the chorus of cicadas pulsed in perfect tempo. "Okay, Alonzo, you sit in the back and I'm taking you home to your wife."

"One prison to another," said Alonzo.

"And you two are in here," said Billy, looking at Leo and Ivory Joe as he opened the trunk.

53

Leo and Ivory Joe stared at each other across the opened trunk and from far in the distance came what sounded like the barking of hounds. Neither moved. Billy circled the car yelling, "C'mon, c'mon. They're gettin' ready to come after you."

Leo stared at the opening chasm. "I'm not getting into any goddam trunk."

Ivory Joe looked from the trunk to Leo. "And I ain't riding in the back of this particular bus."

"Well, shit!" yelled Billy. "Jes' how'd you 'spect me to get you through all those armed men then, mister? By tyin' you onto the hood like so many deer I just bagged?"

The noise of the racing car engines emerged from the chorus of cicadas. "Time is of the essence, gentlemen," said Alonzo.

"Get in the back seat, Alonzo," yelled Billy, starting the police car's engine. "Now, you two idiots comin'? Or you waitin' for Uncle Frank?"

For a moment neither Ivory Joe nor Leo replied. Finally Leo said, "I've never really liked Uncle Frank."

"Me neither," said Ivory Joe as he climbed into the trunk.

The spare tire and the jack were moved out of the trunk and onto the floor next to the back seat. Alonzo sat in pseudo-regal imperiousness, the drunk from the wealthy family being released into the custody of his glowering wife. The trunk of the Ford was still cramped and jarring. In total blackness, Leo and Ivory Joe were folded head to toe. Every pothole reverberated to the depths of their bones. Every stop or acceleration flung them against metal. Or each other.

Each was determined to remain silent. But when the car turned onto a paved road, its tires making a sizzling noise beneath them, Leo said, "You trust this kid?"

From the lurching darkness came the soft reply: "Course I do. If you can't trust a dancing cop who can you trust?"

They listened to the different noises the tires made and the way the metal groaned around them as the car turned and climbed. It was Ivory Joe who broke the silence this time. "Got a favor to ask," he said.

"If it's about taking a bath you're too late."

"If anything happens, I mean, if we run into any trouble, I want you to find a friend of mine. Old guy. Called Red Leg. He's up in Harlem. You ask at the barbershop that's part of Sugar Ray's bar. It's on Seventh Avenue. Between 123rd and 124th. They'll tell you how to find him. And tell Red Leg thank you for me. And that all the money I get from my music is to go to him."

Money? thought Leo. Loose change maybe. Because right now I *own* you, pal. With these typed pieces of paper with Goldin's signature scrawled across the bottom. Papers that'll be turned over to men with dead eyes who will already have killed for them. Men who will take your music and use it to tear strips off your heart and replace it with nickels and dimes. You can sing *Ghost Lover* till you're old and gray and watch Herman and Arnie get fatter. And Genovese. What *is* it with you? Can't you *see* that?

"You hear me?" said Ivory Joe.

"I hear you."

The car lurched and slid and then there was again the drumming of gravel on metal. "Hey, listen, just in case something happens,"

Leo said in the darkness, breathing into Ivory Joe's feet, "I mean, if there's trouble or something—which there won't be, but just in case—I want you to do me a favor. I want you to tell Tina that I never stopped being crazy about her. She's the best woman I've ever met. I mean, just tell her it would have all worked out between us. I know it would. I mean, I know it was all my fault. What with me screwing around all the time while she stayed home."

Only the staccato firing of stones against the metal beneath them was heard.

"You hear me?" said Leo.

"I hear you."

54

When the police car rounded the curve and the headlights first caught the pickup truck parked across the road, Billy braked sharply.

"You'll do just fine, son," said Alonzo quietly. "Just remember that they'll either be at your feet or at your throat. The choice is yours." He smiled as Billy flicked the siren switch for a brief burst and put on the high beams and the flashing light that caught the rustling glint of weapons being held in the darkness beyond the pickup truck. Men emerged into the light, menacing yet tentative in front of the siren that sounded in another burst. Billy stopped the car and barely heard Alonzo whisper at him to stay cool.

He stepped out of the police car into the skipping red light. "We ain't clearing out, if that's what you're here for," someone said. Billy just stared. He walked slowly back and forth, looking each man in the eyes. Many looked away. "Now what all's the problem here, Billy?" another voice said. "We talked it out with your uncle." Billy kept walking slowly around the jagged crescent of men, staring into eyes.

"I know what you talked about, Luther. You don't have to go tellin' me." He walked some more. "Just makin' sure I know who all's here. In case somethin' were to go wrong an' we come lookin' for people."

Billy completed his inspection at the outer edge of the light. He stopped and looked around again as if counting.

"Who's in the car?" asked one of the Cahill brothers, the one with the bad eye.

"Prisoner."

"Alonzo? That you? Looks like you."

"And so it should," said Alonzo quietly from the back seat.

"He get liquored up again?" asked a man in overalls. "Never seen a man go dressed in Sunday clothes jus' lyin' down in the slop like a hog. Alonzo, why'n't you get some proper drinkin' clothes?" There was no answer from the car. Billy started walking back toward it.

"Hey now, hold on. What you doin' takin' Alonzo up here when he lives over near Lake Sydney? I been there," said a thin-faced man with a shock of black hair falling down almost to his eyes. Billy recognized him as the owner of the building supplies depot. And as a member of the local Klan. For an instant something caved in and Billy felt a flicker across his face before he could step out of the darkness.

"Tom, until you sign up with my uncle and become a law officer, you don't go checkin' where I take my prisoners to. But if you're really so hard put to know other people's business then put your mind to thinking about where his wife's daddy lives." Billy stared coldly and then kept walking toward the car as chuckles sounded and jokes were made about Alonzo's father-in-law waiting at the big estate just up the road. Waiting to fire him from the family lumber business. For the fifth time. Or sixth. Or more. The laughter circled the car, punctuated by squirting noises as geysers of chewing tobacco made arcs in the darkness. "Now move the damn truck before I get me another prisoner," said Billy. In the car Alonzo muttered encouragement under his breath as the pickup truck was moved off the road. The police car eased forward and then gained speed, the flashing red light blinking off, as the other lights curled into the darkness on the winding road that climbed toward the foothills of the Great Smoky Mountains and Billy turned around with a jack-o'-lantern grin and let out a whoop that Alonzo returned.

Leo decided he knew what it was like to be blind. In the trunk the darkness was absolute but sounds and motion suddenly took on textures. Tension filled in the spaces and created vision where his eyes could not see. The voices just beyond their thin covering of metal seemed drawn closer by his own ascending fear that left him afraid to breathe. Within his own head every breath seemed like a foghorn.

Then the car started moving again, slowly, and without a sound from the front. There was only the noise of gravel under the wheels, like something being broken slowly. Was there someone else in the car? Why were there now no voices? Was Billy still driving? The seconds and minutes fell in on each other into some pit of fear that had burrowed through the darkness around him. The car began to slow down. It stopped.

Silence. The breath left him.

"I want you to know something. I never had anything against you personally." His whisper was barely audible even to himself.

"Maybe we could talk about this later," came the faint voice out of the darkness.

"There might not be a later."

"Yeah."

"You were just a pain in the ass, that's all."

"*I* was? Huh!"

"It had nothing to do with you being Negro."

"In the dark you guys all turn into liberals."

"I'm serious."

"Yeah? Well, just remember that if a guy with a bedsheet over his head opens the trunk."

"We're both in this together."

"You just figuring that out?"

Footsteps. A rasping noise at the lock. The trunk flew open. A blinding light shone in at them. *Yeeeeeehhhoooooo!*

Billy and Alonzo jumped up and down, shouting and toasting the heavens. Leo stumbled out of the trunk first. Then Ivory Joe crawled out and they all drank out of Alonzo's silver flask of bourbon. "You meant what you said in there?" said Ivory Joe.

"I don't have any idea what you're talking about," Leo said. And then he grinned.

On the road again, Billy looked at his watch and reached for the two-way radio switch. "Should be startin' up pretty soon." Out of the static burst Uncle Frank's angry and intermittent voice. *Billy? Dammit, Billy! Where the hell are you? What the hell happened? Billy?* Billy switched the radio off. "They'll come lookin' for sure. Right up this road."

"We got a good head start," said Leo.

"Not enough," said Billy, pulling over to the side of the road and driving the car into the brush.

"Billy, it's me who usually does this," said Alonzo. "Only my excuse is alcohol. Try and stay on the road, will you?"

"Uh-uh, Mr. Bethan. Can't take the car any further. Gotta ditch it here."

"How you expect us to get away?" said Ivory Joe, looking at Billy with a sudden furrowed expression.

"No choice. Gotta walk it." He switched off the engine when the car was far enough off the road. Distant sirens sounded from the direction they had just come. "We're at the county line. If I take this car two feet over it my uncle'll be having warrants out for me stealin' it. I swear he will. But if I leave it here all he can do is get madder'n hell cause one of his employees up 'n' quit on him." It was said with finality and not even the sirens made any difference. Outside the car, Alonzo turned in circles and stared at the three-quarters-full moon.

"Edith," he yelled, shaking his fist at the sky. The others watched as he turned and yelled again, this time in a howl that caused something in the trees to take flight. He took off his fedora, threw it on the ground and jumped up and down on it with both feet in the air at once. Then he stopped, wheezing for breath. "I'm coming with you," he said. "I've always wanted to see New York."

They walked in single file through forests, among trees that whipped back on whoever was behind. Billy led relentlessly, along trails he knew from boyhood, as he talked about meeting his wife back in Glen Cove. He had phoned her from the jail. Even now he missed her while the sirens settled just over the hill and the baying of the hounds came from the creek they'd just walked through until Leo gasped at the insanity of it all, a place without a deli. And what the hell were they? Boy Scouts? He and Ivory Joe needled each other the entire way until Alonzo told them he didn't care whose fault it was that they were walking through a cloud of mosquitoes in the middle of nowhere.

"You know where the hell we are?" Ivory Joe asked as they labored up the ridge of a small mountain. Billy said nothing. The hounds still sounded but in front of them a faint yellowing of the horizon signaled the dawn. They descended back into the darkness of the forest. The hounds seemed louder. "Those dogs can tree," said Billy in a worried voice.

"Huh?" said Ivory Joe.

"You don't want to know about whatever the hell it is," gasped Leo, as they stumbled through the sugar maples down into the blackness of the pines until they were suddenly stopped by the beam of a flashlight that froze them all in midstep. From the darkness in front of them footsteps on twigs crunched down with a volley of snapping sounds.

" 'Bout time you got here," said Zoot.

"Praise God," said Billy. "I never was sure you'd find this here place."

55

At the Icehouse, Herman Pinsky poured out whiskey from the bottle hidden in the console. Arnie Dalitz paced around the recording studio until it was time to go. In Herman's black Cadillac they drove in silence across the bridge into Manhattan. Neither of them could push aside the weight of this, the next murder that was settling across their thoughts before it had even happened. It had all been arranged, approved by Genovese himself after he calculated how much extra his share of *Ghost Lover* would be worth once Goldin was dead. And the Havana IOU now held by Leo Klein was used to take over his company.

Genovese ordered a favor to be called in from Detroit. A man named Frankie Lavachriccio was sent to New York. He was known as Frankie Lava, and when Arnie Dalitz met him, he decided the name came from the man's eyes. Just being around him made Arnie Dalitz nervous. They drew maps of the street and stores around Goldin's house. Photographs of Goldin from a trade paper were studied. Frankie stared a lot and burned holes in them with his eyes.

Two days before it was to happen, Arnie Dalitz went to a diner in Queens where a man was waiting for him in a booth. Detective Third Grade William Parazader was on his way to work at the 17th Precinct.

From five in the afternoon till nine o'clock the following morning he and a partner would be officially checking the cabarets of the upper East Side. There were the big flashy ones, El Morocco, the Copa, the Inner Circle, and then there were all the dinky joints with the cutouts they looked through after 4:00 A.M. to see if drinks were still being served. Each one of them represented the occasional envelope filled with money. The amount depended on the size of the club and the infractions overlooked. But none of the envelopes had ever been as full as the one Arnie Dalitz passed across the table.

Arnie Dalitz and Herman Pinsky got out of the Cadillac and went into the Inner Circle, making sure their arrival was noticed. They took the table next to the dozen or so garment stiffs who were partying, their wives probably at the Jersey shore. The stiffs were loud and obnoxious, looking to score with the women at the bar, half of whom were pros and the rest were in training. Arnie Dalitz and Herman Pinsky sent drinks to their table and received waves and cheers. More witnesses. And just after eleven o'clock the cop Parazader showed up with his new partner, the rookie who did not yet have the bit in his mouth and could look any district attorney in the eye and say he had seen both Herman Pinsky and Arnie Dalitz miles away from the murder site.

Looking down on Broadway from the fifth floor of the Brill Building, George Goldin told himself tonight he owned New York. The record promoters had left his office after listening to the tape of *Ghost Lover*. All the music guys could read the signs. The avalanche of success was about to pour money down on him. Already Ivory Joe and the Classics had been booked into Alan Freed's big show at the Paramount. Which meant that Freed alone would fill the airwaves with this *Ghost Lover*. Downstairs at the Turf he paid for drinks and acted insulted when Jimmy the bartender refused to let him sign for the bill. Soon he would buy the place, he announced. And fire them all.

For the first few minutes after he arrived at the Copa, everything was as it should have been. Just like the old days. The red jackets fell all over him the minute he walked through the door. It was amazing what a difference a few well-placed twenties made. In a few weeks he'd be dispensing them like sticks of gum. And there was nothing better than dropping bills in ways that turned heads. Except for maybe gambling on the edge for an entire evening.

But tonight the Copa was strangely empty of the people he wanted to be with. There were none of the high rollers. Not even the Pinskys or the Dalitzes. A Wednesday in August. That had to be it. And there was no Peggy Lee or Sammy Davis Jr. performing. Just some tryout act that should have been somewhere else. Goldin sat at the front balcony drinking a highball and staring at tourists.

He left the Copa and walked toward Madison Avenue. He had parked his car halfway up the block. As he started the engine, he was aware of someone beside him, a man he had never seen before. A man who had the most terrifying eyes.

56

Leo is amazing. He can turn anything into a party. We're all driving back up to New York as fast as we can. Everyone wants to get home now. Even Billy the cop who's not a cop anymore and this new guy Alonzo who's nice but smells funny and says he's a poet. They want to get to New York too.

There's three cars now including the one Leo rented. All of a sudden he's friendly with everyone. His car is where the real party is. Even Zoot ends up in there playing cards and laughing like they're old friends. Leo even gets Billy in there driving and Mother has to drive the DeSoto. She stays real close behind Leo's car all the way along the highway. She watches real carefully. Ruthie and I think she wants to be in there too.

Ruthie is really the one who wants to get back to New York. She's got all the gas station road maps marked up and she can tell you where we're supposed to be every hour of the day. She's always looking at her watch to figure out how we're doing. Byron. Byron. Byron. She almost has a bird when Leo and Alonzo the poet decide to stop in some dinky little town to buy a bottle. Booze Leo calls it. Ambrosia Alonzo calls it. He calls a lot of things by weird names. He looks like a hobo in a suit but like I said he's nice. I can prove it. When

Alonzo gets into Mother's Buick he stinks of ambrosia and you can tell Mother doesn't like him. But by the time we get to Virginia she's a goner. She's listening to him reciting all his poetry that even Mrs. Levine couldn't do. Mother's like a cat when you feed it cream. Me too. I decide I'm going to be a poet.

Alonzo is the first one of Leo's friends that Mother really likes. Even if he has been to jail. Arnie Dalitz was in jail and Mother doesn't like *him*.

Even Leo and Ivory Joe are friendly. Sort of. They talk but not really. But you can tell they kind of like each other. Ruthie and I decide that they're the same only Leo's crazier. But Ivory Joe's tougher. When they both get into Leo's car they let Zoot drive and then start playing cards like crazy. This makes Mother drive so close that we have to keep yelling at her not to crash into them.

On Wednesday we get into Maryland. Ivory Joe lets me ride with him and the others. The problem is Clyde. He's really getting nutty and smelling under his arms and shouting *peeeyew* we have to stop and get some new clothes. He's still mad because Billy's weirdo uncle ran over all their clothes two days ago. Who would run over clothes? But by the time we get to Pennsylvania Clyde is real upset. He's waving at the air like there's bugs in it. So Zoot who's driving goes off on some little road that leads to a town where he stops in front of a clothes store. The other two cars follow us and Ruthie comes roaring out of the Buick. She's got the maps and she's going crazy and looking at her watch because she's going to be late for Byron. She just sits down on the sidewalk and says *Fine* as Clyde goes in to buy some new shirt.

I still wish I could say *Fine* like Ruthie says it. When I try it doesn't sound the same. Every time I say *Fine* it just means fine. But when Ruthie says it you can tell it doesn't mean fine at all.

When Clyde comes out of the clothes store he's wearing a new shirt. Zoot kids him and says hey Clyde give us some teeth. This means he wants Clyde to smile. Clyde smiles. Then he looks back and makes a big sweep with his arms and out walks Alonzo too. He's wearing a shirt with short sleeves and big stripes. It's definitely not Alonzo. It's like he and Clyde are old friends now. *Every*body's friends now. It's different from school that way.

Ruthie and I start keeping score of who's been in whose car. By Pennsylvania only Leo and Mother and Ivory Joe haven't been together in the same car. But we're working on it.

The problem is that by the time we get to New Jersey I'm a goner. Ruthie too. I think I remember parts of New Jersey and maybe the Lincoln Tunnel. Then all of a sudden it's Thursday and we're home in our own beds. When we wake up Mother is real weird. She's on the phone all the time.

We hear her talking about Mr. Goldin. He died last night.

57

Even in Maryland, before they learned that George Goldin had been murdered the night before, Leo knew a part of his life was slipping away from him. There was no longer any choice. He would soon doublecross Arnie Dalitz and Herman Pinsky. And worse, Genovese. He knew just by staring at Tina. There was something about the way her eyes laughed. And something about the way she looked when she talked about this song, this *Ghost Lover*.

And something about the way just being with her drove out the fear of what Arnie Dalitz would do.

The drive back to New York from the South had been a glorious refuge from what lay ahead. The laughter of his daughters, scheming between themselves over ways to reunite him and Tina; the bizarre stories told by Alonzo; and now even the wary banter that passed between him and Ivory Joe and the others. And most of all, Tina. Even if she did act as if he was just another member of the group.

For the first time in his life he dreaded New York. On the last night it became something fiery, raging out beyond the darkness where the headlights ended, pulling him in by the force of his own fears from which there was now no escaping. The closer they got, the more he joked, until Alonzo turned in the front seat and asked, "Leo, are you all right?"

The image of Arnie Dalitz's terrible smile vanished before he could answer.

PERSONAL REASONS

58

At Tina's apartment Leo carried Christie in his arms after removing her gently from the car. Ivory Joe carried Ruthie and the two men walked almost in unison into the elevator, standing silently with the two sleeping children. Returning downstairs to their cars, they smiled, each waiting for the other to say what was on his mind, and then finally parted in silence with only a nod.

Leo returned to his empty, echoing apartment where the mail was piled in accusing columns beside the door. And the bottles of bourbon stood like silent sentries on the living room cabinet. He poured from one of them but left the glass untouched on the arm of his chair as he sat staring at the Manhattan skyline until he fell asleep.

The next morning Stanley was waiting downstairs with his car. It was as if time had closed over everything. Havana and Georgia had happened to someone else. Almost. He got into the car, took out the pieces of paper from the inner pocket of his suit coat and told Stanley to drive up to Harlem. Stanley thought it was a joke and began driving south toward the garment district until Leo stopped him.

They arrived at the barbershop next to Sugar Ray Robinson's bar. Leo stepped out of the Cadillac as Negroes on the street stared at him. Inside he asked for Red Leg. "Who wants to see him?" asked the old Negro barber closest to the window, without even looking up at Leo.

"I owe him some money," said Leo. The only reply was the snipping sound of the scissors. The barbers exchanged glances.

"Ain't seen him in a long while."

"It's important."

The barber strafed him with a glance and kept cutting hair. No one spoke.

Leo took a fifty-dollar bill from his pocket and put it on the shelf beside the assortment of combs. "Well, maybe I could give you a part of the money I owe Red Leg. Now it'd be real helpful if you could just get Red Leg on the phone." For the first time the barber stopped cutting hair. Then he went to the phone and dialed.

Leo waited. Waiting had always been an emptiness that had to be filled. With anything. Talk, sports pages, gags, betting—whatever could ward off serenity or silence. But now Leo sat in the barbershop quietly waiting, untroubled by the stillness that settled across the room and the edgy volley of stares that passed among the others. When the phone call was returned, the barber listened, said nothing, and then gave Leo instructions on how to get to the betting joint on Lenox Avenue.

Leo told Stanley to park several blocks away. He walked the last few blocks on Lenox Avenue, reading the numbers until he came to the storefront where a few Negroes were sitting on battered chairs. Leo's nod was met by curious stares. He walked down a corridor that reeked of cigars smoked long ago and entered a large room bordered by trestle tables. Red Leg sat at the back hunched over pieces of paper. Approaching him Leo could not see his face, only the mass of white lamb's-wool hair until Red Leg looked up and the long creases in his face caught the overhead light like chasms. A toothpick worked its way around his mouth. "Care to explain all this mystery?"

Leo pulled several pieces of paper from the inside pocket of his suit coat. "I want to make you the owner of a record company."

Leo found a lawyer in the Yellow Pages. With Red Leg watching, the toothpick tracking the circuit of his mouth, Leo gave his instructions. The Havana IOU for Goldin's company was to be transferred to Red Leg. All the recordings, the music publishing, the royalties for *Ghost Lover* and the other songs were to go to Ivory Joe and the Classics. Herman Pinsky and those he represented were to get nothing.

"Why?" On the street afterward Red Leg stopped Leo before he could leave.

"My business."

"Mine now."

"Yeah? Well then, there's something I want you to do for me. Make sure *no one* ever knows about this. Not Ivory Joe. Or Zoot. And not Tina. Understand?"

"Why?"

Leo said nothing.

"You're gonna get yourself in some deep shit."

"I told you. My business."

"Yeah." Red Leg shifted his toothpick and nodded. And for the first time that day he smiled.

Leo stood in the dress store feeling strangely calm. Christie and Ruthie were rummaging through the dresses, running in and out of the changing rooms. Ruthie had been promised a new dress. To meet this chess player, this Byron. Or whatever his name was. Leo wandered into the perfume department, squeezing the atomizer bulbs on the samples and wondering if this was the right time to buy a present for Tina. He returned with eight different perfume bottles and found Ruthie standing protectively over a dress box. Behind her was a saleslady trying quietly to attract Leo's attention. The saleslady was shaking her head, mouthing *No!* Leo looked from the saleslady to Christie, his barometer of all things relating to his daughters. But she had gone blank on him. Just staring at everything and everybody but him. He looked back at Ruthie and recognized the signs. That tiny tight-lipped smile was all that stood between him and a rampaging torrent of thirteen-year-old female insecurities.

"We'll take it."

Carrying the dress box, he walked along the southern edge of Central Park watching his daughters race among trees playing tag. When they got to Columbus Circle, he told them to wait while he made a phone call. Herman Pinsky picked up the phone in the Icehouse, almost breathless from irritation. "Leo, for christsakes, we've been looking all over for you. Where the hell have you been?"

"Herman, I just got in late last night. One lousy crisis after another at the company." Trying to sound irritable instead of nervous.

"Well, get the hell over here. We got papers for you to sign. You gotta turn over control of Goldin's company. You heard about him? He got whacked last night."

"Yeah. Too bad."

"Terrible. Now listen, Leo, Arnie's on his way over here—"

"I was just trying to phone him."

"—and you get over here, too."

"I can't. Not till tonight."

"Whadya mean you can't? You know what's riding on this?"

"I'm with my kids."

"What the fuck is this with you and your kids? I'm sick of this, Leo," Herman screamed into the phone. "Now get over here."

"Herman, goddam you, don't you ever yell at me again."

"Leo, nothing can go wrong on this. Or do I have to spell it all out to you?"

"You don't have to spell out anything."

"So why the hell didn't you even return our calls?"

"I told you, for christsakes," Leo yelled back, looking around to make sure Christie and Ruthie were far enough away not to hear. "You think you're the only one with problems?"

"Leo, sometimes I'm not sure I understand you. If anything went wrong on this, certain people would be very, *very* unhappy. And you're talking to me about your *kids*?"

"Herman, I'm calling from a pay phone on Fifth Avenue. I gotta go. I'll call you later tonight and we'll get it all straightened out." He hung up and leaned against the side of the phone booth for a moment until Christie came running back with panic in her eyes. "I think you should take a look at Ruthie's dress," she said.

During the summers most of the family was away on weekends, so the gatherings at Mother Ackerman's were held only on alternate Thursday evenings. On the few times when Leo would show up he would usually barge in, giving Mother Ackerman a vociferous hug and acting louder and more raucous if the Berman side of the family was there in force. It was all part of Leo's act. He knew it drove them crazy to have to go to the trouble of being condescending to someone who couldn't even figure out he was being condescended to. A couple of times Leo even slapped various Bermans on the back.

But this evening he sent Ruthie and Christie in ahead of him like human bird dogs, sniffing out cousin Arnold, whose zigzag smile disappeared the moment he saw them. Arnold left quickly, claiming there was a patient he had forgotten about.

When Tina arrived it was noted by all that she and Leo seemed more friendly than they had in months. But no one seemed to notice when Leo nodded to Morris and the two of them quietly left the room.

Leo and Morris went upstairs to their old bedroom, the one they shared when they were boys. Within minutes Leo realized all over again why he was the outside man and Morris was the inside man in the company. Morris could hide nothing. In middle age, his brother's face was now a road map of every worry, of every detour in the ceaseless journey to an organized world. To Morris, life was a serious matter and humor was a luxury. Yet Leo could make him laugh, especially when they were away from the office, sitting around the remnants of their boyhood. The old Giants pennant on the wall. The high school yearbook class photos where Leo was listed as *absent*. Hung next to Morris's framed report card.

They talked with an openness that neither shared with anyone else. It was part of a boyhood trust they had never allowed the years to alter. "I've got some problems," Leo said, lying across his old bed. "And I hate to tell you, but I think they're going to affect you."

"Your family? Tina?"

"Uh-uh. After tonight I'm on the shit list with Arnie. And other people."

"Arnie's your friend."

"Hey, Morris. You weren't born yesterday. Of course Arnie's my friend. And of course he takes his orders from Genovese, who wouldn't know a friend from a snake."

"What did you do?"

"Doublecrossed them. Big."

Morris threw himself back across his old bed. "Oh shit, Leo. You were always crazy. But never insane." They both lay across their beds. The room was too small to pace. But Morris quickly sat hunched over. "What did you do?"

"There was a guy they murdered last night. George Goldin. A prick, may he rest in peace. I went down to Havana because Arnie and the others asked me to beat him out of his company in a poker game. I did. Now he got blown away, and I'm supposed to sign over his company to Herman. And Genovese, of course. But I just signed it over to some Negro guy."

Morris stared. His mouth opened but at first he said nothing. "Leo . . . Leo, do you know what you're doing?" In almost a whisper.

"Yeah. I know."

"Those people you don't fool with."

"I'm clearing out for a while. Going somewhere new. It'll calm down."

"What about the company, Leo? Our company?" said Morris, as if he'd suddenly realized what Leo was steering him toward.

"Yeah. Is there a lot of insurance?"

"Oh God, Leo! What are you telling me?" Morris was on his feet, twisting in the small space at the end of the beds.

"I swear to God, Morris, I never wanted to drag you into all this. But it just happened and I couldn't control it."

"And Ida! She'll—"

"Ida's a strong woman when she has to be."

"Oh, great," Morris yelled and whispered at the same time. "But why does she have to be? What did you do it for?"

"Personal reasons."

"*What* personal reasons?"

Leo shrugged and stared into the Giants pennant.

"C'mon, Leo! What's more personal than the company?"

"My kids."

"What are you talking about?"

"Right now they think I'm a good guy."

"So?"

"So maybe I want to keep it that way."

"I don't understand."

"Let's go downstairs."

Morris excused himself from Mother Ackerman's, saying that there was a client with an emergency. Bloomingdale's buyer. Very urgent. Waiting for him at the office. Morris hurried to his car, with Leo following, insisting that he go too. Morris refused. Not since they were very young had Leo seen his older brother so firm and in control. It was too dangerous, Morris said. Arnie Dalitz and the Genoveses had too many eyes in the garment buildings—the night watchmen, the cleaners, truck drivers, barbers. Who knew? They might already have been told to watch out for him. "I don't want you anywhere near the place."

"Yeah? Well, what are you going to do in there on your own?"

"Leo, I don't have any idea. But leave it to me, will you? I mean it, Leo."

In the darkened offices of Frolic Frocks, Morris filled a large cardboard box with accounts receivable ledgers, invoices, checkbooks, order books, buyers' addresses, insurance policies and inventory lists. Then he made plans to ship most of their stock to a warehouse in Pennsylvania early the next morning. He couldn't bring himself to leave. Like a general reviewing the troops, he walked stiffly among the endless rows of dresses hanging on the racks and stretching out into the blackness of all the years it had taken to build the business. His mutterings rose into the gloom as he marched around, the bald spot on his head showing as a moving white dot in a labyrinth of cloth.

Then he stopped and burst into tears.

59

Leo sat in the hotel room staring at the phone. On the other side of the wall Alonzo called out in his sleep. The traffic noise from Park Avenue far below had lapsed into the occasional bleat of a horn. Morris sank into the overstuffed armchair on the other side of the phone, his face falling into haggard repose. Only his eyes seemed capable of movement. "You scared?"

"Of what?"

"Don't bullshit me, Leo. I'm your brother, okay?"

"What do you want me to do? Shit a brick in Times Square?"

"Just be honest with your feelings. That's all."

"Oh, Christ. You been hanging out with that dink Arnold too much."

"Leo. I'm just trying to help."

"I don't want to talk about it, okay?" Leo stared at the phone until

Morris wondered if he was missing something. Then Leo reached for it as slowly as if he was getting ready to swat it.

"Leo, don't."

"No choice." Leo dialed the number from memory.

"Just get out of town. Before they find out. They're gonna come looking for you."

"Not yet. Byron's showing up tomorrow."

"Who the hell's Byron?" Morris was on his feet, pacing and rubbing his forehead in nervous circles.

"Arnie?" said Leo, staring at the floor.

Arnie Dalitz had answered the phone on the first ring with a voice tight with exhaustion and anger. "Leo, where the fuck are you?" he snapped. "It's two in the morning. I been waiting all goddam night with Genovese on my ass."

"I'm not going through with it, Arnie." Leo felt the same strange calmness descend on him. As if it was all over with.

"What the hell are you talking about?"

Herman Pinsky came on the extension line, his voice squeaking with fury. "Leo, get over here."

"There's no point, Herman."

"What are you? Crazy? I want *Ghost Lover.* Now! You listening to me?"

"Too late, guys. I signed Goldin's company over to one of Ivory Joe's friends."

"Very funny, Leo."

"I'm serious, Herman."

"Wha—?"

"Arnie, he's a goddam maniac. He means it."

"To a nigger?"

"He did it, Arnie."

"Leo!" Arnie Dalitz screamed so loud that Morris could hear the words across the room. "Are you outta your fuckin' mind? What the hell for?"

"It felt right."

"Right?" screeched Herman Pinsky. "You fucking idiot! You wanna know what's gonna feel right? When Genovese tells Arnie to take a sledgehammer to your face and—"

Leo hung up.

He and Morris sat staring at each other. "Surprise, surprise."

"Hey. It's just Arnie, you know."

"*Just* Arnie? How about *just* a snake? Ever since you and he beat the shit out of each other when you were shoeshine boys he's been waiting for the rematch."

"Oh, bullshit. Me and Arnie are friends."

"*Friends!* For christsakes, Leo. You're a total moron sometimes. Arnie's your friend cause you always made him money. But *lose* him money and then just watch what happens. He'll cut your heart out just to prove that no one can fool with him."

Leo stared out the window. "Lay off, Morris."

"Yeah, sure, Leo. So tell me, do I have to hire my own gangsters just to force you to get out of town?"

"I'll leave tomorrow."

"Where will you go?"

"Somewhere that's got corned beef sandwiches. How the hell do I know?"

"Just don't show up anywhere around the office. Arnie'll have his goons out looking for you."

"What—you think I'm crazy?"

"You want the truth?"

Sitting alone in the hotel room, Leo stared out the window and wondered who to phone. Maybe Christie and Ruthie might like to talk. It was only three in the morning and he remembered some wonderful conversations they'd had when he'd woken them up.

60

We've been back in New York for three days and already it's a disaster because today's B-day. B for Byron. This afternoon at three o'clock is when we meet him.

Ruthie's a goner. I could see it coming. This morning after she washed her hair she put curlers in it and then took her pillow out to the living room so she could lie with her head sticking up over the hot-air grate in the floor. To make her hair dry properly she says. But it's not wintertime and Ruthie couldn't turn the heat on. So instead she goes out to the kitchen and turns the oven on full. Then she lines all the kitchen chairs up in front of the oven so she can lie on them with her hair hanging down. Pretty soon the whole place gets like a furnace. While I'm roaring all over opening the windows Ruthie's slowly rolling around on the chairs the way they cook hot dogs at Coney Island. To get her hair dried evenly she says.

It gets worse.

Leo's not around and the only thing in the icebox is some food that died a long time ago. So I go out to get a pizza for me and Ruthie at the place where Leo always tells us to charge it to him. When I get back Ruthie is getting dressed in the dress she got yesterday. It's the one she was holding up in front of her and asking me if I thought Marilyn Monroe would wear it. I said yes. Which is true. Marilyn Monroe but not Ruthie. Now it's all my fault. I should have said no. But how was I supposed to know that was the dress she'd end up with?

But now when I'm standing there with her pizza she's there staring down at herself wearing the dress. The dress is okay. It's Ruthie that's the problem. Where the dress is Ruthie isn't. Marilyn Monroe would be. But definitely not Ruthie. Maybe in a few years when she gets a chest. She asks me what I think of the dress and the only thing I can think of is having to put the pizza through a hole in the bottom of the bathroom door if I say the wrong thing. I tell her the dress looks okay. Which is true. I don't know what else to say. So I just stand there and look at her. You can tell she's waiting for me to say more but my mouth just stops working. She has a conniption. She starts bawling and for the first time with Ruthie I don't have a clue what to do. So I roar off to get Mother. But Mother's not here. She had to leave quick when Ivory Joe phoned her and told her the good news. Red Leg owns the record company now. Mr. Goldin lost it in a card game up in Harlem on the night before he died.

"My life is over," Ruthie says. "I'm ugly."

No you're not I tell her. You're pretty.

"No I'm not." She's bawling again. "And I don't even look like Marilyn Monroe."

You sort of do I say.

"*You* don't even understand." She's really bawling now. And pointing at her legs. I start looking at her bare legs sticking out the bottom of the dress that's all taped up at the back. Her legs look like the tent poles we used at camp. But I don't say that. "I'm hairy," she yells.

You are I ask her. She sticks her leg up on the armchair and wants me to look at it.

"See?" she says.

See what I ask her.

"My legs. They're hairy. Marilyn Monroe doesn't have hairy legs," Ruthie bawls. I never thought of that before. I look at her leg again. I don't see any hair on it but she's looking at me like I'd better not say that. So I say yeah. It looks like any old leg to me. What do I know? So I shut up.

But Ruthie just keeps staring down at her legs like they belonged to Mrs. Cooper's spaniel. You know she almost sees the hair growing while she watches.

Ruthie is still going bananas when Stanley shows up instead of Leo. We have to meet Byron in an hour and Ruthie's a mess. But I get a brainwave like in the cartoons. When I tell Ruthie my idea she throws her arms around me. I think I remember us seeing a newsreel where Marilyn Monroe did that.

Stanley is always pretty weird but now he's extra weird. Instead of parking out in front of the building Stanley's parked down by the garbage in the back. And it's not even Leo's car. It's someone else's. He keeps trying to hurry us up when we're walking toward the car. When he's driving he keeps looking in the rearview mirror like someone's after us. Then instead of driving over to Leo's apartment he stops in front of a deli way up on Third Avenue. He honks the horn and Leo comes running out and gets in the car. Something's going on. I've never seen Leo run before. And since when does he go to a deli up on Third Avenue? Leo looks different. Like nervous different.

But you can tell right away he's real happy to see us. He reaches over and gives us the goobery kisses that make you squeal. He sits in the back with us and says things. "Well, guys, big day today, huh?" I say yeah but Ruthie just sits there. Leo figures out that Ruthie's winding up for another fit. You can tell right away that he's thinking Miami Beach just like I did. His eyes go all funny and he keeps looking over at me like I'm supposed to know what to do. "What's the problem with your sister?" he says like Ruthie isn't even there.

Which is not such a good thing to do with Ruthie because she's got all sorts of ways to let you know she's there. She's wearing the raincoat I told her to put on. I nod to her just like we rehearsed it. She unbuttons the raincoat and sits there looking like Marilyn Monroe in that dress. Sort of. Actually she looks like Uncle Fred's boat when the sail fell halfway down. The dress bulges at the top and flags all over.

"Where did you get that dress?" Leo looks like the Goldmans' cat when the firecracker went off beside it.

"*You* said she could buy it," I say. We're not going to let him off the hook.

"I did?"

"Yeah. In the store yesterday."

"Well she'll have to wear something else."

"Like what?"

"Like blue jeans."

This was not in the plan. "Blue jeans to meet *Byron*? You think my legs are hairy too." Ruthie's lower lip is starting to shake like jelly. It's not such a good sign.

"What are you talking about?" Leo doesn't get it yet.

Ruthie whips her leg up onto the back of the car seat. "*This*. Marilyn Monroe wouldn't go out to meet Clark Gable with hairy legs." The lip is really going now.

This is when Leo really blows it. He sort of laughs. Just a little tiny laugh. You can tell he doesn't really mean to. It just comes out. And right when he does it he knows he shouldn't have because Ruthie starts crying. Not bawling like before but with big fat tears that don't make any noise. "Byron's going to laugh at me," she says in a voice like a hamster. "And you're ashamed of me too."

"Stanley, stop the car," Leo says, looking like something's on fire. We're somewhere around Times Square. "Ruthie, honey, I'm not ashamed of you. I'm proud of you. Aren't I, Stanley?"

"Yeah," says Stanley as if *that's* supposed to make it all better. He can't find a place to stop the car. Ruthie's still all scrunched up in the back seat blubbering away to herself and making noises like she's drinking from a hose whenever she tries to breathe. Leo keeps looking over at me. So I decide it's time for the plan. You can stop at your barbershop I say. The one under your office.

"And do what?" says Leo like I said something wrong.

You can have your barber shave Ruthie's legs I say and Stanley jams on the brakes so hard we all go flying forward.

"No way," says Leo.

"Why not?" Ruthie says making her hose drinking noise so loud it scares Leo. And me too actually.

"Ruthie honey I just can't do it."

"Why not? It's right in the same building as your office."

Just when Leo's talking about how he's got some problems at the office and he can't go there right now Ruthie lets go and bawls so loud that Leo has to roll up the windows because people are looking in.

"Ruthie honey come on now." Leo says this while he's licking his lips and looking around like he wants out.

"You don't want me to be a woman."

"I don't *what?*"

Ruthie's really going now. Even I'm impressed. "And Byron's going to see what an ugly scrag with hairy legs I am." She's slobbering all over like the Finemans' dog did when it got old.

"Okay, okay. We'll go to the barbershop," says Leo as Stanley makes the car jerk again and looks at Leo like he's crazy.

All I can think of is if Marilyn Monroe has to go this far whenever she shaves her legs.

61

As Christie and Ruthie chattered and wriggled on either side of him, Leo put his arms around them and stared into Stanley's sad eyes that were burning holes in the rearview mirror. "Boss, I don't really think you want to go there, do you?" Stanley said, clearing his throat.

"Well, of course I do." Leo stared into the mirror, not wanting the girls to sense anything wrong. It was the first time in the nine years Stanley had worked for him that his expressionless Slavic face had shown anger. Or maybe it was fear. Leo couldn't tell. The cars behind them honked but Stanley sat with both hands gripping the wheel and his foot on the brake until Leo said, "The office, Stanley," in a voice so tight the words barely came out. And when they did, they went unheard within the turbulence of his own thoughts, muffled by the other voices, voices that said *today* his older daughter needed him.

And no mere punk was getting in the way of *that*.

"We're late, we're late." Ruthie bounced up and down and Christie looked out the back window as Stanley slowly accelerated through Times Square, his eyes still flickering into the mirror. As the car jostled through the traffic onto Seventh Avenue heading toward Frolic Frocks, Leo felt any residual composure drain away, replaced by fears that rushed in and stiffened the smile he showed to Ruthie and Christie. The car cruised to a stop at 525 Seventh Avenue.

"Boss . . . "

"Back in ten minutes, Stanley." Leo avoided looking into the rearview mirror. On the sidewalk, he hesitated for a moment while Ruthie fidgeted and told him how little time was left until they met Byron. He took their hands, ignoring the greasers who gawked through the big glass door and then yelled to the man on the lobby pay phone. "Ready, gang?"

"Ready? Are you kidding?" Ruthie tugged at his hand, lurching through the door into the lobby where the clatter of their feet echoed off the marble floors all the way to the entrance to the barbershop. Leo left the girls outside and entered the shop, which rippled into silence as his presence was noticed along the row of chairs. Men with steaming towels swaddling their heads or lather circling their faces lay in rumpled masses in the five chairs. The barbers hovering over them stopped in midmotion and stared. Philly, his personal barber, was working the fourth chair and Leo had to force himself to take the next step. And remind himself to smile like he did when he won the daily double.

"Philly, howya doing? Need your special talents. Upstairs in my office in five minutes." Leo pulled out several bills and pushed them into the shaving mug filled with lather. "And bring your shaving stuff." He pulled the towels off the face of Zelinski the furrier. "You're done, Louie. And your shave's just been paid for."

At the elevators, he felt the eyes darting across him like needles. As the polished brass doors opened he looked into some infinity and a blur of faces swept past him. He heard his name whispered in various stages of exclamation and was almost into the elevator when

Ostriker from the eighth floor grabbed his arm and said, "Leo, you shouldn't be here! They're look—"

"David, have you met my daughters?" Leo smiled into the closing doors. On the eleventh floor, he walked toward Frolic Frocks amplifying the chatter of his daughters in his mind. He opened the door. A stricken knot of employees stood outside his office, nervousness flickering across them as one by one they realized that Leo was there.

Morris hurried out of the office, not seeing Leo until he noticed the others looking toward the entrance. "Oh, God, Leo! No! Oh, Leo, no, please!"

"Say hi to Uncle Morris, girls."

"Leo, come here! Girls, you wait there." Morris was a flurry of unconnected motions, his words shooting off in fragments. "Are you out of your fucking mind?" he whispered, clutching at Leo's arm after he had maneuvered them away from the girls.

"Morris, don't do anything that's gonna upset the girls. I'm telling you."

"Yeah, well then keep them away from *this*!" Morris pushed through the employees into Leo's office. Leo followed and stopped abruptly in the doorway. Morris's feet made crunching noises, like the breaking of bones, as he walked over the wreckage of Leo's desk. Everything was smashed. Files were emptied and papers scattered. The desk looked as if someone had taken an ax to it. "And this is just the warning, Leo!" Leo thought Morris was going to burst into tears. "Just get out of here. While you still can."

"I can handle myself. It'll be okay. I'll straighten it out."

"Leo, ever since we were kids you've been able to straighten things out. I always envied you for it. But this is different. Arnie Dalitz ain't your friend anymore. He's looking to do something awful to you. Just get out of here."

"I can't."

"Why not?"

"Ruthie's legs need shaving. I got Philly coming up here."

"Are you *totally* crazy? Why did you have to come back *here*?" Morris was almost screeching now. "You coulda had any goddam barber shave her legs!"

"Are *you* nuts? I'm not having just *any* barber touch my daughter's legs. Philly at least I know."

"Leo, I don't be*lieve* you!"

"Morris, I'm telling you I got no choice! Ruthie thinks today's the day she becomes a woman."

62

Sometimes Leo gets all jittery when he doesn't have to.

He's been jumpy ever since we got to Frolic Frocks. Everyone has. They're all walking around talking to each other like they've got rubber bands around their mouth. Uncle Morris especially. You can tell they don't want us to hear what they're saying. But now it's worse. He's running around making sure that no one's going to be able to see Ruthie when she's having her legs shaved. He's got Mimmo hanging up curtains on the dress racks and putting them together like when you're in a hospital. Only this time the doctor's Philly the barber. He looks like he just wants to get out of here. Leo's making him crazy.

I get to watch. They wheel Ruthie in on a chair like she was going to have her tonsils out. Only me and Ruthie and Leo and Philly are inside the curtains. Leo's yelling for towels and Mimmo comes running up with a lot of white cloth that Leo drapes over the top of Ruthie's legs so Philly the barber won't be able to see her underwear while he's shaving her legs. Leo doesn't say that but you can tell that's what he's thinking. He keeps walking around saying, "She's almost a teenager for Godsakes."

Philly the barber doesn't want to see anything. He just wants to get out of here. "Mr. Klein, please," he keeps saying. "I do beards. Mustaches. Nose hairs even. But please. I don't do legs."

"Everything's going to be fine. Just calm down, Philly," says Leo, who's way more jumpy than Philly the barber is. He's bald like all Leo's barbers and he's little so when he moves it's sort of jerky like the wind-up dolls we used to have. Ruthie has to lie down on Mimmo's cutting table with her legs sticking up in the air while Leo's wrapping her up like she's a present. "She's almost a teenager," he says again. Ruthie's just lapping it all up. She's got all these men roaring around her like bees. She looks over at me and puts the back of her hand on her forehead like the old silent movie stars do. Maybe this is how Marilyn Monroe shaves her legs after all.

Philly the barber stands there with his shaving mug staring at Ruthie's two skinny legs sticking out toward him like they were the railroad tracks and he was Mr. Wiseman's mongrel dog the time that the train was heading straight toward it. "Philly! Let's go," says Leo but Philly the barber just stands there with his mouth moving but no words coming out. Then he starts putting the white foamy stuff all over Ruthie's legs with his little brush. He's shaking his head while he's doing it.

I can't watch anymore. So I get up on the chair and if I stand on my tiptoes I can look over the curtains hung over the dress racks. Mimmo is out there walking around talking to himself and waving his arms in the air. Uncle Morris is talking to *him*self. They're all doing it. Except Leo. He's going nuts now because Philly the barber is taking the white foam off Ruthie's legs with the razor. "Not so high up," he's yelling. "This is my daughter you're shaving!"

"Mr. Klein, please. Maybe you'd like to do it."

"You're doing fine, Philly, you're doing fine." Leo sticks a bunch of money into Philly's pocket.

Right then there's a *blam* from the door over on the other side of the big room. I look over the top of the curtain and see Arnie Dalitz and two men come in like they're walking right through the door. I figure right away this is going to be a problem because already we're late to meet Byron and Leo and Arnie Dalitz always waste so much time slapping each other on the back and saying nothing to each other but talking crazy. But today Arnie Dalitz is just like all the rest of them. *He's* talking to himself even. In exactly the same way. They all talk like they've got that elastic band around their mouth. He can see Leo over the top of the curtains. He comes walking toward us but when I wave he doesn't even look at me. Uncle Morris and Mimmo just stare. They both look strange. Maybe scared. Even old Mrs. Weissman comes out and makes a little noise and then hurries back to her switchboard.

Arnie Dalitz comes right up to where we are. You can't come in here I tell him. But he pulls the curtain back and walks right in anyway. He looks grouchy but he changes real fast once Leo sees him and goes bananas. "What are you, a pervert? A peeping Tom?"

yells Leo. "Walking in on a little girl when she's having her legs shaved?"

"Huh?" says Arnie Dalitz. He doesn't get it yet.

"Cheap thrills! Is that it, Arnie?" Leo yells. He's really angry I can tell. "Just who the hell do you think is lying there with her feet in the air? One of your dollar-a-night broads?"

"Huh?" says Arnie Dalitz again. He doesn't look so grouchy now. You can tell he's never seen Leo so nuts either.

"That's *my* daughter there!" Leo just walks straight toward Arnie Dalitz who keeps backing up.

"Okay, okay." Arnie Dalitz looks mad and scared at the same time. I know the feeling. All of a sudden he's out on the other side of the curtain. That's when I hear a crash behind me. It's Philly the barber. He fainted. He's lying on the floor looking like he's asleep. His razor has landed over near my feet. You can tell Leo doesn't know what to do. So he sticks another ten dollars in Philly the barber's pocket and says it'll be all right. Philly the barber just moans.

But then Ruthie looks down and pulls her movie star routine like *she's* going to faint too. I figure she's secretly mad at Philly the barber because now Leo's fussing over *him*. "Oh no," she says. "Now I'll never see Byron." Her lower lip's starting to go all quivery again.

Leo gets that jumpy look in his eyes again. He picks up the razor. "Christie honey," he says, "you're going to have to help me with your sister's legs."

I mean honestly.

63

All the way over to the Biltmore Hotel Ruthie's real happy. She keeps looking down at her legs. But for a long time Leo doesn't say much. I ask him if we did something wrong. I don't think we did but I ask it anyway. He sort of smiles and then rubs his hand through my hair and keeps staring out the car window.

But all of a sudden he changes. It's like he's the old Leo. The crazy one. He starts laughing and making Ruthie tell him which chess player is which. Ruthie's getting nervous about what will happen when Byron starts asking around for *R. Klein*. But Leo says leave it to him. We do.

We get to the Biltmore and just when we're getting out of the car Arnie Dalitz and a whole lot of men come roaring up in his big Cadillac. "Oh swell," I say. "You invited *them* too?" But it's the same old thing. Everyone is weird. The men just stare at us. Arnie Dalitz just sits in the car. And Leo doesn't say anything.

All this because of Byron.

Leo takes our hands and we go into the Biltmore and up the stairs to where the tables are in this special part of the lobby where the big clock sticks up out of the floor. All of a sudden Ruthie stops and says, "You guys aren't going to sit at the same table as me are you?" Like all of a sudden me and Leo smell bad.

Huh? I say.

"Well after all," she says, "I *am* meeting Byron you know."

All I can think of is oh boy is Leo going to have a hairy over this one. But when I look up at him I can't believe it. He's smiling. "No problem," he says grabbing my hand and dragging me away.

"Well I mean I *am* going to be with Byron you know," Ruthie yells out as we're leaving her behind. I look around and all of a sudden she looks real little and nervous with all these people walking around her.

"No problem," says Leo.

"Well what's wrong with that?" Ruthie yells. But she doesn't sound like the old Ruthie.

"Nothing," says Leo. "It's just that whenever Marilyn Monroe meets anybody she has all her people around her. See you later."

"Hey wait!" Ruthie yells.

Honestly. Sometimes Leo can be so smart.

So we all go over to a table with Ruthie sticking to us like glue. We sit and wait and talk. Leo and I tease Ruthie. Everyone who comes into the lobby we say hey here's Byron. One old guy with a cane comes in and Ruthie giggles when we point to him.

I see Arnie Dalitz's friends come in. Leo doesn't see them. They stand out in the lobby behind Leo's back. They're still not smiling. I decide I'm not going to say anything. I'm not sure why.

All of a sudden we hear someone asking a man at the next table *if he's Mr. Klein*. Ruthie lets out a little squeal and then claps her hand over her mouth. We all turn around. There's this real gawky-looking guy about Billy's age. Almost goofy-looking but not quite. Ruthie almost falls through the floor. This ain't Marlon Brando for sure. "Over here," says Leo in a loud voice. I see Ruthie try to kick him under the table. Ruthie's face is like a piece of chalk. Byron turns around with this big grin and walks over. He shakes Leo's hand. I can see Leo is pleased that Byron looks so goofy. Leo's sneaky that way.

"Barry Lewis," says Byron, shaking hands. I see Ruthie's nose wrinkling up and her head going sideways as she says *Barry*? without making a sound. Leo is Mr. Smoothie. He introduces this Barry to us. But he'll always be Byron to me and Ruthie. And that's that. He's not quite as goofy when he sits down. But tell that to Ruthie. She just gawks. Leo makes a big deal of being best buddies with Byron. They talk about everything. Chicago. New York. The weather. All the usual junk.

"How come you ever got to be a doctor?" Ruthie says all of a sudden. Like he was full of it.

"I'm an optometrist," he says. "Just graduated a couple of months ago."

"Hah!" says Ruthie.

We don't know what to say after that. Everyone just stares. Until Leo starts talking about more junk. This goes on and on. Ruthie starts putting her head in her hands. She's seeing Marlon Brando in her mind. Or maybe Paul Newman. But then there's this Barry who should be Byron sitting in front of her with cake crumbs on the side of his mouth. And an optometrist. At one time Byron was a brain surgeon.

"I want to congratulate you," Byron says to Leo.

"For what?"

"I've been playing chess since I was eight and I've never come up against such a brilliant strategist."

"I have a confession to make," says Leo with a big grin. "I'm an impostor," Leo says. I can see Ruthie reach under the table and try to kick Leo with her foot. But it's too late.

"Impostor?" says Byron.

"I wouldn't know a chess board from a football field."

"But you played superbly."

"It was really my daughter," says Leo pointing to Ruthie who squirms and wriggles all over her chair like when you catch a fish on the dock. She makes all kinds of *tssk* noises but Leo doesn't pay any attention because right then he sees Arnie Dalitz's friends on the other side of the big lobby.

"You're kidding me," says Byron. He looks like he's been hit over the head. He turns to Ruthie. But she won't even look at him. Her mouth is very tight and crinkly. "Ruthie? It was you?"

"Naw," says Ruthie staring daggers at Leo who just smiles.

"That four Pawns attack was brilliant."

"Naw," says Ruthie.

"It was. And the White Bishop to Queen Three in the fifth game was amazing."

"Naw," says Ruthie.

"I'm serious. And then rescuing the Queen like that?" Byron is drawing a chess board on a napkin. Ruthie won't even look at it. "I was completely fooled."

"Naw," says Ruthie. But now she sneaks a look at the napkin.

"You were three jumps ahead of me. You're easily the most fascinating person I've ever played."

Now Ruthie just keeps quiet.

"I'd expect you to move your Knight to Rook One," says Byron making little squiggles on the napkin.

"Oh, for Pete's sake," says Ruthie grabbing the pen. "Why would I move my Knight there when you could have moved the Rook up to here?" And she makes her own squiggles.

Byron just gawks now. "You are brilliant," he says.

"Well thank you," says Ruthie.

I know what's coming. I just order another Coke and settle in for it. Byron and Ruthie are jabbering away like two parrots. The Rook this and the Knight that. Leo and I just watch the squiggles on all the napkins. And Arnie Dalitz's friends. Have you ever listened to two people talking about chess when you don't know what they're talking about? It's like being stuck in an elevator with two Chinese people. But even more than that Ruthie's getting to be a goner. It's like Mother when Alonzo was talking poetry. Only different. Because

Byron is suddenly starting to look like Marlon Brando to Ruthie. I can tell. Just because he's saying all the right things. Another cat with the cream.

But that's not the worst. When he mentions Mozart I want to throw myself on the floor. I know I'm trapped here forever. Ruthie goes babbling on about Mozart. And then it's Brahms. Two brains together. All of a sudden Ruthie gets all gooey and says, "How old are you?" Leo almost has a fit.

"Twenty-two," says Byron. He doesn't look it. But all of a sudden Leo's telling Ruthie to pull up the front of her dress.

"I was going to say what a nice dress it was," Byron says. "Most female chess players really don't have much style."

"I shop in Miami," Ruthie says immediately. Leo announces he's late for something and we have to go. But Ruthie and Byron have already made plans to write. And phone too. Of course it's all about chess but Ruthie doesn't think so. Neither does Leo.

When we go out Leo looks over at Arnie Dalitz's friends. They look real angry. Leo just talks to them with a big smile and introduces Byron who they don't even say hello to. "Very rude," Ruthie says but Byron doesn't mind because he can talk more to her about chess while Leo is staring at these creepy friends of Arnie Dalitz's. When Leo just turns and walks away I can hear one of them tell Leo he's making a mistake. Who cares I think and we all leave.

But you can see Leo's real jumpy all over again.

On the way back to the car Leo keeps looking behind us. Like Stanley. Ruthie's in a daze. She keeps asking me if I think Byron looks like Paul Newman. I think about it for a while. And then I finally say, "Absolutely."

64

Again the news came through the rearview mirror. The black Oldsmobile followed like a shadow. Leo forced himself not to look at it. There was no more time left. It had to happen now. But beside him Ruthie wriggled and swooned and told him he was the best father in the whole world. Which Christie said she agreed with.

"Boss, we've got our friend following—"

"Don't worry about it, Stanley. Everything's just fine."

When they got out of the car in front of Tina's building, Leo made an excuse to go back to talk to Stanley while the girls waited in the lobby. "Wait a couple of minutes, then take off like you're ditching me."

"But they're right back there in the Olds. I can't leave you here." Spoken with fears and loyalties warring.

"Just do it."

The noise of his own thoughts drowned out everything else. Walking into the building he heard none of his daughters' giggling demands to see him tomorrow. And even Tina's soft smile barely adhered when he followed their tumultuous entrance into the apartment. He remained a mask of enthusiasm until he could excuse himself long enough to go into the laundry room at the end of the hall, where he remembered pieces of lead pipe being left in a closet.

On the way down in the elevator, he positioned the pipe, about the length of his forearm, under his suit coat, which he carried slung over his shoulder. When the doors opened at the ground floor, he remained in the elevator, riding up and down for several minutes and smiling politely at the occasional passenger until the roaring in his mind had to be stopped. After all the years it was just him and Arnie again. Full circle. With odds about three to two in Arnie's favor. He had whatever greasers were with him in the Olds. And the killing machine of the Genoveses behind him.

But then he had himself to beat. Arnie was always Arnie. Loud and brash, everything for show, the tough-guy strut that covered up all that cowardice that no one ever got to see anymore. If Arnie had been ordered to kill, Leo knew it would be done so efficiently he wouldn't make it across the sidewalk. In the jumble of thoughts he saw the faces of Ruthie and Christie and Tina staring down at him, sprawled and bloody on the pavement. *But* there were still the odds—always with Arnie there were the odds and right now the money was going on a grudge match, a blustering detonation of all the years of Arnie Dalitz's encrusted resentments and envies, fought not for the efficiency of the kill but for the need to see fear in the eyes of a friend, the same eyes that since boyhood had never ceased to bore right through the flashy suits and profane smiles into the vast cavern of emptiness that was Arnie Dalitz.

Leo made the bet with himself and realized he had smashed the lead pipe against the elevator railing hard enough to bend it. In the lobby he stood not far from a back entrance leading to an alley. But it would be covered by Arnie's men. And even if it wasn't, running would only prolong what had to happen.

Leo walked straight out the front door into the twilight.

"We're taking a ride," said a voice from behind him. A voice that started to say something else before it was silenced as the lead pipe struck home in a small explosion of flesh. A second man stepped out of the shadows and clubbed Leo onto his hands and knees and then moved in for another blow that never fell as the lead pipe smashed against the lower part of the man's leg with a dry explosive sound, like a bough breaking off a tree. Leo staggered to his feet clutching at his side, swinging at the blurs that circled him until something crashed against the side of his face and sent rockets of pain screaming into the uncharted reaches of his senses. Ribbons of blood spun from somewhere on his face. He tumbled onto the edge of the street in front of the Oldsmobile.

And through the shards of his vision saw the cubist fury of Arnie Dalitz's face. "You never learned, did you, Leo? You tried to fuck with me. Tried to show me up."

"I didn't have to try, Arnie," rasped Leo, trying to form more words as Arnie Dalitz screamed and kicked the breath out of him.

"Fuck you, Leo. You listenin' to me, asshole? You listenin'? Cause you're gonna have a little traffic accident." Arnie Dalitz turned to the driver of the Oldsmobile. "Run the sonofabitch over."

But the instant before the driver would have pushed his foot down on the accelerator, a pistol was jammed through the open side window against his temple. And simultaneously Arnie Dalitz turned to see a small revolver only inches from his face, held by an older Negro with white, woolly hair and a toothpick that circled his mouth. "Just ease up or your brains'll be all over this nice clean car of yours."

"Okay, okay," said Arnie Dalitz, noticing that suddenly the street seemed to be filled with Negroes.

JUST A MATTER OF TIME

65

Word spread in the music industry. The story was that George Goldin had lost his company on one of the countless nights he spent gambling up in Harlem.

It was pointed out that Herman Pinsky and Avalon Records did everything they could to destroy the chances of the new song *Ghost Lover* ever becoming a hit. With the active assistance of the Genovese family they pulled it from all the jukeboxes they controlled. Avalon Records found a white group with a lead singer who sounded like Pat Boone and recorded their own version of the song which was heavily promoted with disk jockeys who received plain envelopes filled with twenty-dollar bills. In spite of these efforts, it was the version of *Ghost Lover* recorded by Ivory Joe and the Classics that became the hit. The group appeared on *American Bandstand* and then *The Ed Sullivan Show*. Extensive tours were arranged by their manager Tina Klein, who had just opened an office in the Brill Building.

It was rumored that Arnie Dalitz had tried to stop the tours, but his efforts were interrupted when he was indicted by a grand jury for the murder of George Goldin.

In the week before *Ghost Lover* went to number one on the charts, a fire destroyed Frolic Frocks. It was listed as arson but no one was ever charged with the crime. Nor did Leo and Morris Klein pursue the matter. Morris Klein immediately moved to Florida. Leo Klein was severely beaten by unknown assailants after leaving his wife's apartment building on the upper West Side of Manhattan. A scattering of his assailants' teeth were found beside him as he lay unconscious on the street. He remained unconscious for almost two days. His jaw was wired shut for seven weeks. Physical therapy was begun to teach him to walk with a cane.

66

After the bad accident he had, Leo's in a kind of hospital up in the middle of nowhere. It's like Camp Wig-A-Mog only it's not a camp. There's people in iron lungs here. And people on crutches and all sorts of awful things. It's a kind of hospital in the woods. There's lakes and forests all around it. And a big lawn out front where people sit in their wheelchairs. It's still in New York State but Canada's not far away. That's how far it is.

Sometimes Uncle Morris comes all the way up from Florida. When he shows up it's a big deal. None of his other friends like Arnie Dalitz ever bother to show up. Even though Leo still can't talk properly with all the wires around his mouth he laughs and they make jokes. Once Uncle Morris brings up Mimmo too. Leo likes that. And Ruthie and I try to come up on the train every other weekend. We stay in a special room that Leo gets for us.

For the first couple of months after his accident Leo's not too good. There's wires and plaster and tubes all over him. But then he starts getting better. We can tell because we see him playing cards in the next room with a guy who's supposed to be dying but doesn't. Leo skunks this guy out of his expensive gold cuff links that were supposed to go to some nephew when the guy dies. The nephew comes up and starts yelling at the people who run the hospital. Leo just yells right back at the nephew and goes on skunking the guy who doesn't die. Leo says he's keeping him alive more than the hospital is. And for sure more than the nephew is.

We bring up a radio for Leo. You hear *Ghost Lover* on it all the time. Even up here. When Leo hears the song he gets strange. Sometimes he just lies back and starts talking about the good old days in Georgia.

What good old days in Georgia? we ask him but he doesn't answer. But other times he doesn't look so pleased and talks about what it was like before we all met Ivory Joe.

Ruthie and I still go on Ivory Joe's tours. But just for a few days at a time when they're around New York. Mother goes for longer. But we know that she phones Leo a lot. Leo gets real mushy when they talk. He did even when he had the wires all over his face and all he could do was make noises. Once when Mother was up here she cut her lip when she reached over to kiss him. Before she comes to see Leo she takes a long time getting fixed up. She always tries on about four or five dresses before she figures out what to wear. She never used to. She always looks prettier when she's up here. We tell her that but she thinks we're just saying it. You can tell. And Leo always puts the Vitalis on his hair and shaves around the wires when he knows she's coming.

Until they find something to argue about they always look real happy. And sometimes even afterwards.

67

Now that all the wires and tubes are coming out Leo is really starting to be Leo again. We come up one weekend and all of a sudden a lot of nurses are trying to be nice to us. Too nice. Ruthie and I look at each other. We both think the same thing. Doxies. Just like the stewardesses. But *nurses*? We can't believe it.

The next weekend we come up here with Ivory Joe. He wants to. We say sure and then look at Mother who looks like it's all normal. But it's not. Because Ivory Joe changed everything for us. He didn't mean to but he did.

It's sort of like a dream. We leave with Ivory Joe after he and Zoot and Clyde and Clarence are on *The Ed Sullivan Show*. We're in the audience and I know even Louie Makin is watching at home on television when Ed Sullivan tells them to turn the camera around on the audience. After the show everyone's jumping up and down all excited. Even Ivory Joe who was great and drove them all wild when he did *Ghost Lover*. He hugs Mother and then me. Then Ruthie and I get in the DeSoto and start driving up to see Leo with him. Just us.

We stop at Red Leg's place in Harlem where there's all the smoke in the big room behind the store. And the men marking down things on pieces of paper. Ivory Joe's a hero when he walks in. Everyone saw him on *Ed Sullivan*. I feel famous too. Red Leg gives Ivory Joe a lot of money. He puts it in a paper bag and we leave. It's real late. On the way up to see Leo, Ivory Joe sees how tired we are. He starts singing songs in a real soft voice and we conk out. We don't even remember getting there. I wake up when I hear voices and we're in bed in one of the rooms in the place where Leo is.

The voices are Leo and Ivory Joe. I can look out the door and see them in the big room across the hall. No one else is around and it's dark. Leo sits in a wheelchair and Ivory Joe stays standing up. You can tell they like each other but each of them doesn't want the other to know it. Just by the way they try to be tough but they're not. Ivory Joe has the bag of money in his hands. "It's yours," he says to Leo.

But Leo just shakes his head and says, "What, are you crazy?"

Ivory Joe just keeps staring at him. "I owe it to you."

They keep talking like this for a long time. Ivory Joe says the money is to help get Frolic Frocks going again. Leo acts real insulted and says since when do I need charity?

Ivory Joe just stares at him again and says yeah? Well I feel the same way. And on and on like this. Until I can't stand it anymore. Then Ivory Joe just puts the paper bag down on the table beside Leo and smiles in that mysterious way he has. Leo sort of smiles too but tells him to take the bag with him.

But Ivory Joe doesn't.

In the daytime when we get up Leo plays father again. He goes for walks with us and takes us down to the little pond which we all pretend is like the one in Central Park. Leo's still slow with his cane.

But that night after he thinks we're asleep we can hear the noise from our room. We creep down the hallway and all these sick people and the nurses are having a party. Even the dying guy's there looking like he's not going to die. Leo's right in the middle of it playing cards. He's won a lot more gold cuff links. Probably off the dying guy again. And right on the table is Ivory Joe's paper bag of money that Leo uses to pay for the champagne when it comes.

Even after we get back to our room and go to sleep we still keep waking up because we can hear Leo's voice somewhere. Everything is quiet now. It's real late. Leo's laughing. And some doxie is giggling. Like he's tickling her or something. They're telling each other to *Shhh!* but boy can you hear them.

But Ruthie and I know that this is just while Leo's up here. It's his way of getting better. He can hardly wait for Mother to come up and visit him. He talks about it all the time. And when he gets out of here we know they're going to get back together again.

It's just a matter of time.

MY THANKS to those who helped inspire the threads that wove together into the lives of *Ivory Joe*:

Linda Chandler, David Ostriker, Billy Ward, Milton Murrill,
Aerlyn and Kelly Burke, Ruth Brown, Morris Levy,
Sandra Goroff, Kay Ferry and Liz Walker.

ABOUT THE AUTHOR

Shortly after finishing college, MARTYN BURKE paid his own way over to the war in Vietnam. From his experiences there came his novel *Laughing War*. Since then he has traveled above the Arctic Circle in Russia and in the tributaries of the Amazon. He has made undercover documentaries on the Mafia and the KGB and gone inside Afghanistan with rebels attacking a Soviet garrison. He has won numerous awards for his films—many of which provide the research for his novels. A native of Canada, he divides his time between Toronto and Santa Monica.